WILD FRUIT

Sheng Keyi was born in Yiyang in Hunan Province, and later moved to Shenzhen and Beijing. She is the award-winning author of several collections of short stories and novels, which include *Northern Girls*, published by Penguin Random House, and *Death Fugue*. *Northern Girls* was longlisted for the Man Asian Literary Prize. Sheng Keyi's works have been translated into more than ten languages, including English, French and German.

Shelly Bryant is a poet, writer, and translator. She is the author of nine volumes of poetry, a pair of travel guides, a book on classical Chinese gardens, and a short story collection. She has translated more than twenty books from the Chinese. She has translated Sheng Keyi's *Northern Girls*, and her translation of You Jin's *In Time, Out of Place* was shortlisted for the Singapore Literature Prize in 2016.

WILD FRUIT
A Novel

SHENG KEYI

Translated from the original Chinese by
SHELLY BRYANT

VIKING
an imprint of
PENGUIN BOOKS

VIKING

UK | USA | Canada | Ireland | Australia
India | New Zealand | South Africa | China

Penguin Books is part of the Penguin Random House group of companies
whose addresses can be found at global.penguinrandomhouse.com.

Penguin
Random House
PENGUIN BOOKS

This paperback edition is published by Penguin Group (Australia), 2018

1 3 5 7 9 10 8 6 4 2

Cover design by Di Suo © Penguin Group (Australia)
Text design by Steffan Leyshon-Jones © Penguin Group (Australia)
Calligraphy by Chris Pui Yan Owens © Penguin Group (Australia)
Printed and bound in Hong Kong by Printing Express Limited
A catalogue record for this book is available from the National Library of Australia.

ISBN: 9780734399014

penguin.com.au

FSC
www.fsc.org
MIX
Paper from
responsible sources
FSC™ C012285

'The four of us were like wild fruit falling from a tree.'

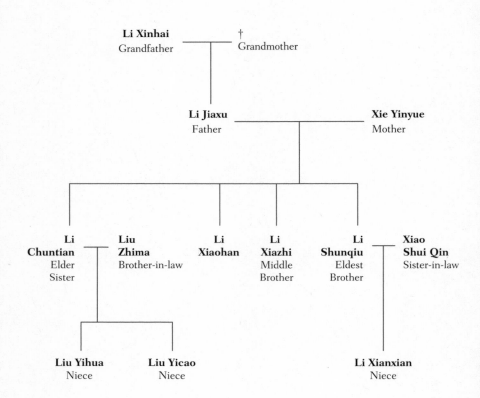

Li Xinhai
Grandfather

†
Grandmother

Li Jiaxu
Father

Xie Yinyue
Mother

Li Chuntian
Elder Sister

Liu Zhima
Brother-in-law

Li Xiaohan

Li Xiazhi
Middle Brother

Li Shunqiu
Eldest Brother

Xiao Shui Qin
Sister-in-law

Liu Yihua
Niece

Liu Yicao
Niece

Li Xianxian
Niece

A Note on Chinese Usage and Names

In Chinese, a person's given name always follows their surname. Therefore, the protagonist of *Wild Fruit*, Li Xiaohan, has the surname Li and the given name Xiaohan. Depending on the occasion and the familiarity between people, given names can be shortened to a repetition of the final syllable, such as Hanhan for Xiaohan.

WILD FRUIT

Chapter 1:

Li Xinhai, Grandfather

As far back as I could remember, the ancestral photo of a beauty was hanging high up in the main hall, mouldy and spotty, her face covered with fly faeces under the glass frame. She was a pale, frail woman, looking a little disheartened. Under scrutiny, her features looked as if they had been chiselled with a knife, with the coldness of late spring in her eyes. When the first shots of the Xinhai Revolution were fired and her life was lost in a pool of blood, she was just eighteen. Please do not misunderstand – I do not mean to imply that this woman, the matriarch of our family, lost her life in some heroic revolutionary sacrifice. She died in childbirth. It was my grandfather who tortured her to the point of death, as husbands often do.

My grandfather was called Li Xinhai. Unlike most Southerners, he was lanky, pale, and beardless. He was refined, without the dullness of most country folk, and always elegantly dressed. He was widowed when he was around thirty years old and did not remarry, remaining a bachelor. Only two things mattered to him: reading and gambling. He would occasionally pen the calligraphy for funeral or wedding scrolls or make offerings for his neighbours, as a way of making a bit of pocket money. He had a mysterious distant relative who none of us ever met. We only knew it was a woman who occasionally sent something over, like the brown beret that once came in the post. My grandfather always wore that strange hat wherever he went, whipping around as if on wings, making the willow sway and the surface of the river ripple when he passed. Some said the mysterious woman was the result of the wild oats my grandfather had sown in his early years.

It was said that my grandfather and my father had some entanglements. For the lack of anything better to do, my grandfather had raped my father's first wife. My father did not care if my grandfather disturbed other men's wives, as long as his was left alone. This was a matter of family tradition. Not long after my father sent his first wife away, her body was found floating in the river. Some people fished the body out and returned it to my father, who dug a hole in some forsaken field and buried her there. From then on, father and son were bitter rivals, like two old oxen used to grazing on their own, having nothing to do with each other. If they were forced to talk, they ended up butting heads and fighting, their horns crashing like pebbles knocking against each other. My father was strong and had a loud voice. Because my grandfather was dependent on my father for his livelihood, he was somewhat restrained. Not wanting to have his food source cut off, he usually just returned silently to his own room, took a deck of cards from his box, and picked a good hand to suppress the resentment in his heart.

My grandfather was playing cards when my grandmother died. When someone came to give him the news of her death, he was reluctant to put his cards away. Furious over this, my father sought every opportunity to reprove my grandfather for it. He criticised him for having no regard for the propriety, wisdom, sense of right, wrong, shame, and compassion of card playing culture, despite his many decades of gaming. My grandfather, who was actually very alert, feigned deafness, putting on a calm expression and a manner that indicated that at the end of the day, he was still my father's father.

My father loved to tell people off, cursing animals, trees, crops, and his busy manual workers in colourful terms. My grandfather squandered the family fortunes, losing the land and the ancestral home early on. When he was old and no longer of agile mind, he made many ill-fated, confused decisions in his gambling, giving away all sorts of advantages, losing even his old ivory cards and his ten-volume commentary set from Japan, *Book of Songs: A Textual Exposition*. My grandfather said the cards had been stolen, and he had used the pages of that sacred book to wipe his arse. My father knew they had been sold and the money gambled away, disappearing altogether in the space of two nights. News of these things got around, causing my father great mental anguish. If my grandfather had not made a mess of things, the money would have been sufficient to pay half the cost for the building of a house. But those treasures belonged to my grandfather, so if he did not leave them for his son or grandson, who could blame him? My father could only turn his back on my grandfather, caning the pig that had left its shit everywhere, scolding it for being a spend-thrift and a selfish ghost, and asking if it would need someone to take care of its burial when it died.

My grandfather was not only empty-handed throughout life; his heart was also devoid of all feeling. He had long ago cast every-thing aside. His face and chin were tilted slightly upwards, giving him a look of arrogance, as if those before him were his subjects and he could utter a divine edict that they would have to kneel and receive. When he was, on occasion, invited to speak about poetry, he would drop his pretence and turn eloquent, sometimes creating suspense while he explained in lively detail the context of a literary quotation. It was in those instances that a rare smile would appear on his face and you would witness a moment of simple joy. Perhaps he was too lonely, so even when people had had enough of his performance, he refused to let them go. He would take treats or his other prized toys from his treasure chest, just to detain them. Later, only small children would listen to his poetry, coaxing a snack from him. Eventually, though, even they grew bored and started to ignore him.

Chapter 2:

Li Chuntian, Elder Sister

My elder sister often went to the temple of the God of Earth to pray for my father's sudden death.

Before my sister grew up, she was not considered attractive. On reaching puberty, she suddenly acquired some beauty and, throughout the Lanxi River area, she was considered quite good-looking. She was 1.68 metres tall, large-framed and fair-skinned, like a Northerner. Her face was not small but, since it came to a point at the chin, she was saved from being called barbaric or stupid. Her short, black, shiny hair was cut to show her beautiful temples at their best advantage, highlighting her thin ears. Her arched eyebrows added to the intelligence of her face and, coupled with dark, narrow eyes, it was all quite lovely. Unfortunately, her lips were on the thick side and had a black lustre. When she was angry, they puckered up like a chicken's arse. Even so, it was those thick lips that made others believe her to be honest. Someone as honest as that could only look life squarely in the face, bite the bullet, and embrace the disadvantages it sent her way, not cutting herself any slack for what fate had dealt her. It was fortunate she had no religion to serve as an additional burden on her.

There were many God of Earth temples in the countryside, some very simply built, piled stones forming the walls and standing lazily under a tree or along the roadside. The one my sister often went to in the rice paddy was properly built. It was small and square but completely whitewashed with flying eaves at the corners. Inside was an altar dedicated to the God of Earth. There my sister knelt, clasping her hands together and calling down curses on my father, asking for him to drown or be gored to death by a buffalo, or perhaps attacked by a mad dog or run over by a car. She did not care how he died, as long as it happened, one way or another. But apparently, this lowly little emissary of the God of Earth did not watch over who lived or died, because my father was still alive and swearing, not even getting the sniffles.

Discovering that the God of Earth was just a big fraud, my sister tossed several clods of mud at his temple. Sometimes she sat in the fields chewing on grass roots, feeling helpless and waving birds away. Other times she caught frogs, then started flaying them from the legs, the frog croaking miserably as she peeled away layers of skin. Before long, the creature lay splayed in the water, dead. My sister would lie down, expression-less, listening to the insects rustle in the grass. Eyes turned to the sky, she smiled, as if she were carried off into the distance with the clouds. She said that if she had wings, she would fly hundreds of thousands of miles away and never come back.

*

In the spring of 1965, when the flowers were in full bloom and the river high, my sister uttered a few feeble sounds as she reported for duty on this earth. My father's expression was dark. He wanted a son who crowed as loud as a cock, with the ability to rise like the sun and bring joy to the world; he did not want a 'useless' girl with her mouse-like whining. My father never hid anything, wearing his emotions on his face. He wanted others to keep their heads down, waiting to read his decrees or his pleasures in the godlike image of his face.

He lit a cigarette, his frown as thick and dark as night. Even the weak light in the house was swallowed up by this darkness.

Now two in the morning, it was a muggy night. It was unusual, but three kerosene lamps were lit in the house. The lit glass lampshade was like a giant stalk of golden barley. It was shaded by dirty black rings that had not been cleaned from the lamp's glass. Wisps of black smoke rose from the aperture in its cover. The column of flame was quiet and sober, giving out a golden light which lulled one to sleep.

My father finished his cigarette and went over to snatch the baby girl up in one swoop. Feeling the roughness of the external world, she opened her mouth to cry, but no sound came forth. Smothered, her little face turned red. My father held her upside down by her feet, took a torchlight, and walked silently to the water's edge. He was going to drown her in the Lanxi River behind the house before she could become a burden. The last thing he wanted was something this unlucky. The midwife, who was cleaning up after the delivery, caught up with him and stopped him. She rescued my sister and put the newborn back in her swaddling clothes. The midwife spread this story around with great interest, treating it as a joke. Eventually, many years later, it made its way to my sister's ears.

My father put great effort into arranging hard labour for his daughter. Only when she was toiling did he have peace of mind. He secured a mud pond a great distance from the house. Fearing it would not be fertile, he covered it with straw and ordered my sister to tread over it until the straw was buried in the mud. She laboured for two days. When I took food to her, I saw that her feet were raw and bleeding. She sat in the field, weeping.

Several years later, my sister said she always felt she was being held upside down by her feet. She almost tried to go back in time to save herself, but actually, she rather wished she had never been saved from drowning all those years ago. She often wept at night. Sometimes there were crunching sounds as if she were eating something, and a strange odour would come from inside the mosquito net. The headless matchsticks I found the next day were evidence that my sister had chewed them off in the night.

My sister only employed methods that did not guarantee death to attempt suicide. It seemed she loved to loathe herself.

Chapter 3:

Li Jiaxu, Father

In 1934, Hunan suffered a drought that was called 'the great drought of the eleventh year' in the local literature. The ground dried and cracked, killing many people. My grandfather was still playing cards in Shatou Village, hoping to win back what he had lost. He played fair, never cheating. Generally, he won small and lost big, and when he went to other people's turf, he lost so badly he did not even have money left to pay for the ferry ticket home. At such times, his true nature – that of a poet – was revealed as he stood on the riverbank watching the enveloping mist, composing an impromptu poem for the dark maiden in charge of checking tickets, waiting for her to bow her head to hide her flushed face. Then he would turn nimbly and step aboard the ferry. My grandfather often sought to bribe the dark maiden with a New Year picture or a sweet but in the end, it was his scholarly looks that fascinated her. After my grandmother had departed this world, my grandfather continued to go to Shatou Village to gamble but by that time, the dark maiden was already a mother of two children.

One particular day, my grandfather lost everything in his pockets. By the time he had finished joking with the dark maiden, taken a ferry to the opposite bank, and walked ten miles along the Lanxi River to reach home, it was already dark. As soon as he came in the door, he heard the baby crying and smelled the fresh odour of blood. The midwife gleefully pushed my grandfather to have a look at the baby. His mind still on the poker table, he could not quite adapt to his new role. He walked indifferently into the room and found the baby's face among a heap of blankets. My grandfather glanced at it, then turned to go. The midwife quickly picked my father up and peeled back the swaddling clothes, exposing the little penis before my grandfather's eyes. My grandfather said, 'Oh,' and my father cried loudly.

From then on, my father started crying every night at that exact same time, and he cried all night, torturing my grandmother until both her eyes were sunken. My father cried for a full hundred nights, and my grandfather did not come home to sleep. My grandmother got used to this. People who saw my grandfather emerging from the house of one girl or another kindly hid it from my grandmother.

Two years later, my grandfather had another son. The child died on his first birthday, sending my grandmother into a deep depression. She came down with breast cancer not long after and did not survive it. Later, we could not even find her grave anymore, it was so heavily covered in grass. When my father and grandfather quarrelled, this issue always came up. My father did not miss his mother, and he was not bothered by his father's heartlessness. He really just wanted to frustrate my grandfather on many different fronts, hoping thereby to prevail and prove that he was the true boss at home.

My grandfather's childhood could be considered ostentatious, and his family had large tracts of land. He had a nanny, he went to a private school, and he never went hungry. My father would starve for one meal and glut himself for the next. He dabbled with school for a few years and then at the age of twelve, he ran away to the city and got a taste of true hardship. Later he served for a while as an unregistered soldier, marching with the troops and helping to carry arms and food. Fifteen years later, he suddenly returned home, now as a man enjoying imperial gains. He joined a shipping company and started a floating life on the waters. The Xiangjiang, Zijiang, Yuanjiang, Liuyang, and Laodao were all rivers he traversed, learning well which sections were wide and which narrow, and where the bends and the rapids were. He also took advantage of the chaos in the country to make a catch or two – including his beautiful first wife, who later drowned herself.

*

My mother, my father's second wife, Xie Yinyue, was a dimpled girl from the mountains of Xielingang. She was pretty, but had a hard life. Because of the war and unrest, she had been orphaned as a child and was sent to live with her brother and sister-in-law. I do not know if she might have suffered any harsh treatment from her sister-in-law, but it is enough to know it was not a very happy childhood. She was full of old-fashioned ideas and her smile revealed red lips and white teeth. She was ten years younger than my father. The first time he saw her, she was washing clothes in the Zhixi River. The waters of the Zhixi were like my mother's eyes, crystal clear. My father was domineering, telling my mother that the river was now under his control, and his office was at the dam, all of which was true. This was about six months after his first wife had died.

Later, when my father proposed marriage, my mother's oldest brother did not agree. He felt that my father had the look of a gangster and feared my mother would suffer ill fortunes with him. At any rate, a widowed man had to be somewhat unlucky.

My mother was determined to go with my father, who was not the least bit worried since he had fought his way from the country to the city, and from the old society to the new China, conquering everything on Earth. In the territory of Yiyang, there was nothing he could not accomplish.

'I am only discussing it with you out of courtesy. If Yinyue and I run away together, what can you do about it?' my father said to my uncle. Being a wise man, my uncle quickly yielded and gave them his full support.

Xielingang had a lot of bamboo. It was said that, previously, the emperor liked the bamboo sleeping mats from there and expected the residents to send some in tribute each year. My father said the emperor was a real novice – he should have travelled to the place and picked the most radiant, vivacious girls there to be his concubines, then he would have known that it was more comfortable to sleep with them than on the mats.

My mother was the prettiest, most charming daughter-in-law within a hundred mile radius of the village. She wasted no time, quickly giving birth to a litter of new villagers.

When my elder brother was born, my grandfather was pacing in a circle outside the room. Until his grandson had turned one month old, he would be kept in the room, as was traditional for newborn children, and my grandfather would not be able to see him. Actually, my grandfather was not that eager to see his grandson, but he was very keen to show off his great learning. He had selected several possible names for the boy, and he could not wait to start explaining to the other villagers the meaning of the names. But my father did not use any of them. He did not want my grandfather's interference in family affairs and was intent on depriving him of all powers.

The treatment and ostracism my grandfather received at home was basically that usually reserved for a concubine.

My grandfather was not yet sixty at this time, so still had some spunk and was not so easily pushed aside. He was particularly adept at acting pitiful. He was eloquent; even without swearing, and even though he might have made some errors, people's sympathies still inclined toward his side. Once when father and son clashed hotly, my grandfather called on our ancestors for mercy. He went on a flight of fancy, breaking down history, analysing Confucius and Mencius, citing the four classics and eight virtues, calling for the three cardinal guides and five rites, until finally the hammer of judgement landed squarely on my father's head. But the judgement was revoked by my father's single phrase: 'You're not worthy.'

My grandfather was always smouldering after a fight, and when my father was not home, he made things difficult for my mother. My mother was generally a woman of few words, but when provoked into an argument, her thin lips would clap as lively as cymbals, and she used slang and proverbs perfectly. My grandfather never won an argument with her. When it was all over, he would sit alone outside the door, and his aloof expression would slowly give way to sorrow over his hopeless situation.

My father was the lord of the family; his wife and children were his people. The weakness and gentleness of the women and children not only failed to evoke any tenderness in him, they actually contributed to his violence. My father often beat my mother. Once, he beat her so badly she rolled all over the floor, her hair dishevelled and her body covered in blood, and it finally prompted her to leave home. A month later, my uncle brought her back, and my father accepted her like tribute from a vassal. My mother took out snacks and dry goods from her bag, and once the light went out at night, she rolled in the sack with my father.

Chapter 4:

Li Shunqiu, Eldest Brother

The distinction between city and rural people is as clear as that between black- and white-skinned folk. My father had it very carefully calculated. He arranged for his own retirement, citing ill health as the reason, and for my eldest brother to quit school and replace him. My brother's official residential status was immediately elevated from from a rural one to an urban one. He started 'enjoying imperial gains,' and everyone else nearly died of envy.

My brother, Li Shunqiu, was born good-looking, bashful, reticent, and soft-spoken. When he occasionally laughed out loud, he would emit a couple of syllables of *ha-ha*, then stop abruptly. He was prone to nostalgia, and never let go of friendships forged in our village, but always gathered with his friends when he came home. By the time the nationwide anti-crime crackdown started in 1983, his old pals had become real peasants with dark skin, thick knuckles, slipper-clad feet, and smoking low-grade cigarettes. When they gathered, it was just like old times when they were kids going to the fields to pluck gourds or to the river to fish. My elder brother had a complete set of fishing equipment. When they were not used, the nets hung in the backyard neatly, like polished weapons. He could quickly straighten out messy nets, and knew how to repair the holes. He knew which sort of net to use to catch which type of fish at different stages, just as he knew which kinds of fish spawned in the shallow waters and which kinds liked to come to the surface in the dark of night.

Summer nights in the village were as docile as an unspoilt maiden. The moon parked itself in the night sky. Fireflies flitted around the grass field and thorn bushes. The Lanxi River lay on the ground basking in the moonlight. My brother was fishing on this sort of night, his body cutting across the satiny surface of the water like a pair of scissors.

There was no warning sign for the bad turn of events.

The night the incident occurred was livelier than when the folk theatre group came to perform in the village. The people had come out in force, flocking towards the Brigade Department, surrounding the police cars, taking stock of those powerful and forceful people. Leaning from the window, they watched the police shave half the hair of the young people, covering their mouths as they snickered. Nearly seven decades earlier, during the Anti-Manchu County Criticism, the Brigade Department was the interrogation room and prison, imprisoning the farmers who could not pay up their commissariat, and later it was converted into a mill. Now, it was the temporary interrogation room.

The village Party Secretary tried to find out the sense of propriety of the matter from an armed man. 'Young people watch open-air films, sometimes jeering and engaging in group fights. This is not unusual. . . But why are the armed forces alerted this time? Will there be a problem?'

Looking arrogantly at the Party Secretary, the armed man took a cigarette from his mouth and said, 'Don't you know this is a special crackdown period?'

'Do you think you could send the trial back to the township

government for verdict? If anything happens here, my skull will be cracked.' The Party Secretary lit a new cigarette for Minister Cai, then tossed the match away. He looked at the other party helplessly. 'The neighbours meet frequently and they are under the mistaken impression I am colluding. . . No, of course, it is cooperating. As a member of the Communist Party, I have always cooperated unconditionally with the work of my superiors.'

Minister Cai wore a uniform that was stretched around his body like a ball. He seemed like he was about to raise a hand to slap the secretary's face. Smoke swirled from his nostrils and mouth, as if his whole person were being consumed in flames. 'Just do as I say. You're so short-sighted. You can't see any farther than you can piss.'

The Party Secretary stared at the minister alertly, his facial features all bunched together. 'But, how far I can piss depends on the minister's orders, right?'

Minister Cai said slowly, 'There is too much chaos in society right now. The central government had a meeting and is launching a nationwide "severe crackdown on criminal offences" movement. Those who can be caught and those not easily caught will eventually be swept up in an iron grip. Those who can be sentenced, will be; and those who cannot be sentenced, will also be dealt with resolutely. Those who must be killed and those who can't be killed, all will be eliminated without delay. The population of our county is large, so the crime index is also higher than other counties. This is no good. There is so much to be done I don't even have time to sleep at night. These people today are gangsters. They gather to fight, molest women, fish in the river, and steal state property. . .'

'Gang crimes have to be settled with a bullet!'

The Party Secretary was shocked. 'These. . . young people were watching an open-air film, jeering, and fighting, but they always do this! They are law-abiding people who have never committed any outrageous act. It was not a gang, nor a gang issue,' he protested.

The minister said that whether or not they had done anything outrageous, or committed a crime, everything would be clear after the interrogation. The law functions on evidence.

Two hours later, six handcuffed young men with half-shaved heads were squeezed into the police car.

A week later, the verdict was handed down. Li Dage, the leader, was given the death penalty, along with several of the other participants. For his role in the fight, my oldest brother received the lightest sentence, eight years in jail.

The Lanxi Middle School's drill ground served as the site for the mass trial meeting, but this was not what was most important. After the trial meeting, the condemned prisoners were to be dragged to the Lanxi River and executed. Nobody had seen a killing before and did not want to miss the opportunity. It was as if a public holiday had been declared.

My sister was still at the factory and had no idea what was happening at home. My mother's tears flowed and her nose ran. My father was no longer cursing, but kept his mouth tightly shut. My second brother, Li Xiazhi, quietly filled a bucket of water, then obediently went to the vegetable field and hoed for a while. I snuck up the dam and rushed to the school to watch the mass trial meeting.

The weather was not bad. It was hot, with a wind blowing in from the south and the river's layers of ripples moving north. I went on the causeway, where it seemed a crowd of people had sprouted from the ground. All of them were rushing toward Lanxi Town, where there were organised groups of orderly students looking especially stern and confident. The causeway was usually only this lively during the Dragon Boat Festival. The burst of festive atmosphere gave me a thrill. I was soon swallowed up by the crowd, feeling nervous and excited. I became so sweaty as I walked that perspiration dripped from the ends of my hair, falling to the ground and producing a soft, tough sound, transparent and sticking thickly to the ears. I was not even sure where the school gate was. I just followed the crowd and made my way straight to the drill ground.

Many photos were taken, forming a record of the scene I witnessed. A large poster was hung, and a shrill loudspeaker pierced my ears. The heads of the condemned hung low. On Li Dage's chest hung a sign with the words 'gangster' on it, with a huge red X. A few who did not have red X'es on their signs stood in a row at the back, their hands behind their backs. The drill ground was surrounded by a packed crowd. The air turned muggy. A huge mushroom-shaped cloud formed overhead, like a lion watching the proceedings, its profile greyish-white. After a while, it turned into a ball, then became formless. There were periods of total silence. One of the marked criminals collapsed, unable to stand any longer. Two uniformed personnel held him up after that. Later the crowd began to loosen and expand. The trial was over. The people turned and followed the vehicle parading through the streets, escorting the offenders to the execution ground. They wanted to see for themselves as the bloody red flower came into sudden bloom across the chest of the condemned when he was shot.

I twisted my ankle as I squeezed through the exit of the drill ground, so I did not make it to the execution ground, but this had no effect on my later boasting to my classmates when I described all I had heard, as if I had seen it. I said ten people with guns stood in a row before the ten kneeling criminals. There was a gunshot, and it was as if the condemned had been kicked. The bodies lurched, blood-spattered, and a burnt smell instantly filled the air, like the smell of a barbecued kebab.

Chapter 5:

Li Chuntian, Elder Sister

When my brother went to jail, a decree from my father brought my sister obediently home from the factory. All day, her lips were sucked in like a chicken's arse, but she cried all night every night, both for our brother and for herself. If not for my brother's misfortune, she could have remained at the factory. She was sixteen at the time, and there was a fellow at the factory who always smiled at her. It was the first time she heard the sound of her own heart pounding like a drum. After she returned home, she was still obsessed with his smile, thinking of it until it finally floated away like the evening clouds.

My sister returned to her old life, the brief three months she had spent in the factory were like a scratch that did not even leave a scar on her skin. Even so, that period flung open the gates to my sister's emotional life, thanks to that fellow at the factory.

I was too young to understand the implications of my sister's next entanglement, this time with the recently divorced Li Letian, son of the village Party Secretary. One night, my father slapped my sister and said, 'You're a shameless hussy, why do you want to be stained with a divorcee with kids; do you think it's so easy to be a stepmother?'

The next day when Chuntian spoke with the son of the village Party Secretary at the riverside, she said, 'My father won't agree.'

The son of the Party Secretary, clearly of the same mind as my father, said, 'You're a virgin. I don't deserve you.' Then he walked away.

My sister sat alone in the grass slope crying. When she found that I had crept among the willows to eavesdrop, her anger erupted. 'What are you looking at, you little bitch?'

I retorted with words learnt from my father, 'Shameless hussy, wanting to be a stepmother. Hussy!'

I cursed as I ran. Half of a red brick flew behind me, hitting me right in the hindquarters. I immediately wailed in pain. Chuntian was so scared she started to examine my injury and, applying spittle to it, she started to cry with me. She cried even louder than I did, as if it were a competition. I stopped and watched her cry. I had never seen my sister cry so openly. Up until then, I had even thought she didn't really know how to cry, only knowing how to twitch her shoulders like in the silent films.

My father really hated the Party Secretary.

For a while, our house was as sombre as a grave, and there is never any light in a tomb. My parents' hair greyed rapidly. They were like an earthen dam that had suddenly collapsed, its dust covering the bodies of me and my sister. We were all coated in grey.

My father made things increasingly difficult for my sister. He would pull up and replant the rice planted by her, criticising my sister for not planting neatly enough, saying that the gaps between the plants were lopsided. He was like a teacher correcting home-work, cursing as he made corrections, then finally driving my sister to stand in the field as punishment.

My sister stood on the ridge of the field with the evil sun overhead, as still as a statue. It was as if everything was her doing, and she could never do anything to please my father, as he scolded her every day, cursing her like livestock. My sister acted as docile as a lamb, sometimes with tears in her eyes, going wherever my father pointed. If he said to hoe up weeds, she hoed up weeds; if he said to pull weeds, she pulled weeds; if he said to stop work, she dropped her tools immediately. One would think my father would be quite satisfied, but he continued to scrub and polish my sister, as if working a piece of jade.

When the fields had been sown, my father tied a piece of red cloth on a bamboo rod and told my sister to use it to chase away the sparrows, coordinating her time of rest with the birds'. After seven or eight days when the seed grains had sprouted into rice shoots, my father brought home bundles of nylon yarn for my sister to weave into nets, pocketing the money he got as a deposit for the nets for himself.

The old man did not let me off either. When he went out fishing, he would call me, the 'unlucky ghost' following him with the fish basket. We lived in the lake area. There were always many open loti in the ponds, and water chestnut leaves covered the face of the water. It was beautiful in a dull way. As I walked on the turf, shellfish-like objects often dug into my soles. If I stepped on a water chestnut shell, it would make me scream, but my father never even looked back. He could tell from the underwater debris in the puddles on the roadside where the previous fisherman had fished. If he pulled out a dripping snail or clam, he did not slow his pace at all. Like a general clad in armour and carrying sharp weapons, he led his endless army forward. He rarely caught any fish. At most a small fish or two would sit in the bottom of the basket. It was as if he had not really gone out to fish, but to relax.

Since my father felt betrayed by my oldest brother, he turned double attention to my second brother, stipulating his bound duty to study. He was basically not expected to touch any farming work. When it was harvest time and my sister had set the threshing machine to roaring with her quick steps, my second brother volunteered to run errands, only to be scolded by my father. My oldest brother's diploma had been taken down, but my second brother's new diploma made the rear of the house shine once more. When my father saw that I also received various 'awards,' he made it a point to never encourage me himself. The better my results were, the more disappointed my father was. This was like a blatant provocation. He clearly preferred me to be a stupid, reckless troublemaker, which would allow him to make use of the various punishment tactics he loved.

My father often sat in the rear of the house smoking, with Chairman Mao smiling upon him like the Mona Lisa as he spewed clouds of secondhand smoke. Every New Year, he would remove the portrait of Chairman Mao, his teeth stained yellow by the smoke, and replace it with a fresh picture. The new image would show Chairman Mao's teeth in all their white purity, practically reflecting the white light when the weather was fair. When I pulled a stool up beneath the picture and added a moustache for Chairman Mao, my father picked me up like I was a shadow puppet, swinging and pulling me, until I dropped to my knees on the ground, kneeling there the whole morning.

After my sister broke up with the son of the village Party Secretary at my father's insistence, they had nothing further to do with each other. She farmed all day, and at night silently bit on matchsticks with her chicken's arse mouth; her shoulders continued twitching as if she were in the silent films. In the winter, she went out with my father to carry mud to repair levees to earn work points. The matchsticks cost 2 cents each, which meant that my sister's chosen method of suicide was quite cheap. Perhaps that was why she continued on in this fashion, as if it had become the only pillar of her survival. She felt that her problems came from her appearance; her earlobes were not long, her fingers too stubby, and her palms too hard. Women of good fortune had soft hands, as if they had no bones at all. She often rubbed my hands, saying that they felt as if they had no bones either. She was envious. She also envied the daughters of this or that man, hanging on to their father's necks as they whined. She was driven to tears by her jealousy.

The son of the village Party Secretary remarried. When his new wife's belly started to bulge, my sister had an epiphany, thinking of a way to escape from home. She should marry. Why hadn't this occurred to her earlier? When the matchmaker had come to her door, she had been of the mind that she would never marry. She now forced apart her metal can and counted a heap of loose paper money. Within a few days, she had made a pair of fashionable bell bottoms. But she was only allowed to be pretty for a few minutes. My father could not stand it. He thought permed hair and sunglasses and bell bottoms were symbols of rebellion and a lack of proper upbringing, so he cut the new pants to shreds.

A creature like Chuntian would be quite a hot commodity, if she were led to the market. The fingers of the buyers and sellers would be vigorously calculating prices in the cuffs of their sleeves, almost pecking blood out. My sister had no clue about her own value. She nodded her head on the first blind date, even though the potential husband was like a black mule with a foolish smile. His name was Liu Zhima, and he gave out betel-nut and cigarettes to everyone he met, not even sparing the little children. At this point, my father became aware of how reluctant he was to let my sister go. She was a good worker, and hers was a vacancy he could not afford to fill. My father first grew melancholy, then anxious; then finally, he set an exorbitant bride price, which made him feel slightly relieved. A few days later, the necessary ceremonies were held. The wedding was set before spring ploughing next year, roughly six months away.

*

The autumn rains wouldn't let up. My father again became worried. Chuntian was getting married. He should prepare a few items for her as a dowry, just to keep the neighbours from talking. The nightstool was easy to manage, and did not cost much to make. My father worried that the wardrobe was too big to transport. He said so, as if to justify himself, making clear it wasn't just about saving money. He did not want to be remiss in his treatment of my sister, so the issue of the wardrobe gnawed at him as he sat in the rear of the house smoking and thinking, glancing at Chairman Mao from time to time as if a suggestion might come from that front. My father thought it through quickly. This generation was bad, making this popular and that popular, with nobody knowing who started each fad. This caused people to make a big show of the dowry, as if it were some sort of competition to see who could get the highest bride price. It was all quite crass. My father cursed, then turned and caught sight of the rotten wardrobe in the room. The Mona Lisa smile crept across his face.

The carpenter was called to our home. Wood shavings rolled up merrily on the floor after the nightstool had been made, new doors placed on the wardrobe, and the other riveting parts reinforced. When the carpenter left, my father started polishing the items, repairing as needed, then covering them with a coat of paint. When the weather was fine, he put all three things on the flat ground, bending over and busying himself here and there like an artist. He touched up here, polished there, as if there was nothing on earth more important than his handiwork. No one in the village personally made their daughter's dowry. They said the crucial moment revealed that the dog-fucking Li ultimately couldn't bear to let his little girl go. 'Dog-fucking' wasn't an especially crude term, but was just an expression often heard from the lips of the village men to add weight to any emotion expressed, making it seem more sincere.

If the professional standard of the carpentry was not so high, my father would have undertaken the whole task himself. My father did not know where to start in carpentry, and this rattled his all-encompassing confidence. Only when he had set to work, did my father discover that painting was not as simple a job as he had imagined. The nightstool was brushed with tung oil, requiring only a few more coats. But it was harder to apply the red lacquer evenly on the wardrobe. It ended up looking like the face of a dark-skinned woman in white powder, not of uniform thickness, and very patchy. He ultimately had quite a battle with that wardrobe. Because the weather was bad, the painting project lasted three months. When he finally announced that it was complete, he was like a triumphant soldier returning home at the end of a long campaign. My mother prepared a good meal as a reward. This episode had cost my father a great deal of energy, turning his hair even whiter than before.

*

Before the New Year, my mother and the mothers of several other men in prison undergoing reform met together to discuss visiting their sons as a group. For some of them, it was as if they were waking from a dream, realising that the prisoners would have to celebrate the New Year too, so they rushed to prepare food, clothing, and other necessities, accidentally creating an early New Year atmosphere. Most of these women hardly ever left the village, but now they began to establish a link to the outside world. I felt there was nothing more enviable than this group of mothers of convicts setting out to see their children. Their hair was grey. They made themselves clean and tidy, with scarves covering their heads. They wore their good clothes stored at the bottom of the chest, those reserved for visiting relatives, and carried sacks stuffed with salted fish, eggs, preserved meat, and pickles. Slinging the sacks over their shoulders or arms, they tottered out on their journey with vigour and vitality. They wanted to walk to Lanxi, where they could take a rickety minibus to Yiyang County, then change buses for a four or five hour ride to the prison, where they would wait at the gate like a flock of speckled hens for the doors to be thrown open.

As our mother was preparing, she asked my father whether he was going too. With his expression dark and fierce, my father smoked. When he inhaled a stream of smoke, he wanted to go; when he exhaled, he did not. He inhaled and exhaled half a pack of cigarettes, filling the room with smoke. Finally, my father's voice swam through the cloud toward my mother like a bunch of tadpoles in a murky pond. He said he would not go, saying the expenses of the journey were not worth it. After that, visiting the prison became my mother's business alone. She never described the proceedings, and my father never even bothered to ask.

*

Just after the New Year, the flower drum opera group began their show, with dragon and lion dances, rice-begging, songs, and performances for the God of Fortune and Buddha. My mother flattened her bank notes and hid them in her pocket. Whoever performed at her door could get a share of them. When the flower drum opera group came to perform, they put up electric bulbs, one to hang for a celebratory welcome and one for a happy send-off. This sort of performance was worth at least five *yuan*. The lead actor was beautiful, and the singing was good. We gave them one 'peasant worker soldier' edition banknote worth ten *yuan* without feeling the pinch. In some places, believers lived frugally for a lifetime, saving for pilgrimage. During the first month of the year, the villagers' generosity was basically similar to that. Just this once, they acted with panache. This year we collected money and invited the opera troupe to sing and act out a popular local drama. They sang from the sixth day of the Spring Festival to the fifteenth day, and I even got to play the part of a little imp who waved its streamers.

My sister did not like crowds, preferring to stay home by herself and sleep. When she would wake up, she would look for something to eat, occasionally going out to play a game of Chinese dominoes. Nobody bothered about her for the first month of the lunar year, and she did nothing to draw attention to herself. The first month passed. The cotton-padded jackets were packed away, green shoots sprouted on willow twigs, and peach blossoms laughed in the wind. I was the first one who noticed my sister's swollen belly. Even so severely sick, she did not go to see a doctor. I had to tell my mother. She checked my sister's belly, and I could see from her face it was catastrophic. That night, my parents whispered in the room next door. I heard my father curse loudly, and my sister and I both heard the word 'shameless.' My sister covered her face with her hands, and her shoulders started to shake convulsively. Before long, I realised she was laughing – in fact, laughing so hard she could barely breathe. Actually, since her blind date, my sister had not chewed anymore matches worth 2 cents a box. Sometimes she even made sweet snoring sounds.

The day my sister, Chuntian, got married, the weather was especially good. She wore a pink jacket, wide skirt, and her waist was so thick it was hard to hide. In the early 1980s, a pregnant bride was a rarity. My sister did quite well. Under countless strange looks, she went over to her husband's house with her protruding tummy. My father decided to have no part in any of it. He did not want to lose face along the way. He was a real bastard, always making sure his own behaviour appeared stately. He always stood on the side of righteousness.

At nine o'clock in the morning, my sister and mother, each shedding some tears, stepped out of the house. I was exceptionally pleased in my new rose-red outfit. The three of us got on the causeway with vigour, followed by our relatives, lugging the night-stool and wardrobe behind them. Two long poles were tied around the wardrobe, and its top was covered with several red and green quilts. They carried the wardrobe like they were carrying sedan-chairs, with their hips moving in rhythm. Those carrying the items walked at a fast pace, and they eventually had to leave us behind.

The three of us flowed gradually across the winding causeway. Though, actually, there were four of us. Everything around us was deserted. The ranks of our procession were both neat and solitary. No one spoke. Chuntian's mouth was in its usual chicken-arse-tight pucker. It was more like a funeral procession. We walked for four hours. I could not remember clearly if any of us issued a sound the whole time. No impression was left in my mind at all. I felt we were walking toward a hole, and it was getting darker and colder. The weeds around us stood higher than my head, and the reeds rustled. We noticed a cluster of Chinese roses blooming by the roadside, the same colour as my sister's new jacket. I should have picked one and given it to her, but neither I, my mother, nor my sister herself thought of it at the time. We were focused on walking. The weather that day was the only thing worth mentioning.

Chapter 6:

Li Xinhai, Grandfather

I was spinning a top at the door. When it was spinning, it seemed to stand still. I lay the rope down and stared at the top as it turned. My grandfather had much experience with boredom. Seeming to think I was bored too, he took compassion on me. He called my nickname and waved to me. Staring at a thing spinning blindly was in fact quite boring, but I did not expect my grandfather to step in with anything of interest to me either.

I walked lazily over. For the first time, my grandfather disclosed the contents of his treasure chest. A smell of old must and fragrant food rushed out of it. All my grandfather's possessions were locked inside. I was like a thief checking to see what treasures I would like. I saw some bottles, cans and several books that were starting to turn yellow. A set of ivory Chinese dominoes flashed vaguely, and then my grandfather fastened the lid again. He put a large piece of rock sugar into my mouth, saying, 'Let Grandpa teach you some calligraphy. We in the Li family have this one excellent craft. It would be a shame not to pass it on.'

I asked what was so good about writing calligraphy. What I really meant was, would there be rock sugar every day when I wrote.

My grandfather said the benefits equalled that of playing dominoes. It built character, nourished one's nature, and if he did not care about winning or losing, one would be free of worry, unhappiness . . . that kind of crap.

Later, I listened to my grandfather's lofty rhetoric regarding gambling as he flicked open the box. He pushed a piece of rock sugar into his own mouth, teeth crunching on it as he spoke, like he had pebbles in his mouth. He deftly retrieved a brush and some ink from a chaotic pile and told me to hold them. I felt that he was thinking quite highly of me. He moved a small square table over and continued saying that the feeling of having a good hand of cards is the same as writing well, both were worthy of pride. It was many years later that I came to understand my grandfather's analogy, but he had extended the meaning of having a good hand of cards.

That day I copied the phrase 'Guan! Guan! Cry the fish hawks.' My grandfather said the words had endured for three thousand years. My hands were shaking so much, as if I were on death row. I thought something must be wrong with me. I continued to seek my grandfather out to practice calligraphy with him every day after that. When my hand stopped shaking, I felt that writing calligraphy was as interesting as rolling a metal hoop through the street, or playing with a slingshot, or spinning a top – or perhaps even more interesting. Before long, I got a taste of the pride my grandfather had talked about when my teacher praised my writing in front of the rest of the class. I memorised a good deal of poetry. Thinking that Li Bai, Li He, and Li Shangyin might be my ancestors, I found it even more exciting to memorise their work.

That summer, my grandfather found a boil as big as an egg on his buttocks. He felt the opportunity had come to get revenge on my parents, so he took this ailment as an excuse to lie in bed and not get up at all, expecting them to serve him as he ate, drank, peed, and pooped in bed. When anyone came by, he would scream as if dying, shouting, 'I'm dying! I won't last long. I just want a bowl of chicken and noodle soup before I die, with a fried egg and chopped chillies.'

Sometimes my mother sent me to see whether or not my grandfather had died yet. When I returned, I said it seemed he still had plenty of spirit left, and had even explained the rhyme scheme of a poem to me. My mother called the old man a coward, saying dying scared him half to death.

With the dressing on the festering boil, my grandfather's room smelled strongly of herbs. He was like a hen sitting on soon-to-hatch eggs for half a month. When the boil did finally hatch, it gave birth to a bowlful of pus. Collapsing inward, it left a pit on his skin. He lay for ten more days before he was willing to get up. After that, whenever he saw anyone, he made a show of having recovered from a serious illness.

Logically, once he had recovered, my grandfather should have sat at the entrance to our house, smiling and thanking passersby, or counting the stars at night until bedtime. Instead, he vanished. This made my parents very unhappy. They had not cared for him like a wounded soldier just so he could return to the battlefield of the gambling house. Before he vanished, my grandfather did not have any money, so he pretended to be so sick he could stay in bed. He wanted to continue being sick, but a mysterious distant relative suddenly sent a rather huge sum of 200 *yuan* to my grandfather. He could lie still no longer then.

When I came home from school, my grandfather was sitting on the floor staring at the pond outside the door. A few ducks were frolicking on the surface of the water, the male duck flapping his wings and squawking loudly. I felt instinctively that there was something mysterious coming between the ducks and my grandfather. That mysterious matter was his real concern right now.

My grandfather waved to me like a generous lord. He told me to go to the consignment shop and buy some liquor for him, along with a pound of snacks shaped like cat ears, reminding me to make sure the snacks would crackle when he chewed on them. When I returned, my grandfather invited me to share his snacks. At this time, my grandfather suddenly seemed quite young, pouring his liquor into the dirt-covered iron sheet cup and taking a swig. Each sip he took was followed by a slurping sound, so content he sounded like a vampire finding blood. The 'cat ears' were burnt yellow, thin and crispy. I focused on eating the snacks, my heart not really in my grandfather's chatter.

My grandfather pinched a piece of 'cat ear' between his long fingers as he talked about a place called Anhua, which sounded far away and mysterious, like my grandfather's past. For a while, his story caught my attention, so I asked, 'What happened then?' But it was just for show.

Half of the liquor had disappeared inside my grandfather by that point, turning his cheekbones blood-red. He opened the wooden box, pulled out a well-thumbed-through book, and took out an old picture. It was a woman with hair coiled at the back of her head, revealing a shiny forehead. Though the face was faded by this time, I could still see how delicately pretty and elegant she was.

My grandfather stared at it for some time, then sighed, put the photo back into the book, and carried on drinking.

When he started to recite poems and sing, I decided I had had enough to eat and abandoned him.

Chapter 7:

Li Chuntian, Elder Sister

My sister Li Chuntian's house was like a wild mushroom growing on a hillside, and later, a small mushroom sprouted next to it. My sister was very capable. During the weeks that she was building the house, as soon as she finished nursing the baby, she would start carrying mortar, then put down the shoulder pole to cook, still managing to find time to move a few bricks while the fire was burning out. Everyone said she came and went like the wind, but was as silent as a tree. The trees rustled loudly when the wind blew. As if gunpowder had been ignited, smoke filled my sister's mouth when she chewed on matchsticks. Now that she had rid herself of my father, she worked happily in her own home. This happiness was a sort of revenge on my father.

Once my sister married, she never returned to her girlhood home. When she had her child, my father did not go to visit, and my mother did not go to help. . . Of course, my mother did not have time for that. If she were away from home, those of us left at home would not even know where to find the oil or salt jars. And why would my father go to visit, since the newborn beast would not bear the surname Li? And anyway, he did not like the plum wine and Torch brand cigarettes the 'black mule' gave him – he liked to call Chuntian's husband that. He was almost fed up enough with my brother-in-law's offerings to throw them away right in front of the fellow.

My mother, on the other hand, had a better way of handling things. She re-gifted, passing the gifts on to the master worker in the field. After the master had drunk the plum wine and smoked the Torch brand cigarettes, he ploughed the fields deeper than a foot, even digging up the fertile soil of past centuries. The seedlings were so full of nutrients that the leaves were big, fat, and dark, but the grains were like old breasts, half-shrivelled. Of course, this account was not the master's responsibility, nor was it on the black mule's head. My father was the only one to blame. Chasing the dreams he harboured in his head of 3000 *jin* per *mu* of land, he secretly put many times more fertiliser than anyone else on his field. At harvest time, my father cursed over and over while he worked the mill. Most of the grain fell in front of the mill, with only a small portion of it ending up in the basket. What dropped in front of the mill was considered slop fit for pig feed. When there was a food shortage between harvests, we mixed the bran in with rice and shared with the pigs, too.

While she was building the house, my sister's appendix started to hurt. She had to lie down to rest several times, making her in-laws unhappy. The black mule dragged my sister to work, thinking it better for her to finish building before going to the hospital. This rationalisation received great praise from all, aside from the still nursing infant, who could not yet voice his opinion. My sister understood the fact that the truth lay in the hands of the majority, so she could not break the truth with one kick. The good temperament she had acquired in her maiden home was put to good use at this time.

When Chuntian finally collapsed and was unable to pull

herself up from the ground, the majority, who determined the truth, finally sent her to the hospital. They were not the least bit concerned about my sister's intestinal problems, but they were extremely worried about how much it would cost to cut out the useless little appendix. It did not matter to them that this rotted bit of gut nearly cost my sister her life; they felt the delay in the work on the house was the biggest loss.

This experience led my sister to better understand life's truths, but she did not share her experience with anyone. The sun rose as usual. There was no deviation from their daily routine until one day, when their son was two years old, the boy fell into the ditch and drowned. It happened in a flash. There was so little water in the ditch that no one had thought to be concerned about the possibility of an accident. The truth was once again held in the hands of the black mule's family, and they decided my sister was to be condemned as a sinner through all the ages. They did not even allow her to shed a tear, and the black mule slapped her so hard he drew blood. My sister had to swallow her blood together with her tears.

Our family knew nothing of this. It was only after I graduated from university that I heard my sister mention it, even though it happened before my second brother started university. I remember my sister once came home, like a returning cat that has wandered as a stray for many years, dishevelled and eager for a hot bath and a hot meal. But my sister ate very little. She shared my bed that night, and I saw that her mouth was no longer stubbornly puckered like a chicken's arse, but her brow was furrowed – this was when I discovered that she had started chewing matchsticks again as she convulsed silently. She stayed one night, then left the next day without a word.

My father cursed into the air, complaining that it was inappropriate for a woman to come back to her maiden home empty-handed. Then he cited examples of so-and-so's daughter giving her parents living expenses after her visit.

I despised my father.

One year during the summer holiday, my second brother, Li Xiazhi, and I cycled to our sister's place to visit her. My brother, then in his third year of university, wore glasses and spoke in an extraordinary language. We chatted as we cycled, him saying he was a product of our father's tyranny and violence. It was our father who had pressed my brother's nose to the grindstone during his school days, taking away all his joy in growing up and depriving him of freedom. He liked to write poetry, and he wanted to major in Chinese, but my father forced him to choose science, not wanting another whiny poet like our grandfather in the family. My brother told me to not take orders, as he had done, and said he would support me.

I did not believe him. The previous year, I had relied on my brother's presence to speak up against our father, and it had resulted in the riling up of a hornets' nest. My father picked up the carrying pole which lay nearby, but my brother snatched it away. It was the first time anyone had stood up to my father so blatantly and so, determined to suppress this evil air, my father went into the kitchen and charged out with a glinting meat cleaver. Scared out of his wits, my brother ducked to one side and hid.

I later said, 'If I hadn't run fast, who knows which part of my body might now bear a scar from that knife.'

My brother stopped his bicycle and said, 'Under those circumstances, I was right to hide, and you were right to run. Father had gone completely crazy, but we can only reason with a normal person.'

I said, 'Father's never normal.'

My brother replied, 'I still need to talk to him. If not, no matter how far we fly, we can only be kites in his hand. We need an enlightened monarch.'

My brother had a great deal to say about the 'monarch,' spending half the journey going on about it. He was our father's favourite, but he did not want my father's affection.

I said, 'Why don't we rebel against our father?'

He replied, 'Before long, he will be against himself.'

I didn't understand what he meant.

The mushroom on the hillside appeared in our view, with smoke rising from the roof. My sister really was cooking. When she saw us, she smiled from ear to ear. She reached into the chicken coop and pulled out a few eggs, then went to pluck several peppers from the garden to fry with slices of pork, and picked a few stalks of amaranth, too.

Chuntian had separated and lived apart from the family. Xiazhi and I took liberties. He scooped some water from the cistern and drank directly from the ladle, asking after her husband, Liu Zhima. My sister said he was out of town selling mosquito nets, and one trip took him away for anywhere from ten days to a month. My brother commented that it was the 'rush harvesting and planting' season, and yet Zhima left the house. Chuntian said this was the worst season for mosquitoes, so it was the best time to sell mosquito nets. Xiazhi and I thought this did not sound right.

Chuntian's house was quite empty, with nothing worth seeing. The only decent furniture was what had been sent as dowry, and even the wardrobe's paint was fading. My sister opened the door and pulled out a drawer. She reached in to grab something, then pushed the drawer back. The door was out of shape and could not be closed properly, so she had to lift it, close it, then slap it shut. My sister pressed a few crumpled notes into my hands so I could buy myself something to eat and need not envy my classmates. She knew I loved to eat. I was very happy, except that I could see she had aged. In fact, she looked like our mother. She did not share naughty jokes with my brother and me anymore. It was like an invisible veil had fallen between us.

Chapter 8:

Li Xiazhi, Middle Brother

As the years passed, my father was no different from other farmers. He was keen to talk about his crops, and the first thing he did early every morning was to take a turn around his fields. He always came back carrying a bunch of barnyard grass, which he threw on the ground for the chickens to peck at. When he was free, he took his hoe and dug in the back garden, planting vegetables in every inch of wasteland, even planting soybeans and building bamboo frames for sponge cucumbers and bitter gourds to climb, placing them beside the pond. The pumpkin vines crept up the big earth grave, with the fruits hidden under the broad leaves. My father took on a rosy tanned look. His hands did not look like they had once been fed by the government. The produce grew so wildly we could even hear the jolting sound of the bones of his hands in the night. Every other day, my mother had to carry a load of vegetables into town and sell them cheap. If she made it in time for the morning market, she could sell them for a good price, so she had to set off before the sun came out. She often asked me to go with her, since she was afraid to walk while it was dark. I was always happy to eat the noodles, fried buns, pancakes, rice tofu, or some such thing in town, so it was my belly that benefitted from this arrangement.

The money from the sale of our produce often went to pay for my second brother's living expenses. He loved to eat the local speciality, pork fried with peppers, but he painfully sacrificed money set aside for meat so he could buy school books. University changed him into a young man with a serious expression. His glasses were so thick each lens looked like the bottom of a bottle. Once, he put away his glasses when he came home and pretended to have good eyesight, but he ended up putting his chopsticks into my rice bowl.

The rhythm of my brother's speech changed drastically. Even more, he learned to play with pauses and employ the art of silence. My father was not sure how to take him.

Xiazhi spoke to me privately saying that the following year our elder brother, Shunqiu, would be home, and he himself would graduate and go to work. 'We need to concentrate our firepower and have a long talk with Li Jiaxu. A harmonious, warm family should be democratic, and we should also talk about the status of women. Chuntian – our own sister – is still living under the old society's rules.'

My brother called my father by his name. It made our father seem just like an ordinary member attending a meeting, immediately making us equals.

Once, Xiazhi brought several classmates home with him, both men and women. At night, they went out to catch frogs, steal melons and dates, and throw nets into the river to fish. It was just like the time when our elder brother, Shunqiu, had got in trouble. The difference was when they closed in on their prey, they hopped about as lively as the fish, yelling and squealing. It had been five years since the 'crackdown', and people were no longer forced to eat a bullet or were sent to jail because of a bit of fish poaching. But just as the dead do not rise again, no sentence was ever overturned. When Xiazhi and his friends mentioned this, they raised their voices against injustice. They also talked of corruption and the rigidity of the system. They debated, criticised, and bullshitted. The female students raised their eyebrows in anger because of this, saying that once changes had been made, a solution would emerge, and if there was no reform, the path only led to death. My brother felt that if the root was damaged, reform was of no use. He went on to say that the patriarchy and the stifling of individual rights could only lead to an illusion of peace, but a plant would always grow in the direction of the sun. My father had no idea what my brother did at school. In fact, he published a good deal of poetry and was one of the main forces behind the literary society.

In the evening, they recited poetry under the bitter jujube tree. When the wind blew, the purple jujube flowers, as fine as grains of rice, floated down one after another. Some leapt into their teacups, and others hid in their hair. The flora and fauna around our village were playful like that. Later someone took out a guitar and a book full of musical scores and lyrics and started playing and singing. The head of the literary society, Yu Shuzong, sang through three songs all in one breath, his hair standing up straight like a hedgehog's quills. The onlookers gathered under the jujube tree, so full of envy as they looked on that they were practically drooling. Xiazhi was tone deaf, so could do nothing more than sit and listen silently while he rubbed the jujube flowers. The guy playing the guitar wore glasses and his hair covered his ears, making him look as docile as a lamb. He sang 'Walking on a Path in the Countryside', from time to time looking up at the rural scene around him. His eyes occasionally lingered on my face for a brief moment. I clearly remember that night as my first experience of puppy love. He was called Tang Linlu.

I was in my second year of Junior College, studying in town. It was late May and the school was suddenly half-empty. Students everywhere were copying what was going on in Beijing in the spring and early summer of 1989, skipping classes to take to the streets in protest. The atmosphere was restless, so the teacher cancelled classes and dispersed us. My mother was surprised to see me, thinking I was expelled from school because I had done something bad. My father always watched the news, so he knew of the situation that was spreading. He was only worried my second brother would do something outrageous, and even said he would break Xiazhi's legs if he made trouble. My father was always making such cruel threats, but he never thought of setting out personally to look for my brother and confront him face to face.

My father stopped all work and remained glued to the television. Voices chattered non-stop on the black and white television set. The host said there had been riots in Beijing. Burning cars and dead bodies appeared on the screen, along with tanks and troops in action. My mother came over and assumed he was watching a war film. She could not stand watching. I too went into my room. We felt it was all so far away from us, and that it had nothing to do with us.

A week later, as I got ready to go to school, Tang Linlu graced our house with his presence. When I saw that docile lamb's head, my heart stopped instantly. The news he brought struck me even harder. 'Xiazhi went to Beijing ten days ago, angry at someone or other, and he sat in the square not eating or drinking. He could not be persuaded to leave or be chased away. All night he slept under the open sky with countless other students, refusing to move even when it rained.'

As he went on, Linlu's face grew paler, as if he was frightened out of his soul by what he was going to say. He paused, then said,

'Xiazhi disappeared. We later found him in the crematorium, with his student identity card hidden in his pocket. His whole body was in ruins.'

My parents' expressions were blank, as if they did not understand what had been said.

Linlu said, 'I brought Xiazhi home.'

He placed a wooden box on the table. A strange aura surrounded it.

We sat in silence for some time. No one dared to touch it. Finally, my mother's voice broke the silence, uttering a shocking sound.

Chapter 9:

Li Shunqiu, Eldest Brother

Autumn brought with it a look of lamentation. The sky was like a swath of grey cloth, and a blackbird uttered a shrill cry, shooting like a sharp arrow through the fabric, but the rip immediately patched itself up. The field was a centenarian's face. The ponds and ditches were frozen into thin ice, and withered yellow leaves of vegetables drooped on the bare soil, painted with autumn frost. Withered vines were tightly wrapped around the empty melon shed. Chilli plants stood like skeleton specimens, with a few shrivelled red peppers hanging from their branches. The wilted grass dyed with frost became as fluffy as a dog's tail.

My father burned everything belonging to my second brother, not even leaving a single scrap of paper behind. He was ashamed of Xiazhi's participation in the riots, saying it was even more humiliating than Shunqiu's imprisonment. My father's rage was greater than his sorrow. If my mother cried, he started to yell, coughing and spitting, and dusting off dirt from his body. I was staying in school then, and only returned home for a couple of reasons. One, was because I missed my mother, and the other was the lack of funds for boarding expenses;

occasionally both reasons brought me home at the same time. Once, the son of some rich family in the village was getting married, and my mother gave me twenty *yuan* and told me to put it in the account books. She asked me to eat and drink as much as I wanted at the feast. I skipped the wedding feast and put the money in my pocket. My mother was willing to give other people this much money in one go, but was not that generous towards me, and that did not please me. That day, the men in the village drank half the night, and the women were dressed up in pretty clothes. After sipping a bit of strong liquor, their cheeks turned a festive red. Even the skinny folk were looking prosperously complacent.

It had been more than six years, but I had never visited my oldest brother in prison. My father had not been to see him either, and my mother only went once a year. She said Shunqiu did not want to see anyone. Like in any other prison, all the things we sent him were swallowed up by a mysterious monster. He was no longer as temperate as before, but answered all my mother's queries impatiently. He did not bother about the family either, only once asking what year I was in at school. The last several times my mother had been to see her son in his prison uniform, she did not say anything at all. The last time they met was like they followed diplomatic protocol, it was dull and courteous, without joy or conflict.

After my second brother died, my father burned all the fishing nets in the back garden, sold the old bike to a rag and bones man, and tore his awards off the wall, completely cleaning the place up. Before winter set in, my father quietly cleaned out a room, whitewashed the walls, and replaced the plastic layer on the wooden windowsills. My mother stepped on the mosquito net in the foot-soaking basin until foam splashed. When I chanced to go home and saw that my parents' life had suddenly taken an enthusiastic turn, as if they had received a blood transfusion, I thought it was highly unusual.

The night before the Lunar New Year, when the five-watt bulb in the house had just come on, a ghost suddenly drifted in from the back garden. My father scolded, 'Fucking thief can't even come through the front door, has to come through the back door.'

When he'd finished cursing, he came into the main room and lit a string of firecrackers with a thousand words written down its length, throwing it onto the floor. The sound was ear-splitting. Smoke billowed into the room. In the dim lighting, it was hard to see the shadowy ghost clearly. At this time, our house was full of people. They all knew Shunqiu was to receive an early release, and they had come to congratulate us, and also hopefully catch sight of what someone newly released from prison looked like.

The ghost was afraid of firecrackers. When they started crackling, it floated out the back door again. At any rate, it never showed up again.

Everyone was a bit disappointed, but they said they understood. The mothers of several of the concerned parties stood with misty faces and mixed feelings, sighing even as they wiped away tears of joy.

To my memory, our house had never been this lively before. That was also why our dinner was delayed. I sat beside the stove and lit the fire. When the rice started releasing the aroma of rice crust, I doused the fire and covered it with soot. My mother started to cook, spicy fermented black soybeans, garlic braised bacon, oily, fatty pork, and of course, pepper fried with pork slices. She deliberately cut the fatty pork into slices so thick it was like biting into a radish. It was very tasty. She also prepared a fish soup and a chilli omelette. Grey smoke rose from the chimney, but a portion of it found its way into the kitchen. It smothered my mother, and she lifted the edge of her apron to wipe away her tears. I realised then that tears had always been her favourite means of expressing herself.

If we say Shunqiu had formerly been like a green date hanging on a tree, he was now like a dried date turning black. I did not know the past life of the dried date, and could not imagine the future of the green date. The seed of the date was now stuck in my throat. My brother stood in the kitchen, asking where I was. I just stood up from my usual place behind the stove and said nothing. With her typical roundabout way of expressing her concern for her children, my mother said, 'Damned girl can't even speak up when she's addressed.'

Shunqiu was shocked. He had expected to find a little girl less than ten years old, but I was already as tall as my mother. He was overwhelmed.

My father and brother spent a little time sizing each other up, then found several trivial issues to quarrel loudly over.

'Why would anyone want to set off a bunch of firecrackers when a reformed prisoner comes home?' Shunqiu asked. He had loitered in town for a few hours, intending to wait until dark so as not to disturb the neighbours. Could the firecrackers have been meant for any purpose other than to embarrass him?

My father was sure he had the upper hand. He said, 'This fucking ghost comes lurking in the middle of the night and doesn't know how to appreciate what's good. I'll set off firecrackers any time I fucking please. There's bad luck all over the house, and I'm going to get rid of it!' My brother retorted, 'So I'm bad luck! Don't worry; I'll leave in a few days.'

My father said, 'You wastrel. If you leave, don't come back.'

My mother used her tears to break up the fight.

We started to eat. My brother wolfed his food down. When he had eaten half a bowl of meat, he asked where Xiazhi was. Clutching her rice bowl, my mother left the table, while my father kicked our yellow dog. I said my second brother had gone to Beijing as soon as he'd graduated and was quite busy at work. Then, I changed the topic and started to talk about my sister, since Shunqiu had heard so little about her in the years he had been locked up. 'She had a son,' I said. 'He died when he was two years old. Drowned. Now she's got two daughters. Yihua is three, and Yicao is one. She wants to have another baby. She said she wants to bring her son back.'

My father grumbled, 'We don't bother about the Liu crew. If they cannot afford to pay the fine for having too many kids and their house is demolished, they better not come running here to stay with me.'

My brother slowed his pace of eating, as if he was stuffed.

I thought of what Xiazhi had said, *Wait until Shunqiu's back and we'll have a talk with Li Jiaxu,* and I started to feel very uncomfortable.

*

The chilly wind seeped into our bones on the causeway. The moonlight was pale and ailing. My oldest brother's figure was still ghostly. He had become careful and agile, as if tentacles protruded from his body and he flinched at the slightest obstacle and changed directions or bounced off it quickly. He did not talk to others face to face or look them in the eye. He was a vigilant hare, focusing only on the world within a ten-metre radius of himself. He sometimes jumped down the causeway slope, circling the jetty where he fished. I said, 'You were unlucky. There's nothing wrong with fishing in broad daylight now. It's a game of cat and mouse.'

Shunqiu didn't answer, except to say the water was narrower, and the world of fish smaller. We never inquired about his prison life, which might seem cold or heartless, but it was like we were keeping a secret, bottling the matter up, as if we were accomplices hiding a body after committing a murder. We wanted to bury my brother's inglorious history a thousand metres underground.

'What do you want to do in the future?' Shunqiu asked.

I said, 'I want to be a lawyer, to defend the innocent.'

'Lawyers are more effective for the guilty.'

I didn't understand.

'What's up with Xiazhi. Are you all hiding something from me?'

I thought about it, then said, 'He's dead.'

Early the following year, the snow piled a foot deep after a blizzard in early spring, and like fat meat, a layer of snow was added to the causeway. The north sides of the trees were wrapped in icy armour, and their leaves turned into onyx stone. The lake wore a shield, and the grass had grown into corals. From under the eaves, luminescent sword-like icicles hung. The whole village was filled with the sheen and sharpness of weapons. My father set a big tree stump on fire in the back garden. In the picture hanging on the wall next to Chairman Mao, the ten generals on their mounts looked like they were rushing to the battlefield. The pictures of the ten generals were hung apart on the eastern and western walls, their mighty horses facing south, orderly and mighty. It filled the back garden with an extraordinary momentum.

When my sister came back with her family for the New Year, she stayed one night, then left. My father despised Yihua and Yicao, just as much as he hated the plum wine and Torch brand cigarettes. Liu Zhima chewed betel nuts, spitting the juice as he talked about what he saw and heard on his business errands. He told us which black dogs bit people, which roads had stupid people willing to buy his lousy nets, which folk custom was the most fierce, which widows had attempted to seduce him. . .

And finally, he always had to talk about prison, as if it held great charm for him.

When he was arguing with my sister, Zhima was sure to mention reformed prisoners, then supplement it with 'Cultural Revolution hatchet men'. When my sister had first got together with Zhima, they used indicting our father as a sort of foreplay when they went to bed. Zhima had loved to listen to Chuntian complain. A suffering woman was easy to please, because all he needed to do was say a few gentle words and she would feel he was the best man in the world, and when she worked, she was like well-fed livestock. But these things had all become Zhima's offensive weapons now. What he meant was that our family only produced thugs and reformed inmates, nothing good.

If Zhima spoke ill of my father, my sister was not angry. But if he spoke ill of Shunqiu, she would retaliate. She said, 'What's so great about your family? Your father stammers and your mother is cross-eyed.'

What she said was true, but Zhima could not accept these facts. Or, to put it more accurately, the facts were there, but they were not there to be dragged out and talked about. So Zhima slapped my sister. She always felt no one in the world was allowed to slap her, except my father – and him only – because she had come from his seed. Zhima was not qualified to slap her, so she slapped him back, but her aim was bad, and she ended up putting two long bloody scratches on his face with her nails. This riled Zhima up. He struck back, and the pair started to scuffle. Finally, Chuntian picked up a cup and smashed it on her forehead. The one who shed more blood had the right to make the judgement call. Such was the pattern of their marital life.

Zhima was always in a good mood in our home, without showing any signs of his love for hitting others. When he talked to my brother, he was especially nice. Shunqiu acted as though he had long lived in darkness and was now finally let out into daylight; his eyes had not even fully adapted to the light yet. In order to protect his eyes, he would look down, or sometimes hide in the corner to be able to talk to people.

When Chuntian came back and saw how Shunqiu looked, her resentment towards my father grew another layer. She felt everyone at home had been ruined by my father. Xiazhi had gone to Beijing, but it was in rebellion against my father. I was taken aback by the thoughts going on in the skull that had spent so many years eating matchsticks.

I secured glutinous rice cakes with tongs and grilled them over the red-hot burning wood, not saying much. I turned each cake over several times until it finally turned golden brown and aromatic. Yihua stood leaning against me. She was quiet, instinctively quite sensible, unlike other children who were always clamouring to eat this or that. Yihua also liked to squat beside Shunqiu and watch him organise the fishing nets, asking many questions. Shunqiu liked Yihua, and she liked him. In the spring he brought her to the riverbank to put out the nets. Yihua was as lively as a fish, and so was Shunqiu.

In previous years during the spring, we would still have preserved fish and preserved meat left over at home. This year, we had eaten them all by early February, and even the cats meowed in disbelief as they saw the empty hooks where the preserved meat used to hang. When my father's mouth, which was usually shut tightly like he was biting a seed, loosened up, it was like a machine gun extended from the fort, sending bullets flying in Shunqiu's direction. 'Good for nothing', 'sit idle and eat', 'fruitless commodity', sometimes he lumped my grandfather and brother together in his cursing. As soon as the spring seedlings took root, my father's dislike of Shunqiu was magnified. He hated gluttons, especially the bottomless pit released from prison who could not be filled to satisfaction with even a hundred pigs.

My brother stumbled out of the house to the Township Enterprises to do some odd manual jobs. My father got him these jobs. Shunqiu had no social resources, nor skills of any kind, and had only spent his time in the reform prison farm developing his physical strength. There was a screw factory in Lanxi Town, about five miles from our house. Shunqiu left home early and came home late, appearing and disappearing on the causeway like a thief, coming and going under the inky black sky.

When about a month had turned on time's wheel, the matchmaker had found an older woman for Shunqiu. My brother's left knee suddenly started to hurt. It was so painful he was hopping about on one leg, and he could not go to work. Instead, he sat at home, resting his ailing leg on a stool, watching it as it gradually swelled and turned as pink as a baby's flesh, shining like the skin of ripe fruit.

Before he had started earning any wages at all, his medical expenses started to come in. My father saw that his condition was not getting better, so asked his childhood friend, a rural village doctor, to come see him. This helped create some business for the doctor and kept expenses low for my father. Most importantly, he could delay payment. My father's friend was called Wang, balding and red-faced. Smoking and half squinting, he rambled to my father as he poked my brother's knee like he was inspecting a treasure. Wang said that it was septic arthritis and the inside had rotted. He drew a few tubes of blood and pus from the knee with a syringe, making the skin above collapse. He hung an infusion bottle beside Shunqiu and said it would be fine in a few days.

A week later there was a rotted wound on my brother's knee, open and exposing the bone. The air flowed through the exposed bone, bringing out the fishy smell of pus. As soon as Wang saw this, he knew something was not right and felt he was betrayed by the knee, so he recommended an amputation of the rotten thing.

I have said my father was very calculative. When he started adding up the cost of amputating a leg, he realised that the burden of a disabled person was worse than that of an amputation, so he gritted his teeth and borrowed and gathered enough money to send my brother to the hospital in Changsha for recovery. As soon as he arrived at the hospital, he was taken in for surgery. The doctors there said it was a very dangerous situation, and that if he had been any later there would have been no way to save the leg. My father breathed a sigh of relief. It had been quite some time since he had done something that made him feel this proud, so he went around boasting about his wise strategy. Every time he and my brother clashed after this, he always brought up this instance, using it like an ace up the sleeve to quell the other party.

When Shunqiu was discharged, he was recuperating for a while. He sat admiring his bad leg every day, paying close attention to its development and changes. The doctor said that post-surgery rehab depended on the patient's initiative. If the muscle atrophied, there would be a relapse and he would lose the leg. A person who has broken a bowl before will naturally take special care with the porcelain he holds in his hands. Gritting his teeth, my brother started walking on crutches, spending the late night hours walking up and down the causeway every night. When summer had passed, his skin had turned pale and he had rid himself of extra flesh. His illness and pain had reduced him to a ball of crumpled paper, but he now looked more like his old self, before prison had interrupted his life.

Chapter 10:

Li Chuntian, Elder Sister

My sister kept her hair long after giving birth to Yicao, adopting the fashion of pulling her hair into a bun, like the people in the city. Hers was nothing like theirs, only creating a messy hairball and exposing her narrow forehead, and since her fringe had always covered her forehead, it was whiter than the rest of her face. On this particular day, my sister was coaxing Yicao to sleep. The village director of women's affairs, Auntie Cui, was ploughing her way in with her thick legs, laughing even before she came near. Her hair was naturally curly, like African hair, fluffy around her whole skull. Auntie Cui's ample flesh shook loosely all over her frame. When she sat, she looked like a hen hatching eggs, spreading her wings over the bench where she perched. She stared at Yicao for a while, then praised her for being obedient and looking good.

My sister put Yicao back in the cradle and rocked it as she said, 'She sees you, so she won't be naughty, but she torments us in the night.'

Auntie Cui said, 'Now she's a torment; in future she'll turn into quite a little padded jacket. Look around, see which naughty boy does not forget their mother after they have taken a wife.'

My sister did not pick up the thread of the conversation.

Auntie Cui went on, 'I really have no luck with giving birth. I had two sons one after the other, and I really want a daughter, but I have to respect the family planning policy, right? So I went to the hospital to get my tubes tied. Getting a ligation is a trifle. After a couple of days, I was healthier than ever.'

When Auntie Cui finally got started on this topic, she looked quite happy, as if having a tubal ligation was some wildly enjoyable thing. My sister did not tear her story apart, knowing that Auntie Cui was married to the younger brother of the village secretary, a position of real power and prestige. Auntie Cui had gone to the hospital with an air of importance and pretended to have her tubes tied, and was carried home in a wooden cart, moaning and groaning. Later, somebody noted with a furtive glance that there was not even a scar on her belly.

My sister nodded and grunted perfunctorily, saying she would go to the hospital when her menstrual period was over. Looking like she had won, Auntie Cui went joyfully on her way. My sister touched her belly. She was already four months pregnant. It would soon begin to show, exposing her intent. If it was discovered, she would be bound and taken to the hospital, and the child would be aborted. She would then be neutered, like an animal. At least if she walked into the hospital of her own accord, she would be left with some measure of dignity.

When Zhima came home, my sister discussed the matter with him. He said to check and see whether it was a boy or girl. If it was a boy, they would keep it; if a girl, they would abort. My sister said whether it was a boy or a girl, this was their last chance. She did not want to keep sneaking around, living in fear. It was such an inhuman life.

Zhima bought a pound of fresh meat and brought it to our house, asking my mother to look after Yihua for him for a little while – several months at least, he said. At the time, Shunqiu was still recovering from the injury to his leg. He could hobble a few steps on crutches, but was also an idle mouth to feed, and now Zhima wanted to add another dead weight, and this one did not even have our surname. My father said, 'No way. We are surrounded by ditches on every side here, and if anything happens to a member of the Liu family, we can't afford to bear this responsibility.'

Zhima knew my father's temperament, so he begged Shunqiu to intercede. Zhima did not know that my father had borrowed money to help treat my brother's leg, depriving my brother of all rights long ago, leaving him no more qualified than Zhima to plead the case. But Shunqiu was moved by Yihua's helpless, innocent look. She seemed aware that she was an extra burden, and was like a small animal lowering its head as it listened to buyer and seller bargain over its price.

When Shunqiu interceded for Yihua, it was as if my father had been scalded with boiling water. He bounced up, and his voice got louder and louder. Shunqiu stared at his own knees, listening patiently to the tirade. He had no objection, feeling that my father had the right to express his dissatisfaction. My father repeated the same things over and over. There were two core issues: our house was not an orphanage, and there was no one to take responsibility for Yihua. Shunqiu quietly answered my father, saying he would eat less, to compensate for Yihua's share, and that he would look after her safety, taking responsibility if anything happened to her.

Zhima went home happy. That night he told Chuntian to pack her things. Early the next morning, they snuck out, escaping to his Aunt Liu's house in Yuanjiang. My sister carried Yicao, who was awakened suddenly by the rough journey. Chuntian looked furtively around her in the dark, then someone's dog barked and scared the child, making her cry.

They ate a bowl of noodles in town, then went to the jetty at the ferry crossing to wait for their ride. There were huge red words painted on the white wall opposite them, reading, *We would rather bleed a river than allow the birth of one more child.* Chuntian knew these words. Unconsciously, she lowered her head and imagined bleeding a river. It made her uneasy. Later, she again told Zhima that once this one was born, she would not have any more. If it was not a son, she would just accept their fate. But both Zhima and his father were the only sons in their generations; even if he agreed, his father would not. No matter what, he had to bring home a son.

At two o'clock that afternoon, after an early start on a long journey by land and water, the Liu Family reached their secret destination. Aunt Liu offered a lukewarm greeting, as if she could just barely tolerate them. When Yicao smiled upon seeing Aunt Liu, the old woman was a little embarrassed, so smiled in return. This made Yicao laugh out loud, which in turn pleased the older woman. She rushed to cook some peppers fried with pork, steamed eggplant, and fried eggs. While they ate, Aunt Liu took Yicao off to one side to play. Later, she used bricks to make a bed in the main room where they kept the farm tools. Zhima stayed one night, then left. He wanted to sell his last batch of mosquito nets that he brought with him before the weather turned cold.

Aunt Liu had been widowed for some years. Her daughter was married, and her son was working at a toy factory in Guangzhou. She was lonely, but she was content to hold onto her loneliness in order to freely take care of so many people.

Chuntian was a diligent worker. She passed Yicao to Aunt Liu and set about cleaning the house from top to bottom. The land reclamation skills my father had taught her came in handy at this time. She quickly turned a half acre of wasteland into a vegetable plot, planting cabbage seeds, which grew into tender seedlings in just a month's time. Early in the morning while the dew was still fresh, she picked the cabbages and took a basketful of them to sell in town. Coming back before breakfast with the basket now empty of cabbages, she would always have a few pancakes or steamed buns inside. Aunt Liu was overjoyed. One day she took the initiative to take Chuntian to the hospital to find out the sex of her foetus. When the results showed it was a boy, my sister cried openly in an expression of her own feelings and, in gratitude to Aunt Liu, she complained about my father in passing.

After this, the smoke from the chimney in Aunt Liu's house livened up a good deal. As if the liveliness were meant to incite the envy of others, when my sister's belly began to shake violently, Aunt Liu's son returned, bringing a pregnant girlfriend home with him. They planned to marry, have the baby, then leave the child in Aunt Liu's care while they went back to earn their fortune. When Aunt Liu saw that her son had brought a pair home all at once, she was ecstatic. This naturally brought about a decline in the interest she took in Yicao. She was about to have a descendant of her own flesh and blood. Yicao could laugh and cry all she wanted now; Aunt Liu would not be so easily moved.

Chuntian was seven or eight months pregnant by this time. There was no going back now. Victory was at hand. If she could not escape the fines for having children outside the state plan, she might as well go home and give birth in peace. Zhima, too, had long ago grown weary of life in exile, so they packed up their things, expressed their gratitude to Aunt Liu, and the bloated family tottered out the door and headed home.

Chapter 11:

Li Shunqiu, Eldest Brother

I never quite knew what the convicts did in prison. From what I had seen on television programmes, I thought the prison was like a school: the reforming prisoners like students in clean uniforms, listening to the instructor lecture, watching television, playing basketball, celebrating the Spring Festival, some even preparing for the college entrance exam, and each one eventually looking into the camera to express their gratitude toward the prison. . . This made prison life look more interesting than the world outside its walls, so that there were always people going in – so much so that when some convicts were released, they missed the place so badly they found a way to break the law and be sent back again.

Before school started in September, I asked Shunqiu if his early release was like in school too, where you could complete a four-year programme in two years by working hard and taking extra credits. He smiled shyly, as if he was surprised by his own good results, and said, 'This country has no law whatsoever. Whether to catch you or not, sentence you or not, is all up to a few people to judge and weigh. Whether they let you graduate or not, it all depends on the instructor's mood.'

My brother had worked desperately hard to outperform in the prison reform farm. He cited an example. If his quota was to finish carrying enough soil for 10 000 plots in a year, he worked hard and did it in half a year. He could put down an acre of paddy in three days, and like a reaping machine, he could complete rolling in two. The farm planted two seasons of paddy and he learned everything he needed to know about the labour involved. The instructors all said that he was so honest he did not qualify to be in the labour reform camp. When my brother was released, everyone asked him to add a handful of soil to the ancestral grave in hopes that his filial remembrance would secure their protection for him. Our family only had one ancestral grave. Inside it lay Li Xinhai's wife, her feet bound, who died during childbirth. Very early on, my grandfather had blocked out the others, so nobody else knew what unhappy events had happened among our ancestors.

My brother made the vast farmland sound very attractive, highlighting features such as large plots of reeds, hidden marshes, muddy ponds, lakes, and flood control dykes, all within a hundred mile radius. Sometimes the sky was not variegated, and other times it was quite turbid. The prisoners moved like a flock of birds, sometimes lined up in a V-formation, sometimes in a straight line. The instructors walked back and forth with their hunting rifles, sometimes shouting or cursing, and when the situation got out of control, firing their guns into the air. Those who were disobedient were punished with solitary confinement, sealed in a room the size of a coffin, to reflect on their mistakes. Those who were tired of prison life and tried to escape ended up in one of two situations – either swallowed by the swamp or having their sentence extended. Another violent end came to those who chose to swallow razor blades.

Shunqiu was not affected by any of this. He was very thankful for the protective callous that had grown naturally on his hands, which was even tougher than the handle of a hoe. I asked him what the easiest work was. He said it was weeding. It was only later that I discovered that weeding was not actually easy. The weeders spent ten hours every day in the water, bent at a ninety-degree angle, facing downward, their faces so swollen by the end of the workday, they were hardly recognisable. Imagine that. The artistic quality is no less than Jean-Francois Millet's famous painting *The Gleaners*. One did not know what went on behind the scenes, like what happened to prisoners who did not know how to distinguish between weeds and rice. Pulling the rice seedlings would have a negative effect on production. Prisoners who did that were criticised. A light punishment was given to them, such as a demerit on their record or solitary confinement. Heavy punishment would be extended sentencing. But absent of that knowledge, one cannot deny the poetic quality and beauty of the picture presented by prisoners weeding. When these same people were not working on the farm, they were repairing roads or embankments or carrying silt, with so many people passing back and forth, creating an impression of ants in motion.

My brother looked at his leg and said he had hurt his knee while working in the prison. But there were much more terrible things there, such as the deadly mosquitoes on the farm. These mosquitoes would normally form themselves into an egg-shaped swarm, then when they saw people, would rush forward, surround, and attack, covering the inmates' white clothing so thoroughly it appeared black. While they worked, they tied the cuffs of their sleeves and trousers tightly and covered their faces with cloths, leaving only the eyes exposed. When one of the prisoners had talked back to an instructor, he was thrown into a ditch to feed the mosquitoes. Later, the prisoner's entire body was covered in blood, and his face swollen to the size of his arse. When he returned, he was sent to solitary confinement, where he died two days later.

There were many things that bit in the prison. Besides the gadflies and leeches, there were numerous poisonous things, for which no one even knew the names.

Chapter 12:

Li Chuntian, Elder Sister

Auntie Cui did not come with a friendly attitude this time. She did away with polite greetings and feigned tactics. Even her hair was fluffed really high because of her rage. She pointed at my sister's belly, saying, 'This is a serious insult to my IQ. When the family planning workgroup comes to visit, you have to deal with it yourself. There's not much human sympathy in the face of policies.'

My sister did not know how to engage in artful talk. She thought she had actually deceived Auntie Cui, but she did not feel the least bit bad about it, for she felt Auntie Cui's scam was much bigger than anything she had done. Everyone cheated. Of those who shared a kinship or friendship with the village cadres, not one of them was without mischief, and they were never punished for having more children than was allowed.

My sister was very calm. She rubbed her belly with a circling motion, like a farmer appreciating the fruits of her harvest. When the produce had grown, who could change it back to its original form? But when the birth control group arrived, she started to panic. They were like the Eight Immortals, five of them in military fatigues, and one in a Mao suit. One wore a worker's hat, and one of the women in the group was an accountant. It was like a heavenly host had descended from above, riding the clouds and fog, and when they touched the ground, their celestial aura was not extinguished, and their expression remained immortal. It was the first time Chuntian had seen a group of such creatures, so it really shocked her.

They did not sit. The official in the Mao jacket asked questions, which my sister answered. Another recorded the conversation.

'What is your name?'

'Li Chuntian.'

'How old are you?'

'Twenty-five.'

'How many children have you had?'

'Three . . . one of them died.'

'What is your condition now?'

'I'm eight months pregnant.'

'Do you know about the family planning policy?'

'Yes. One is fine, two is tie, three and four is scrape, scrape, scrape!'

'And?'

'If you didn't tie when you were supposed to tie, we will demolish your house; if you didn't abort when you were supposed to abort, we will destroy your house and take away your cow.'

'Which do you choose?'

'How much is the fine?'

'Twenty thousand.'

'What?!'

'This is considered a light punishment.'

'I don't have that kind of money.'

'You can abort.'

'. . . Can it be reduced? Say, maybe 5000?'

'How can you haggle over the policy?'

'OK, 8000 . . . I can go to 8000.'

'Don't talk nonsense! If you dare to have the child, I will dare to fine you . . . But of course, our aim is not to fine you; our aim is to control the population growth. You have three days. Either get the abortion or pay the fine.'

When they had finished saying this and the ticket had been issued for the fine, the Eight Immortals stepped back onto their cloud and departed from my sister's world. Chuntian was left behind like a heap of rubbish they had dumped onto the floor on their way out. She did not move for a long time. Finally, she opened the cupboard and pulled out a drawer. She touched a cloth bag in the corner, in which she kept all her money. She counted it. There was 183 and a half *yuan*. Before, that had seemed like a lot of money; now she found it was nothing more than a louse or a scrap of skin on an elephant's body. Every time Zhima went on a business errand to sell mosquito nets, he only came back with 180 *yuan*, and she sold a basket of vegetables for about a third of one *yuan*. They might be able to save up 20 000 in ten years.

My sister rubbed the notes, as if working a spell that would turn them into a great sum of money.

Zhima had been afraid he would be caught and forced to have a vasectomy, so he stayed away from home, hiding out. At midday, he slipped in through the back door. Hearing that the fine was 20 000, his face turned bright red and he kept muttering, 'Thieves,' or, 'Bandits.'

By contrast, Chuntian felt she had violated the policy and was in the wrong. She had no right to blame others. She was calm in the face of reality. It was no use continuing to curse. It was better to set about trying to borrow the money. Zhima sat for half a day, thinking. He mulled over all the close and distant relatives, those he had contact with, and those he had long been out of touch with, and mapped out a reasonable traffic route. When he had eaten his lunch, he carried some field rations and hopelessly set out again.

Her belly jolting with each step, Chuntian made her way to the relatives on our side of the family. She first sought out our oldest uncle, whose family situation was about average. It was our aunt who held the purse strings. After a great deal of effort, my sister got 1000 from her. Our uncle then added another 200 from his own private stash. My sister wept as she said goodbye, feeling unsettled. She walked around a bit, then suddenly realised she had no more relatives on our side of the family. She thought it would have been much better if our maternal grandparents had had many children, and better yet, that each of those children had been both wealthy and generous.

When she got to our house, it was already ominously dark. Dinner had just been cooked, so my sister sat at the table with us. All the way to our house, she had been pondering the issue of money. When she realised she had arrived at our door empty-handed once more, she became uneasy. The dinner was as dull as usual. My father was lukewarm. He assumed my sister had come to get Yihua, so he recited all the girl's errors during her stay, such as breaking a bowl or wetting the bed at night. Although Yihua was still small, she knew what it was to be embarrassed. In a small voice, she said, 'I want to go home.'

Several times, Chuntian thought to mention that she had been to our uncle's house, hoping this would create an opening for her to talk about borrowing money, but seeing how Shunqiu looked, she did not say more. When she had finished eating, she took out 200 *yuan* and gave it to Shunqiu. She told him to buy some nutritional supplements with it. Shunqiu took the money, but later placed it in Yihua's pocket.

Chuntian chatted with our mother, all the while in her mind, she went through the names of all her childhood friends. They were generally poor. One had married well, but they had since grown apart. My mother said that the one in the village who was doing best was Li Letian, who had made a fortune from raising pigs and had built a three-storey house. Letian was the son of the village party secretary, the one who had been the cause of the beating my sister had long ago received from my father.

Taking my mother's cue, Chuntian sat thinking for a long time. Stroking her belly, she eventually came up with a shameless idea. Anyway, many years earlier our father had cursed her and called her shameless. She had always felt she owed him for that. Well, now she would repay him; she would prove him right.

Chuntian stopped about six metres away from Letian's house. Light from the house fell on the ground, as if it was the pity in Letian's eyes, carrying with it a little sigh. Chuntian struggled to turn around. With her back to the light like that, it looked like she wanted to leave. She paused for a moment, then turned awkwardly around, looked at the high-rise, and solemnly advanced to the door.

It is not difficult to imagine the scene in which Chuntian spoke up and asked to borrow money from Letian. She did not know how to flatter him, nor to sweet talk in any way. As soon as she sat down, she launched right into the matter, pouring out her heart's desire. Whether he loaned her the money or not was up to him.

My sister's errand was not in vain. The next morning, Letian came to our home and, right in front of my father, handed my sister an envelope with 3000 *yuan* inside. He said, 'You can pay me back when you have earned lots of money.'

Chuntian was so stunned by the amount that her lips, normally clamped as tightly as a chicken's arse, fell wide open. In this way, Letian displayed his wealth in front of my father. He did not know it, but my father had never once regretted anything he had done, and he was not about to be flattered by this fellow's manner today either.

*

It was three days later, at seven in the evening, that Zhima finally came back. He had sought out seven or eight relatives and borrowed money from them, bringing back just 2000 *yuan* with him. They put all the money together in one pile and spread it out on the bed. Neither of them had ever seen so much money before, and the pile seemed alien to them. They stared at the money for a long time, experiencing the joy of some secret wealth. For a moment, the charm of money seemed to overshadow the foetus, and in their minds, the couple separately realised their own dreams with this 6000 *yuan*. For instance, Zhima had always wanted a motorcycle to use in his runnings to and fro in the mosquito net business, perhaps even enabling him to go to the city from time to time to transport customers. Chuntian thought of sending Yihua into the city to attend kindergarten and primary school, giving her a bright future like all the little girls in town. After a while, the foetus in my sister's womb kicked her, bringing her back to reality. She remembered that the money was meant for an almost certainly futile investment, and they still had to find ways to get another 14 000 *yuan* to accomplish even that.

This really was a messy debt. With an anxious expression, Chuntian was distracted as she was doing housework. She really could not figure it out. The people from the family planning group would be there the next day. She would have to ask them to extend the deadline. But even if they gave her a month, or even six months, where could she get that kind of money? This road had come to an end. Whether alive or dead, they could only come up with 6000 *yuan*. The rest of the money they had to pay with their lives, if the Party would even accept it. This was how Chuntian settled her own mind, and she said the same thing to comfort Zhima. Zhima agreed, saying, 'Yes, I don't have any more money. Take our lives if you want.'

The two of them encouraged each other, growing emotional. Zhima said, 'What does my having a child have to do with them? I even find it hard to give up this 6000!'

Chuntian said, 'We have gone against the state policy and should be punished, and we won't cheat, but the fine is all up to them. Some pay a few thousand, some tens of thousands. What right do they have to fine us 20 000? They're just bullying us.'

Zhima was getting more worked up. He cursed the policy. 'Who cares about controlling the population? Control, my arse! If you have money, you can have as many children as you want. If you have power, you can have as many kids as you can spawn. Son of a bitch! They're just targeting us – poor, powerless people!'

That night, Yihua and Yicao slept very soundly. Chuntian and her husband clung on to the 6000 *yuan* and could not close their eyes. As soon as it was light outside, Zhima decided to handle it like a man of integrity. He told his wife to plead their case before the family planning group, and not to anger them. He himself went outside to hide. All along, he had feared they would catch him and take him in for a vasectomy. In the village, any man who was castrated like that would be a laughingstock, ridiculed even by his wife and mother-in-law.

Just after breakfast time, the Eight Immortals turned up again. Yihua and Yicao clung tightly to the hem of my sister's dress, with her bulging belly. She put her arms over each of them. Soon, people heard Chuntian shouting. The two children wailed. There was momentary confusion, and then Chuntian was put into the car and taken away.

'I would rather bleed a river of blood, than have one more kid. They really did it.' When Chuntian told me this, I had already graduated from university, and was eager to contribute to society.

When the son was aborted and the wife given a tubal ligation, the couple did not return the money they had collected. Zhima spent 3000 *yuan* on a motorcycle, and before long, he had an accident. The vehicle was totalled and his leg injured, and he still owed 3000 *yuan* of medical fees. This shattered Chuntian's dream of sending Yihua to a school in town. With no son in his life, Zhima did not care about anything. He started drinking, spending three *yuan* for every quart of spirits. He was drunk every day, taking no interest in anything.

Chapter 13:

Li Shunqiu, Eldest Brother

June was painful to our family, as if silkworms were nibbling away at our hearts. No one mentioned my second brother. Whether he was confused or patriotic was irrelevant; all we had left was a pile of ash. My father did not know where to go to find out the truth, and had no interest in knowing the truth either. Anyway, my brother was dead now and would not come back. When my mother cried, my father did not scold her now, as he usually did in the face of any other displays of sympathy for her children. He drank half a glass of sorghum spirit at lunch, then took a nap. This pattern was repeated for many days.

By June of the following year, my oldest brother's leg had completely recovered. He was able to go about doing farm work, fishing, and catching frogs in his normal fashion. Fishing and catching frogs was no longer just a form of recreation for him, but had become his livelihood. Nobody knew when this sort of sideline work had begun to flourish, when men started relying on this kind of primitive hunting instinct to feed their families.

At dusk, people started out one by one from the causeway on their bicycles, armed with torchlights and fishing devices. Their rations for the journey consisted of cooked corn, sweet potatoes, or bread. They greeted and called out to their friends, ringing their bicycle bells. They laughed raucously, cursed, and slowly blended into the belly of the twilight. These people caught frogs throughout the night, and in the morning they passed by the market and sold them. Then, they took the cash home and lay down to rest, their faces dark with weariness. Those who used storage batteries to fish wore rubber boots attached to jumpers as they waded into the water. The fish floated up after they received the electric shock. If the fishermen were careless, they could be electrocuted themselves.

At this time, people kept introducing older women who were waiting to be betrothed to my elder brother. My mother encouraged my brother to go take a look, so he dutifully agreed to go look at one of them, but at the last minute he refused to make an appearance. My mother said, 'Just choose a woman who is healthy and can have children, and that will be fine. In your situation now, you can't hope to catch someone like Luo Yan.'

Our mother liked to attack others' weak points.

Luo Yan, a girl from the city, had been my brother's colleague. After my brother went to prison, she came to our house. Her eyes were red, and she did not say much. As always, my father behaved arrogantly, not treating Luo Yan nicely at all. She acted like she came to say farewell to Shunqiu's corpse, silently placing a full stop in her heart, and then she never appeared in our lives again. Luo Yan had earlier taken the initiative to pursue my brother, but I never found out what happened between the two of them. I told Shunqiu that she had come to our house after he met with trouble.

He did not ask why she came, but just said that her father objected to the two of them carrying on. Luo Yan did not listen, so her father had kept her under house arrest. This was the only time my brother spoke to me of Luo Yan. He said very little, leaving me in suspense. In my opinion, this was the most mysterious part of his life, an even greater secret than the time he spent in prison.

In a change from his usual appearing and disappearing in the night, Shunqiu gradually started appearing in the daytime. He came and went, like a shadow passing by, never stopping in one place. Had he worn a hat and cloak and carried a sword, he would have been called a knight errant. Then the villagers would have feared and avoided him instead of chasing after him asking, 'Had your dinner yet?' or 'Where are you going?' or 'Is your father at home?'. My brother, though weary of such courtesies, felt obligated by his sense of propriety to treat them seriously. His answer was often thrown like a hidden weapon, and he was gone immediately after he spoke, leaving the questioner startled. Over time, the villagers came to know his habits, so they usually stood at some distance as they called, 'Had your dinner yet?'. Then, they turned and walked away. After all, this was the usual way of greeting. No one really cared whether he had eaten or not. But even this sort of entertainment made Shunqiu miserable. From then on, he walked more swiftly and if he saw someone coming, he would quickly duck behind a haystack or shrubbery. This certainly wasn't the classy style of a knight, pulling his bamboo hat low and quickly diving away as soon as he saw a woman.

Shunqiu felt he was different. He did not like being with other people. Had it been possible, he would have been most willing to live in a cave in solitude.

He was very capable of creating his own world. This world had its own atmosphere and flavour, like a cloud floating over the village sky. When he had nothing to do, he would sit in this world. When he was finished, he would come down from the cloud, fold it up and put it in his closet, where no one could see it. No one asked him about it, because no one even knew he had this cloud. They simply said his behaviour was a little strange, but if you gave him a wife and they had a few children, it would make him normal. This was what my mother believed, too. But she also had an ulterior motive, hoping for a grandson. An old, white-haired woman without a grandson peeing on her trouser legs was a shameful thing.

My mother secretly encouraged those matchmakers who were left out in the cold to continue to look for healthy girls fit to have children so that, if Shunqiu would not visit the matchmaker, she could bring the girl to him. Whether it was a success or not, they would definitely not go empty-handed. At the critical moment, my mother emanated the sheer animal strength of people from the mountains.

Lying awake at night, she could not make sense of it, so she even woke my father, asking whether something might have gone wrong with Shunqiu in prison. 'What man does not want to find a wife and have children?' she asked. 'In a few more years, he might only be able to find a widow who can't have children.'

My father did not care about grandsons, because a grandson would not be under his control anyway. Having a grandson meant he was on the road to decline. Like a rotten straw rain cape hanging on the wall or a rusty tool in a corner of the shed – it was a useless thing.

It was generally not very easy to find Shunqiu at home. It wasn't much easier to find him outside, for that matter. For instance, if someone said they had just seen him at such and such a place, when you went to that place to look for him, you'd find nothing but a few discarded cigarette butts still issuing a tail of smoke, but there was no one in sight, like a warm crime scene. Even if he was out catching frogs the whole night, it was still hard to catch him in bed. Twice girls showed up at our house with the matchmaker, but Shunqiu was nowhere to be found. This caused my mother great distress, as well as great financial loss, since she had to pay their travel expenses, even as she endured their suspicious stares.

But one spinster was more persistent. Without a matchmaker to accompany her, she came to our house by herself a few times. She was quite satisfied with what she saw. Li Shunqiu had a resident's permit in town, and he had no brothers to share the property with and no jealous sisters-in-law, so when our parents passed on, everything they owned– all several hundred square metres of land– would be hers. The chickens and dogs would be hers, and no outsider could encroach on a single centimetre of her territory. This girl was called Xiao Shui Qin. She was thirty years old, and possessed a good measure of stubborn strength. She took the college entrance exam four years in a row, hoping with all her heart to make a success of herself. But she failed every year. Her arrogant spirit made her look down on the rural types. Ultimately, she wound up a spinster. Now that her hopes of going into the city via the college entrance exam had been destroyed, she took remedial action to sort out her own life. She took up sewing, and the clothes she made were quite good. She liked to come up with trendy designs, and all the coquettish girls and daughters-in-law in the village sought her out to make clothes for them.

The fourth time Shui Qin came to our house, she ran into my brother at the slope of the dyke. The moment their eyes met, my brother felt his private world invaded by an alien, and he quickly pulled his imaginary bamboo hat down lower as he brushed past her.

Shui Qin later said that my brother emitted an odd aura that gave her a start. She instinctively felt that this person was the one she was looking for. She immediately turned around and followed him, and saw the proof that she was correct.

My mother liked Shui Qin. The two plotted together to do this and that, arranging things this way or that way. Three days later, Shui Qin's sewing machine was moved into our house, and she stayed there with it, arranging flowers and plants in my room and making it fragrant. The closet was tidied up too, with my side and hers being clearly demarcated in the process. For about half a month, my brother hid in his cloud every day, not emerging at all. He did not chase Shui Qin away either. He watched the vast expanse of white world in his cloud. When another cloud in the distance appeared strange, it was the monster, Shui Qin. This monster was grasping the present and steering for the future, pushing her way into the territory of others and leaving an indelible footprint there. My brother could solve any equation and calculate square roots, but he could not deal with women; they were to him a strange sort of being. They were like a ball of cloud which could not be caught, solid and formless, and also like a gigantic cavern formed by a tornado, trying to uproot him.

Because my brother did not chase Shui Qin away in the beginning, it became more embarrassing to do so the longer she stayed, so my brother decided not to hide any more. He would even smile at the lady sometimes, touching the fabric she had cut and asking what sort it was, much in the way a patient might ask the doctor for an update on his condition. Shui Qin was fully integrated into our family. She told my mother she knew Shunqiu was innocent and that his fate was unfair, depriving him of many things. She hoped he would gradually be repaid for all that.

This made my mother's nose run and eyes tear. She had a special respect for someone who had taken the college entrance exam four times, so she discussed everything privately with Shui Qin. All the mothers and daughters-in-law in the village were natural enemies, but in my mother's relationship with Shui Qin, there were no signs of animosity at all.

The first thing Shui Qin did when she arrived at our house was make a draped coat for my mother and a small jacket for my father. She paid for the fabric, paying for her upkeep even before she married into our family. Such a sincere girl was certainly hard to find. Shui Qin was not considered ugly, nor was she short, and never mind that her skin was a little on the dark side – a matter of no small prejudice in our village. She had a small face, double eyelids, and dark eyes. Her face showed her intelligence. Her self-esteem had not been affected in the least by her advanced age. The other villagers were quite envious of my mother; she was getting a capable daughter-in-law without spending a penny. They said it was a blessing from our ancestors. There was really nothing to say about a gift from the ancestors. My grandfather wrote poetry and gambled, never harming anyone, but also never doing anything particularly good. But then, if you count gambling away the family fortune as a sort of charity, then my grandfather had truly accumulated some old morality. But the key was, who knew where heaven had recorded this karmic debt?

My brother and Shui Qin lived on either side of a wall. She hummed and read stories in her room, and before she went to bed, she tapped on the wall, which was made of earthen bricks. Over time, her tapping made a small depression. Before she chiselled all the way through that wall, the sound of her fist pounding suddenly stopped one day. My mother was so excited she could not fall asleep, feeling the thing she wanted had finally been accomplished.

The marriage date was quickly fixed. My parents vacated the master room, which had red brick walls. Shui Qin implemented her own design ideas, sweeping the walls of dust and painting the bricks with lime, turning them white. She put wild flowers in bottles and jars and sewed flounced curtains and quilts. With her own money, she bought bunk beds, which were popular in the city, and wall unit cabinets. Throughout the whole process, my brother had only to put forth a bit of brute force to move this and that during the day. At night he rolled around in bed with Shui Qin, and everyone was happy.

Chapter 14:

Li Xinhai, Grandfather

While our family home was undergoing renovations, my grandfather inspected the building site, looked at the sky, then looked from the sky back to the building site, as if comparing the two. The ducks in the pond had long since been made part of my brother's engagement banquet, leaving only the big white geese that liked to peck people to serenade us. My grandfather always kicked them for no reason, so they ran to the pond every time they saw him. He stood on the riverbank under the willows now, hands behind his back, enjoying a small victory.

My grandfather's mind was mixed up, and he was often quite confused. When he was alert, he could still write and compose poems, sparing no effort to express his aloofness and pride, as if his mind had not given in to anything.

My grandfather's birthday coincided with the blooming of cole flowers and the buzzing of bees. Early that morning, he had put the table on the floor and started rubbing his ink stick against the ink stone and reciting poetry, repeating it over and over. After working out the draft in his mind, his brush soaked in ink, he leaned over and, like a carpenter at work, he slowly chiseled away at his paper. Before long, a couplet scratched on two long red sheets of paper was pasted on either side of the door of my grandfather's short, thatched cottage. It read: *a celebrity does not complain about his cottage being too small, and a hero always dresses like a commoner.*

Seeing it, my father booed and spat, squeezing ugly words out between his teeth. He said to my grandfather, 'You bastard, shamelessly awarding yourself with silk banners. You're so pretentious, as if you know no shame.'

There seemed to be some complex truth hidden in my father's abusive words, proving that my grandfather was not quite the persona he flaunted.

My grandfather's actions also lacked self-confidence. Not daring to talk back, he just waited until my father moved sufficiently far away, then turned toward me and said, 'What do you know? Who are you to teach me? Shunqiu didn't break the law, and now that he's out, you should go to his work unit and see what the situation is and try to think of ways to reinstate him to his previous position. Now only his registered residence is in the city, but he doesn't have a job there. Being registered in the city, he doesn't even get a share of a third of the land that rural people are allotted. He's losing out at both ends, and not settled anywhere, but you're not the least bit worried. Now *that's* being a bastard!'

As my grandfather poured the remaining ink back into the bottle, his hand trembled and some ink spilt. He used his palm to clean the bottle, then placed it on the windowsill among others.

While we were eating, a puffy-faced woman came to our house. She was one of my grandfather's many goddaughters. She was very zealous, coming to see my grandfather on his birthday every year and bringing the crispy snacks he loved to eat. As she chatted happily with him, their laughter occasionally floated out the window.

My grandfather's voice was especially loud at this time, as if intentionally letting my parents overhear. 'As for me, I'm as good as dead, but not quite buried. I won't live long. There is no flavour to my food, and I can't sleep at night. Each night seems longer than the one before. I don't care about anything and, you can be sure, nobody cares about me.'

The puffy-faced woman used the term for 'godfather,' saying, '*Gandie*, you're wrong. I couldn't bear to lose you. You must take care of yourself. I want you to live to be a hundred!'

'Shufen didn't come?' my grandfather said, suddenly calling another girl's name.

'She'll be here soon,' said the puffy-faced woman, comforting him. Smiling, she came into the house and put down two packets of dried lychees. She greeted my parents and called them brother and sister-in-law, making goose flesh come out all over their bodies.

'*Gandie* is always asking these days, "is Shufen coming?". Who is Shufen?' the woman with the puffy face asked.

'His mind is not clear, and he's always talking rubbish.' My father didn't like the puffy-faced woman, convinced that she had fooled my grandfather out of no small amount of wealth. He was cold towards her.

Shui Qin poured more tea, trying to lighten the atmosphere.

The puffy-faced woman talked about her '*Gandie*' with affection. '*Gandie* is looking healthy.' '*Gandie* still sits up quite straight.' Later, she helped *Gandie* over to the dinner table.

As the woman went on with her prolonged performance at our house, my father quite magnanimously gave my grandfather face, enduring all the different gestures of that puffy-faced goddaughter.

My grandfather sat proudly at the head of the table, looking at everyone arrogantly. Urged on by the flattery, he announced to everyone that he planned to live to be a hundred. He went on to say, 'When I die, wrap me in a summer sleeping mat, dig a hole and bury me, and plant a pine and a cypress over me.'

My father said, 'You just want others to talk behind my back for not going through all the elaborate formalities.'

My grandfather said, 'I can write it down as evidence.'

My father said, 'That's no use. The one who others curse will be me.'

The woman with the puffy face said, 'Today is *Gandie*'s birthday. Don't say those inauspicious things.'

My mother said, 'Yes, let's just eat. The food is getting cold.'

Shui Qin handed my grandfather a bowl of soup. Shunqiu scooped a few vegetables into his bowl with his chopsticks and went into the back garden. Taking the bowl, he moved to a remote spot, squatted, and ate, as he was accustomed to doing in the reform prison.

My grandfather still had a few teeth. When his pursed lips moved, it was like he was chewing with his lips. He looked like a lonely, regurgitating cow, his eyes completely blank. He was actually no match for a chicken drumstick now, but for the sake of his efforts to live to be a hundred, he puffed up his cheeks, doing his best to destroy it.

Oil dripped from his wrist, dirtying his shirt. He strenuously dug out the chicken meat stuck between his remaining teeth, looked at it, then stuffed it back into his mouth.

'How come Shufen didn't come for dinner?' My grandfather mentioned that name again.

The puffy-faced woman's mouth was full of rice. She stopped chewing, her mouth half-open, and stared at my father.

A housefly buzzed around the table. My father shooed it away with his chopsticks and said, 'Eat.'

Chapter 15:

Li Shunqiu, Eldest Brother

My brother got married over the May 1 holiday. I was in high school at the time. When I returned for his wedding, I did not bring any sort of gift. My family did not observe such formalities and, furthermore, I was a student on a tight budget. I had met Shui Qin twice before and had a fairly good impression of her, going so far as to feel my brother gained something by the attachment to her, if I analysed it carefully. Of course, on the emotional side, it was harder to say. That was not something that could be measured. It wasn't some commodity whose shape or size was clearly visible.

This day was also a big day for my grandfather. For once, my father was unable to restrain him, as he was perfectly justified in hanging the couplets he had written all over the house. They were generously affixed to the door frame and lintel of our house, and his own place was not spared either. He explained the content of the couplets to everyone he saw, white foam gathering and drying at the corners of his mouth, breathing hard as he sat down. My father always looked upon my grandfather's couplets with distaste, but he knew he could not heap abuses on the old man at a time like this, so he resorted to ridicule. Even so, his ridicule lacked its usual cruelty. There was even an element of goodwill in it, and perhaps a desire to show off my grandfather's talent a little.

The back garden had turned into an extensive kitchen, with the cooks chopping meat in unison. It sounded like a great host of firecrackers exploding.

Yihua and Yicao were running in an unruly mess. My sister roared at them, first at one child, then at the other. But of course, she was most concerned that they do not touch the silk wedding quilt.

Everyone had heard the couple's bedroom was decorated in a very Western style. They squeezed into it to have a look, pointing and exclaiming over various things. I could read the words in their eyes – how Shui Qin knew how to live life like people in the city. They noted the good technique evident in her sewing, and felt that, for a convict, this was really just plain dumb luck. They also felt that Shui Qin did not lose out in marrying Shunqiu, since Shunqiu had a permanent urban residence and she was, after all, a spinster. Country people were like that. They thought of a couple as a pair of shoes, and they ran their worldly eyes over the two to see whether they might be mismatched. They even went further, taking note in their record books so they could broadcast them at various later occasions.

After a while, the bridal procession appeared on the embankment, a long, colourful parade. Somebody on the terrace cheered, 'They're here!' It got slightly rowdy, with those setting off firecrackers going forward to meet the bridal party, following it and popping firecrackers all the way to the door. The silk quilt, piled in towering layers, was bright and beautiful. Some people reached out to touch it, praising it for its exquisiteness. Shui Qin's relatives stepped through the noise of the firecrackers and over the threshold, taking their seats in the living room and starting to sip ginger sesame tea and munch on peanuts, melon seeds, and sweets. My parents were also dressed modestly, sitting beside them and chatting. This was the first time the two families met and, I hate to say, the only time in their lives both showed so much restraint or attention to etiquette. They were constrained and elegant, with nothing but a spirit of festivity hidden away in each crease on their faces.

Shunqiu and Shui Qin had just finished toasting the guests and were about to sit down and have a bite when someone came over to congratulate them. It was my brother's former partner in crime, Li Ganzi. Shunqiu almost did not recognise him. He used to be thin and tall, and his back straight. The prison had bent him, and when he talked, his body leaned forward like he wanted to please people.

My brother said, 'You're back.'

Li Ganzi said, 'Yes, I've been back for a week.'

'Here, let's have a couple of drinks,' my brother replied.

'I followed the smell of wine here.'

'Next time we'll be toasting you.'

'When pigs fly.'

Seeing Ganzi, everyone at the table made their way over and asked how everything was going. They toasted, and before long, it grew quite raucous.

The party stayed up until late in the night drinking wine. My brother did not know how to decline drinks when they were offered to him but at the same time, he could not tolerate much alcohol. Inevitably, he was forced to drink more than he could handle and before long, got quite drunk and disappeared. The nuptial chamber crashers customary at Chinese weddings were not able to find him, and so all dispersed, each going on their way.

Shui Qin waited half the night in that deserted room. As dawn drew near, my brother finally crept into the bridal chamber. Shui Qin's expression was darker than the night sky.

My brother said, 'I've had a lot to drink. I didn't want to puke on the new bed, so I didn't dare come into our new room. I fell asleep on my grandfather's bed.'

Shui Qin said, 'You should see that Li Ganzi less. He reeks of bad luck.'

My brother was a little uncomfortable. Perhaps he was allergic to all the new things in the house. He sneezed, sniffed at the quilt, then said it all smelt of new money. Finally, he was so uncomfortable he left the room, then went out of the house, desperate for a cigarette.

*

The sun set across the river, turning the water into glinting fragmentary ripples. The heads of the swimmers were like buoys, floating in the centre of the river. Against the backlight on the bank sat two figures silhouetted with a golden lining, completely unmoving, aside from the occasional lifting of a hand, which was soon returned to its original place. My brother and Ganzi were smoking.

Shunqiu said, 'Eventually, Minister Cai got a promotion because of our case. He was transferred to the Public Security Bureau to serve as Deputy Secretary.'

Ganzi spat, 'We went to hell, and they ascended to heaven. God, I've thought since early on that when I got out, I wanted to settle the score with that old turtle Cai.'

Shunqiu sighed. 'How can you settle a score with him? Do you want those ten years back? You won't get them. Why look for trouble?'

Ganzi said, 'Anyway, I'm a convict. What am I afraid of?'

My brother said, 'He's got all the power. It's like an egg fighting a stone . . . Honestly, get over it.'

Ganzi said, 'How? How do I get over it? My face has "convict" etched into it. That's all the capital I have now.'

Shunqiu said, 'This is reality.'

Ganzi was silent for a moment, then said, 'You used to have an air gun. Let me use it for a while.'

My brother said, 'I can't provide you with the tools to commit a crime.'

Ganzi laughed and said, 'You think I want to kill someone? Kill, my arse. He would have his retribution for sure. I'm just bored, and I'd like to shoot some birds.'

He really did go out to shoot birds every day, but he was a poor marksman. With each shot, he only managed to scare the birds, never even knocking a single feather off, but it did not dampen his enthusiasm. Each morning he wiped down the gun, no expression on his face, then loaded it and set out to spend the day shooting at turtledoves. He did nothing at home. A group of children often trailed behind him. If he hit a bird, he gave it to them, and he taught them how to shoot fowl. For instance, he showed them how to aim accurately to hit the fatal point on a turtledove. If they were not confident hitting a one *yuan* coin from twenty metres away, then he said they should aim for the chest. They were never to shoot it in the back, because the feathers on the back of a turtledove were smooth and slippery, making the bullet feel like nothing more than a massager.

After playing with the air rifle for some time, Ganzi got bored and enlarged the air chamber of the gun to increase its power. Whenever he was at home, he was grinding bullets.

One day Ganzi suddenly returned my brother's gun, saying, 'The old turtle's dead.'

Shunqiu stared at him, waiting for him to spit out the rest of the story.

Ganzi said, 'The bastard was killed in a car accident seven years ago.'

Shunqiu said, 'So you did go to the county to look for him.'

Ganzi said, 'I've practised my marksmanship in vain. That old turtle never even gave me the chance for a shot at him.'

Shunqiu spat roughly and said, 'You keep the gun.'

Chapter 16:

Xiao Shui Qin, Sister-in-law

Shui Qin seldom went into the fields. She was too afraid she would get dark with too much exposure to the sun, or that she would be bitten by leeches. When it was the busiest season in rural areas, what we called 'the rush-harvesting and rush-planting period,' she would unwillingly put on a show, wearing long trousers and sleeves that kept her tightly covered all over. She even sewed an additional sun screen onto the brim of her hat, making her look like an alien as she walked through the fields. Only when she lifted the screen could you see her face. She grinned happily and seemed to be in a festive mood, with her chest puffed out as she walked. It was as if she had not gone out into the fields to work at all, but instead was on her way into town to shop. Shui Qin arranged everything according to a plan. She was not even pregnant, but she bought books on how to care for a baby, and she continually reminded my brother that she would need to eat more fruit and drink more milk when that time came, so that the baby would be born with soft, fair skin. Shui Qin's deepest regret was her dark skin. She put a great deal of effort into finding out how she could produce white-skinned offspring, including learning what foods she could eat to bring about the desired result. My brother only had one thing to say: If the child was like him, its skin would be naturally pale. He was just telling the truth, but Shui Qin thought his words were a sort of sarcastic barb at the efforts she was making. At any rate, when it came to the issue of having a child, she really didn't want any more participation from my brother than was necessary – certainly nothing beyond planting the seed. So she turned off the lights early each night, leaving only the table lamp on, giving off a weak orange halo to light the way for my brother's labours.

During the day, Shui Qin looked like an entrepreneurial woman, clear-minded and organised, with a tongue as sharp as a blade, making each cut clean and neat. Her tailoring business went quite well, but she did not wish to work hard at the sewing machine – sometimes she did not even wish to accept orders – so she would just laze about and read. We could not find another woman in the village who was a reader like her, just as no one else spread a tablecloth over the dining table and put a bottle of wildflowers in the centre.

*

The first thing Shui Qin did after she was married was to separate the house between her and my parents, employing a method she had learned from city folks. My brother often felt he had entered someone else's house, and he felt like a stranger there. The conflict between Shui Qin and my parents started with the division of the family assets. The division itself was not a big problem, since my family had little of value, the house itself being just sufficient for our needs. But Shui Qin brought up the idea of splitting the back garden, building herself a sewing room, a space to hang clothes, and a space to store fabrics. The back garden was my father's favourite part of the house. Shui Qin's failure to note this basic fact was a major oversight. She regarded this failure as a mark of shame on her record. From then on, she clearly divided up what was hers and what was theirs, and she no longer spent her idle moments sewing new clothes for them. At any rate, she was now too busy for that, since she soon got pregnant and became my brother's queen.

Shui Qin was a calculating person, and she was very seldom in error. She very rarely stumbled and fell in her calculations.

Now that Shui Qin had become the queen mother and was making my brother wait on her hand and foot, my father and mother were quite unhappy, but because they were also looking forward to enjoying the fruit of her womb, they put up with it. My mother occasionally made soup for her, asked after her, and shared her own life experiences with her daughter-in-law. It was obvious that my mother's experience was useless, since Shui Qin's ideas were so different from hers. My mother had not paid much attention to things when we were small, and the four of us were like wild fruit falling from a tree. Shui Qin, on the other hand, was taught in the city fashion, even choosing precisely when she wanted to be pregnant, and practised early prenatal care, rubbing her belly as she spoke to the foetus. Finding herself of no use, my mother increased her efforts in stew preparation, making Shui Qin a real fatty. She put on forty pounds of flesh, even though the foetus was only around five pounds. When my mother saw that the stew she prepared for her grandson was going to fatten Shui Qin, just the same way the foodstuff she had sent for her son in prison never got to him, she was angry. But even then, she kept a rein on her tongue, saying nothing.

The baby girl that was born was pink and delicate. On the second day, she opened her eyes and laughed, looking quite adorable. My grandfather and father both chose names for her, but Shui Qin used neither. She had taken the college entrance exam four times, and she had a strong self-reliant streak, so she expected no charity from her elders. She chose the child's name herself, and no one dared oppose her. She had considered it carefully throughout her pregnancy. If she had had a son, he would have been Li Yongqi. She named her daughter Li Xianxian.

When Xianxian celebrated her first month, Shui Qin made a public proclamation. In her eyes, a daughter was no different than a son. She would only give birth to this one child, so she would put her best efforts into raising it, including sending the little one into the city for school, where she could receive a good education. Xianxian was going to study at a renowned university. Perhaps she would even go abroad for her studies.

Shui Qin knew my father's bias against girls, and it seemed her intention was to give him a deliberate warning, as well as to air the grievances of us Li girls.

My father immediately said, 'No. This is not just your concern, and you will not have final say in the matter. You must think of the Li family. . . unless you're saying you want to let the Li name die out.'

His words were heavy, but Shui Qin answered like a gentle breeze and rain. 'Father, don't talk about any "future generations." Think back three generations – do you even know who those ancestors were? We don't live for others. As long as we live this life well, that's enough, and that's all that matters. Furthermore, I am a woman, and I am also a human. I have my own plans for my life. I am not a child-bearing machine. I certainly don't want to have my tubes tied, going under that knife for no good reason.'

My father, accustomed to having the last word, had never come across someone who reasoned with him. He did not know how to respond. The status of the parents had vanished into thin air before Shui Qin; they even seemed a little afraid of her.

Later, my mother told me how imposing Shui Qin had been. When I heard it, it sparked my interest in her. I was in Beijing studying journalism then, planning for a future as a reporter, since Xiazhi had said that the lack of law in the land made it impossible for a lawyer to help the innocent, but could only manage to set the guilty free. Shui Qin often asked me about university life, so we got along quite well, and our relationship gradually deepened. I never got involved in her conflict with my parents. Every wife was sure to have problems with her in-laws; there was no way anyone could help that.

Xianxian drank so much of her mother's milk that her flesh was white as powder, and her eyes were bright and black. She loved to laugh. Most of the time she looked like a little cat. When she was awake, everyone fought for a chance to hold her. Even when outsiders held her, they didn't want to put her down. My brother had to wait until she was asleep, then watch her sleeping in her crib.

My brother had good fortune. Perhaps he was finally getting a break.

Chapter 17:

Liu Zhima, Brother-in-law

The year her foetus was killed, my sister also died a little. She caught an infection after the tubal ligation, so had to make another visit to the hospital to have her wound cleaned and redo the stitches. Her whole body was in pain, and it effectively stopped any further interaction between sperm and egg. Since the Liu family had no hope of a male heir, they were inferior to others and so they spoke with less authority. They were even labelled as 'sonless,' as if their ancestral graves had been robbed. Zhima was initially so angry he could not sleep at night, thinking hard, pondering how he could come up with more vicious ways to retaliate. During the day he would join the crowds that formed around quarrelling and fighting opponents. Hearing them scold and observing their fighting moves, he eventually discovered that the worst curse that anyone could come up with was, *May you die sonless*. He also discovered that when fighting, the one without weapons was worse off than the one holding a lethal force.

Zhima learned a tactic. When he heard the word 'sonless,' he would threaten the opponent with a red brick. Over time, everyone came to know that Zhima was not to be provoked, so no one dared to use the phrase in front of him. At least that left his ears unsullied. In fact, he came to realise that his was not the only household that was 'sonless,' and he could look forward to comforting pleasures in the future. Just wait until his two pretty little girls, Yihua and Yicao, got married; good wine and cigarettes would flow in then. Happiness was just a matter of how one viewed life, so the 'sonless' Zhima felt free. He drank, played cards, and left his wife to work the farm like a beast, while he was at ease. In local terminology, he was 'parting his beard to drink porridge, sitting idly waiting for his daughters to honour him.'

Zhima occasionally went out to conduct a little mosquito net business, but it was a mess. His mosquito nets were of poor quality and rotted easily. People could buy better, prettier ones, and so stopped buying from him. He had no choice but to give it up. One night, on the way home from playing cards, Zhima spotted clothing outside a house, and inspiration hit him. He had come up with a capital-free way to make money. All it required of him was that he sleep a little less at night and put forth a little more intelligence. At night, Zhima rode a bicycle, carrying a big basket behind him. As he drove around the village, if he saw clothes or linens, he picked them up. He even got the occasional electric rice cooker or water flask, or perhaps a wok, kitchen knife, or something of that sort. When he had accumulated enough goods, he piled them all on his three-wheeled bike, then rode to the neighbouring village, selling his wares at bargain prices.

The second-hand items were very popular. Women gathered around the three-wheeled bike to pick and choose. He often completely sold out within two or three hours, and the women would ask him to bring more items soon, perhaps mentioning that they really needed trousers for their children, men's T-shirts, or a pressure cooker. Zhima took note of all these hand-picked goods, remembering to raise the prices on them when he got them in stock. When his route became familiar, the women would know Liu Zhima was coming as soon as they saw the bike. They would call cheerily as they flocked towards him, then look over his items, feeling grateful to him for enriching their material lives.

One woman, surnamed Cao, had a rather unusual coquettish energy. She pointed her fingers in a dramatic way at a house about a hundred metres away and asked Zhima to ride his bike to the terrace outside her house. She was cooking and was afraid the food would burn. Zhima stared at her vigorously swinging hips as she departed, and he knew he was in some real luck. He had run into many such situations when he sold mosquito nets. A young widow once asked him to carry the net into her room, then *that* happened. That widow had not even asked his name, but just undressed him. She finally bought a mosquito net she didn't even need.

Zhima stopped the bike on the terrace. The woman, Ms Cao, called him to come into the house for a drink, saying that she was feeding the pigs and that the animals always fought. If she did not watch them closely they would make a mess of the food. Zhima went into the house. It was very dark inside, but he could see that there was nothing of value there. Black ropes, which had been smoked to season them for use, dangled from the roof beam, and the corners of the paper pasted on the wall drooped and were covered with black ash. The Cao woman brought out a bowl of cold tea. When Zhima took it, she curled her orchid-like finger around him and caught him in her grasp. Zhima put the bowl down and embraced her, thinking this was to be like the time with the widow. But the woman did not reach for his crotch. Instead, she reached into his pocket and removed his money, then pushed him away.

'You crook! Trying to steal from a woman like this. If you don't want my husband to break your legs. You'd better get out of here quick!' The Cao woman took the money and put it into her own pocket.

All his sweat and hard work had been stolen by this woman. Swallowing his grievance in silence, he made a quiet retreat and never again returned to that place.

Chapter 18:

Liu Yihua, Niece

Yihua failed her high school entrance exams, falling just short of the score needed for admission. She was told that if she were to pay a sum of money, she could continue her studies, but Zhima was unwilling. The money he had borrowed the year his son was to be born was for the purpose of ensuring a successor in the family. It was a necessity. 'Whether she studies or not is no fucking big deal,' he said.

My sister's dream of sending Yihua into town to study likewise went up in smoke. She still owed large sums to our uncle and Li Letian. That money was owed by her, so Zhima didn't bother about it. All he cared about was drinking and leading a life of oblivion. From the time she was small, Yihua had been quite sensible. She never fussed about wanting to study, and when the other girls her age started to date, she also did not feel the sky had fallen in on her.

Yihua turned fifteen in the autumn, about the time a fishing net factory from the city came to recruit workers. Seven girls from the village applied, the oldest of whom was twenty and the youngest fourteen. Yihua was one of them. She said to Liu Yicao, 'You study hard and I'll pay for your school tuition.'

Zhima was very attentive at this point as he helped Yihua tie her quilt tightly and stuffed various items into her plastic basin and bucket, securing them with a leather belt. Smiling, he walked Yihua to the vehicle, then the seven girls there, or rather nymphs, rumbled their way into the city in a tractor. The tractor, as if it were an invading military vehicle, kicked up dirt like flying war banners, and the pedestrians moved to give way to it. The girls laughed as they sat in the tractor, as if they could pull the excitement over a fresh start to life from the laughter, though it was a journey of only five or six miles to their new home.

Yihua was the prettiest of the seven girls. In fact, wherever she went, she was considered pretty. The other girls called her Black Beauty, and she was both truly dark and truly beautiful, her skin almost as dark as that of an Indian woman. Though it was the dream of all the girls in the village to have very pale, soft skin, Yihua was not of the same mind, which meant that she had a more uninhibited, wilder nature. She was never upset over a broken nail, nor would she spend time picking at a bunch of hairpins. She either left her hair down or pulled it back in a ponytail with a black band. She took little interest in what she wore, but however she dressed, she always looked like she had taken great pains over her appearance. She was quiet, preferring to make use of her eyes instead, observing things, as if the world was screened through them. She did not speak much, but expressed herself through action. For instance, if the food was no good, she would put down her chopsticks and leave, sitting on one side enduring her hunger. For any reality that could not be changed, she did not waste time talking about it. For example, the first important event in her life was dropping out of school. Of course, she did not really place a lot of importance in studies, but she resented her parents' cold attitude and knew that she had to find her own path. So when an opportunity presented itself, she did not hesitate, and in fact felt it was too close to home and not exciting enough.

Yihua had inherited the hidden, suppressed part of my sister's personality – the cold resolution my sister displayed when she prayed to the God of Earth about my father's sudden death, and when she chewed the matchstick heads in the night. Liu Yihua did not think much of herself. She was already 1.65 meters tall, even though she was still developing and had not quite fully blossomed, like the undulating lines of the skyline that would soon be visible when the sun rose in the east. When she had been at the fish net factory for a while, several young men appeared around her, waiting for that sun to rise. The seven nymphs were in the habit of walking to and from work. They lived in a back street, and they had to go through an alley to reach it. The alley lay between the New Moon Bridal Shop on one side and a book rental shop on the other. The boss of the wedding photography shop wore glasses, while the book rental shop was watched by a wizened old man who always sat on a stool. The neighbourhood punks often took advantage of the time the factory shift ended to hang out in these two shops, waiting for their targets to appear. The girls had no idea that the gang of boys already covertly divided the spoils of conquest. Several had their eyes on Yihua, but they'd already resolved this conflict among themselves – they would abstain, leaving Yihua for the most prestigious among them.

The fellow she was left for was named Ma Liujia, but everyone called him Liuzi. Liuzi was from a good family, living in a Western-style building by the river. They had opened a fish net factory in the early days, and had raked in a fortune back then. But it had been closed for a while, partly because they were unable to recruit younger employees with all of them fleeing to Guangzhou, and also because of the later-opened fish net factories that led to poor sales. The fishermen had then also found other ways to earn money. In short, the industry had withered.

The first time Liuzi and his gang approached the seven nymphs, it was as if a shot had been fired into the trees, flushing out the birds. Only one bird was unmoved, Liu Yihua. She stood straight, looking at them. Under this gaze, several of them turned away or ducked their heads.

Liuzi kept his cool. He said, 'You want to go for spicy crawfish and karaoke?'

Yihua said, 'There are seven of us.'

Liuzi hesitated, then said, 'You can bring along as many friends as you like.'

They bled Liuzi that day. It was the first time Yihua and the girls had eaten spicy crawfish, so they ordered plate after plate. All seven ate until their eyes bulged and they burped nonstop. When they got to the karaoke bar, they sat dumbly. Not having been exposed to such a setting, they stared at the screen with mouths gaping. Liuzi and the gang were shy at first, but after a few beers, they raised the mic and yelled and sang without a care in the world.

Yihua also learned to drink beer on this night. Eventually, she could quietly put away horny guys in a private room with her drinking capacity, but that came much later.

Yihua liked to sing Zhang Huimei's songs, but she didn't open her vocal chords. She was thinking about the lives of urbanites, and she thought of her sister Yicao. Yicao loved singing, and knew practically all the hits from Hong Kong and Taiwan. No one knew where she'd picked them up.

Later, when Liuzi asked her out for dinner and a movie, Yihua went alone. In fact, she knew nothing about romance but she thought that although Liuzi seemed like a bit of a ruffian, he actually wasn't a bad guy. Liuzi asked about her family, and said that if she needed any help, she should just tell him. Yihua said, 'My home is a bottomless pit. If you dumped a million banknotes into it, it would be of no help.'

Liuzi had been with many girls, but he'd never seen a flower with quite so many thorns as Yihua. Fortunately, he liked being pricked.

It was only when Liuzi asked her to go to his parents' house for dinner that Yihua realised he was serious. She wasn't sure what to do, so she went to the oldest of the seven nymphs, Liu Lihong, for advice. Lihong was robust and ruddy, and had a loud mouth. She said, 'You're in a hell of a lot of luck! Liuzi's family's got money, and they're from the city. You're climbing above your station.'

Yihua said, 'The fall will be deadly for anyone who climbs high. I don't even dare to climb a ladder.'

Lihong said, 'Did you come to me looking for advice or looking for a quarrel?'

Yihua said, 'I came to ask you to accompany me to dinner tomorrow.'

Lihong said, 'What relative should I pretend to be?'

Yihua replied, 'We've got the same surname. You could be my older sister.'

And so it was agreed.

Later Yihua told me that her first love was not Liuzi, but the bespectacled boss of the wedding photography shop, Dai Xinyue. She described this man to me in great detail, not leaving out the direction of his sideburns, the density of his eyebrows, nor even the shape of his fingerprints. From Yihua's description, it was clear that Dai Xinyue was a gentle scholar, a somewhat gloomy character, unshaven, and looked as if he'd seen some setbacks in life. But in the eyes of the 15-year-old Yihua, this sad, lonely look was a sort of hidden splendour.

Inside the New Moon Bridal Shop hung many shabby clothes. Once the seven nymphs had taken their wages and gone there for photos. They chose their favourite designs, and Dai Xinyue gave them each a makeover. While taking Yihua's pictures, Dai Xinyue had told her that it was best not to get too close to Liuzi. When she asked why, he said, 'No reason. It's up to you whether or not you want to listen.'

From then on, Yihua frequented the studio, slowly getting a clear picture of Dai Xinyue's profile. He had not been successful in the college entrance examination and had been married, but his wife ran away with someone else. This was nothing to Yihua. Later, Dai Xinyue asked Yihua to be his model for advertisements, so he took several photos of her and posted them in the shop windows. One evening after that, Dai Xinyue brought Yihua to the second floor of his studio. There, in his bedroom, he undressed her, and clumsily stuck a white towel under her lower body.

'You want to check to see if there's blood?' Yihua sprung from the bed. Without waiting for his reply, she added, 'I'll tell you, I'm not a virgin.'

Then she got dressed and left.

But it was a lie. No man had ever touched her, but she thought Dai Xinyue's action with the white towel was reprehensible. It disgusted her to think that a person could bother about such trivialities at a time like that. It was like changing a baby's diaper. It was ugly, terrible, and suspicious. Yihua had always been quite childish, showing her temper when unhappy, then running away. At that moment, she didn't care about the swollen appendage on Dai Xinyue's lower body, a thing she had little knowledge of or interest in. All her emotions were focused on Dai Xinyue's face.

Outside, she saw Liuzi in the dim light of the streetlamp. He sat on the curb, cigarette stubs all over the ground.

Liuzi saw Yihua come out. Without greeting her, he turned and left.

Early the next morning, as the seven nymphs made their way to work, they found that the windows of the New Moon Bridal Shop had been smashed, the shattered glass spattered onto the middle of the street, and torn wedding gowns strewn all over the floor. Standing at the empty windows looking in, they could see that the inside had also been ransacked.

From this incident, Yihua's reputation spread back to their hometown via the other six nymphs. The story was that she'd been sleeping with two men, and one had smashed the shopfront of the other.

Chapter 19:

Xiao Shui Qin, Sister-in-law

At the end of the post-delivery confinement month traditionally observed by Chinese mothers, Shui Qin worked her sewing machine madly. The rushing stitches sounded like a machine gun being fired. The continual stitch lines led toward the future, and she was dauntless in her belief that her feet could make anything a reality.

When Xianxian was six months old, and my father could not bear to be parted from her. He carried her into the fields to inspect the crops, to the shop to buy cigarettes, and as he stood by the tables watching people play cards. Later he taught her what different things were, and was very patient. Even my mother was surprised by his behaviour. Everyone said, 'Old Li doesn't love his daughters, but dotes on his granddaughter. So odd!'

In 1999, when Xianxian turned five, Shui Qin started making plans to move to the city. She even went into town to look for a house they could rent, hoping to first set up a tailor's shop.

My father was not happy. He told her to just go to the city and earn money, but to leave Xianxian behind. Shui Qin simply smiled at her father-in-law's childish talk. She reasoned with him until she was tired of it. The whole point of going into the city was so that Xianxian could study there. My father intentionally forgot this, then finally played the trump card and refused to help them take care of the crops. Able to defend against any move my father made, Shui Qin simply turned around and contracted the field out to others. This hurt my father. He truly loved the land, and those people who chose to work in the city and contracted their lands out could only get a bundle of grass as harvest, so they would just let the fields go barren, overgrown with weeds and wild flowers. My father had griped about this many times. Now the Li fields were going to become a wilderness too. Was this not a crime? He was angry, and his hot temper built up a good deal of phlegm in his system. He spat as he cursed, but not in front of Shui Qin. He always vented his anger at my mother, who resorted to her old tactics, fanning the flame and whispering in my father's ear as she went along with his way of thinking. This helped my father release his anger as quickly as possible. For my father, it was not suitable to employ the systematic guidance method. That was like forcing a powerful bull to drink; it would rise up and struggle, and you might even find yourself gored on its horns. After so many decades of marriage, my mother's one real achievement was that she developed a good understanding of my father's temper.

A flower arrangement with flowing ribbons stood at the door, and Shui Qin's Beautiful Tailor Shop opened for business with a crackling of firecrackers. She wore a blouse she had made herself. Business came in very quickly. Women stood all around the shop, asking all sorts of questions. They wanted advice on how large women should dress, or whether a short woman should wear skirts or trousers. Soon, all sorts of fabrics were piled up on the desk. Shui Qin's scissors snipped, and her sewing machine whirred. Day and night she made row upon row of clothes, hanging them and placing the customer's number neatly on the cuff. It looked like business was booming. She got to know some clients with powerful connections, and she deliberately slashed prices for them, sometimes even offering a small gift to them. They liked the tailor's polite, generous attitude. They did not know that Shui Qin's secret motive for doing this was to pave the way for Xianxian's education. Six months down the road, the way forward was clear to her. She knew which primary school was good, and who would provide the most effective assistance in getting her there.

One plump woman, Ms Qian, was the wife of the Director of the Education Bureau. Shui Qin put special effort in dressing her top to bottom in clothing that had been exquisitely designed, inside and out. When Ms Qian was dressed beautifully on the outside, her inward array became lovely too. Listening to Shui Qin's concerns, she patted her own full chest, indicating that she would do her best to help. She was very dedicated and got quick results. She said that the school did not accept students from outside the city, which included the children of the city's migrant workers whose residence permits were registered in the countryside, but she exerted her considerable influence and finally got the principal to give her the nod. However, Shui Qin had to pay 20 000 *yuan* in admission fees. Even though Shui Qin had prepared herself mentally, 20 000 was more than the baseline, so she became greatly perturbed.

At night, Shui Qin discussed these matters with my brother. Since going into the city, he was a little lost. There were people and tall buildings everywhere, with no space for wandering. He grew moody and mumbled when he talked. Shui Qin said, 'You can't think of taking Xianxian back to the village to study. No matter what, we can't try to save money that way. Things will be quite tough, and I won't be able to earn enough money alone. You should try to find a suitable job. You can't carry heavy stuff with your bad leg, and carrying sediment at construction sites is not worth the wages anyway. I think security is your best option.'

'Dogs watch doors,' my brother growled.

Shui Qin said, 'You've got to make some money.'

My brother said, 'I only know how to catch frogs. I'll go home and catch frogs.'

Shui Qin said, 'What will you do when they're hibernating?'

He replied, 'There's no way I can keep them from hibernating.'

Shui Qin started crying. She said, 'Why don't you find a way to keep them from hibernating?'

My brother said, 'I'm not one of them.'

Shui Qin wouldn't let up. 'You either keep the frogs from hibernating, or you go into security.'

My brother cursed those selfish frogs, completely disregarding his needs like that and going to sleep for such a long stretch. Finally, he decided to go back to the village for a while and take advantage of the period when the frogs were not asleep. When they started their hibernation, he would think of another way.

So in the end, my brother went back to the village, where he caught frogs all night and slept half the day, then got up and spent the rest of the day fishing and catching the occasional snake. He saved his money, and went into town once a week to pass it to Shui Qin.

*

By the time the rush-harvesting and rush-planting was over, it was August, time for Xianxian to start school. The frogs were not only still awake, but very active, so my brother's business was even better than Shui Qin's, sometimes equalling her week's income in a single evening.

When summer ended, my brother once again looked like he

had when he was first released, dark and thin, and overworked to the point of being sleep-deprived. Wrinkles crawled all over his face. Shui Qin busied herself counting their money, giggling after she finished counting. She said the frogs really were stupid. When struck by the torchlight's beam, they didn't run, but just sat waiting to be caught. She took no notice at all of my brother's haggard face and bloodshot eyes.

As a show of appreciation, Shui Qin made a fine wool coat for Ms Qian, delivering it together with fine wine and cigarettes. She spent nearly 2000 *yuan* on it all; Ms Qian smiled in satisfaction. The entire month's worth of frogs my brother had caught was thus spent. Only when he saw Xianxian skipping about in her clean, pretty school uniform did he feel some comfort.

Shui Qin took Xianxian back to the village for the Mid-Autumn Festival. Happily, my father tried to pick Xianxian up. She had grown, and my father nearly broke his back.

Everyone laughed, and the atmosphere was very harmonious. Shui Qin got some orders from several of the villagers, giving them a bit of a discount on the clearly marked prices. She wanted to go back to the city after lunch and get right back to work. My father urged her to leave Xianxian behind, promising to bring her back to the city himself the next day, so Shui Qin made her way back to the city in advance. She had not even been there a year, yet she had already become alienated from village life. Her focus had shifted to the city, and if she stayed in the village even for a while, she felt uncomfortable. Each step lost on her sewing machine's pedal made her feel her life had been diminished. To be fair, my sister-in-law was a diligent woman. She always had a clear notion of where she was, and of what she wanted.

*

During the hot autumn period, the temperature was always thirty-five or thirty-six degrees. The hot, muggy weather made the frogs active at night. My brother swooped them into his bamboo basket, feeling as pleased as if it was money he was swooping up. It put him in an especially happy mood.

My brother hated to deal with people. He liked this sort of profession that allowed him freedom. Standing between heaven and earth, in the natural world, shrouded in night's darkness, there was nothing there but some small docile animals, all waiting to be caught up in his net.

He swept the crops with the beam of his torchlight, surrounded by the fragrance of mud. This world was familiar to him. During his years of labour reform, there was not a single day that he did not step in this same mud. Then, it was as if he had forgotten he had had a work unit, that he had a decent job to go to, and that he had had a wonderful girl called Luo Yan who loved him. He only knew that he belonged to the land, and that the city was just another prison. His wife and child were locked in it, and he had to go visit them.

On the last day of the hot autumn period, he gathered his money and went into the city. He made his way straight to the shop, where Shui Qin was measuring a customer. He did not go in, but went back to their rented flat instead. This one-bedroom, one-living room suite had been tidied up and made warm by Shui Qin. She had also brought in some plants and flowers, and Xianxian's pictures were on the walls and countertops. The bedroom was cramped, with a line hung high up, displaying newly-made clothes. My brother pulled on each one, as if calculating the price of labour for each. He stroked the fabric and tried to imagine if the owner was going to be fat or thin, poor or rich. He then set about checking the house, hoping to find something faulty that he could repair. Unfortunately, everything was in good order, so he turned all his energy to chasing a few flies, grinding them to a pulp, then throwing them away. After that, he fell asleep on the sofa. Then, when the time was right, got up and went to fetch Xianxian. Xianxian wore a bow, a floral dress, and pink sandals. She was pale and clean, like all the other girls in the city. She was not at all happy to see her father. As soon as she spoke, her words made him turn cold. She said, 'From now on, you don't need to pick me up; I'll go back on my own.' Then she glumly abandoned him.

When he got home, Shui Qin was cooking. The ingredients had all been brought over by my brother from the village, including vegetables and eggs, along with fish reared by my father and pickles made by my mother. Things bought in the city were full of pesticides and chemical fertilisers, or had been fed growth hormones. My father had opened half an acre of barren land for growing vegetables and had dug a fish pond. He had kept very busy. He might not have time to go into the city, but he also had no time to mess around. Shui Qin always boasted about how competent her in-laws were, making the other women envy her, especially the rural women who had gone into the city to make their living, just like a herd. But Shui Qin did not hang out with them; they did not give her any business, so there was really no benefit to her in dealing with them.

As Shui Qin fried the vegetables, the large, greasy black exhaust fan overhead roared, and the choking smell of chilli spread throughout the house. The three of them had to speak loudly until the hood was switched off. In the sudden silence, they laid out the dishes, coughing a little amid the lingering smoke, and started to eat. Before long, it was time for Shui Qin to describe their family ambitions. Usually, it was a monthly plan, an annual target, a five-year plan, and a ten-year goal. Xianxian was at the heart of it all; it always ended with sending Xianxian overseas for university. Shui Qin had already calculated the costs. She had to work overtime at night, and she had plans to expand the storefront within three years. She would also expand the scope of business, offering training and apprenticeships. She did not read anymore, except for her passbook. She could memorise every line of figures, each expenditure, making sure it was accurate to the smallest fraction of a *yuan*. She knew what each transaction was, whether it was an ATM withdrawal, a transfer, a cash deposit, or anything else. My brother could only look on from the side. When she finished inspecting it, she locked it up and did not let him even touch it. Fortunately, it was not something my brother wanted to touch, no more than he wanted to touch Shui Qin. His mind was full of frogs, contemplating where to go that night, and the next night. This was because there were many people catching frogs now, and the frog families were declining, trending towards extinction. Sometimes he had to cycle ten kilometres, going to some fresh site just so he could have a successful night.

Shui Qin again raised the question of him moving to the city to work. She had recently met the sister of the director who was in charge of personnel at a betelnut factory. She had agreed to make arrangements for my brother to work in the factory. The salary was not high, but not low, and it was an eight-hour workday. There was extra pay for overtime.

My brother asked, 'What would I do in the factory?'

Shui Qin said, 'Mostly move the betel nut shells and push carts of the product. It won't be a breeze, but it won't be that difficult either. The money doesn't come in as quickly as it does from frog-catching, but it is more dependable. Anyway, if you go on too long with this upside down schedule, getting day and night mixed up, it will do no good for your health.'

Shui Qin thought it was just a matter of time before my brother went into the city to work. She had once even encouraged him to go and look for the work unit to which he had originally been assigned, to see whether he could be reinstated. Even if they wouldn't reinstate him, it would be enough to do some temporary work.

My brother absolutely refused to go. Later, Shui Qin secretly sought out the leader of the work unit, not telling my brother. But after that, she seemed to have given up, and did not mention it any more.

Xianxian said. 'They're preparing programs for the celebration of the school anniversary, and I was chosen to dance, but the teacher said we have to come up with the cost of the costumes ourselves.'

Shui Qin said the school was always coming up with many useless expenses. This was most unreasonable, but she had to go along with it, since this was her only child. When she finished saying this, a sudden thought flashed into her mind. If she designed and sewed the costumes, couldn't she earn a bit of money from that?

She mentioned this thought. My brother thought it an excellent idea, but they needed to deal with the fat Ms Qian again. He said Ms Qian was practically a parasite. Shui Qin did not agree with this assessment, since parasites had their own positive parasitic uses. If Ms Qian did not serve as their bridge in the middle, they might not even have anybody to give gifts to. In fact, she would pay Ms Qian a visit as soon as they finished their dinner, hoping to clinch this business deal. She grew quite excited as she rubbed her palms together.

My brother had a gentle temperament and was quite content. He stood up and started to pick up the bowls and chopsticks, then suddenly fell to the ground.

Shui Qin was frightened half to death. She struggled to get him to the hospital's emergency ward. A checkup revealed that he had bilharzia, or 'snail fever'. It was already too late.

Everything went downhill after this. Shunqiu had to fight with the blood-sucking worms infesting him. He took praziquantel, furapromide, nithiocyamine, and Mida, all the while enduring dizziness, headaches, nausea, vomiting, and alternating between drowsiness and insomnia. He could not work, certainly earning no money. His diseased body needed looking after; he had to return to the village to recover. When the poor have a rich man's disease, it is a thing to be despised. An unblessed person enjoying a 'blessed' life meant he was a waste. But even so, no matter what happened, he would not be despised more than he already was as a reformed prisoner.

Chapter 20:

Li Chuntian, Elder Sister

My sister really rounded out. Her face started to show signs of her advancing age, though she still looked younger than other women in the village. Years of manual labour had not damaged her appearance too much. Other women envied her good fortune. She was just in her thirties and her daughter was already earning enough to support the family.

Whether her fortune was good or not, only my sister knew. She didn't bother with the gossip – she just wanted to play cards. She had become completely hooked on cards in recent years. She was so caught up in card-playing that she often forgot to eat, and even when she did eat, she didn't leave the card table. She sometimes played overnight. In the village, we called this sort of local card game 'running the beard' or 'simmering the beard.' It consisted of eighty long strips of cards marked with numerals in capitals and in lower case, in red or black. The situation changed constantly, with layers of mystery, and Chuntian's genius was opened up fully in the game of cards. I could easily understand the joy she found when she threw herself in the game. With cards in hand, she was in command; she was the mastermind, the field commander who had the final say. Everything she could not do in real life, at the card table, she could.

Of course, my understanding might have been off. An alternative explanation was that, perhaps now that Yihua and Yicao had grown up, they could take care of their own affairs. It was alright if the pots and stove were cold when they came home from school. They could just prepare some egg fried rice for themselves. That means they were basically at an age at which they could be self-reliant, so my sister had nothing to busy herself with at home, leaving her quite bored. At the end of the day, no matter how much a girl studied, in the end she would hit that 'oh no' point and just get married. My sister felt that she had gotten ahead a little now, and she could find her own entertainment. But this was just my own blind analysis. I did not truly know my sister's mind, and she never told me what appeal gambling held for her. What I did know was that when she did not work during the day, it was boring as hell. As the sun sank over the mountains, it was so quiet it made one's scalp crawl with goosebumps. Her nearest neighbour might yell as loud as they could, and still might not get a response. They had to walk a bit of a distance and turn a corner before they could see the light from the neighbour's window. In the past, as soon as it got dark out, my sister would lock the doors and sleep. Later she couldn't sleep at all, and she waited through the long night for the day to come. She listened to Yihua talk in her sleep, Yicao grind her teeth, and Zhima snore. She listened to the night bugs chirp in the dark, along with the leaves rustling. The moon was hidden, the wind was strong, and she could not see her hand in front of her face. She was bored to tears.

In short, she could not bear to be at home. At first, she would rush home before night fell. Later, she extended her playing time, then would crawl home just before midnight, and eventually it expanded to just after midnight, and it gradually kept increasing until she ended up staying out the whole night. Her face was often bloated, and her expression dark. Twice, Zhima dragged her from the card table and, when they got home, beat her until she was bruised and bleeding. But her battered flesh did nothing to discourage her. The next time, Zhima had no choice but to overturn the card table and warn the players that he would beat up anyone who played cards with my sister, and even create trouble at their houses. After that, whenever Chuntian showed up at the card table, everyone scattered; when she left, they regrouped around the table.

By the third time this happened, Chuntian started to think clearly. She would not bring harm to others, so she gave up. But cards were as addictive as drugs. When her withdrawal hit her, she grew itchy physically and mentally, and her muscles twitched. The image of cards flew in front of her eyes. Food was tasteless, and her sleep was restless. She was in a trance. Eventually, she could stand it no more. She rode a broken bicycle to a town miles away and played cards there. When her passion cooled, she went home and lied, saying that she had gone back to her girlhood home and stayed for a few nights. If playing cards was a form of military exercise in the village, then the village recreation room was a battlefield, with real knives and guns. Chuntian barely made it through. Eight times out of ten she lost, and when she lost, she would borrow money. Some people claimed she even slept with men to get the money to keep playing cards.

But in the end, the cat was out of the bag. People who saw her playing cards at the recreation room reported back to Zhima. He came to the village searching for her. However, Chuntian had won that day, and the person who lost to her was not willing to let her leave the table. There was a security officer in the village, and one must play by the rules. Zhima could do nothing but stand obediently to one side, talking nicely and begging her to go home, then pouting as he stood waiting at the door. Later, some of the players said that Zhima sitting there waiting like that affected their mood, and they finally forced my sister to leave the table. When they left the recreation room, Zhima raised a fist. Without a word, my sister just started fighting with him. A crowd surrounded them, watching the excitement; Zhima had apparently heard the rumours. He kicked her while cursing, tore her clothes, and made a wreck of her hair.

Some people tried to discourage him. Zhima said, 'What the fuck do you people have to do with me beating up my woman?'

It was only when a great number of people had seen my sister's exposed body that Zhima was satisfied. She did not cry, but just pulled the rags across her chest and, puckering her lips as tight as a chicken's arse, left the crowd's field of vision. Zhima, pushing the rickety bicycle, followed her, spitting betel nut juice at intervals.

When all was done, Chuntian still sat on the back of Zhima's bike and went home, as if nothing had happened. She continued along, very proper and honest, for a week. But her old ailments returned, and she pedalled into town and continued playing cards. After some time, Yicao was also less anxious to come home to eat fried rice, and was likewise too lazy to do her homework, so she started fooling around with boys on the sly.

Zhima realised he could do nothing about Chuntian, so he went to my father to complain. My father rained curses on him. My mother said, 'Whether or not you can manage your own woman is your own affair. Don't come knocking on our door about this sort of thing again.'

Zhima had no ally. He decided he could only leave Chuntian to her own devices. He cursed her, saying, 'I hope you die at that damned card table.'

Once, Chuntian did not go home for two consecutive nights. At ten in the morning, Zhima showed up in the gaming hall. The whole place was full of smoke. Chuntian sat, face dark, in that tobacco-filled room, the floor covered with cigarette butts and betel nut dregs. She glared at him with black-ringed eyes, pulled her mouth into the usual chicken arse shape and looked at the cards in her hand.

Zhima said, 'Go home. Something's happened.'

Chuntian did not say anything. Zhima patiently repeated himself twice.

Upset, my sister asked, 'What happened? Who died?'

Zhima hesitated, then said, 'That's right. Your uncle died.'

My uncle and aunt did not have children. My uncle had always liked my sister, and had even wanted to adopt her when she was small. My aunt did not agree; she wanted a son. Chuntian had many adversaries in her life. Had it not been for this sort of aunt, she would have been my uncle's little princess. My uncle was very good to Chuntian, and she always went to visit him on holidays, receiving gifts or cash on such occasions. Later, when she complained of my father's coldness and violence, she always raised my uncle's kindness and affection as a point of comparison.

My uncle died of a cerebral haemorrhage. Chuntian did not get to see him one last time. When she arrived, the coffin had already been sealed. My aunt leaned on it, howling. The candles, incense and even firecrackers all reeked of the smell of death and burial. My father's face showed the restraint it required for him not to scold; he was furious with my sister for being improperly late. If it had not been for the special occasion, he would have certainly taken the opportunity to unpack all his old grievances against her and air them. Chuntian had married into another family so long ago, but he had never let go of his right to teach her a good lesson.

My mother, brother, sister-in-law, and nieces were all there in mourning apparel. Yicao's eyes were filled with spookiness. She was developing, with small blossoms beginning to show on her chest. She was intrigued by this new scene. Her fascination had nothing to do with death; at first, she was even chewing gum. My mother dug it out of her mouth and threw it away and said, 'You don't learn from good examples. You're acting like a hooligan.'

My mother liked Yicao. She had a sweet tongue. When she went to our house, she would pester my mother to make her delicious snacks. None of us siblings were sweet talkers, so with just this tactic alone, Yicao captured my mother's heart. A character like Yicao's was at complete variance with ours. No one like her was to be found in either the Li or the Liu house. At this moment, she supported her old grandmother, comforting her with care.

As soon as the funeral gun sounded, the firecrackers exploded hysterically. The sixteen people who carried the coffin let out a sudden cry and raised it onto their shoulders. The crowd around it was in a commotion. But before they could move from the terrace, the coffin suddenly cracked. My uncle's head drooped from the crack in the coffin. My aunt had bought the coffin and, hoping to leave a little more money for herself to live on, she had chosen the cheapest. She had never imagined the wickedness of the coffin-maker, that he would do a shoddy job and make the coffin loose and baggy. It was too late to change it, so the people stuffed my uncle's body inside once more, but the quality of the coffin was too poor, and it was too thin and short. The top of my uncle's head and his heel pushed against the ends of the coffin and the gaps could not be closed, so the people just tried to nail the coffin shut forcefully. The long nails penetrated my uncle's head and feet. The wood around each nail was soaked in blood.

After so many frustrations, my uncle was finally laid to rest in his grave. The crowd dispersed, and the grass started to grow on the grave.

For a very long time, my sister did not go into town to play cards.

Chapter 21:

Li Xiaohan

To those of us in the village, Beijing was as distant as heaven. It was not real, but just something we could see on the television, and it disappeared with the press of a button, no different from our dreams. Before I reported to my university, the village had a bon voyage celebration for me, sending me off with fireworks. They held a banquet, everyone drinking until they were red in the face. Everyone came with great kindness, as if ushering me into paradise. They even mentioned my second brother, Li Xiazhi, saying my family produced scholars, saddening my parents. When Xiazhi had gone to Changsha for university, it had not been such an event. Those he had close contact with came to congratulate him, but everything else was normal. I gave the Li household a good name, elevating my grandfather's status, and most people attributed my success to his influence. For a time, we had become a scholarly family. Perhaps times were changing. It seemed the academic atmosphere in the village was improving. Some parents in the village came to my father and mother, trying to learn the secret to raising a university student. I can imagine my parents' naive expressions. If a sapling grew from bird shit, how could they find the bird that deposited the shit? That was most likely the case, in my situation.

My father was even more vague, describing the smoke of burning incense rising over our family's ancestral grave. When he said that, he had no intention of following the trail of smoke to find its source.

My mother was more flattered at the compliment. In fact, I credited my success to her. For so many years, she got up when it was still dark each day to make me breakfast, then cooked hot meals for me when I came home. She was never lazy. I was my mother's occupation.

Long ago, Chuntian had said she wanted to go to some distant place and never come back. I became interested in distant places then, always feeling they must be nice places. At the very least, my father was not there, and anyplace that did not have my father was a fun place to be. At that time, Shunqiu and Xiazhi always praised me for being naturally intelligent, which became the root of my self-confidence. To me, going to the university was a normal thing; not going would have been strange. If I had said that aloud, people would have scolded me for being insincere, seeing it as a form of blind arrogance, so I chose to keep my mouth shut and stay low-key, simply letting the smoke continue to rise from the ancestral grave.

*

I did not become a class cadre during university. I spent all my time studying and falling in and out of love. I studied in the library or on my bed. I dated under the willow tree and on the banks of the lake. Later, I dated in the library and in bed, and left studying for the willow tree and the lake. Eventually, I could do either anywhere I pleased, until the two activities finally merged completely. I had four boyfriends, the longest lasting for a year, and the shortest for three months. Some of them later became 'sea turtles'– overseas graduates who returned home – and were completely transformed into elite businessmen. Some of them became famous reporters, supporting various important news and media, writing current political columns, making indiscreet remarks or criticisms. The best-looking was a boy a little older than me, Qin Huaihe. I took him home to show him off. My father was more enthusiastic than before, catching fish from the pond in front of my house and slaughtering chickens in the back garden. He brought out all the good wine he possessed. But in the end, Qin Huaihe still went to England. Of course, he could have taken me with him to England, or at least not just abandon me like that. But ending our relationship was not all his decision. Mostly, I felt that dating became fictitious if the distance was too great, while being in the same location was somehow more real and reliable. So I broke off the relationship, and Qin Huaihe slipped away and decided to try the local girls in England instead. Later, we became close friends.

Aside from a few casual boyfriends, I had another hidden relationship. If I say it openly, it takes away the mystery, but the fact is, my college life was quite ordinary.

I dated an English teacher the semester I graduated. We called him Mr Zhu. He was around thirty-eight, and his complexion was good. He had a photo of his wife and daughter in an embrace on his desk, and they fluttered on his computer screen. They were also firmly embedded in his wallet, so whenever we went for dinner or to a hotel, as soon as he opened his wallet, I saw them. It was like they were raising a hose and spraying cold water at me. I acted out of boredom, and this made it even harder for me to warm up to Mr Zhu. It put me in the state of ambiguity; I was not sure if I was hungry or not, and I could eat or not eat. I had to admit that Mr Zhu was a good cook. He had experience, and I knew that, and he could cook a good dish. The quantity was small but the flavour was good, lingering even when we parted. That's how things were between us.

But none of this affected my studies. During my four years at university, I read the twenty-four histories, the four classics, and the five great books of Chinese literature, and I read all the philosophers, the Tang and Song poems, the Ming and Qing novels, hundreds of biographies, Western philosophy, and Eastern stories. Later, I did an internship at a Beijing television station. Mr Zhu opened that door for me. When I had slept with him, I had never imagined there would be such tangible benefits. Later, when I thought about it, if Mr Zhu had not carried his wife and daughter's picture in his wallet, he probably would have delayed me for my entire life. I was like a ball of fire which, once ignited, had no boundaries and did not care about consequences. I can say without shame that Mr Zhu met all the criteria I dreamed of in a relationship, and I hated myself for not being like a vixen with a firm grasp. In one swoop, I could have made a wasteland of Mr Zhu's family and then, in one more fell swoop, I could have built the richly ornamented home he would share with me. Fishing in these emotional waters, I was still like Jiang Taigong, not using a hook, but just assuming that the fish would leap into my hand of their own volition. I learned soon enough, though, that twenty-first century fish were not like the discerning fish of the ancient Shang dynasty, when Jiang had waited them out. That was probably why I was single when I left school, with no male arm to cling to.

While I was an intern at the television station, the director who guided me was Yehe Nara, and she was an idler. Her ancestors were high officials of the Qing court. She retained remnants of her aristocratic legacy, and was very particular about food and clothing. She always paid careful attention to image. She liked me very much. Yehe Nara drove a VW Beetle, and there were always perfumed sachets and cartoon dolls in the car. When she was free, she would take me to wander around. I went to many famous lanes, celebrities' former residences, and time-honoured shops. If it were not for Yehe Nara, my four years studying in Beijing would have been in vain.

Yehe Nara had been working for ten years. Seeing me as little more than a child, it was fortunate she felt no contempt, but instead took me under her wing, as if she were my sister. She had made up her mind that I would graduate from her excellent school in three months, so she embarked on the mission of giving me a full education, including teaching me about food, drinks, entertainment, and love. She taught me how to get along with men, and how to give and receive affection freely. On the weekend, she dragged me to bars and taught me the art of flirting, and how to drink red wine or Champagne without paying for it. Yehe Nara did not touch beer or spirits, feeling they did not match her image. I deeply enjoyed Yehe Nara's lack of restraint. Her mantra was the English phrase, 'Why not?'. I did not know what I did in my past lives to deserve being blessed with such a mentor. I had learned how to dress. In three months my talent in dealing with worldly affairs and emotions grew exponentially. I even had a one-night stand with a long-haired artist. I had never imagined women could enjoy this sort of life, too.

Yehe Nara had soft, thin skin, long eyes, fine eyebrows, and small, narrow lips. She looked like a typical Southerner, but had a Northerner's personality. She was articulate, precise and accurate in her use of words. Once, when she had had too much to drink, she spoke of her past boyfriends. The focus was on a pilot who was her childhood sweetheart. Not long before they were to be married, his plane crashed into the sea. Her lover now was the boss of Xingke

Book Garden. She wanted to take me to the Book Garden to see where they committed their love act, where the boss had raised her skirt and fucked her behind the bookshelves. Just ten metres away, the guests were drinking coffee and chatting.

We got in the car and left Sanlitun. As we drove, Yehe Nara spoke nonstop of the boss's new tricks. Once in the dark of night, he had pushed her against the bough of a tree in the park and fucked her where she stood. On the other side of the park were residents of the city and Peking Opera fans having late singing practice. She said doing it in public places had an unexpected appeal. Yehe Nara's descriptions whetted my appetite. The boss of the Xingke Book Garden provoked my curiosity and filled my fantasies.

The entrance to the bookstore was not large. The black bricks and red window frames were in the old Beijing style, but when you entered the door, it felt broad and open, and a few cats napped atop the books. Walking past the book bar reading area, there were several rows of bookshelves. They were meticulously organised, starting with a row on democracy, freedom, and constitutionalism, then followed by a row of Chinese intellectuals, a row of Western philosophy, and so on. Yehe Nara stopped in front of the literature section and, laughing, said softly, 'This is it.'

She said her lover nearly knocked *Love in the Time of Cholera* and *A Hundred Years of Solitude* off the shelf there.

I said, 'If people had walked by then, what would you have done?'

She said, 'Very few people come to this row to look for books. Most people just come for the atmosphere at the book bar. I realised that early on.'

I said, 'I like Marx. I read him during my first year of university.'

She glanced at me. 'I didn't know you were a literary youth. Books are the cheapest thing to buy. For the price of one pair of shoes, you can buy a basket of books. Pick whatever you want. I'll buy it for you.'

I showed no restraint, choosing a whole pile of books. At the cash register, Yehe Nara asked if the boss was in. The cashier said he was out, but would be back in half an hour.

We found a quiet corner and sat down. A fat cat woke from its nap and tiptoed over, leaning against me so I would pet it. Yehe Nara ordered a cappuccino. I did not like coffee's bitterness, so ordered a lemonade. I said, 'I look like a cow when I drink. I've always been like that. I'm not stylish enough to drink coffee.'

Yehe Nara added, 'I used to like reading books, but stopped doing it completely. There are so many interesting things in life. It's silly to sit holding a book all the time. You will later find that it's a waste of time, especially if you cry over a book or think too much – we have to live in the real world.'

I did not quite agree with her thinking, but perhaps in ten years I would see things in the same way, so for now, I did not want to argue with her. But I did ask, 'Then why do you want to give me books? Are you trying to sabotage me?'

She said, 'It's your own life. If you want to waste it, it's up to you. Sometimes you need to waste it. I'm only telling you a principle; I'm not trying to change what you do.'

We carried on at the bar for a while. I could not win against Yehe Nara. She seemed to be a person with no weaknesses.

She pulled out her phone and sent a message. I started reading the prologue of Sartre's *In Camera*, and quickly got lost in it. I looked up suddenly, and I found there was a man sitting next to Yehe Nara. Entranced, I sucked in a deep, cold breath and did not exhale.

Yehe Nara said, 'This is the famous boss of Xingke, Tang Linlu.'
I still did not respond.

'Oh. . . you look a little familiar. Maybe we've met before?' Tang said, looking at me, with an expression like he was trying hard to identify me.

It had been many years, and the flower was now in full bloom. He did not recognise me. And that young person, so full of ideals and sorrows, from all those years ago, his eyes pure and transparent, smart and cynical; he was older, too. The boy who had sat under my family's jujube tree, playing his guitar and singing, his gaze falling on me like a dragonfly flitting on my face. I waited for him to say my name.

But he did not remember. He swept right past me, and they went on talking vaguely in front of me. I could not understand what they were saying.

I opened the book and hid my face, pretending to read, listening to my heart pound in my chest. It was exactly the same as it had been ten years earlier. The words on the page turned purple, like the jujube flowers, floating in front of my eyes, their smell light and elegant. The last time Tang had been to our house, he brought Li Xiazhi's ashes, and when he left, he said to me, 'Study hard and develop a good conscience, and that will be enough.'

Several acquaintances came into the store, and Tang went to socialise. Yehe Nara got up and went to the washroom.

I patted the fat cat. It purred, perfectly content.

Tang was soon back at his seat. He said. 'I keep seven or eight cats here, Scottish Fold, American short-haired, Russian blue, a Norwegian forest cat, a Himalayan cat, and a Persian. This one is called Xiazhi. He's a ragdoll cat. If you like him, I can give him to you.'

'Xiazhi?' I asked. The fat cat purred and look at me.

'You're Xiaohan. I knew it the moment I saw you,' Tang said.

'I don't have anywhere to keep a cat . . . I'm just an intern.'

Yehe Nara's training was of no use. I had reverted back to my

EQ level of ten years earlier. I hoped he would talk about that distant past, talking about what he thought of me in his memories.

'You've already graduated from university,' he said, handing me a business card. 'Where did you study?'

'At the Renmin University of China. I studied Journalism,' I said. My mind was full of images of his affair with Yehe Nara.

'Not bad. Do you remember that year when you sneered at that porcupine head fellow at your house? He founded *Today Newspaper* and is the editor there now. He was Xiazhi's roommate.'

'Right. Yu Shuzhong.'

'You've got a good memory. He's very successful. The media in the South is very advanced. I suggest you go to Guangzhou to further your development.'

Chapter 22:

Liu Yihua, Niece

Dai Xinyue did not make a big fuss over his smashed shop, but simply went about repairing it without complaint.

That winter, Yihua stood up to her boss. Because the temperature suddenly dropped, the boss gave her old sweaters and cotton jackets to the seven nymphs but announced that she was going to collect rent money from them, deducting thirty *yuan* for each piece of clothing, straight from the wages of each worker. Yihua leapt up onto the table, scolding her boss, 'You were a product of the Japanese, so no wonder you want to bully the Chinese people.'

The boss really had been the child of a rape by Japanese soldiers, but it was a matter no one ever mentioned, especially not in public. The woman could not take it. White foam formed at her mouth as her eyes rolled up, and she collapsed, falling under her desk. Her son-of-a-bitch son and grandson took her to the hospital, then came back and settled the score with Yihua, the son-of-a-bitch grandson slapping her until she bled from the mouth and nose. Yihua wiped the blood stains off her face and went in search of Liuzi. He only brought three people with him and laid out three conditions: one, the seven nymphs' pay would not be short a single cent; two, the son-of-a-bitch grandson would apologise to Liu Yihua; three, Liu Yihua would be given 5000 *yuan* for medical fees.

The son-of-a-bitch son promised to meet the first two conditions, but wanted to negotiate on the third. Liuzi laughed and said, 'I never give discounts. You better figure out how to settle it.'

The son-of-a-bitch son and grandson huddled together. They knew Liuzi was ruthless, untouchable, and that losing a little money here would be the best approach. They apologised, restored the full salary, paid damages, and finally dismissed the seven nymphs. When the other six went back to the village, Yihua became a legend. There were all manner of rumours, all of them describing her as a loose girl.

The 5000 in damages was split fifty-fifty between Yihua and Liuzi, ending up in their pockets. They formed bonds of complicity and common profit through this incident. Money is a lubricant for everything. Yihua did not have to be grateful to Liuzi, nor was she in any way committed to him. Liuzi had only had to talk, whereas she – to her great credit – had borne physical pain.

After this, without giving any thought to her future, Yihua spent several abstinent nights in a cheap hotel with Liuzi. When they were having *mifen* for breakfast one morning, she saw in the social commentary section of the newspaper that many people from Hunan were looting and vandalising in Guangzhou, giving people from Hunan a bad name.

Yihua told Liuzi, 'Let's go to Guangzhou and further the bad name of the Hunan people.'

Liuzi rolled his eyes and said, 'Desperate love birds. That sounds good. I'm your bodyguard. I'll go where you go.'

Yihua did not go home. She went to the post office and remitted

500 *yuan* to my sister. She attached a message, saying, *I've gone to Guangzhou.*

*

The hard train seat was still bearable at the beginning of their journey, but halfway through the night their backsides began to ache, their bodies were sore, and they wanted to lie down. Yihua had never missed a night's sleep before. It was so unbearable she kept cursing, turning this way and that, but could not get comfortable, so Liuzi generously offered his thigh. Yihua lay on his lap, and he leaned across her back, then they swapped, going back and forth this way several times until they finally slept all the way to Guangzhou.

When they arrived, day had just broken. They followed the crowd out of the train station and looked around, petrified. Of all the places, they had travelled all the way to Guangzhou, and now they didn't quite know what to do with themselves. Liuzi smoked to keep himself awake, while Yihua plopped down on her luggage, as if in a stupor. All around were people yelling loudly and dragging snakeskin bags. A security officer came and hustled them along, saying the square was only for passing through, not for staying. Liuzi resented the officer's rudeness. The hot-headedness of a mob boss rushed to his brain, and after only a few words with the other party, they started fighting. The officer was there just for show and was easily knocked down. He quickly spoke into his walkie-talkie and five or six others appeared as if from nowhere, dragging Liuzi to the police station without another word.

Yihua waited outside the police station. An hour later, Liuzi walked out, face bruised and swollen. He said, 'Fuck it. This is their turf.'

Yihua said, 'We haven't broken out the guns yet, and you've already taken a beating, so we'll just have to follow the rules for now . . . My uncle was put in jail for fighting. By the time he got out, he had wasted away.'

Liuzi argued, 'He should have been even more imposing when he got out. It would be intimidating, like a scar on his face.'

Yihua retorted, 'No job, poor health, a hatred for night, and a fear of other people . . . my uncle is very honest.'

Liuzi said, 'You mean I'm not honest?'

She replied, 'If you had lived at that time, you would've been the first to be shot.'

He said, 'I'd show those bullies a thing or two before I was shot.'

'Where are we going?' Yihua asked.

A middle-aged woman handed Yihua a paper, printed in black and white. It was a list of recruitment advertisements for Dong-guan City.

'Dongguan? Where's Dongguan?' Yihua asked.

Liuzi said, 'It's near Guangzhou.' One of his friends from primary school had worked in the Hsu Fu Chi biscuit factory, but he had been fired for stealing.

Leaning against a sign at the bus stop, they studied the advertisements in their hands. *Electronics factory worker, toy factory labourer, nanny, sales assistant, retail, cashier, hotel hostess, bartender*. . . the pair read until they were dizzy with the prospects. Thinking of how many jobs were waiting, their hearts were lifted. They started to feel hungry.

They found a small food stall and ate bowls of fried rice noodles. It cost five or six times as much as noodles in Yiyang. Even Liuzi pouted over this, 'If we don't watch our pockets, we'll go broke in Guangzhou.'

Because he got beaten up in Guangzhou, Liuzi did not have a

good feeling about the place. But, the advertisement had fallen from the sky, and he had long ago heard of Dongguan, so it seemed to be fate. Liuzi advocated going to Dongguan, so he asked the food stall keeper for directions. There was a bus to Dongguan at the stop outside the stall. It would take less than an hour to get there. By the time they had inquired thoroughly, it was only a little after nine in the morning.

Liuzi leaned back and tried to look through the densely packed buildings to the sky, but he could only see grey everywhere. The wind brought a deep chill, sometimes stirring the fallen leaves on the ground, crawling over the backs of cold, rushing feet.

Liuzi said, 'I never imagined Guangzhou would be so worn that it would look like a rag.'

'I've never seen such a good rag. It's just that the sun hasn't come out yet,' declared Yihua.

Liuzi added, 'No matter how good the weather is, it's still just a worn-out rag.'

He touched the wounds on his face, as if he would not be able to find anything good to say about Guangzhou in this lifetime.

Yihua said, 'The noodles were good. I like the big city. I like how you can be sucked right in all at once, then you have to try desperately to swim your way to the surface for breath. I'm sure Guangzhou is more interesting than Dongguan. Since we're already here, there's no need to fiddle around and go to a smaller city.'

When Liuzi tried to persuade her, Yihua retorted, 'If you want to go to Dongguan, go.'

Liuzi hung his head. He had said he was her bodyguard, so he should play the part, but he was depressed. Yet, Yihua could afford to act this way, relying on the fact that he liked her to get her way.

Liuzi was six or seven years older than Yihua. There was a question he had turned over in his mind more than a hundred times, but could still not figure out. He could not understand her. If she did not like him, why would she stay in the hotel with him, or take the train with him, or come to Guangzhou with him, or lay her head on his lap as she slept? But if she liked him, why did she build this wall between them, not allowing him to touch her. He often felt like he was ready to explode. It was embarrassing.

'What are you thinking about?' Yihua gave Liuzi a push. 'Look at this.' She pointed to a wall plastered with colourful flyers.

Liuzi looked it over for a while, then said, 'Factory life is hard, and the pay is low. You've got more to offer than that. You should go to a hotel and be a hostess.'

Yihua asked, 'What's a hostess?'

'It means you wear a *qipao* and stand at the hotel's entrance. When customers come, you take them to their table to eat. The hostess wears pretty clothes, and doesn't need to wash dishes or serve food, but she gets higher pay.'

'You think a hotel would want me?' Yihua asked, stirred.

Liuzi looked her over. He said, 'You won't have any problem, even at a five star hotel.'

Yihua laughed. 'Liuzi, you finally tell the truth. Of course, someone looking half-Indian like I do is pretty rare, so I must be in demand.'

Liuzi looked at the advertisement again. 'North Tianhe Bingsheng Hotel. Serving congee . . . recruiting hostesses . . . requirements: at least 1.65 metres tall, good-looking . . . *Aiyoh,* Huahua, can you speak Mandarin?'

'I told you to stop calling me Huahua. It sounds awful. Like you're calling a dog.'

'It says you need to speak Cantonese and Mandarin . . . If you're really pretty, you can receive preferential consideration.'

Yihua said a few words in Mandarin. The pair nearly died laughing.

'It feels awkward to speak Mandarin in front of you. Back when I was studying, my Mandarin pronunciation was very accurate. I won't have any problem speaking. But what about you? You don't mean you plan not to work and just let me support you?'

'This isn't my territory. I'll wait until you get settled into a job, then when I run out of money, I'll go back.'

'Actually, my youngest aunt is in Guangzhou, but I don't want to look her up now.'

'Since when did you have relatives in Guangzhou?'

'It's true. She's a news reporter.'

'Then it would be good to look her up.'

'My aunt looks down on the uneducated . . . If you haven't studied and you go out into the world, is that really as good as death?'

'So you don't want to rely on your relatives. With as strong a backbone as you have, I don't think you'll die.'

Chapter 23:

Xiao Shui Qin, Sister-in-law

Shui Qin returned home to visit Shunqiu as he recovered, carrying back various herbs to boost the blood and nutrition, along with peanut oil and rice, showing that she was not going to eat for free. She poured pleasing words right into my mother's ear. She came in calling 'Mother,' as if she were a schoolgirl coming home at the end of the day. My mother always fell for this. Shui Qin's sweet words washed away all the former complaints she harboured inside. Added to this, they were no longer living under the same roof, so there was less friction over trivial matters. The old grudge was no more; it had been replaced by joy and happiness. Xianxian was more loveable than ever. Her sweet talk was just like her mother's, and often left my parents quite speechless. She loved to perform, and was not shy and reserved like the village children. She sang when she talked and danced when she walked, as if the sunlight had broken the soil, allowing new flowers to bloom and butterflies to flit into open graves. She brought spring-time with her.

When she next came back, Shui Qin looked quite cheerful. She told my brother privately that she had signed a contract with the school and taken over the design and production of the costumes for their show. She would be very busy. She needed to employ at least five or six girls who could sew, and she had already spoken to the shop next door about taking over its storefront.

My brother said, 'Where will you get the money?'

Shui Qin replied, 'I got an advance payment when I signed the contract.'

She stretched out five fingers.

'Five thousand?' he asked.

'Add a zero,' she replied.

My brother stared in disbelief. He had grown very thin. His nose looked as if it had been sharpened, his chin like an awl ready to stab the ground, and even his smile looked pointy. His expression quickly collapsed. He thought of how he was of no help, and there was a hint of shame in his new expression.

Shui Qin said, 'After a while, you should come to the city to recuperate. You'll be able to take care of Xianxian. She's learned to go online and play games now, so she needs to be controlled.'

My brother promised to go into the city to keep an eye on Xianxian. He then added, 'Chuntian learned sewing. Add her to your group of seamstresses. Anyway, all she does is play cards all day and night, and fight with Zhima.'

Shui Qin said, 'What about Yicao?'

My brother replied, 'She'll be in secondary school and living on campus soon.'

Shui Qin agreed, feeling it was better to keep good things in the immediate family. Most of the women in the village had learned to sew when they were girls. Very quickly, she finalised the rest of the candidates, who agreed to be paid by the piece for those that passed the inspection. This sort of flexibility was meant to cater to the village women who had to take care of farming duties while they worked. Each time they received the money, it would enrich their housekeeping fund; this would provide real motivation.

From the beginning, Shui Qin had possessed an entrepreneurial style. Now she had even more confidence. She said that if they were satisfied with this year's cooperation, the whole school would have its uniforms done by her next year, including their design. Good things were waiting to happen. When she spoke of the principal, Ms Wu, the wrinkles at the corners of her eyes were full of good will and her descriptions of that 50-odd-year-old woman made her seem like Kuanyin, the Goddess of Mercy.

Ms Wu had been through a lot of hardships, and she had seen her dreams shattered. When she was sent to work in the countryside, she almost died, thinking she would stay there forever. But, she went back to the city and sat the college entrance exam, taking it twice before she finally passed. Her life had been complicated, so she could understand Shui Qin. In short, Shui Qin felt she had met her fairy godmother. She set aside all the money she made so she could send Xianxian overseas for university. Her immediate plan was to buy a house, and to buy a resident's permit for the city. She wanted to change her identity as quickly as possible, to no longer be the sort of country girl people always discriminated against.

Faced with Shui Qin's grand ideas, a pointy, shy smile appeared on my brother's face, and he just listened. After he was released from prison, he stopped fantasising about the future. It was like he was standing on a cliff and did not have the courage to look down as his legs quivered. Shui Qin was demonstrative. Other people's reactions did not matter. She would continue to spread out the scroll of her life, presenting each wonderful inch in its turn. But even when my brother had seen the whole painting, he did not utter a word in praise of it. He just continued to sit there with that shy, sharp smile on his face. It could be taken as a smile of encouragement, tolerance, trust, support, or just about anything. Shui Qin could understand this well enough, so she did not ask for his views. Instead, she just rolled her scroll up again and tied the string securely around it, storing the secret away in the drawers. She suddenly thought of something important. When my brother was well, she wanted him to take the test to get a driver's license in case it was needed. Everything was planned, so they would not be caught in a rush.

My brother nodded, as if this sort of arrangement could not be more properly made.

When my brother had spent half a month more recuperating at home, Shui Qin gave someone a message, asking him to go quickly into the city. She was working herself to death, and Xianxian often had to go with her when she was out, eating fast food, which didn't agree with her stomach. My brother took a bag and started packing to go into the city. My grandfather shouted at him, stuffing prescriptions of Chinese medicine for improving blood levels and kidney health into his hands, saying they had been handed down since the days of Emperor Qianlong. Shunqiu was the only person who would talk to my grandfather, so my grandfather took him as a confidant. Since he had had Shunqiu as an ally, he had dared tweak his nose in front of my father. My father's interest in bickering with him had waned. He was now ageing and growing lonely, like my grandfather, and was likewise starting to look like him.

Shunqiu threw the prescriptions away while he was on the road. He did not want to continue doing anything that would cost money.

Because it was on the way, he went to wait for Xianxian so they could go home together. Shunqiu stood against a phone booth, looking at the entrance to the school from time to time. He was afraid the place he stood was too conspicuous, so he retreated to a spot behind the phone booth. The students exited the building and dispersed in many directions. Xianxian was walking his way with several of her classmates. She did not look happy, as if she were quarrelling with someone.

'If you were capable, you could get the top score in the exam too!' Xianxian said.

'What's the big deal about a top score? Top score or not, you're still a village girl,' one girl said in an obstinate tone.

Another girl chimed in, 'Yeah, and not only a village girl, but a village girl whose father is a reformed prisoner!'

Xianxian froze, then suddenly rushed at the girl who had chimed in. Unprepared, that girl fell to the ground the moment Xianxian pushed her. Xianxian did not give up, but pressed her knee against the girl and started swinging her school bag at the fallen figure. The girl on the ground covered her head with her arms and cried.

My brother hid there, not moving. He watched Xianxian walk quite a distance away, then followed slowly.

Later, he went to the tailor shop. He could hear nothing but the machine-gun-fast sewing machines. Chuntian sat on the first row. When she looked up and saw Shunqiu, she got up to speak with him, reminding him to take good care of himself. My brother smiled sharply, asked after Zhima, then added, 'The education in the village is no good. I hope Yicao will study hard and do well enough on her exams to get into a junior college in the city.'

Chuntian said, 'I don't know if she'll do well enough or not. Every person's fate will come about naturally.'

Shunqiu said, 'Is Yihua still working in the fishing net factory?'

'She's gone to Guangzhou,' my sister said. 'I guess she went to look up her aunt. She's clever and mischievous. There is no place in heaven or hell that girl doesn't dare go.'

My brother nodded his approval. 'She's brave. She's not afraid of anything. Yicao is also very sensible, but she should still study hard.'

Shunqiu said this as he was turning to walk away. He spoke softly, as if talking to himself, and his voice was lost in the excitement of the sewing machines running at the same machine gun pace. Chuntian did not hear the last half of what he said, but assumed it was irrelevant. She smiled and sat down again, then went back to sewing.

Shui Qin rushed out when she saw my brother and asked, 'What happened to Xianxian? She was crying when she got back. Did the other students bully her?'

Shunqiu said, 'I went to her school, but didn't pick her up. . . She's very ambitious. . . Is she down because she didn't do well on her exams?'

'When has she ever done poorly on exams?'

Shunqiu nodded, agreeing. He had long ago quit smoking, but he wanted a cigarette now. He searched his pockets, as had long been his habit, patting his thighs. Then he remembered he had quit. He turned to look at Shui Qin, offering a pointy, embarrassed smile, and said, 'I'll go cook dinner.'

Chapter 24:

Li Chuntian, Elder Sister

When my sister had been in the city for several months making clothes, her skin started to look much healthier, a bit of rosiness coming back to her pale cheeks. Shui Qin cut her two sets of skirts and two blouses, one set navy blue and the other beige. My sister worked overtime so she could sew and iron them, then hung them up, but she could not bear to wear them. One day, Shui Qin finally forced her to try them on. She did it unwillingly, but when she stood in front of the mirror, she was surprised. She did not know that she, now nearly forty years old, could look like this. She filled out the skirts and blouses fully, and they fit her nicely at the waist. She was fascinated by this strange, Western-style woman in the mirror. She alternated between these two outfits for a while, then asked Shui Qin to cut her some more new styles, gradually discarding those she brought from the village. She permed her hair wavy. She put it up when she worked, but left it down otherwise. She complained of being too fat, so she dieted, starving herself until she dropped ten pounds. Her face and body were reduced by one size; only her chicken-arse-shaped mouth grew thicker. She started talking more like people from the city, reducing her volume and paying attention to the way her sentences tailed off. She even started talking logically, with 'I feel . . .' entering as a part of her regular speech pattern. Her legs were no longer as sloppy when she walked, but clamped, her steps closer together, and very light-footed.

When my sister was young, she loved to dress up, but her bell bottoms had been cut to shreds. She had never recovered the love of beauty that my father had killed inside her. Later, she had had children and worked on the farm, treating herself as nothing more than livestock.

Zhima stopped by a couple of times. The first time, he came to take money from her, saying someone was getting married, and he was invited to the wedding banquet. The next, he came to tell my sister to go home, saying Yicao had brought a boy from school home and slept with him in their house. Zhima had given her a good beating.

Chuntian said, 'You've taught her, then, haven't you? What do you want me to do, go back and give her another beating? Can't you just leave me in peace and let me make a little money?'

The third time Zhima went into the city, he got a room in a small hotel and asked my sister to stay with him there. Chuntian suddenly felt great despair. She felt a great physical repulsion, not even wanting to undress. Finally, out of habit, she stripped herself naked, then lay spread out on the bed, waiting for Zhima to finish all that he had in mind, as she asked how things were at home.

Zhima said, 'You're thin, and your body has hardened. Your waist isn't soft anymore.' As he was doing her, he tried to persuade my sister to go home, saying he was bored at home alone. Without his woman at home, it was cold and he couldn't sleep.

My sister said, 'If I go back, it's to the card table. I don't want to live like that anymore.'

Zhima replied, 'You've got a lot of new clothes. You've become fashionable.'

She said, 'People who work in a salon cut their own hair. People who sew for a living make their own clothes. Isn't it just a matter of convenience?'

As Zhima continued to work on my sister, he said, 'Chuntian, you don't have anyone else, do you?'

'Who wants a sallow-faced woman like me?' she said.

Zhima replied, 'I think that pale-skinned chap is interested in you.'

She thought for a moment. That day, the lawyer, Sun Xiangxi, had come to have clothes made. While she was taking his measurements, he had told her a few jokes. She had laughed loudly. When she raised her head, she saw Zhima at the window staring.

Since Chuntian did not answer, Zhima stopped and asked, 'Do you have a lover?'

Hearing this, she was annoyed. She pushed him away and sat up. 'You motherfucker, what did you say? I haven't worn such nice clothes in decades, and now that I wear it to please myself, why is it such a big deal?'

Zhima was like a bottle of wine, suddenly uncorked. With a bang, he stood up, naked and angry. He said, 'Filth,' and picked up the dress my sister had taken off to rip it, like it was the culprit.

An attack on my sister's beloved dress was like an attack on her life. Her breasts jiggling, she flew across the room, snatched the clothes from him, and clasped them to her chest. She said, 'Liu Zhima, you've bullied me for too many years. That's it. I'm going to divorce you.'

Chuntian even scared herself with these words.

Zhima stared, eyes growing round. He was growing more convinced that my sister had someone else.

Chuntian got dressed to go back to the workers' dorm. Zhima

stopped her, his teeth flashing white against his dark face in the dim light of the room. He wanted her to tell him who it was. Face hard, my sister said, 'There's no one.'

Zhima could not hold back the ruffian side of himself. He said, 'You still want to lie to me? You bitch!' He pushed her down on the bed and blocked the door, shouting, 'Tell me and I'll let you go! This won't end until you tell me!'

She said, 'You can't force me.'

Zhima let out a strange sound. Chuntian's hair stood up and she lowered her voice. It came out solid and hard as she said, 'Zhima, you motherfucker, I love myself. And it's none of your business! You messed around outside plenty of times yourself, and even got extorted. You think I'm as filthy as you. I didn't even say anything about it, and you turn around and make a fuss about me? What man could possibly be as lazy as you?'

Zhima suddenly felt he had been punctured. Waving his arms like a drowning man, he stammered, 'What big mouth has been spreading rumours? Fuck him, and his mother too! I hope he dies . . . Chuntian, I know you don't have anyone else. I just saw you dressed like that, and felt that the cheeky fellows' eyes were on you, and I was uncomfortable. I'm your husband. I'm jealous. Do you understand that?'

My sister had always been more responsive to a soft approach. She grew calmer. She didn't want to go back to the dorm in the middle of the night; she'd be a laughingstock. She undressed once more and went back to bed. Zhima put his arms around her contentedly and set about the business he had left unfinished.

The next morning, after the couple ate rice noodles, Zhima looked back three times for each step he walked before he finally left. He still hoped Chuntian would go back with him. He said everyone in the village was laughing at him, saying his woman had left him and he was guarding a vacant room. Zhima was easily stirred up by others, and once he was stirred up, he took a big gulp of mannish pride and set angrily about to settle scores. He had boasted, saying he would bring his woman home and teach her a lesson; instead, he had to back down.

Chuntian promised that, if Yicao did well enough on her exams the following month to get into a school in town, she would rent a flat there and they would open a fruit stall in the city. They could contract their field in the village to others. When Zhima returned home, he started to take Yicao firmly in hand, but it was Liu Yihua who motivated her to work hard.

Yihua wrote to her constantly, saying that it would not be easy to go out into the world if she did not study, because people would always look down on her. If she saw a chance for a good job, without a diploma, she would not even be given the opportunity to try. She could only rely on her looks working as a hostess. She even sent a stack of test questions to Yicao.

Yicao eventually did well enough to enter the Number Five Secondary School, which was located on the outskirts of Lanxi Town, not far from our home. My mother was thrilled, because she now had a new occupation – cooking for Yicao.

Zhima became a commander without a post. There was only an old cat left at home, so he went to look for my sister regularly, intending to bring her home. At first, he acted pitiful, hanging around outside the door. Later he tried arguing, getting more vigorous when there were spectators, making it difficult for the tailor shop to conduct business normally. In the end, he even found fault with Shui Qin, saying that his own woman had been perfectly content staying at home, but then Shui Qin just had to lure Chuntian out, destroying his family.

Being that they were relatives, Shui Qin did not pull a long face. Rather, she smiled and said, 'Zhima, you need to understand something. Chuntian is a person. She's not a belt you put on and take off as you please. She has her own ideas. You wait for her to get off work, then the two of you have a good talk. Isn't it humiliating to stand on the street quarrelling?'

Confronted with this soft rebuke, Zhima was drained of offensive energy. He sat on the pavement across the street from the shop, looking like he would not give up unless Chuntian went back with him. But he did not hang around until the workday finished. It cost money to stay in a hotel. He would rush home and sleep in his own bed.

A week later, Zhima showed up again. He went to have a look in the tailor shop. A stranger was sitting in my sister's place. He went in, but no one entertained him. Shui Qin was busy cutting fabric. The scissors were long and sharp. The glint of the scissors and the *ka-cha, ka-cha* rhythm as she cut the cloth made Zhima feel a little frightened.

'Where's Li Chuntian?' His voice followed the scissors, coldly tearing the fabric apart.

Still, no one answered.

'Shui Qin, where's my wife?' he asked politely.

'Oh, Chuntian? She resigned a few days ago,' Shui Qin replied.

'Then where did she go? She didn't come home!'

Zhima felt he had fallen into an icy cave.

'I don't know. She didn't say,' Shui Qin said, not even looking at him.

Dumbfounded, Zhima stood there for a few moments. Then, he turned and walked slowly along the pavement.

My sister burrowed out from behind a pile of cloth. The women laughed, collapsing in a heap. When the hilarity finally died down, they went back to work. Chuntian resumed her old seat and continued making clothes. To her surprise, Zhima wheeled around and struck back, catching them red-handed. Because he had been the butt of a bunch of women's joke, he was especially brazen. The fire held inside him exploded on Chuntian. He pinned her on the sewing machine, ordering her to go home with him immediately.

This time, those who had interfered earlier were too embarrassed to help, so they left the couple to tear each other apart on the street. The pair fought as they walked, finally fading into the distance until they could not be seen anymore.

Chapter 25:

Liu Yihua, Niece

The restaurant in the Bingsheng Hotel was old and famous in Guangzhou, and business was good. Reservations had to be made for a table one day in advance, and three days in advance for a private dining room. Those who had not made reservations had to queue up and wait. Yihua wore a red silk *qipao* embroidered with gold flowers. With her hair pulled to the back and the required light makeup, with black eyeshadow and red-painted lips, she had suddenly turned into a real beauty. She ushered the guests into the main hall or private rooms, serving drinks and melon seeds to those waiting in line, sometimes alleviating their anxieties.

Usually, Yihua was not particular about her clothing. This was the first time she was so neatly coordinated and dressed with such care. She felt very restricted. When you added the wobbly high heels she wore, which made her afraid she'd fall, she walked like an old woman with bound feet. But she learned quickly, and was soon able to move to a steady rhythm. She mastered a method to do so, pretending she was angry, standing with a straight back, puffed out chest, and lips protruding. If she could keep her hands and legs from awkward movements, it really made her look quite dignified. Occasionally some offensive man, seeing her flat breasts and buttocks and guessing that she was a virgin, would tease her. She was not intimidated, but just spoke her mind. When she was bored, she would look at the passing cars, recognising the BMWs, Mercedes, Land Rovers, Maseratis, and Cadillacs. She was most interested in the people who got out of those cars. She did not like domestic cars, nor was she interested in the people who got out of them.

Yihua first learned about cars from Liuzi. Liuzi had not gone back, nor had he said he would stay to keep her company. He worked at a nearby hotel, as a security guard at the car park there. Liuzi was accustomed to an idle life, but he worked just to pass the time. He had plenty of money on him, so he rented a one-room, one-hall flat for 700 *yuan* a month, where he and Yihua settled in. Yihua slept on the bed, Liuzi on the sofa. Sometimes they both slept on the bed, but Yihua made him promise that he'd never touch her, nor even think of touching her, or she'd go straight to the dorm and stay there. Liuzi stuck to the rules, never deviating. Sometimes he would even cook peppers fried with pork slices for Yihua to remind her of home, and would accompany her to the shops, to the movies, or to the roadside stall to eat Cantonese congee.

Once, the pair were eating kebabs and drinking beer at a roadside stall in the hazy Guangzhou evening. Liuzi watched Yihua as if through a haze. He asked, 'You don't like me at all?'

Yihua said, 'So what if I like you, and so what if I don't?'

Liuzi had no reply to that.

Yihua said, 'You're the one who chose to stay. I didn't ask you to. You shouldn't expect anything from me.'

Liuzi said, 'You're really overbearing.'

Yihua curled her lips and said, 'It's not like you just met me today.'

Liuzi scolded, 'You're a devil woman, a sucker.'

Yihua thought, then added, 'I don't ever want to get married for as long as I live.'

Liuzi said deliberately, 'Don't dream. I've never asked you to marry me.'

Yihua smiled, 'All right. I'll take it that you're giving up.'

Liuzi wanted to take back his words, but was afraid it would only result in further teasing, so instead he drained his cup.

As a key male character in the drama of my niece's life, Liuzi plays no small role in this long story, so it is reasonable that I carve out his appearance for you. Liuzi was not ugly, but not handsome either. He had a crew cut, an ordinary square face, and features that were properly positioned. His physique could be considered burly, and though he liked to use force, his temperament was not necessarily rude. When he grew stubborn, he was not afraid of blood or pain. Yihua was something of a nemesis to him, having subdued him with ease. In his relationships with women, Liuzi was very gentlemanly. Take, for instance, how he had waited for Yihua to grow up. After all, she was only sixteen or seventeen. But he had underestimated her savviness – and she was more aware of this fact than anyone else.

Guangzhou's summer had a sort of street hoodlum meanness to it, leaving no trace of anything praiseworthy. The tall buildings made the streets feel like a canyon floor, with a fusion of various waste gases rising from it. The sun made faces look like they had been smeared with butter, turning the skin sticky and the breath hot, with the thick, scorching wind making it even more stifling. Short little girls swung their dark, thin arms and legs, while fair-skinned, voluptuous women from the north exposed their cleavages. Foreigners of all different colours could be seen gazing through the windows of cafés along the road, with cups of Blue Mountain, Brazilian coffee, or mocha in front of them.

Yihua stood inside the glass door of the Bingsheng Hotel, her legs aching, feeling as bored as a plant exposed to extreme sunlight. She usually got along well with Lu Mingliang, a girl from Chongqing. Mingliang was straightforward and happy, and was never arrogant over her good looks. She even tended to make fun of girls with pretty faces and deep cleavages. She said their faces had clearly-marked prices and a blatant, *Can you afford it?*, arrogance written all over them. As soon as they met a rich man, they turned into lap dogs.

But Mingliang had resigned and gone to work at the Pearl of the Orient nightclub. She said to Yihua, 'Hurry up and come with me. Working at the Bingsheng is a waste of your youth.'

So one night she went to the Pearl of the Orient to look for Mingliang. Mingliang was working, and she moved through the dim light and shadows. She wore a white princess dress with a tiara, very vibrant makeup, and heavy perfume. Yihua asked, 'Why are you dressed like that?'

Mingliang said, 'It's my uniform.'

Yihua saw several other girls dressed the same way, busily showing the guests to their private rooms, flitting around like fairies. Yihua stared, seeing the elaborate decor inside and feeling like she was in a royal palace, and she was dazzled and lost amid its resplendence and magnificence.

Mingliang said, 'Those who go to the Bingsheng are there to take the family to dinner. Those who come here, come for pure pleasure. If the men want to approach you, they approach without scruples. A couple of days ago, one of the girls won the favour of a boss from Macau, and he took her home.'

Yihua claimed that she hated working during the day, and thought working nights suited her better. She'd have no problem working all night. Mingliang led her along a brightly lit corridor to a snack bar, dim and full of sultry music. Mingliang went up to the woman drinking at the bar, leaned over to talk to her, then waved Yihua over. Only when Yihua approached did she see that the woman was a man, and her heart almost stopped. He was the manager of the Pearl of the Orient, a man named Zhou. He had long hair and an ear stud. He looked Yihua over, but seemed to feel this was not enough, so he asked her to sit down at one of the tables for a chat. Zhou wore all black, and was as skinny and pale as a vampire. His speech and actions were both soft, and Yihua thought maybe he really was a woman. But it didn't actually matter whether Zhou was male or female. He seemed to be testing Liu Yihua's ability to respond under the ambiguous lighting, asking her various questions. His expression was alert, and she was afraid he would disappear in a cloud of smoke right before her eyes.

Yihua said she'd really like a beer, since her throat was dry from all the smoke. When Zhou asked whether she was a good drinker, she smiled and said, 'Well, I've never been drunk.'

Zhou asked, 'How about some whiskey?'

Then, without waiting for her consent, he caught the eye of the waitress and ordered two glasses of black label, asking Yihua if she wanted ice.

Yihua said honestly that she'd never drunk whiskey before, and had only had ice in a cola. Zhou smiled elegantly. 'Then I'll make the call.'

Before long, the waitress returned with the liquor, along with plates of cashews and peanuts. Yihua looked at the dark colour of the drink and, seeing that it looked like cola, she took a big gulp. She immediately realised it was a strong spirit. Fortunately, she'd had a few drinks of *baijiu* with Liuzi before, so her mouth did not explode.

Zhou asked Yihua how old she was. Adding a couple of years, she said nineteen. Zhou smiled as if he were tired, saying, 'The first requirement for working at the Pearl of the Orient is that you are beautiful. The second is that you can drink. The third is that you don't get emotionally involved with the patrons. Any questions?'

Yihua said that she had a boyfriend, giving Liuzi a status upgrade. Zhou's mouth twitched contemptuously. 'Once your emotions are stirred, don't talk about boyfriends, even marriage is nothing. Humans are lustful things. I have a friend who says that ecstasy is but a heap of beautiful ashes. These words are easily understood, but hard to live by. You appear to be transparent. To tell you the truth, in the working world, emotions are the greatest pitfall.'

Yihua fell in love with the dark drink and gradually began to feel a little intoxicated. Though she didn't understand what 'beautiful ashes' were, she knew more or less how to behave in the working world. She had experience with Dai Xinyue and Liuzi, and she had worked at the Bingsheng for quite some time. She had seen all sorts of people. You might even say she had seen the world.

Chapter 26:

Li Xiaohan

Out of friendship for Yehe Nara, I told her my story about Tang Linlu. She laughed at me for falling for him at one glance. She had never experienced a secret crush; she always expressed her feelings if she liked someone, and the other party's response was of no consequence. She felt it best for a person to travel with as little baggage as possible, and one certainly should not spend a whole lifetime carrying garbage – picking it up along the way and discarding it; get it, leave it, throw it away, and be done with it.

I asked her whether she had experienced a period of shyness in girlhood. She said, 'No. If the head is stuffed full of too many things, it will get cloudy. From the time I came out of the womb, I've hated beating around the bush or hiding things. It's no secret who I've loved or who I've slept with.'

I thought she was a glass house. At a glance, the inside of the structure, the furnishings, and its style could be seen clearly, and were not hidden in darkness. There were no dead ends and, though the sun might momentarily cast a shadow, it would move before long. I studied with Yehe Nara for three months, but I could not achieve that sort of behaviour so quickly. Maybe after ten years, I could be like her, rising above everything.

I had not yet let go of Qin Huaihe at that time. When he came back to China, he went to my school to find me, and I fell for him again. We spent two nights together. Unfortunately, we felt more like fuck buddies. When his girlfriend called from England, he hid in the washroom to answer the call. I could hear him lying. I knew I was the one who made the situation so terrible, that I had turned such an open love into betrayal, but without any of the joy of betrayal. When it was over, my heart was full of sorrow.

I had also not expected to encounter Tang Linlu again after so many years. He did not sing and play the guitar anymore, but he had become a skilled veteran womanizer. Yehe Nara said he womanised for fun, while he also had a lover who was a painter. She did not mind his straying, because an outstanding man was rarely single-minded. The couple gave each other appropriate space, which was why their relationship had always been fairly good.

That day, I went alone to Xingke Book Garden. There were two instincts that made me seek him out; I was a reporter, and I was Li Xiazhi's younger sister. I wanted to hear Tang Linlu talk about what happened that year. This matter was always weighing on my mind, just as it shrouded my parents.

Tang maintained a sort of respect for the relatives of his deceased friend. His conversation was not light and frivolous like with Yehe Nara. The atmosphere was solemn. He wore a navy-blue cotton Chinese shirt, his moustache was well trimmed, his chin clean-shaven, and he had a bracelet of brown sandalwood beads on his right wrist. Yehe Nara had told me before that each one of those beads cost 1000 *yuan*, and he also had a priceless jade pipe that he did not like to show to others. I had a difficult time linking this person to the Tang Linlu who sang and played the guitar under our jujube tree so many years ago.

When I asked him about my brother again, Tang seemed reluctant to describe the scene from that summer in 1989. He took me to see his collections of CDs. His office was like a small cinema, with a projector aimed at a white wall. He pulled out a music CD from a row of disks entitled 'La Marseillaise.' He asked if I was afraid of blood, and told me not to look if I was. I asked how music from 'La Marseillaise' could be bloody.

He said, 'The cover is fake. The real thing is inside.'

I said, 'I can watch a Stephen King film in the middle of the night without so much as blinking.' He weighed the disk in his hand. He still hesitated, as if afraid I couldn't accept the contents of the disk. I snatched it from him and put it in the machine, but did not know how to make it play. He taught me how to operate it, then left, closing the door behind him.

*

Watching it, I understood Tang's reluctance to talk about that time. Even now, I cannot bring myself to talk about what I saw on the disk. Even if I were to tell, no one would believe me. I can hardly believe it myself. It was like I was just watching a movie, witnessing the experiences of my second brother and his friends in that year.

I sat silently, waiting for the blood that boiled inside me to cool.

When I left the mini-cinema, I noticed that the sky was indecently dark. Tang sat in his Mandarin chair, smoking. He looked like he had been waiting for me. He said there was going to be a storm, and that people would be able to swim or row boats on the streets again. There was a heavy smell of cigars in the room. In a daze, I seemed to smell the burning smoke I had seen on the screen and saw people swimming among fire and smoke.

We did not talk for a long time.

After a while, I said, 'Give me a cigarette.'

He stood up and passed me a cigarette. My hands shook badly. I could not light the cigarette. In the end, he lit it and handed it back to me.

This was the first time I had ever smoked. I dragged too hard. The first inhalation of smoke burned my tongue, and tears came to my eyes.

The rain started to fall heavily against the window, pounding it like bullets, in a thick decisive burst. Scar-like stains were left on the window after the onslaught.

We could not see anything outside.

'I mentioned you to Yu Shuzhong. He very much hopes you'll join his team,' he said.

I watched the bloody water pouring down the glass like a waterfall.

One needs emotions to be a reporter, but cannot act on blind emotions, I thought.

The rain suddenly slowed. The window was a mess.

'Don't cry, Xiaohan. Go find Yu Shuzhong. He's still idealistic, not like me. I'm just dawdling,' he said.

The ginkos were blooming in Beijing; turning yellow like roaring flames, flickering when the wind blew. The sparks, undying when they fell, continued to burn.

There was a good media outlet in Beijing waiting for me to report to my post, but after watching the 'La Marseillaise' disk, I changed my mind. When I left Beijing, the autumn wind was blowing in my heart, bright and sad. Yehe Nara taught me to put down my baggage as I moved forward and travel light. But, I did not do it. Instead, I carried Beijing's autumn and the past years, wrestling with them the whole way of the jerky train journey, until all traces of them were gone. Yehe Nara and Tang Linlu drove me to the train station. They had prepared food and drinks for me. Tang gave me a set of *Javier's Collected Works*. Yehe Nara said, 'You might not adjust to Guangzhou. Your mentor is always here for you in Beijing. Don't worry, I'll always have a place here for you.'

She was sunny and cheerful, laughing the whole time. Tang was like a bird circling in a dull sky, flying lazily in his own pattern. At the time, he was frowning as he puffed out swirls of smoke, ascending as if from a bottomless pit.

'Please take care of my mentor. Be good to her,' I said to Tang, laughing. Then, I boarded my train.

*

Guangzhou's autumn was hard, the people's spotted expressions as cold as the concrete surface. Reality covered everything, and nothing could lift my inner melancholy. I climbed into a taxi dully and looked out the window throughout my journey. I had never lived here before, but I already felt a sort of weariness, as if I already had for a long time.

I told the driver I wanted to go to *Today Newspaper*, *Jin Bao*. He did not say a word. Fearing he had not heard me, I repeated it. He just said two words. In his Cantonese accent, they came out as, Chicken Street, *Jin Dao*.

The car moved coldly along. I looked at the things outside the window. The sound of the train chugging lingered in my mind. I'm not sure how, but I fell asleep. When I awoke, the metre had already leapt to seventy-two *yuan*. Five minutes later, the car stopped at the entrance to the press offices. I paid and told the driver, 'I know you took the long way round, but I won't make a complaint. From the beginning, I didn't like Guangzhou. Thank you for making me actually hate it.'

I registered at the door. Honestly, I had forgotten what Yu Shuzhong looked like, but we hit it off rather well this time. He was a year older than Xiazhi. He was not actually a young fellow anymore, but at first glance, he seemed to be the same person from years ago; he had not changed at all. When we met, it did not feel distant. He stroked his short hair, which had replaced his wild curled-up hairdo. We chatted about the scene under my jujube tree so many years ago, recalling that mischievous little girl. He wore a T-shirt and blue jeans, looking free and fresh. His usual expression was serious, and his mouth had a slightly stubborn set to it. When he laughed and chatted, his face was completely transformed. That night he took me to eat Chaozhou cuisine, and we went on chatting over beef balls, grouper, and beer. He talked a lot, but seldom mentioned my second brother, only saying in passing that history would eventually make a fair evaluation of Xiazhi and his group. Mostly, he talked about his work managing the newspaper and his ideals in connection with it. He even asked for my views. I knew he was testing my news sensitivity and professionalism. I had already learned from Tang Linlu that Yu's staff was carefully selected. He would not retain a blockhead on account of personal relationships.

When it was over, Yu told me that this meal had been my interview. He had confidence in me. He arranged for me to be in the News Department and run the news line.

Chapter 27:

Liu Yihua, Niece

On other people's territory, Liuzi was quietly frustrated, given to moody silences. His expressions were always cold. Having nothing better to do, he would wear his flip-flops and stroll the streets. The stifling heat was relentless, making him bad-tempered. He was used to walking tall, having his own boys in a small town. They always settled scores for him, but now that he had ventured out on his own, he went everywhere with his tail between his legs. If it weren't for Liu Yihua, he would have gone back long ago. What was really exasperating was that Yihua couldn't be bothered with him. Without a word to him, she'd up and gone to the Pearl of the Orient. Liuzi had been very irritated, finally blowing his top, and eventually resorting to ridiculing her for working in a filthy place like that. Sooner or later, it was bound to tarnish her.

Yihua said she was free, and she'd do as she pleased. What was pure would remain untarnished everywhere, and what was impure would be tarnished anywhere. She dropped these words, then moved out. Liuzi had apologised, but it was no use. She said she didn't want to tarnish him.

They had lived together for over a year. If Yihua was a valuable possession, then Liuzi was the security guard in charge of looking after it. This was the only responsibility into which Liuzi had ever put all his effort, but he had not received a single reward for it. He had never even seen Yihua naked, let alone smelled, kissed, touched, or screwed her.

As soon as Yihua left, Liuzi felt there was no point in going to work, nor staying around in Guangzhou, nor even staying alive. Liuzi knew he'd committed a big taboo. The other six nymphs had gone back to the village spreading rumours, and Yihua had cut ties with them. Now Liuzi had been cast aside by Yihua – he had said she was tarnished, so his fate would be no different from the six nymphs. Yihua was not a person to hesitate or deliberate over things, just like when she had left the fishing net factory and had immediately decided what to do with those people, deleting them with a single keystroke. Several times, Liuzi went to the door of the Pearl of the Orient to wait for Yihua. He called her, but once she had decided to turn her back on something, she was like a dead flower, unable to blossom again.

When Liuzi got his pay cheque, he resigned. He called Yihua, saying he was planning to go back to Yiyang, and would like to take her out for dinner, as a sort of farewell. Yihua said, 'There's no need for that. Just be careful to go back untarnished.'

That was April 2003, the wettest season in Guangzhou. It was muggy and sticky, and the laundry refused to dry even when it had been hanging out for days. Water oozed out from the tiles and formed droplets, as if they'd been sweating all day. When Liuzi came across one of Yihua's hairpins or her socks while packing his things, he would throw them away, then pick them back up, thinking of returning them to her. His chest hurt, as if the tip of a cold blade was lodged there. He did not blame Yihua. He was filled more with self-condemnation and remorse. From the day he had met Yihua, he knew what sort of person she was. He thought of how she had been misunderstood by the world. He was the person who knew her best. Even if everyone else betrayed her, he would stay beside her. He had never said this, but it was certainly how he felt. If she were here now, he would definitely say it clearly.

But now Yihua was even colder than a blade, and all Liuzi could do was cry. After crying for a while, he was ashamed of his tears. He wiped them away and thought of how very soon he and his boys back in Yiyang could rule the world again. Then, he was overcome by the spirit of brotherhood. He thought to himself, *Love affairs are nothing compared to world affairs.*

At seven or eight that night, Liuzi ate a dozen grilled oysters, ten lamb kebabs, and three steamed buns and drank two bottles of Zhujiang beer, loitering around the bustling Tianhebei area. Nighttime in Guangzhou was very different from daytime – like a woman in love, it suddenly turned fascinating and charming. In fact, he felt that Guangzhou was not nearly as bad as his first impressions of it had been. Now he could hardly bear the thought of leaving it. It held a sentimental attachment in his heart, an attachment entangled in a dead knot with Yihua. He stood staring at the neon signs in Citic Plaza. With every scene displayed on its huge screen, a heavy heatwave passed over him, pushing against him.

He walked with his head down for a while, covered in sweat, stopping at a dessert shop in Xuliu Shan for a cup of herbal tea. It calmed him down.

In the distance, he saw Laoshu Street, where he and Yihua had once shopped. The things there were mostly smuggled goods, authentic and of decent quality. Yihua's pretty clothes had all come from there.

Liuzi remembered that the last time they had been there, Yihua had seen a royal blue sling dress. The shopkeeper was adamant in his refusal to cut the price, and he was arrogant, so she gritted her teeth and gave up, but her heart lingered over it. Liuzi decided to buy it for her. He had certainly never given her a decent gift before, though he had received many belts and wallets from her. Recalling these things, Liuzi became uncomfortable. If he hadn't been such a bastard and said those hateful things, Yihua would have eventually been his.

Only when Liuzi strode toward Laoshu Street did he notice that there were fewer people idling there than usual. He thought it very strange that several uniformed men stood in front of him and asked to see his papers. Liuzi smiled and said, 'Who brings his papers out for a walk? They're back at my quarters.'

One of the uniformed men waved Liuzi onto a bus. His posture was strange, like a clown performing on the street. Liuzi laughed more heartily, as if he really appreciated the act, or was even flattered by it. He said, 'Do you want to give me a lift home? I live on East Tianhe Road. My papers are in the drawer of my nightstand.'

Another uniformed officer politely placed Liuzi's hands behind his back, even taking him by the shoulder to keep him from falling. This sort of close contact made Liuzi feel very uneasy.

A jeep with small windows was parked outside, about twenty meters away. A few hands held the iron fencing at the window, and a fuzzy face squeezed against the metal, watching Liuzi. Liuzi realised he had been picked up by the legendary 'homeless catchers,' the guys enforcing the C&R – custody and repatriation – policy. From what Liuzi had heard about the shelters, men and women were huddled together without food or water, the smell of sweat gathering around them, and they were subjected to plenty of blows, kicks, and foul language. Liuzi wasn't afraid of any of this. He was only afraid he would see Yihua there, bringing money to rescue him. It would be humiliating – not the least bit romantic.

SHENG KEYI

Liuzi walked limply, in an obedient attitude. When he reached the car, he twisted and suddenly broke free and ran. But before he could kick off the slippers from his feet, he was wrestled to the ground. Several hard shoes kicked him. 'Motherfucker, damn beggar! Who asked you to run? Where'd you think you'd go?'

Lying on the ground and suffering kicks had never been Liuzi's style. He wanted to stand up and play his usual role, showcasing his own talents on the other end of this transaction. But unfortunately, his arms and legs lost their freedom. He was like a pig pushed into the slaughter car, carried by his four limbs. Everything around him was dark and smelled of blood.

*

The jeep, crammed full of people, drove to the police station, where it was unloaded, then went back onto the streets to make more collections. The whole courtyard was crowded. Men and women sat in a disorderly mob on the ground. Mosquitoes and moths flew around the incandescent lamp. Liuzi was singled out and enclosed in a cell of five or six square metres. A dozen or so people, men and women, were packed inside, skin to skin. There was only room to stand. Those at the front stood against the iron gate, waiting for release. Those in the back could only stare at the back of the heads of the people in front of them. As the night grew more solemn, some people were bailed out, while others were left behind.

It was hot, and everyone was sweaty. Body odour spread around the room. Liuzi was pressed against a heavily made-up woman. She was calm. Her hands clutched the iron gate, and she constantly watched the sky across from her, waiting for her boyfriend to bail her out. Seeing that Liuzi was also from Hunan, she was quite friendly toward him. She loaned him her cell phone, saying that if they did not make bail that night, they would be taken somewhere else the next day. Nowadays, if the cops in other parts of the country did not catch people, they had no income, so they came here to buy people, earning a higher bail price when they got back. Those who were not bailed out there, would live a slave's life or would be sold to other shelters.

The heavily made-up woman said it was her third time 'entering the palace.' The last time, she had been a step too slow and had been passed along to another shelter.

Liuzi laughed and said, 'Well, that's good. At least you get to travel for free.'

The woman spat and retorted, 'Shit, I spent 2000 *yuan* in bail over there. It's at most 500 here.

'It's a little expensive over there,' Liuzi said.

Yihua did not answer the phone. Liuzi guessed she was busy. He called five or six times before he finally heard her voice.

He said, 'Huahua, it's Liuzi. You OK?'

Yihua grunted and said, 'I'm at work. If something's wrong, tell me. If not, I need to go.'

'Huahua, I'm really not a good bodyguard. . .'

'Are you being annoying?'

'Yeah.'

'Ma Liujia, go do what you want to do. Don't you know I'm busy at work?'

'I can't do anything right now. I've been sent to the police station.'

'Serves you right. What did you do?'

'I went out without my ID.'

'Where are you?'

'Lancun. Damn. I just wanted to go to Laoshu Jie and buy that blue dress for you.'

'Don't worry. I'll just call Lu Mingliang to come cover my shift.'

'OK. You have my keys, don't you? You could bring my ID. Also, you'll need to bring five or 600 *yuan*. I can't get out without money.'

'Got it. Just wait for me.'

'Whatever you do, don't make me wait until tomorrow morning. That would be goodbye forever!'

'Then I'll go collect your corpse.'

*

By the time Yihua rushed to Lancun Police Station, it was already midnight. The gate was closed, and there was a man on duty. She knocked on the window and explained her purpose. The officer on duty was a stocky young fellow, badge number 007. Seeing Yihua was quite pretty, he smiled and asked if she was half-Indian. She had not yet removed her makeup before coming out. The false eyelashes curled lusciously, her eyeshadow was heavy, and her eyes dark and round. She was anxious to bail Liuzi out. She did not want to carry on and on with this fellow.

Officer 007 flipped through the data, and asked who Ma Liujia was to her. Yihua said it was none of his business, and she had brought the money and ID. She lay the documents out. He picked up Yihua's ID card and compared it to her person. He said, 'You're originally from Hunan. I hear Hunan girls are passionate.'

Saying this, he took out a City Shelter Registration Form and read, '. . . loitering in the street, met an officer and was questioned by him. Officer discovered that he did not have a Temporary Residence Permit, and took him to the Lancun Police Station. . . Oh, Yihua, this Ma Liujia was just taken to a shelter.'

When she heard 007 say her name, it felt very familiar. She thought he was a nice fellow, so she asked why Liuzi had been sent to the shelter. Double-o-seven said he was going to be sent home.

Yihua laughed and said, 'Going home is alright. He's about to go home anyway. Just means he saves the ticket fare.'

Double-o-seven wrinkled his mouth and said, 'If the incentive was that good, everyone would hang a "homeless" sign on themselves and wait on the streets to get picked up.'

Yihua thought the same thing. It made the police station seem like a welfare organisation. But she still didn't quite understand, so she asked 007, 'Ma Liujia isn't a homeless person or a beggar. Why do they want to pick up an able-bodied fellow like him?'

Double-o-seven said, 'You need to look at the regulations and see what sort of people we have the authority to pick up under the C&R system.'

He wrote down his phone number and gave it to Yihua, saying that if she had any more questions she could continue to ask him. Then he added, 'The shelter is quite far from here. There won't be anyone there to take care of bail procedures tonight. It's best you go in the morning.'

Yihua could not sleep that night, thinking of things that had happened with Liuzi; the smashing of Dai Xinyue's shop, the threats to the fish net factory's owner, and the train journey southward. Inwardly, she admitted that Liuzi was a good bodyguard and a good scoundrel. He was much more reliable than those self-righteous, successful people. Mingliang had been played by a gentleman, and his manner had been quite underhanded, so she had come to see things in the light of Mr Zhou's advice of not being emotionally involved, and was forever warning Yihua. In fact, Yihua did not need these warnings. She had watched her parents fight since she was little. She had no illusions about how things were between men and women, and certainly no illusions about romance. She did not understand how two people who had battered one another so badly could still share a bed. She even hoped they would divorce. Once, she had asked Liuzi if he would hit a woman, whether he would beat his wife, when he married. Liuzi had replied, 'A man who beats his wife is an inferior man.'

Just as well, Yihua had already forgotten that blue dress. When Liuzi mentioned it, she thought about it again. She lay on the bed staring at the ceiling and could not fall asleep. She thought about going to bail Liuzi out of the shelter, going straight to Laoshu Street to buy that blue dress, then finishing up with a bowl of Xuliu Shan mango fish. Later in the night they could enjoy some spicy crawfish, watch a movie, and then afterwards, go back to Liuzi's place, where she would remove the obstacles between them and take off every piece of clothing they wore, then the two of them finally engage in a solid embrace in bed. Yihua had thought it all through, and her heart was now filled with delight. Her spirit relaxed, and she suddenly felt very sleepy. Before long, she was sleeping so soundly she could have been mistaken for a corpse.

Chapter 28:

Li Chuntian, Elder Sister

My sister, harassed by her husband until she could no longer take it, was forced to leave the tailor shop. She had been to apply for all sorts of jobs: a nanny, restaurant staff, hotel cleaner. The pay was low at all of these places, and there was no freedom, so she was not quite willing to take them up. Jobs that involved technical skill offered higher wages, but always had academic requirements. If Zhima had not come making trouble, my sister would have been happy working in the tailor shop. She was also unwilling to return to the village and live her life with both feet stuck in the mud. The night my sister had screamed at Zhima that she wanted a divorce, she woke herself up. She went back and consulted the well-educated Shui Qin.

Shui Qin advised, 'It's better to destroy ten temples than break up a marriage. I won't encourage you to divorce. You have always lived for others, but if you decide you want to live for yourself from now on, I'll support your decision.'

My sister said, 'So, do you mean it's better to divorce or not?'

Shui Qin said, 'I'm not you, so I can't make the decision for you. It's you who has to live with the decision. Give it more thought.

If you really can't carry on, there's no point in forcing yourself.'

Chuntian added, 'You're so ambiguous, like the fortune teller in Lanxi Town.'

Shui Qin smiled sadly and replied, 'Aren't we all calculating our own fortune. You calculate as you live, and sometimes it pans out according to your calculations, but sometimes you come up empty. Look at me, my golden goose is flying away.'

The principal, Ms Wu, was soon to be transferred to the Propaganda Department, destroying the plan to cooperate on the deal for the school uniforms, and also affecting Xianxian's future. This was all simmering in Shui Qin's mind, but she did not talk much about it. The tables turned as she complained to my sister. She said that life had not been easy for her since she married. Shunqiu was always sick, not earning a cent and always running to the hospital. Everything at home depended entirely on her, so it was hard to say which of the two of them was actually better off. She also mentioned which families' husbands could earn money, and how blessed their wives were.

My sister grew uncomfortable as she listened, thinking, *But Shunqiu was so exhausted when he was out catching frogs all night, and he earned so much money for you. How can you forget that?* Chuntian did not want to turn against Shui Qin, so she just said that there was no one who cared more for his family than Shunqiu. If his health allowed, he would not be idle for a moment. His luck was just too bad. He had met with one misfortune after another. He had really fallen on evil days!

Shui Qin sensed that Chuntian was defending our brother. She grunted and steered the conversation back to the question of Chuntian's divorce.

At first, my sister really had intended to get Zhima to go into town and manage a small stall. Working hard in the fields always ended up incurring a loss, and the work was hard. Every time she saw someone who had gone into town to work, coming back in gold and silver, brilliant and refined as they celebrated the New Year, she was jealous. That detestable Zhima did not like the city, and he repeatedly brought her back to the village. It was utter chaos. In the past, she had always given way to him; it had been going on for more than a decade now. She did not want to give way anymore. In fact, at this point, she didn't even want him to give way to her.

Chuntian went to an agency again. It was a small shop of about two or three square metres wide with a table, chair, telephone, and small fan. There was a wooden noticeboard plastered with many recruitment notices, which all looked old.

The girl who worked there had a ponytail. She flipped through a dirty little book filled with words and numbers, her eyes followed her finger as it slid down the page. The finger stopped at a row of numbers, and her mouth read out the number. The girl with the ponytail made several phone calls. In each case, either the position had already been filled or the party on the other end of the line said Chuntian was too old. Even a small restaurant said they didn't want anyone over twenty-five. The girl with the ponytail said, 'My client is quite nice looking. She looks young, and she's good-tempered. Why don't you just interview her, then see what you think?'

She went on persuasively, then put down the phone and cursed. Chuntian laughed and said, 'It looks like I'm a real waste.'

The girl with the ponytail felt my sister should not talk this way about herself. Looking angry, she said, 'I've never seen such a nice-looking customer. I don't believe it's that hard to find you a suitable post.'

Saying this, she pulled her book over and flipped through it again, this time starting from the back.

My sister sat at the door, half dazed as she waited. Her old client from the tailor shop, the lawyer Sun Xiangxi, came by just then, carrying a basket of vegetables. 'You looking for a job?' he asked.

'Yes,' Chuntian replied.

Sun said, 'Why aren't you at the tailor shop anymore? It's a pity to see your craft go to waste.'

She smiled, but did not explain.

Sun asked, 'Have you found a job?'

The girl with the ponytail interrupted, 'No, she hasn't found one. They are all blind, where could you find anyone as good as Chuntian?'

Sun said to my sister, 'Come with me. I want to bring you someplace.'

Without saying a word, Chuntian followed him.

Ten minutes later, they reached the Peach Blossom Teahouse. Sun went in and called the owner of the place, Mr Gui, who answered and then came out. He was thin and had a humped back, even though he was not very old. He greeted Sun, saying, 'You came at just the right time. A new product came in yesterday, a good quality black tea. You can try it.'

Sun said, 'Don't worry about tea yet. Aren't you lacking someone to look after the front of the shop? How about her?'

Gui inspected my sister carefully, from head to toe, then said, 'Sure. If she passes Director Sun's inspection, then of course, there should be no problem.'

Gui made the tea himself, brewing it, then warming the pot and washing the cups. As he went about his work, he asked about my sister's situation. She gave him an honest report. When he had finished preparing the tea, he called the manager over and in turn explained everything to her. Chuntian moved to the Peach Blossom Teahouse that night. She did not tell anyone, not even Shui Qin, out of fear that Zhima would appear and make trouble for her.

Teahouses in small towns do not require any special skills, so my sister was able to get right into the swing of things. Sun often came to the teahouse, and Mr Gui always called Chuntian to serve him tea when he arrived, and to keep him company. She gradually got to know him. He had divorced five years earlier, and his daughter had married and moved to Guangzhou. He was about to retire. He planned to go to Hong Kong for a holiday, and hoped to find a travelling companion. He asked Chuntian if she would like to join him, saying he would pay for the trip if she would go with him.

My sister was not stupid. While she was working in the tailor shop, she thought Sun might be interested in her, but because of her circumstances, she had not thought too much about it. But now that she knew he was alone, she felt like she was keeping a fish in an aquarium in her heart, and that it was now beginning to stir the water with its tail. Sun was mild, kind, steady, and practical, but also playful and humorous. It was not surprising that Chuntian was moved by him. None of the men in her life could make her feel relaxed. My father was gloomy and stiff, Zhima was dull and boring, and Li Letian had not been important enough to even merit a mention. Sun was like a ray of sunlight on the water's surface. She saw a new world sparkling with golden light and rippling with gentleness. When she closed her eyes, that world was imprinted on her mind, and its glow followed her wherever she went.

Chuntian wanted to go to Hong Kong, but she was afraid of trouble from every side. She was apprehensive, so she again went to Shui Qin for advice. Shui Qin asked how old Sun was, his occupation, what sort of house he had, and various questions about his children and his retirement package. My sister said, 'It's just a holiday. Why do you have to ask about him in such detail?'

Shui Qin said, 'Don't be stupid. You think he would innocently sponsor your holiday, just a single man and woman? Do you know what you're getting into? Have you mentioned Zhima?'

Chuntian nodded, saying Sun supported the idea of her getting a divorce.

Shui Qin warned, 'Chuntian, you need to separate things clearly. Getting a divorce is your business. It has nothing to do with Sun. You shouldn't get him mixed up in all that. Right now, you're a married woman. If you went to Hong Kong – or even America – if you just run away with someone, it's very difficult for you to explain things clearly. I suggest you take it step by step. If Sun sincerely likes you, he won't mind waiting a bit.'

My sister asked, 'You mean I should divorce first?'

Shui Qin waved her hands. 'You know the proverb. "It's better to destroy ten temples than break up a marriage." I'm just telling you, no matter what, don't mix the two issues together. Otherwise it will become all entangled and messy.'

Chuntian had never really given careful thought to the matter of divorce; it was just a weapon, which she could wield like a knife and potentially address any problem that arose. For instance, if she fought with Zhima, she would roar, 'I want a divorce,' at him, and he would stop; when her mind was extremely troubled, the thought of getting a divorce calmed her down. She often fantasied about getting a divorce and riding into the sunset with a certain man, and she was satisfied with the sweet momentary feeling in her heart. If she travelled now and got entangled with the issue of divorce . . . but Sun had not even asked her to marry him, so wasn't that putting herself forward a bit too quickly?

She still wanted to go to Hong Kong, just to see what it was like. She went back to the village to get her resident's permit. She opened the door of the house and called out, but no one was home. She guessed Zhima had gone to the vegetable garden or stopped by a neighbour's house. The smell of alcohol filled the place, and it was as messy as a pigsty inside. It smelled very bad. Out of habit, she thought about tidying up, but she felt she should deal with the urgent task first. She opened the cupboard door, pulled out a drawer, and reached inside to grab the cloth bag she kept at the very back, in which she kept all the family's valuables, including the resident's permits, a gold ring, and a passbook that showed a handful of transactions and a balance of just three figures.

She hid her resident's permit on her person and put the cloth bag back in its place, then closed the cabinet door. A pair of her pantyhose slid down and got caught in the gap between the doors. Her heart fluttered. She was like a thief caught in the middle of committing a crime, and she was quite excited. She had assumed there would be some obstacles to this task.

She let out a breath of relief and turned around almost cheerfully, only to suddenly encounter Zhima standing right in front of her. Frightened, she screamed. Her face blanched for a moment, then turned red.

'Your resident's permit . . . what are you doing with it?' Zhima asked gloomily. He looked right at her. His voice made her heart pound and tremble.

I'm . . . making . . . making a temporary permit,' she said feebly. It was clear at one glance that she was lying.

'That place no bigger than newly spawned eggs . . . is also setting up temporary permits?' he said, his breath reeking of alcohol.

Steadying herself, my sister said, 'Let me put it bluntly. Do you think Yicao's thousands of *yuan* in school fees just drop from the sky?'

Zhima's face glowed with drink. 'Chuntian, I've been looking for you for days, and I haven't so much as seen your ghost. What wild man's house have you been hiding at?'

'If you go on like this, I will divorce you,' she said, weakly.

'Don't start . . .' He approached his wife and said blandly, 'Chuntian, stay home. I'll go out and work, OK?'

He stooped and disentangled the silk stockings stuck in the door of the cupboard. He reached for my sister's hand. She thought he wanted to be affectionate, but in a flash he was pulling her hands behind her and tying them with the pantyhose. He went on, 'I'll work hard. Won't that be good?'

'Are you going crazy?' My sister became alarmed.

'I just want you to stay home.' He picked up a mess of things from the floor and tied her to a chair. 'Now you can finally stay here.'

A drunkard is detestable, but drunken words are pathetic. Chuntian's heart softened hearing Zhima's words.

'I went everywhere looking for you. I even slept under a bridge a few times. I told Yicao that her mama had disappeared. She just ignored me and said that since both of us were always fighting, it was better that we divorced. This shameless girl who messes around in bed without even closing the door – she even dares to look down on her own father. I tell you, Chuntian, I really want to quit drinking. I want to work and earn money, to make a decent home . . . Ah, where did you hide? Why won't you tell me?'

Zhima went on and on, whining and crying by himself. Later, he lay on the floor and fell asleep.

The knot he had tied was not tight. Chuntian broke free, ripping off the stockings and torn scraps of cloth. She put Zhima to bed and sat down in a daze. Then she got up, cleaned the house, and left.

Chapter 29:

Liu Zhima, Brother-in-law

My parents came to look down on Zhima more and more. They called him a sack of cow shit, not even fit for plastering a wall with. Zhima did not dare show up at their door too often. Only as a last resort did he pick up a bottle of wine and show up timidly one day. Of course, the wine was not the green leaf liquor he used to bring years ago, but it was at least Jin Liu Fu from the old Luzhou cellar, a spirit of reasonable quality. My father was quite particular about his wine, so Zhima did not dare be too stingy.

Yicao was close to our side of the family, not going home even over the long holiday. Zhima did not see her and was terribly bored with no one else at home like that.

He had always wanted a son, so had never really cherished his daughters. Now that he was getting older, his feelings changed, and he suddenly grew very attached to them. He always called Yihua, asking about this and that. He was alone from sunrise to sunset. He found that his life comprised these three women. When they dispersed, he fell apart. But what really riled Zhima up was Yicao's harsh ridicule, saying all he did was drink and play cards all day. He did not do anything, but hung around waiting to share in others' crops. She did not want such a father. She even said she would try to persuade her mother to divorce him, leaving him on his own.

Zhima thought of his own desolate situation, of how he was deserted by everyone in his old age, and he realised he was a little afraid. He drank to drown his worries, and then his long-lost wife appeared, as if she descended from heaven. He was drunk. He didn't know what he was doing.

When he awoke, he was lying on the bed. The house had been cleaned, but there was no one to be found. He knew she had gone back to the city, not even spending the night at home. She did not treat it as her home anymore. His heart was filling up with bitterness. Immersed in such self-pity, his spirit grew even more sluggish.

There was a widow in the village whose husband had been gored to death by a water buffalo. She was called Chai Fengying, and she was on good terms with my sister. When Chuntian left, she kept criticising Chuntian in front of Zhima, asking what kind of woman had turned so wild that even a team of eight horses could not drag her back . . . Finally, she even accused my sister of abandoning her family. It made Zhima feel like he had found a bosom friend. He poured out many grievances to her, and even shared all of the couple's most private secrets, including Chuntian's lack of focus during *that*, saying she either cracked melon seeds between her teeth or bit her hangnails, telling him to hurry and get it over with, or talked about how she needed to pee, which made him lose interest, too. Maybe he was actually impotent by now!

Fengying was like a piece of farmland which had long suffered a drought, so she lost no time in letting her own maternal instinct come out, offering considerate comfort and acting flirtatious, her voice affected and saccharine. Such coquettishness gave her an advantage that covered her ugly flaws. Zhima was ready to clutch at any straw he could find, so before long, they were in bed together.

But the event soon turned into just an interlude. Fengying was a sensible person, and she did not intend to attach herself long term to an incompetent drunk. She also had a pair of children herself, so she knew that, if her own mind was flooded over, it would end in wretchedness for them all. She warmed herself with Zhima for about a month and was rejuvenated, decreasing her lust with each encounter. Ultimately, she cut him off.

Zhima was a married man. Being used and chucked aside like that was humiliating, but he was helpless in the face of it and could only suffer in silence. It was strange, but it was only after the affair ended that he realised how ugly Fengying was. Her face was round like a wash basin, her eyebrows sparse, her small eyes were painted with a dark ring of eyeliner, framing a pair of dead, fishy eyes, and her skin was splotchy. Even so, this was was the woman who had yelped like a young dolphin, whispering to his lustful instincts. He was bewitched for a while, and that made him feel a little ashamed.

After this little setback, Zhima felt that other women were even less reliable than his own. Some people encouraged him to go into the city and set up a stall, selling kebabs or polishing shoes while he went about looking for his woman. No matter what, it was better for husband and wife to be together; offering more stability.

Zhima settled things at home and, carrying his snakeskin bag, made his way to a construction site with another fellow from the village. Yiyang was developing rapidly then, and houses were being built everywhere. New high-rises popped up all along the banks of the Zijiang. Variegated lights were scattered across the land- scape each night, like a flourishing dream. Zhima was not used to doing heavy work at home. After a few days of carrying concrete, both of his shoulders were swollen and aching. When he climbed the scaffolding, he was afraid of heights, so his coworkers looked out for him and asked him to shovel concrete, mix cement, and move bricks instead. At night, he slept in a shed with a dozen other people. The air was stale with mixed smells as they quarrelled, played cards, laughed, whistled, and told dirty jokes. It was a happy life.

When he had free time, Zhima went out to restaurants, shopping malls, hotels, and recreation centres, searching for Chuntian inch by inch. He went back to the tailor shop a few times, but found no happy surprises there. Instead, the place was not doing so well; there was no more rapid fire rhythm of the sewing machines. There were just three or four seamstresses left, calmly fiddling with fabric and occasionally stepping on the pedal of the sewing machines, making them sound like a cold gun.

Zhima had a look, then left. But then he turned back and told Shui Qin he was working at the Taohua Warehouse Construction site. He wanted her to tell Chuntian, if the two of them met.

When Zhima had been gone for a while, the women in the tailor shop started to talk.

'If he knew his woman was with another man, he would kill her.'

'As long as a woman never acknowledges it and she is not caught in bed with another man, her husband can't stir up trouble.'

'Liu Zhima is too rotten to even be turned into plaster for my walls. Chuntian should divorce him right away, then find a retired cadre to settle down with. She would be just fine then.'

'Sun Xiangxi is quite something. He got a secondary school teacher pregnant some time back. I'm not sure how, but he settled that problem.'

'It seems he is still in touch with his ex-wife. Who knows whether they'll get back together someday.'

'With his former woman's tough character, there's no way she'll forgive him for fucking around.'

'Why would Sun look for a village girl? Is he just toying with Chuntian? She's so honest, she'll be easily fooled.'

'Chuntian isn't a girl. Whether her relationship is good or bad is her own business. Just don't wag your tongues in front of Liu Zhima and it'll be fine.'

*

Zhima did manual labour until his muscles ached, finally experiencing the hard work Chuntian had always done in the past. At night he was so full of regret, he could not fall asleep. Once, he called Yihua and said, 'Your mother changed her cell phone number. Do you have the new number?'

Yihua answered, 'That's between the two of you. If she wants to see you, naturally she will look for you.'

Zhima said, 'What do I have to do to get her to see me?'

'She wants to divorce you.'

Zhima was confused. 'She's not serious, is she?'

'I don't know. Anyway, even if you two divorce, you're still my father and she's still my mother.'

When Zhima and his friends had been at the work site for three months, the project was completed. When he and the other workers went to the contractor to settle things, the contractor said the account had not been paid, so he could not pay the workers yet. After the workers went to him time and time again and still did not get their money, they decided he was cheating them. Finally, they all went to the office as a group and asked for their pay. Zhima was owed the least, and even his share was several thousand *yuan*. Conditions at the site, bearing both sun and rain, had been quite tough, so he intended to receive his money, then use it to open a stall and sell kebabs. So Zhima was in the front of the pack, shouting fiercely, as if all the bitterness of his marriage and the difficulties in his life had come about because of this payment in arrears. He carefully recounted the fatigue of the worksite, showing the wounds on his shoulders, arms, and legs. He said, 'This is hard-earned money. You have to pay up, every penny of it!'

Thinking Zhima was the leader of the workers, the contractor went to speak to him privately. He waited on Zhima with tea and was very polite. But the soft approach did not work on Zhima. He grew arrogant, talking like a big hero. He said to the contractor, 'Everyone is waiting for the money to support their families. We will only go away when you give it to us.'

The contractor changed his attitude. 'You don't fucking know how to appreciate kindness, choosing the hard way instead,' he said, then kicked Zhima out.

When the workers came to Zhima for an update, he said the contractor was looking for a solution, but that if they did not get their money that day, then they would ransack the contractor's place. His words just came out, and everyone immediately responded, wanting to beat the contractor to a pulp. It seemed Zhima really had become the leader of the group.

Just as things were getting riled up and everyone was determined to carry out their threat, two black cars pulled up and slammed on the brakes with a screech. In the cloud of dust kicked up by the vehicles, five or six young men got out. The hooligans had their hands behind their backs as they walked quickly towards Zhima and the group. In the blink of an eye, Zhima had been hit with a brick. His face was covered with blood. The workers recovered and started to pick up various objects with which to fight back. But in the end, they lost to the evil thugs, suffering injuries.

Badly wounded, Zhima had to be hospitalised. He had two broken ribs and needed ten stitches on his head.

Chapter 30:

Li Xiaohan

It was only when I worked as a reporter that I came to know how chaotic society was, and only when I went to the hospital that I came to realise how many sick people there were. As soon as I took up the job, I was like a donkey at the grinding wheel, immersing myself totally in the insane, endless turning of the wheel. I had no time for a love life. There was a private joke among the staff, saying that the newspaper office treated women as if they were men, and treated men as if they were beasts. It was purely out of willingness on both sides, everyone acting according to a virtuous competitive mechanism. It was not complaining, but self-mockery. So our newspaper office obtained the lofty name of 'the Whampoa Military Academy of the Newspaper World.' University graduates sharpened their brains to squeeze in, got gold-plated, and when they went out, they were worth double what they were before. In fact, this was a place that could even straighten the hump out of a camel's back, righting all wrongs. A journalist with healthy penmanship and good stamina could write to death and earn over 10 000 yuan. I did not relax under the high pressure, but instead sacrificed sensual pleasure and girlish crushes in order to fight my way toward becoming a famous journalist.

I put a spring on myself, and with nerves taut, I conducted interviews about the driver of a BMW that ran someone over, carcinogenic ageing grain flowing into the market, a girl from the music school quitting education to become a dance hostess, and even investigated a serial robber-cum-murderer and a university student who had stabbed his girlfriend thirty-eight times with a knife.

I was a bit addicted to such reports, and often kept my ears open to capture any unusual stirrings. I rushed to the scene like I had been given a blood transfusion, sometimes interviewing witnesses and onlookers. When they recounted what they saw, they were usually quite excitable, not the least bit shy, and I let their original passionate expressions play out to the fullest.

The first time I went to a crime scene, I saw the person who had been run over by the car's wheels. The body had been turned to mincemeat, but the face was still intact. I ran away, retching, thinking Xiazhi must have looked like this when he died. At night I had a nightmare in which I was pursued by the victim who was crushed. Later, after much practice, I learned to observe the bloody bodies of the deceased closely, as calm as a surgeon. Yu Shuzhong said I had 'a clever angle on the story, and the writing was quite outstanding.' Readers especially loved to see my detailed, bloody descriptions of the scene of an accident, finding my questioning in the article 'sharp and penetrating.' It was refreshing.

I had a cot in the office. Sometimes I wrote all night, or until three or four in the morning, and was too lazy to go home when I had finished, so I just opened my simple bed, fell down and slept.

It went on like this until no one else was willing to fight me for interviews when there was a major event. I was the number one reporter. Some people thought it was because of my relationship with Yu, when in fact, because of how dangerous the interviews were, Yu had tried to stop me. But I said, 'I'm a reporter, not a woman.'

Once, I was held hostage by a murderer. After twenty-four hours, he let me go and gave himself up. I knew all the ins and outs of the situation. He was not cruel. He was a good man, but the reality of his situation had forced him to become a murderer. I wrote an in-depth article, 'Twenty-Four Hours with a Murderer,' and I heard his sentencing was a little lighter because of my report.

The paper sold out quickly that day, but Yu criticised me fiercely. He said he did not appreciate journalists who did not care about their own safety. I heard from others that he praised me behind my back, and even told others to learn from me. A colleague from my village told me that, during that twenty-four hours, 'Chief Yu was so anxious his comb turned black.'

I immediately thought of Yu's head sprouting a cockscomb, and thought it was funny.

My colleague said to me secretively, 'Yu likes you.'

I told her to stop talking nonsense.

Yu rarely joked with me. He was eight or nine years older, and he maintained a senior's demeanour with me, never talking to me of any private matters. But when my colleague threw those words out, it made waves in me. Bystanders had a clearer view, and I was not ignorant either. Yu had a family, and he would not walk over my second brother's corpse to treat me without proper respect. I had no taboos when it came to love. I was always elegant and solemn in front of Yu, partly for my brother's sake, but had our background been different, I would have done it with Yu long ago.

I had met Yu's wife, and there was nothing special about her. If anything, she was too ordinary. She had a head shaped like a mushroom, and she dressed conservatively. She had a follower's attitude toward life. But she was always proper in speech and action, not rash, and I gradually came to feel her charm. She was above girls who exposed their cleavage and twisted their waists, but it was these girls who were always in line with a gaming man's appetites, and many boats had capsized in the depths of those cleavages.

Yu was always cautious, and his power of self-control was very strong. I found this quite provocative. I always thought that I would sleep with him, and I thought he always felt he would sleep with me, but neither of us knew when it would happen. The matter was like a huge stone submerged in the middle of the lake in our hearts, keeping the water level high. It might freeze, but as soon as spring came, the thaw and the spring rains would make the water overflow, and that flood would be like a beast rushing towards the wilderness. Years earlier, it was Tang Linlu that pierced my girlish heart at just one glance. First love was hidden away like a disease in the body. Now, my heart was filled with live fish, wanting to jump out, constantly beating against its confines. This was the mental game going on between Yu and me.

People say feelings are like springs. The more tightly they are pressed, the stronger the recoil. At night, I would feel a weight, and the provocation of the spring. It made me feel a little dizzy. Because of this, sometimes the night was beautiful and some-times sultry. The moon was like a drop of water, shrouded in mist. I wanted to write a poem and dedicate it to someone, but the impulse was like a shudder. I shivered, and it was gone.

Chapter 31:

Liu Yihua, Niece

When Yihua woke up, it had just got light outside. She got up and washed, then put on light makeup and a low-cut dress. Liuzi liked for her to be made up. Even though she had not yet let him touch her or screw her, he had been satisfied because he was closer to her than anyone else. Liuzi had once said to her, 'Even if you want to test me my whole life, I'll just keep waiting for you.'

Yihua had almost decided to give in to him.

But then she had decided to wait until his birthday and surprise him. He was born in May, and that was when the japonica was most fragrant in the village. She could smell it everywhere that time of year. Then Liuzi had said the wrong thing, enraging her so much she moved out. Her heart was still with him, but she had wanted to make him reflect a little, and to suffer.

She had recalculated now. It was still a while until Liuzi's birthday. She didn't want to wait. After she bailed him out today, she would take care of things in the bedroom. She would not make him suffer anymore.

She remembered that one night she had turned over in her

sleep and inadvertently brushed against Liuzi. He had been hard down there, like a pestle standing straight up.

Yihua said, 'You're taking advantage of me.'

Liuzi replied, 'It's *that*, not me.'

'You're in it together,' she said.

'I swear we're irreconcilable. You take care of it; I won't help.'

Yihua thought, then said, 'Let me look at it.'

'If you want to see, it's at your own risk,' he warned.

She asked, 'What will the consequences be?'

'It's enraged right now,' answered Liuzi.

Yihua turned on the light. Liuzi pushed down his underwear and let the creature out. Yihua was scared half to death and jerked away. 'Don't turn it my way next time you sleep,' she said.

Liuzi turned over obediently. Without her permission, he would not violate the rules. It was Yihua who kept secretly thinking about that hard object.

As Yihua thought about these things, she packed merrily and quickly. It was still early, and there was no one on the street. She ate a box of steamed buns and drank a bowl of soya milk, then bought some to take to Liuzi and got into a taxi.

The driver was unfamiliar with the route, so he kept pulling over to ask directions. By the time she reached her destination, it was 9:30 in the morning. The security guard at the gate stopped her and checked her ID. When she walked into the building, she was lost for a long while in its confusing structure, and she did not know where to go to find Liuzi. She walked boldly into an office, and found herself facing a man and a woman in a dishev-elled state. The woman's painted lips were all messed up. The pair took some time to get over this surprise.

Yihua said, 'I'm sorry to disturb you. I'm here to bail someone out. His name is Ma Liujia. He was sent here last night . . .'

Because they were caught doing something on the sly, the

pair was especially polite to Yihua. The woman took out some material and flipped quickly to the second page. Running her finger over the paper, she stopped and said, 'Ma Liujia was sent to the treatment station this morning.'

Yihua was shocked. 'Treatment station? He's sick?'

The man looked younger than the woman. He said, 'We don't know, but the person who transferred him here said he could not be trusted and kept reminding us to keep an eye on him. Last night, just after he was sent here, he kept demanding to make a phone call. After that, he did not make a sound.'

Wanting to please, the woman nodded and said, 'He was strong. Even with two people, they couldn't hold him down.'

Yihua thought, *He was an important person back home.* She was proud of him, but also worried about his current condition. She asked for the address of the treatment station, then hoofed it over there as quickly as she could. She threw the steamed buns away along the journey. She thought, *This will be an eye-opener for Liuzi. In two days, he's visited the police station, the shelter, and the treatment station. Those three places should provide him with plenty of entertainment, along with free food and drink. It will give him material to brag about for a good, long time.*

Liuzi loved to eat hot peppers fried with meat. She figured he had not had any to eat in a while, or if he had, it had not been authentic. She decided to buy pork tomorrow and fry a big bowl for him.

*

Yihua could not believe there was still such a shabby place in Guangzhou. The street was dirty and chaotic, with rubbish and sewage everywhere. A blood-red sign hung from an odd-shaped two-storey building with the words *Detention Treatment Centre* written on it. The whole place looked like a bunker with the machine gun holes plugged up. Yihua searched everywhere, stopping at the only entrance – a tightly shut iron gate with a little hole at the door. She looked through the hole, but did not see a living thing. It was lifeless. Even the sun seemed bored, shining onto the sand-covered courtyard. Yihua's body was sticky, sweat streaming down along her cleavage. She stuck her index finger between her breasts a few times to scratch, then flung her hand a couple of times. There was nowhere to rest at the entrance. No one either came out or went in. She thought she must have gone to the wrong place, so she carefully read the words *Detention Treatment Centre* again, just to be sure there was no mistake. Just as she was getting desperate, she glimpsed a shadow of white clothing inside, like that of a doctor. Yihua shouted to him, but she only heard her own echo, making her a little embarrassed. Because her tongue could not curl itself sufficiently for standard Mandarin, when she called, 'Doctor,' it came out sounding more like the word for *monk*. 'I'm looking for someone' was transformed into, *I want you now.*

She knocked hard on the door to attract more attention, soiling her hand with rust. In this empty world, there was no response. She panicked and cried Liuzi's name loudly in the Yiyang dialect, 'Liuzi! Ma Liujia!'

Even his name would sound wrong to someone more used to Mandarin.

She felt that her voice sounded like a temple bell, penetrating all barriers as it rolled across the lakes and over the mountains, spreading all the way to Yiyang and floating through all the streets she and Liuzi had ever walked, echoing across all the waterways they'd crossed. The current surged on the river, the sound of boats rumbling along, mingling with the horn blared from a ship . . .

Yihua walked from east to west, then back again, to and fro, forming a megaphone with her hands and shouting as loudly as she could. In the hot, humid weather, the sweat made a muddy mess of her makeup. Her mouth quickly became dry and her throat mute.

Then, the metal gate banged open. A man with blond hair and camouflage clothing walked out and the iron gate boomed shut. He walked east toward the car park. Yihua started to shout, 'Doctor,' but how could this be a doctor, with his camouflage uniform? He looked more like a commando, but this was a detention centre, not a special forces training ground. Yihua couldn't make up her mind about him. Then she thought, *Who cares who he is? At least he came out from the building where Liuzi is being held. Maybe sucking up to him can do something for Liuzi.*

Yihua wanted to use an honorific title to capture part of his spirit, but before she'd gotten 'commando' out, a series of titles flashed through her mind. She suddenly remembered the title that always pleased the men who frequented the nightclub so much, so she shouted after the commando, 'Hey, boss!'

She was too loud. She startled the commando, knocking his hat off.

'Sorry, boss . . . I'm here to redeem someone . . . '

'What're you being so noisy for? If you keep it up, I'll throw you inside.'

The commando picked up his hat, spitting out these words. He walked to an iron shed nearby, straddled a motorcycle, and started the engine. Her only hope would soon be carried away by this motorcycle. Yihua suddenly rushed over and stood in front of the bike.

'Brother . . . Uncle . . . No . . . Ah, Sir . . . ' All those titles that had been crossed out in her mind came flowing out all at once. Like forgetting her PIN for her bank account, she tried all the various standard passwords she could think of, but none were quite right. The commando's face did not reveal any login instructions. Yihua was so nervous her cleavage kept sweating, but she didn't care to wipe it dry. She remembered how Mingliang had taught her to make the patrons who were depressed happy. She pressed down her anxieties and worries and turned herself instantly into a different person. Her posture and tone softened and she exhaled bitterly, putting on a sincere front, at the same time flattering the commando with a few chosen words, such 'dignified,' 'righteous,' 'friend,' and 'handsome.'

The commando finally killed the engine. He pulled out the bike's key, stood back up next to it, and looked with great interest at Yihua and the groove between her breasts.

'Well, if I help you get someone out, how will you thank me?' the commando asked bluntly.

Yihua wanted to say she would not be a noble person if she didn't repay him, following Mingliang's mantra. But apparently, this was not a time to talk of noble folk and villains. Yihua emptied her pockets, laying out all she had before the commando's eyes. 'This is 600 *yuan*. If it's not enough, I'll bring . . . '

'Six hundred *yuan*?' The commando laughed contemptuously.

'How much do you want?' she asked.

'I want you to sleep with me.'

Chapter 32:

Li Chuntian, Elder Sister

My sister had already made her travel documents and was preparing to go to Hong Kong with Sun Xiangxi. As she packed her suitcase, she hummed 'Green Island Serenade'. Sun's hair was dyed raven-black and his face was rosy, like a monkey in heat. He took turns touching my sister's buttocks and pinching her waist, and said, 'What a waste, you sleeping with Liu Zhima all those years. Consider yourself lucky, now that you've met a man like me who understands a thing or two about women.'

Chuntian laughed at everything he said. Her heart was already in Hong Kong. When she was a girl, she had a calendar that had pictures of Hong Kong's skyscrapers and yachts at the bay. She tore each page from the calendar and hung it on the wall. People always said Hong Kong was paradise. Today, she would go to paradise and have a look around. Her heart was so full of vanity, it nearly burst.

'Isn't Hong Kong part of China?' she asked.

'Of course,' Sun replied.

'If it's part of China, why can't we just travel with our ID cards?'

'Hong Kong was a colony. In 1997, when it returned to China, it could not be managed properly, so they came up with the idea of "one country, two systems." It's different from here.'

My sister said, 'What "one country, two systems"? That's obviously two countries.'

Sun replied, 'Be careful. If you try to split the motherland, you might be picked up by the police.'

My sister was so scared, she shut her mouth immediately. The thing she most feared was the police. As soon as she saw anyone in uniform, her tongue got entangled, and her legs trembled. But after a while, she asked softly, 'What language do they speak in Hong Kong?'

Sun replied, 'Cantonese and English. Some speak Mandarin, too.'

Chuntian thought of the couple of Cantonese phrases she had heard from the operator when Yihua called. It sounded like a foreign language. She laughed.

Sun ran his hand down my sister's buttocks and started exploring it, like a blind man. His face turned bright red very quickly.

My sister pushed him away and said, 'How can you take that tonic in the middle of the day?'

'Who cares whether it's night or day?' Sun said. 'I'm going to take you anyway.'

Sun's words accidentally rhymed, and he found it funny when he heard it himself. He laughed as he and my sister rolled into a ball. Just then, her cell phone rang.

'Don't answer it,' Sun said. 'No matter who it is, it can wait until we're finished.'

The ringing stopped. After a moment, it started again.

Chuntian was distracted. She picked up her phone and as soon as she looked, she said, 'Oh no. My mother rarely calls. Something must have happened.'

Sun's arrow was already en route. He said, 'You answer, and I'll take care of myself.' Then, he really began to fiddle with himself.

My sister answered the phone. 'Ma. . . Huh?. . . OK, I see.'

And in just those ten seconds, Sun cried out twice. His body pumped a couple of times, then he fell onto my sister and did not stir.

*

I'm so long-winded, I have fallen behind a bit. When Zhima called my mother, he had just been admitted to the hospital. He said he was badly injured, and needed 3000 *yuan* to be admitted, but he could not find my sister. It was a matter of life and death. My mother called urgently, and within five minutes had gotten through to Chuntian. She said Zhima's skull had been cracked and the wound was still not even stitched, and the place where the ribs had been broken collapsed, and was completely covered in blood – but he knew he would see my sister soon, and that made him so happy he did not even feel the pain. But, when my sister rushed to the hospital with the money and Zhima wanted to greet his wife calmly, all the wounds woke up and he cried out in pain. My sister had just heard Sun's cries, and now she was hearing Zhima's cries. All these cries became louder and louder in her ears, making her dizzy.

Chuntian got a hold of herself and said, 'If your bones are itchy, why don't you find a tree and rub yourself against it. Why must you fight with people?'

Zhima stopped moaning. He wanted to yell something back, but his body hurt like it was being stabbed with a knife, and it made him docile.

Chuntian went on, 'Yihua called and said she's busy. That bad girl.'

Zhima waved her off. 'Don't ask her to come back. It's too expensive. It isn't worth it.'

Chuntian said, 'It was money that landed you in this state. It's always money, money, money with you.'

Zhima moved slightly, then cried out. He had capital now. All he had to do was groan a couple of times and my sister leapt obediently to his side, feeding him, giving him a drink, or wiping his backside.

On the surface, Chuntian seemed calm, but she felt as if a cat were clawing at her innards. *With Zhima looking like this, how could she go to Hong Kong with Sun?* This golden goose had started to fly, and she hated dawn for coming so quickly. Before she even had time to enjoy it, she had already awoken from the lovely dream. She wished so much this moment was a dream instead, and when she awoke from this dream, she would find herself on a plane on the way to Hong Kong. She had never been on a plane before, or even seen one. But, that's not quite right – she had heard the roar of a jet before and, when she lifted her head, saw a trail of white smoke. The plane was tiny, like a sparrow. That was the largest plane Chuntian had seen.

Sun did not care if Zhima lived or died. He had said to my sister, 'Go to the hospital and see him and, if he isn't dying, we'll go to Hong Kong tomorrow. Anyway, you're going to divorce him.'

She looked at Zhima now, all wrapped up like a bound foot, and she simply could not harden her heart. She found an opportunity to call Sun and said, 'I can't go. Zhima is hanging on by a thread. I have to take care of him. After all, he's Yihua and Yicao's father.'

Sun said, 'But I won't sleep in that huge bed in the hotel all by myself. I'll find another woman.'

Chuntian was not the sort to take threats. 'Do what you like,' she said.

She hung up the phone, feeling more confused than ever. Zhima had stopped being lazy and learned to work hard. What more could she ask of him?

Out of a sense of humanitarian goodwill, my parents went to the hospital, bringing half a basket of eggs for Zhima. My mother thought no matter how insensible Zhima was, it was better than Chuntian being widowed, since widows had a hard time remarrying. So she set aside concerns about carsickness and travelled into the city, vomiting most of the way. When she got off the bus, she carried a plastic bag half-full of vomit. Her face was pale, and her legs felt like cotton. It made one wonder how she had ever survived those long journeys to visit her son in prison.

My parents were not too concerned about my sister. After all, when they were visiting the patient, it was more like a leadership inspection. My father said some words, the sort of good wishes one might hear during the Spring Festival, and my mother maintained a dark countenance, conveying the image of a heavy burden and a long journey. Zhima listened respectfully. It seemed he even wanted to bow, but his body was immobile. His expression was a confused mix, impossible to describe.

Chuntian looked lightly at the floorboards of the hospital, heart filled with hidden bitterness. When she had married Zhima, it had been nothing more than an attempt to escape my father's control. She had never said this, and my father did not know. In fact, he had no idea how much she hated him. Dictators never care about how the little people feel; they are never introspective, and certainly have no sense of remorse.

But Chuntian had told me everything. I have said she was especially superstitious about the skeleton. She touched the back of my head and said, 'You have a rebellious bone. One day, you will grab the right to speak, and you will avenge me.'

My father presented a lot of arguments that day. Suddenly, he felt he wanted to smoke. He had just taken out a cigarette when the nurse saw him. She snapped at him, and he put the cigarette back and kept his hand in his pocket.

'I already called my youngest, and she wants to come back and interview you about this,' my father said, as if specifically to let the nurse hear. 'What kind of a world is this, cheating a worker's hard-earned money? All conscience is eaten up by wolves and wild dogs.'

Zhima was quite moved when he heard this. He cried out a couple of times.

'Xiaohan's newspaper is in Guangzhou. Why do they care about what happens in Yiyang?' Chuntian muttered.

My father had seen the world. He said, 'As long as the matter gets reported in the newspaper, they'll at least have a look.'

My mother added, 'If you can get your wages and medical expenses, that's enough. Those big bosses all have friends in high places. You just can't win when you work for them.'

Amid all the warm concern poured out for him, Zhima could not get a word in. When he thought of his toil at the work site and how this was the first time he had even been at the centre of my family's attention, all kinds of pain occurred simultaneously and tears flowed silently down his cheeks.

Chapter 33:

Li Shunqiu, Eldest Brother

Shui Qin, my brother's wife, was like a plant withered by the sun. If she could take in a night's dew, she would be full of vitality again, getting up quickly after a tumble, and never sighing or complaining in the midst of ruin. She always carried an invisible assault rifle, firing her missiles over obstacles and right on target. My brother had always been like a flag in her hand. When there was no wind, the flag hung limp, but when she waved the flag pole, the flag floated in the air, without volition of its own. But now he had blood-sucking worms in his body, making him prone to dizziness, so if the flag danced too quickly in the wind, the dizziness worsened. In order to prevent the giddiness, he no longer squatted at dinnertime. He could not squat in the latrine pit in the countryside anymore either, so he would control his urge to clear his bowels and rush to the city. The rotten toilet at his house would clog up with every flush, but he did not feel dizzy sitting down to take care of business.

Shunqiu had no choice but to accept the symptoms. He didn't want to feel faint, so he had to carefully serve the 'Fainting Master' all the time. Because he could not look down too long, he often held his head up, making him look proud – in fact, making him look like the master of the 'Fainting Master' instead of its servant.

My brother's body was a hospitable environment for the blood flukes. Shui Qin was willing to contribute and she fought them with traditional local remedies, frying pork liver and cooking blood-enriching soup for him. But in the end, she always felt she was only feeding the blood flukes, so she would get frustrated and scold the worms, while at the same time scolding this country's backward medical technology.

In order to control the spread of the illness, many healthy cells had been destroyed, and it took a toll on my brother. His intimate relationship with the blood flukes often made Shui Qin feel jealous. She said, 'A lot of couples don't even get to grow old together!' She threw tantrums and threw things around, then picked up the mess she created. All the while, my brother just sat to one side, looking ashamed. He was afraid Shui Qin would say she wanted a divorce, and that made him extremely anxious. If she said the word, the limp shell of my brother would collapse completely, lying helpless on the ground.

But Shui Qin never mentioned divorce. She said, 'You have no skill, no qualifications to sit in an office, and you don't want to be a security guard. You won't make it at a construction site. What will you do? Anyway, you need to at least earn back your medical expenses.'

Shunqiu felt she was right. At the very least, he did not want to be a burden. He said he would try the betel nut factory. He thought he could handle loading and unloading betel nuts. Shui Qin had asked someone to help him find a position. When the time came, my brother did not want to take it. There were two shifts, and he knew he could not take the night shift. But then, if he did not go to the betel nut factory, though that was easier on his body, he couldn't take the mental stress of unemployment. So the next day, he finally went to the betel nut factory. After his first day of work, the roots of his hair were all soot, his nostrils white, and he smelled of betel nuts. After seven or eight days, Shui Qin could not stand it. She said, 'Don't keep working there. If you go on like this, your lungs will break down.'

My brother quit, not earning a single cent for his labour. Those seven or eight days had been for nothing, and now he was back where he started.

Before long, he developed a craze for cutting down small canes in the countryside and shaping them into thin strips of bamboo to make paper kites for Xianxian. Due to his dizziness, he could only make one kite in two or three days, shaping them into dragonflies and butterflies. On the weekend, he took Xianxian to the river and flew the kites. Sometimes they crashed into the river, and sometimes they soared high into the clouds. Occasionally the line broke, and no one knew how far the kites flew, nor where they went.

When he was flying kites, my brother was very happy, as if everything that was burdening his body floated off into the sky, and he no longer felt dizzy. Later, he started selling the bamboo and paper kites he made. Many people bought them, but he was chased here and there by the city authorities. That was a blow to his self-esteem. Finally, he hung them in the tailor shop to sell, but a layer of dust gradually settled on the kites, and my brother's interest in them waned, too.

After sitting on the toilet for too long, my brother developed haemorrhoids, and they ran rampant. This ailment was very powerful, keeping him from sitting or standing, and disturbing his sleep and diet. When others showed their concern, he was too shy to talk about it. My brother's weird actions finally caused Shui Qin to suspect something. She coaxed, using both soft and hard approaches. My brother resisted for a while and then, disarmed by shame, exposed his buttocks for Shui Qin to make a clinical examination. Shui Qin was never one to drag her feet. She chose an auspicious day and dragged my brother to the hospital, getting rid of the blood-dripping haemorrhoids. She even told everyone she met about it, embarrassing Shunqiu. He felt that since he had come to this world, he had troubled many people. He had troubled our parents and his wife, and he had troubled the police and doctors, and he had even troubled all his neighbours, who were very concerned about what kind of work he did in the city and how much he made each month. Some even asked him to introduce them to jobs, or take them with him if he found a good job.

I don't know whether, during those turbulent days, my brother thought about taking his own life as a show of his gratitude to everyone. There was an old saying – there was a limit to how long bad luck could go on – but Shunqiu's life had been upside-down since 1983, and there were no signs of improvement. But, as I see it, my brother would not think like that. He was always gentle, but these endless days of fatality were his belief, his religion. He believed that his relationship with the world was set and could not be violated. He was comparable to the Christian martyrs loved by God. His gratitude was obvious, especially when he looked at Xianxian and Shui Qin.

Chapter 34:

Xie Yinyue, Mother

My mother was not very colourful; she was always grey. After she married my father, she had nothing of her own. She never spoke one on one to other men, and she never had letters come from afar. When I was three or four, the president of the marketing cooperative, Mr Ma, came to our house and spoke to my mother in the bedroom. My father was still working on the river at that time. I heard Mr Ma ask about Xiazhi, and my mother said he was so wild she could never be sure where he had gone. Mr Ma said, 'Xiazhi looks more and more like me the older he gets.'

My mother desperately warned Mr Ma not to say such ridiculous things, shooing him out. She remained in her room crying after he left.

I agreed with what Mr Ma had said. Xiazhi really did look like him, with a round face and narrow eyes. Once when I was quarrelling with Xiazhi over an eraser, he said I was nothing but a foundling my mother had picked up, so I retorted, 'You belong to the Ma family.'

When my mother heard that, she rushed over and whipped me, then passed me the eraser. I was very proud to have received a beating and the prize. I had not started school at the time. The eraser had such a strange fragrance, and I eventually chewed it to nothing. Xiazhi complained to my mother, but she did not punish me. She simply sat there, lost in thought.

Whenever my mother grew a little melancholy, I became especially obedient, voluntarily helping her with the housework. When she wanted to paste paper shell, I handed her the paste. When she wanted to dig plaster and mix powder, I shovelled the ash for her. When she wanted to raise silkworms, I helped her pick the mulberry leaves. When she planted pepper bushes, I watered them. When she cooked, I fed the fire under the stove. Year after year, the relationship between my mother and me was quietly built this way, and it became too deep to fathom. My mother was the person I loved most in the whole world. She was a huge tree, and I was a sapling growing in her shade. When Mr Ma came around to my mother again, I would put caterpillars on his neck, or spit in his teacup, or let the air out of his bicycle tyres. Mr Ma seemed to have learned my tactics, so he did not come to our house again. When he passed by our door, he would only take a quick glance inside.

Before long, my father returned from his work on the riverboats. He and Mr Ma had a good relationship. They would often stand together under the jujube tree, chatting and sharing cigarettes. Mr Ma would say he had some good-quality tobacco and invite my father to smoke it. My father would light a cigarette for him. They always had lengthy chats while they smoked. My father was macho, while Mr Ma was gentle and frail. He did not lose to my father, but he was mellow, never in a hurry, and completely free of temper. He often carried his daughter on his shoulders and let her pick flowers or ripe fruit from the trees. I thought of how interesting it would be to have a father like Mr Ma.

Mr Ma's daughter was my classmate all the way through middle school. She did not like to study, but she passed the exam to get into nursing school. After she graduated, she always wore a pink peaked cap, white uniform, white shoes, and a white mask, over which you could see only her narrow eyes. She would rub the patient's hand, squeeze the blood vessel, and poke the infusion needle in. Nursing was a good profession. The nurses who worked in the better hospitals could have a meteoric rise, but Miaohong did not get into a higher ranked hospital. She was stuck in the county hospital, so she had a tough time succeeding. She married one of the hospital's gynaecologists, a bespectacled fellow who had washed his hands so often they were now ghostly white. At the time, the women in the village did not know anything about gynaecology. When they found out what it was, they blushed and said talking about such a thing would shame them to death.

In private, the village women often spoke of Ma's daughter's marriage to a gynaecologist, snickering over it. My mother was one of their ranks. She consciously believed that women were beneath men. Their underclothes should never see the light of day. If I hung such items out where they could be seen by a passerby, my mother scolded me fiercely and quickly put them out of sight, leaving only my father's and brother's pants to flip about in the wind.

Chuntian was greatly affected by my mother. When she first started wearing a bra, I was curious about the little garment, so took it out where everyone could see it. Humiliated, she cried and hit me. In an act of revenge, I once peeped at her while she bathed. Half a red brick came flying out of the washroom, striking me squarely on the hind end. I cried hysterically until my mother punished Chuntian. Even years later, every time Chuntian mentioned this, it saddened her. She said my mother had protected me ever since I was small, and that my father also treated me better than he did her. I felt quite guilty and indebted to her after that.

When our family built the new house, we cut down the jujube tree that had always stood next to the door. This humble, useless tree was actually quite pretty, especially when the flowers bloomed into purple cloud clusters. When the wind blew, they fell like snowflakes. My mother wore a cloth tied around her waist as she sat under the jujube tree rubbing rapeseed, pounding beans, mending the soles of our shoes, or knitting sweaters. I had fallen in love for the first time under that tree, as Tang Linlu played his guitar.

The tree had grown when my father was away from home. He had no special attachment to it, so he cut the tree, dug up the roots, and used it all to reinforce a ring fence. I told my mother, 'You should stop him from cutting down the tree.'

She said, 'There's no use keeping it.'

She spoke so dully that I could only bear the pain in solitude. I did not tell my mother that, for me, the tree was connected to her. I was already in university at the time. I should havehad much to share with my mother, but I still continued in my old ways.

This part of my family history may not seem very important. After all, there was no longer any way to verify whether Xiazhi's surname was Li or Ma. I even doubted my own suspicions. Perhaps I felt that my mother's life was too monotonous, and having one such fantasy would at least prove she was a woman of flesh and blood. It would also prove that she had once cultivated a lively lust, and that she had experienced moments of ecstasy. It was true – I could hardly imagine how my young mother, like the Virgin Mary, could have survived those lonely nights. Of course, in our twenty-first century village, gynaecology is no longer a taboo for women, and stolen pleasures are commonplace. Women say all the dirty words under the sun out loud, their underclothes fluttering in the wind like flags, and when their amour is exposed, they no longer feel suicidal.

Chapter 35:

Li Xinhai, Grandfather

By early 2003, rumours of an infectious disease were spreading, and so many people wore masks when they went out. I called my mother, and she said the price of a bottle of vinegar had gone up tremendously, and the shelves and warehouses had been emptied of vinegar. The price of a Chinese medicine called isatis root, normally sold in medicine halls, had likewise skyrocketed and could not be bought anywhere. I said, 'No wonder there's been such a soar in pharmaceutical stocks.'

My mother asked me to go home and hide for a while. If one caught the disease, death was quick. She told me that when the chickens got bird flu, they were just standing dozing off in the yard, then fell over one after another. When swine flu struck, the pigs would not eat or move, and spots appeared on their bodies. They died soon after that, too. One year, the river had been full of dead pigs, all covered in white spots. I did not say anything else, but just thought of the napping chickens and the fasting pigs, and their white, spotty corpses. I said, 'Mother, don't worry. There are so many people in this country who are still working. Don't believe the rumours. If there really was an epidemic, the government would issue an emergency notice.'

My mother said, 'Two people from the vegetable market already died. Xiaohan, don't let anything happen to you. It's been so many years since your brother died, but I'm still not over it.'

My mother was not prone to sensationalism.

My eyes were red. I asked my parents not to go out unless it was necessary, to be extra careful about hygiene, and to make sure there was plenty of ventilation. 'When the turmoil is over, I'll come back and eat your peppers fried with meat,' I said.

Several days earlier, my grandfather had suddenly become paralysed. He could not talk, and he was incontinent. It was said that just before he suffered this paralysis, he had lost a large bet and had used that bronze jar for oil and salt sitting at the bottom of his treasure chest to pay his debt. He was already ninety-three years old, and everyone said his time to meet the God of Death had come. My father went ahead and reserved a coffin. Because my grandfather's back was not bent and he had not shrunk, maintaining his height of 1.8 metres, he could only fit into a standard-sized coffin if his legs were broken.

There were some people who said that my grandfather was bored with life, faking the paralysis – the same way, when he kept drawing a bad hand, he would become bored and just wanted others to draw on his behalf while he sat and watched, until his addiction stirred and he would enter the battlefield once more. My grandfather certainly knew the pleasures of card-playing, and the taste of being alive.

My father disagreed with this speculation, assuming no one would like to sleep in their own filth. My father called his child-hood friend Wang to come see my grandfather and feel his pulse.

Wang too was old by then, and his fingers trembled slightly.

He said there was no one healthier than my grandfather, whose pulse was jumping like a pot of beans put on to boil. He was very strong, according to Wang. My father was both happy and worried – happy that my grandfather was healthy, but worried the old man would live healthily in bed for another eight or ten years. That would be torture for those around him, just like the time when my grandfather had suffered the deep-rooted boils and was bedridden for two weeks. The whole household was in chaos around him. My father would rather my grandfather get up and go on gambling, feeling the best thing would be for him to die at the card table.

Reality proved harder than what my father had foreseen. My grandfather's bowel movements were sudden and irregular – sometimes two or three times a day. Sometimes my grandfather would throw up after my father had cleaned up, throwing up even the juices from his gallbladder. My father, with the bitterness still in his mouth, called my brother to come home, then made him take over the dirty work. Having faced the indignities of prison, my brother felt there was nothing that could compare with the suffering caused by the loss of freedom. He happily took over bathing my grandfather, washing the mosquito net, cleaning the house, and deodorising the place.

My grandfather lay peacefully. With his eyes closed and his face towards the ceiling, he was like a philosopher contemplating the meaning of life. He had a good appetite, especially for meat. Chicken was his favourite. Miserably, my father slaughtered a laying hen. When he had to slaughter a second one, he started cursing and shouting. After consuming three chickens, my grand-father still did not get up. My father put his knife away, and my grandfather became a vegetarian. 'If he wants meat badly enough, he'll get up,' my father said.

My father's trick was very effective. After eating vegetarian food for ten days, my grandfather suddenly appeared in the kitchen's doorway.

'I want to eat peppers fried with meat.' he said, sounding like a child. 'I want plenty of fat and grease.'

My mother was as shocked as if she had seen a ghost. Still in shock, she immediately went to the market to get some meat, and she fried it with half a red pepper and half a green pepper, heaping the food like a mountain in a bowl. When my father came in, my grandfather was picking at the remains in the bowl and licking the oil from his lips.

'Eh? You're up? I knew you couldn't stand it without meat!' My father was inwardly pleased, but his expression was angry as he fell into his old habit of digging at my grandfather.

My grandfather did not glance at him or return the unkind tone. He merely looked upward and sighed, saying, 'Ah, when you've recovered from a serious illness, fried peppers and meat are so comforting.'

As he said this, he went back to his room.

My grandfather had been bedridden for two months. My father could not let him off so easily now. He chased after him and stood leaning against the side of my grandfather's low door-frame. He shouted, 'You've lived to this ripe old age, so why do you still want to torture people like this? When you want to eat chicken, you just say the word, and I slaughter a chicken. When have I ever withheld it from you? Whatever you've asked for, haven't we tried our best to provide it for you? When have we mistreated you?'

Mr Ma was passing by and stopped, looking at my father. He laughed and said, 'The elder is treated like the babe. Just let it go.'

My grandfather went outdoors then, enjoying the fresh air outside the house. He said, 'The 800 *yuan* in my box is gone. I don't know who stole it.'

'You still have money saved? You've lost your underpants and a lifetime of face gambling. What do you think you have left?' My father was really fired up. 'Talk about your 800 *yuan* . . . even if it was 8000, no one would touch your things! You've thought about money until you've gone crazy. You just got over your paralysis, and now you're making trouble out of nothing!'

Feeling he had the duty to mediate, Ma did not dare to leave. He persuaded, 'Come on, Li, don't be angry. He's nearly 100 years old. Surely his mind's a little cloudy.'

In fact, things would have been better if Ma had left. My grandfather liked to act up in the presence of visitors, and the bigger the audience, the more worked up he became. He decided to employ a 'selective listening' technique this time, pretending he had not heard a word my father said.

'Eight 100 *yuan* bills. I wrapped them in a handkerchief and put them under my martial arts novels . . . They were new notes. I couldn't bear to use them . . . ' My grandfather said to Ma. He really cherished this participant in his drama, this witness, this turtle in the urn.

'Go back and have another good look. Maybe you put it some-where else. You wouldn't lose it.' Ma had to move closer and walk into his role more seriously. 'You are nearly a hundred. Don't play cards anymore. It's the same as giving away money. If you give it away openly, others will appreciate it, but if you give it away at the card table, people just laugh it off.'

My grandfather heard this clearly, and laughed. 'I didn't play cards. I played very little this year. My health is bad. I don't think I have long to live.'

My father was so agitated it hurt. 'You . . . it'll be all right if you die. Who enjoys a better life than you? Ma, you don't know. From last year until now, he brings it up every time he's free. He always makes it seem real.'

My mother came out then and pulled my father away. 'You really love to quarrel, too. You know he's old and confused. Let him be.'

Ma laughed, then slipped away.

My father cleared his throat and spat, swallowing the bullet he had prepared to fire, ending the battle, then turned and walked away. My grandfather was the only person left standing on the terrace. He suddenly seemed lonely.

Staring at the sky for a while, he said to himself, *Well, you think I don't know the mischief your woman and Ma had done?*

Then he went into the house and shut the door.

Chapter 36:

Liu Yihua, Niece

Hearing that the 'commando' wanted to sleep with her, Yihua whirled around on one leg like a compass, looking at the sky, then looking at the ground. The sun was like a cake turning to paste, all grey and hazy. Her whole body felt sticky, and her mind was lost in a dense chaos.

Liuzi was still in that strange building. She did not know if he had had anything to eat or drink, nor whether he had been beaten. When they had first arrived in Guangzhou, Liuzi had been taught a lesson by the police. When they were in Yiyang, Yihua felt they were like crocodiles, but now that they had come out, she felt they were just geckos. They had shrunk to a fraction of their size and were only fit to crawl through cracks in the walls. Yihua had seen many men – fat, thin, tall, short, with cross bite, cross-eyed, and with bellies that made them look pregnant. It was only with such men that she became a crocodile, sitting on their laps, plying them with drinks, and teasing them.

She was momentarily at a loss. Then, she decided to negotiate with the commando.

'If I were not a virgin, I would go with you right away . . .' she said. 'But you know, a girl's first time is to be cherished. It should be something beautiful.'

'You're a virgin? Ha!' the commando sneered. 'If you're a virgin, sows can climb trees.'

'There was a big flood in my hometown one year, and a sow really did climb a tree. She survived,' Yihua said. 'I swear I'm not lying.'

'You've got sows that climb trees there? Ha!' The commando's laughter intensified as it went on. Eventually, he just squatted where he was and laughed, then finally he stood up and wiped his tears. 'Well, if you're a virgin, I won't sleep with you. And I'll do better than that; I'll help you get your man out.'

'Really?' Yihua asked incredulously. 'You mean it?'

'I, Hu Lilai, never lie to women,' the commando said leisurely.

'Your name's Hu Lilai? Where I come from, that means "womaniser."'

'It's a different "Li", the one that means "courtesy". Don't you think I'm quite a polite fellow?'

She noticed he was only about twenty or so years old. In fact, the more she looked, the younger he seemed.

'Yeah, you seem like a good guy.'

'Flattery is useless. So, how are you going to prove you're a virgin?'

Yihua rolled her eyes. 'We'll go to the hospital.'

He said, 'Ok, I want to up the ante. If you're not a virgin, you have to sleep with me ten times.'

'A hundred times is fine,' Yihua said emphatically.

Hu put on his helmet, got back on the bike and stepped on the throttle. The motorcycle spat black smoke.

'Get on,' he called to her.

She hesitated, looking again at the closed iron gate, then climbed on behind him. He stepped on the accelerator, then stepped on the brake. Yihua's chest felt like a mechanical spring coming into contact with his back. The rebound scared her so badly she automatically threw her arms around his waist. The motorcycle howled as they shot out into the street and rode toward the hospital.

*

The doctor wore an unusual expression from the beginning to the end of the consultation. Finally, he said, 'I've seen many men bring women to me for abortions, but I've certainly never had anyone like you two, asking me to check for the hymen.'

In his defence of women, the doctor advised Hu not to concern himself too much with that membrane. What was most important was that she was a good person. Hu laughed, and he now seemed very young to Yihua. She said, 'I was the one who wanted to come here.'

The doctor looked askance at her, but said nothing. He waved her into the waiting room.

When Yihua dared to go to the hospital, Hu believed she was a virgin – and even believed the sow had climbed a tree. He read the text beneath an image on the publicity material in the hospital's corridor, then secretly shook his head and clicked his tongue. He was not as sophisticated as he appeared to be, when it came to women.

He was taking a closer look at the picture of the woman's ovaries and uterus. Suddenly, he heard Yihua wailing inside the room.

'No! How could that be? Honestly, no man has ever touched me!' Yihua cried.

'Ah, don't be so agitated. Just because your hymen is torn doesn't mean you're not a virgin. Vigorous exercise, some vaginal medications, or using devices when you masturbate can all lead to this result. But we can repair it, if you need.'

'I don't need some fake thing. I wouldn't use it to cheat anyone anyway.'

Yihua snatched the medical record and strode out of the examination room. She walked straight out to the hospital's car park before she even turned around. Hu was following close behind. She said to him, 'Damn me. I don't have a good explanation for this.'

'I believe you,' he said.

'I'll do what we agreed. I'll sleep with you ten times. But, my first time will be with my boyfriend.'

'You have a boyfriend?'

'I don't know if he's dead or alive. Let's go bail him out.'

'OK. But you owe me ten times.' He stepped on the throttle, and black smoke rolled from the bike's rear end. 'When this is over, I want to get my fill.'

Chapter 37:

Li Xiaohan

I was browsing the internet when my colleague shouted, 'Li Xiaohan, someone is here to see you.'

I stood up, ran my eyes over the grid of cubicles in the office, and saw Liu Yihua. I was so surprised by how she had blossomed that I neglected her distracted look.

'Auntie,' she called, looking sorrowful.

I thought her father must have died, and my heart did a flip and sank. Although I did not like Zhima, his death would certainly not be a good thing.

I took Yihua into a small conference room. As I poured her a glass of water, I noticed that she was trembling slightly.

'What's wrong?' I asked her. We did not see each other often, and there was a little distance and awkwardness caused by our generation gap.

Yihua made a lengthy case, relating to me the entire history of her and Liuzi in Guangzhou. This was the first time I had heard Liuzi's name. At the time, I did not have any idea that, two months later, his name would rewrite the whole C&R system and be recorded in history.

I was not interested in Yihua's love affair with this tough guy from the streets, and even resented it. I was aware that she had come to Guangzhou to make a living, and I had said harsh words early on, telling her that I did not introduce jobs contacts to anyone who did not like to study or go to university. Unexpectedly, I felt guilty when I met Yihua. We were in the same city, but I had been indifferent to her situation. As if to make up for it, I asked now, 'Where are you working? Is everything going smoothly?'

She did not answer, but went on talking about Liuzi getting picked up and taken to the police station, then shuttled from the police station to the shelter, then moved to the rehabilitation centre.

'. . . He's dead.' She looked at me as she came to an end of her story.

'Dead?' I had always been intrigued by death, and I felt my interest perk up now.

'At the rehabilitation centre, they said he had a heart attack . . . but he didn't have any heart problems at all!' She was getting a little worked up. 'Auntie, I have never bothered you, but Liuzi's death is mysterious. You're a reporter. You have to help me investigate.'

I tried to get the measure of Yihua. She had a childish face, but a deep cleavage. This combination did not match. She was tall and had long limbs, and she possessed the trouble-causing appearance that could control all living creatures, while unfortunately also leaving her brain empty. Of course in hindsight, my point of view was all wrong, as proven by life's realities. In fact, men are never critical about a woman's intellectual capacity, and what they want to hold is not a woman's knowledge or the wisdom in her brain.

'It is definitely strange. Don't panic, wait here for me. I will go speak to my editor,' I said, leaving Yihua and going to search for Yu Shuzhong.

In Yu's estimation, this was a case worth investigating. There certainly was something not quite right about Liuzi's death. He talked about the notorious system of custody and repatriation, saying it was not concern for the weak but rather exploitation of the weak, and a human rights violation. He wanted me to start with the deceased and dig deeper. 'Remember what I've said. We have to abolish the unjust detention system. Perhaps it will start from here, from the *Today Newspaper*.'

I did not doubt Yu's professional sensitivity, but I suspected that what he said might be too idealistic. The *Today Newspaper* had limited freedom. Yu had written numerous reviews on the matter.

'What about the hospital interview?' I asked. 'Two people from my hometown died. Maybe this really is connected to an epidemic?'

'I've already arranged for another reporter . . .' Yu was always quick to sort out his ideas. 'Xiaohan, when you see a corpse, does it still give you nightmares?'

'No. On the contrary – right now, I'm quite keen to observe anyone who died under mysterious circumstances.'

I smiled. I did not want him to worry.

Sometimes, I felt Yu and I were already in a romantic relationship.

Chapter 38:

Liu Yihua, Niece

We took a taxi to the Detention Treatment Centre. Yihua said Liuzi must certainly have been beaten to death. When I asked her why she said this, she replied, 'Lu Mingliang, a friend I met at work, has a friend from her village who was beaten to death. Liuzi was in good health. He didn't have heart problems. He never had a cold, or even a touch of diarrhoea, and now he's suddenly dead. There's definitely something wrong. We have no education and no backing. If we die, we die, and no one cares. Our relatives from the countryside can only come and collect the corpse – what else can they do?'

Yihua said she knew a support worker at the treatment station, Hu Lilai, and he had promised to grant an interview. He was waiting for us there now.

Yihua even provided me with a source. I felt like hugging her, but I didn't. This sort of gesture was too intimate, and I was not used to it. I asked her how she knew Hu Lilai, and she told me the whole story about the deal she had made with him and their trip to the hospital.

I was shocked. 'Are you really prepared to sleep with a stranger?' I asked.

As soon as I said it, I recalled my own indulgences during my time with Yehe Nara, and I felt ashamed to no end. I thought, *How did I become such a self-righteous person?*

Yihua said, 'Whether Liuzi died or not, I still have to sleep with Hu Lilai ten times.'

I nodded. 'It's good to keep your promise, but you can't gamble with your body.'

'What do I have, other than my body?' Yihua said.

I did not answer.

I felt confused, both because of what Yihua had said and because of who she was. It was like I was dreaming. To think that she was our next generation, my own niece, and she was so beautiful, like a mare. And now she was just like me, in this complex society, acting like a philosopher. Her family name was Liu, but she had inherited the piercing coldness of my ancestral beauty. This made me secretly envious. But when I thought of my blood ties to her, I felt I should do something for her. Several years earlier, I liked to preach; every time I met Yihua and Yicao, I told them to study and think diligently, constantly going on about ideals and goals. It was one ear in and out the the other for them. They kept a respectful distance from me.

I asked Yihua, 'Why didn't you sleep with Liuzi?'

'Sleeping together is the easy part,' she said. 'Once you do it, it's gone . . . Like when you eat sweets and are left with nothing but the wrapper.'

The driver glanced at us in the rearview mirror. I could see that he was a little excited and hoped to participate in the conversation.

I did not want to satisfy his lust. I shut up and donned a thoughtful expression.

Before long, we reached the shelter. Yihua pointed to a camouflage-clad, dark-skinned boy straddling a motorcycle. 'That's Hu Lilai,' she said.

A police car stopped at the gate of the Detention Treatment Centre. The gate was wide open. Several officers went in and out. They were carrying away Liuzi's corpse.

'I reported the case,' Yihua said. 'As soon as I did, I went looking for you.'

'That was the right thing to do,' I said, secretly admiring how capable Yihua was. 'Be careful. The police might have been bought.'

'Right. I don't believe them. I believe you, and I believe in the media. In these past few days, I've learned what those old feudal government offices were all about, and what people in such offices still do now.'

Hu rode his motorcycle over and stopped in front of us. He wanted Yihua and me to get on the bike with him so we could find a place to talk.

Yihua sat in the middle, and I sat behind her. Two minutes later, we stopped under an old banyan tree. It had luxuriant foliage, and fine roots hung all over its body. Its branches were old and black.

Hu had a lot to say. For instance, his salary was less than 2000 *yuan* each month, and he often worked overtime. When new patients came in at midnight, he had to tell them the treatment code at the Detention Treatment Centre. He had a 70-year-old mother who was in poor health and bedridden. From his pile of nonsense, the only useful information I got was that the night Liuzi had come to the Detention Treatment Centre. Hu had not only lectured Liuzi, but had also kicked his stomach twice. He said that, because of this, he would cancel the debt of 'ten times' that Yihua owed him.

I told Hu, 'This is no small matter. The more you tell me, the better it will be for you.'

He said, 'Every newcomer to this place has to be beaten. It's a sort of "regulation" before one crosses into the warehouse.'

'Warehouse regulation?' I was a bit confused.

'The sickroom in the Detention Treatment Centre is called the warehouse. Transferring rooms is called transferring warehouses.'

'Then what do you call the people you take in?'

'Rats.'

When he had said this, he started to leave. He wanted to go home to help his mother eat, drink, and empty her bladder and bowels. He did not feel he was a bad person for kicking Liuzi twice. When he had ridden away about a hundred metres, he turned back and offered one last parting comment, 'Go look for the head nursing worker, Qiao Feiyan. He knows everything.'

Yihua and I made our way back to the Detention Treatment Centre. The police had left, and the centre was restored to a state of calm. The gate was closed, and everything was silent.

An hour later, Yihua and I visited the shelter and the police station. We did not finish the interviews until it was dark outside.

Yihua had lost her lover, and I felt society was a real mess. The weather was a bit oppressive.

For dinner, I took Yihua for Teowchew cuisine. I knew which dishes were the best.

'Let's go for a drink,' Yihua said.

'What kind of drink?'

'Beer.'

'No problem. Teowchew dishes go well with alcohol.'

I ordered oysters, roasted goose, bittern, vegetables, porridge, and four bottles of beer. Yihua took a couple of bites and said, 'It's pretty plain. I want something spicy – like peppers fried with meat.'

'It's as hard to change one's tastes as it is to change the accent.' I couldn't help but laugh. When Yu had brought me to this place, I had wanted to eat peppers fried with meat too.

'You don't have an accent. Your Mandarin sounds like the people on TV,' Yihua said.

'I spent three years correcting my accent. If you want to do something well, you just have to be serious and work hard, then you'll most likely succeed. I bet you don't have any desire to learn Mandarin.'

'I do want to learn.'

'Oh, I haven't asked. Where in Guangzhou are you working?'

'If I tell you, you'll look down on me more than you already do.'

'Try me.'

'Promise first that you won't scold me.'

'I'm not your mother.'

'. . . At the Oriental Pearl.'

'A nightclub?'

'But believe me, I've kept my hands clean while I worked.'

'Who would believe a girl in a nightclub is pure? I believe you, but will your parents? Or other people?'

I had already guessed she worked in a hotel or entertainment facility. Only those places required youth and beauty. But hearing it with my own ears, I still felt a little uncomfortable.

'Auntie, you are not much older than me. We're basically peers . . .'

'Hey, hey, hey . . . Have you had too much to drink? I'm clearly your senior, you know.'

'Seniority in the family is just seniority, but we belong to the same generation in society. Don't you also like Leslie Cheung? When he committed suicide, you even wrote an article in memory of him.'

'You read that?' I was a little surprised Yihua read the newspaper.

'I stumbled across it. I just mean to say that the only difference between you and me is that you went to the university, and I didn't,' she said lightly.

'Why didn't you look me up?'

'I wanted to make something of myself first.'

'Well, you have good prospects.' I meant it. 'What do you hope to make yourself into?'

'My teacher at school always loved to ask me that. To tell you the truth, I still don't have an answer.'

'Give me a rough idea.'

'I want to open my own company.'

'You still can't open a brothel legally in China.'

'Li Xiaohan, if you talk like that again, I'm out of here.' Yihua called me directly by my full name.

'You've got a temper.' I pretended to be severe, but inwardly, I liked her more and more by the minute.

'If you don't set aside the empty facade of being my "senior," we can't really talk because we won't be equals.'

'OK,' I said, persuaded. 'I'll reconsider.'

'What do we do next, for Liuzi's case?'

'I need to find a way to get into the Detention Treatment Centre for an interview.'

Chapter 39:

Li Chuntian, Elder Sister

When Sun Xiangxi came back from Hong Kong, Chuntian slipped out to see him. Sun had brought a cheap hairpin back for her. It seemed to be inlaid with small diamonds, and it sparkled. My sister was just happy Sun thought of her. Laughing, she asked him which woman he had taken with him. He said, 'There's no woman. You mean you took my little joke seriously?'

Chuntian said, 'Even if there was a woman, I wouldn't know.'

Sun pulled two pairs of socks out of his bag, and a condom came out with them. The red package fell to the ground. It was quite striking.

My sister picked it up. The words on the package were English, so she did not understand. She rubbed and pinched it with her fingers, and it was slippery. It dawned on her now, and her face slowly turned red. It looked like she was biting something in her mouth, and it escaped her teeth, then her emotion burst forth. It was a big monster, and it was closing in on its goal, bringing with it disappointment, contempt, and pain.

'Bringing this along, you were quite well-prepared.'

Sun was an old pro. This little flaw would not deter him. He laughed and embraced Chuntian. 'What nonsense are you talking about? I meant to use this with you.'

This was a huge insult to my sister's intelligence. She was not stupid, and he knew she had had her tubes tied. She pushed Sun away forcefully, and he almost fell.

'You think you're fooling a small child? When did we need this? When did we ever use it?'

Sun still grinned. 'Don't worry. Let me explain. This thing is different, it has spirals.' Sun moved to whisper in Chuntian's ear, 'You'll enjoy it.'

These words suddenly broke down Chuntian's stand. She gave herself a moment to consider, and she thought maybe she had accused him unfairly. Perhaps he just wanted to do something a little more interesting; he was after all a romantic fellow. Sun saw her hesitation and knew it was a turn for the better. He understood the train of her thoughts quite well. She could not handle two issues at the same time. As long as one issue had the upper hand, with a bit of effort, it could squeeze the other off the cliff.

Sun put forth that bit of effort. 'You're talking about me . . . But you, what have you been doing the past few days? Day and night you're with Zhima. It makes me uncomfortable. Who knows what you two have been up to?'

Sun changed targets, focusing on her weak point. She immediately fell in line. After all, he was single, while she was a married woman. Feeling a little ashamed, she argued hotly, 'He's injured. His ribs are broken. I've been waiting on him hand and foot until I'm exhausted. Do you think it's a holiday for us?'

Inwardly, Sun laughed with joy. He put on a magnanimous front. 'You two can get up to any sort of mischief you want, and what can I do? You're his wife.'

She said, 'With Zhima in this condition, I really can't mention anything to him.'

Sun felt now that the issue of the condom was settled, he could use that foreign plaything with her, consolidating his lies. But she refused. As soon as she saw the red package with English print, it was like cold water had been poured on her, waking her up. On top of that, she had been gone too long. She had to go back to the hospital. She was an emotional wreck, and had completely lost all interest in Sun.

'Some time back, I heard you got a secondary school teacher pregnant. Was that true?' she said suddenly.

Sun froze. His mind spinning, he searched for a defence. 'Ah, yes . . . I wanted to tell you about that myself, but I felt like it was a relationship in the past, so I didn't tell you. I didn't think you'd like to hear me talk about having loved another woman. We were together for a year. She wouldn't get a divorce . . . You know how it is. I'm an old man, and I can't wait forever. We had broken up, but she showed up one day . . . I just saw her once. We lost our minds. We did it again, but I never imagined . . . '

'Why did she refuse to get a divorce?' My sister had some sympathy for the male lead of this tale.

'Sometimes, I really don't understand what you women want . . . She had a kid,' Sun said. 'Maybe I had more money than her husband, and was more cultured . . . But in the end, she played me.'

My sister thought for a moment. 'Are you saying that to accuse me?'

'No. How could I? I know you. You're not like her.'

'What am I like?'

'You . . . You're upright, and kind, and simple . . . And you're beautiful.'

'Forget it. I know what I'm like. You're just trying to flatter me.'

'I think you're beautiful. I love the way you look. What about you? Don't you care about me?'

She wanted to leave. She answered lightly, 'I like ordinary men. I don't mind if a guy's old and ugly, as long as he doesn't fuck around.'

Chapter 40:

Li Xiaohan

Yu Shuzhong got hold of an important document that made the Detention Treatment Centre open their gate obediently. The staff obliged, but coldly. The atmosphere inside the facility was strange. They did not allow me into the warehouse, saying that some of the mental patients were unruly, and it would not be safe for me. I could not differentiate between doctors, nurses, and nurse support workers. Their identities were confusing, and each person seemed to have multiple roles. They were like ghosts, their eyes shifting and their faces expressionless. When they answered my questions, there was no logic, as if they were all psychotic. When they finished their interviews, they turned into busy worker bees, very abruptly leaving me like a dead branch in the midst of flowering shrubs.

I smelt a bloody stench – a hot, disgusting smell. The warehouse was silent. The whole facility was quiet and stifling. There was a pot of devil's ivy outside every window. At a glance, I knew they were all newly bought. Obviously, the staff heard that someone was coming to interview them, so they had made a series of arrangements, sprucing up the Detention Treatment Centre, but I could still detect the chaos underneath the surface. I conducted interviews for two hours, but got nothing.

When I asked about Qiao Feiyan, everyone became imbecilic and incoherent, as if a gun was secretly pointed at their forehead. One by one, they all praised Qiao fervently. From my interviews, I found out Qiao was ex-military, and he was strong. He had been recruited the previous year to work in security, and had done very well. He was quickly made team leader. The security and nurse support workers were the same at the Detention Treatment Centre, and everyone followed his orders willingly. One girl panicked a little. She was Qiao's girlfriend, but she said she had just come back from a holiday and did not know anything.

When I left the treatment centre and the metal gate clanked shut behind me, I felt like I had been released from a prison for ghosts. The little ghosts I had interviewed floated in my mind, with their blood-red lips and their teeth stuffed with human flesh, making my back feel cold. A motorcycle suddenly slammed on its brakes. A cloud of dust and black smoke came out of the bike's rear end. Hu Lilai appeared riding on a cloud, as if the God of Earth had appeared from the ground.

'Get on,' he said. 'I've got something to tell you.'

We went to a herbal tea shop. There were two fans mounted on the wall, rattling and circulating the warm air. I turned on my recorder and wrapped my hands around my cold drink, hoping to cool off. Hu tossed his straw aside and took a couple of gulps of his mango smoothie, then puckered his mouth as if he had been burned.

'Can you please introduce yourself briefly?'

'I'm Hu Lilai, a nurse support worker at the Detention Treatment Centre. I've been working there for three months.'

'What does a nurse support worker do?'

'We wear camouflage uniforms and carry rubber batons. We

keep the patients from making trouble, and also assist the nurses when they distribute meals or medicine.'

'What sort of people are the patients?'

'All sorts. They come from different shelters.'

'Are they all ill?'

'Not necessarily. Some are delinquents, so they come here for "treatment."'

'Was Ma Liujia one of these?'

'When Ma Liujia came in, I was on duty. He kicked up a big fuss as soon as he came in. He was really strong. Some people had just been released that day, so he shouted for help. Before long, Qiao Feiyan said to me, "Someone is way too noisy in there. Put him in Warehouse 206; let them have some fun. Play hard, but be careful not to hit his head, and don't draw blood. Anyway, if you kill him, it doesn't matter. A person dying here is like an ant dying." So I put Ma Liujia in Warehouse 206, and I kicked him a couple of times. I did that just so Qiao would see. If I didn't kick him, Qiao would kick me. He's very strong. He can kill a dog with one kick. We're all afraid of him.'

'What was the warehouse like?'

'A dozen or so cement bunks. Those who pay the nurse support workers money become the warehouse chiefs. They get to sleep next to the window. They're responsible for snitching.'

'So who are the ones who beat people up?'

'They're also sent from the shelter. They don't want to beat people up, but if you're told to beat and you don't do it, you'll be beaten. It's miserable. Warehouse 206 is especially for beating people. When those sent there have been beaten, they'll be transferred. They go in standing erect, but they're carried out.'

'Tell me about Ma Liujia's beating.'

'Seven or eight people surrounded him. They hit him with their fists and elbows, and they kicked him, then picked him up and threw him to the ground. When Ma Liujia squatted and covered his head, some of them jumped on his back and stepped and stomped. He knelt and begged for mercy. Qiao's girlfriend tried to stop them, but Qiao scolded and chased her away. Feeling the beating had not been severe enough yet, he wanted them to continue. The warehouse chief said if the instructions of the security were not carried out well, everyone would be in trouble, so they should keep beating him for another half hour. When they finished, Ma Liujia was moved to Warehouse 208. I saw him through the window. A nurse support worker was using a police baton to poke Ma Liujia. Ma went from screaming to groaning. He lost his voice quickly. The next morning when the nurses were making their rounds, Ma Liujia was lying on his stomach on the cement bed, his face purple. He was hardly breathing. They carried him to the emergency ward, but he died shortly after.'

I imagined his dead, purple skin, like a yam.

The electric fans whirred.

'I've resigned. I smuggled some material out for you.' He stood up. 'Actually . . . The Detention Treatment Centre is a prison. Those who aren't ill will become sick.'

He put the material in front of me. Without waiting for me to shake his hand or thank him, he turned away and left the teahouse. His motorcycle roared, and its rear kicked up a cloud of black fog.

I immediately looked at the material and found some amazing data. There were only four medical professionals in the treatment centre. It had been open for over a year, and had received more than eight hundred patients. More than a hundred of them had died, and the cause of death had not been specified.

No wonder Qiao Feiyan had said a person dying was no different from an ant dying.

I called Yu. 'A storm is coming,' he said.

*

Yu did not go home. I wrote, and he waited for my article. He said that when this report came out, it would be earth-shattering. This was Yu's form of praise. His two dimples appeared every time there was a major event. They were not sweet, but solemn and full of worry. Even so, I had the desire to swim nude in those dimples, especially when I thought that in private, they also had their non-serious moments. The small claw in my heart was scratching. Weariness did not dull my instincts. The wearier I became, the greater my desire. I really wanted to finish the article, then have a go with him. If he were willing, he should reward me according to my demands.

As my thoughts strayed, Yu answered a call from his wife. He told her not to leave a light on for him; he would be at the office all night.

The words 'leave a light on' hit me like a dart, striking coldly in the bull's eye of my desire.

The lights in the office were incandescent. They made it look like a morgue.

Yu was beside me; he was the light left on for me. So, I was like any wife in the bedroom, heart warm as I went about my day's work. We were all preparing for battle, though each battlefield was different. Theirs was the bedroom; mine was the newsroom.

By three in the morning, I had finished a 4000-word report. Yu read it, then tweaked the title to read, *Death of the Lowly*.

When day broke, we went to a small restaurant for breakfast, waiting for the paper to hit the streets. We ate green bean porridge, eggs, preserved vegetables, and dumplings. Yu suddenly started talking about my brother, saying how much I was like Xiazhi, sharing his stubborn streak. A bicycle sped by. Wearing a yellow Mandarin jacket, the newspaper delivery man pedalled on, desperately. I smelt the fragrance of ink. My words flew about. The number of diners around us gradually increased, their topics of conversation behind the time. We silently munched on our dumplings. Yu said something was sure to happen. I did not want to go home and sleep.

Not long after we returned to the newsroom, the phones started ringing. We answered the calls one after another, listening to the angry voices of readers, calling to share their own experiences. A middle school student got lost in the streets, was sent to the shelter and, when he returned home four days later, he was black and blue all over and incoherent. Two 13-year-old girls in the shelter were pimped and forced into prostitution. When a young woman showed her temporary residence permit to the police, the other party ripped the document up and detained her. She was gang-raped by a group of rabid men in the human warehouse in the shelter.

Traffic to our website increased rapidly. People were sharing the story everywhere.

At ten o'clock, Yu called for an emergency editorial board meeting.

'We've just received instructions from above, telling us to stop reporting on the Ma Liujia case.' Yu went straight to the point, 'We all know the situation of the *Today Newspaper*. I think if we put a temporary stop to reporting the Ma Liujia case, we can continue to report on other similar cases. Even if they prohibit us from reporting similar cases, we can still attack the C&R system. In short, continue questioning, and attack the detention system until the whole thing is finally abolished.'

'The C&R system was first set up to help vagrants get back home, but when the police started using it for their own economic gain, it became government-sanctioned kidnapping and ransom. It's black gold politics,' the deputy editor said, 'But this system has been around for twenty years, and just one small newspaper will not be able to abolish it.'

'When you have a sword in hand, you have to polish it. You can't let it get rusty,' Yu said. 'A thousand miles of embankment can be broken by ant nests, and we'll be that small ant colony.'

'Mr Yu, the C&R system involves very solid interests. In five years, one of Guangdong's shelters have earned four million. If you trim the fat, you make yourself their enemy. And anyway, we've been warned twice now,' reminded the director of the editorial department.

'A good newspaper should promote social progress,' Yu said. 'Perhaps each time we are warned, we should wear the mark proudly.'

The atmosphere in the room was quite dignified. Yu started telling stories. He spoke of Xiazhi and their generation. A new young reporter was shocked. He had never known that sort of thing had happened in his country.

'The reason a newspaper exists should be for the rights and well-being of the public. We have come into this world, and we should do something.' Yu's words gradually heated up the atmosphere, and everyone was eager to get into action. This group of ordinary editors and reporters was transformed into soldiers during peace-time. Suddenly, we felt the adrenaline of being armed with live ammunition and sent to the battlefield.

'Before, we would lose our lives. Now, at most, we might lose our jobs.' A young reporter made the worst of calculations.

'Li Xiaohan, you continue to interview Ma Liujia's family. Any problem?' Yu asked me.

'No problem,' I said. 'We're all from Yiyang. We speak the same dialect, so we should be able to communicate easily.'

One of my colleagues pushed the door open and came in, her face flushed. 'Mr Yu, a CDC interview turned up a death suspected to be SARS-related. Do we want to report it?'

Yu nearly stood up from his seat. He adjusted his position and said, 'Let's discuss it. I want to hear everyone's opinions.'

'It's the first case. We'll be the first to offer media coverage of SARS.'

'But there are the unified propaganda specifications from above. If we . . .'

'Right. With both of these issues together, the *Today Newspaper* will be dazzling.'

When he had heard all the pros and cons, Yu asked, 'What is the beast trainer's whip made of?'

'Just ordinary material. Nothing special.'

Yu asked, 'And why are wild beasts afraid of an ordinary whip?'

'They're afraid of hunger and punishment.'

'They're afraid of the pain inflicted by the trainer's whip.'

No one spoke.

'No,' Yu said, smiling faintly. 'The beasts are afraid because they have lost their freedom and their savage ambition.'

Chapter 41:

Xiao Shui Qin, Sister-in-law

Shui Qin valued saving money more than her own life. She became a piece of fabric. Threads grew out from her head, her hands were scissors, and her feet were fastened to the sewing machine's pedal. Her voice mingled with the sounds of the machine, just as rapid and precise, as if she was constantly trying to avoid being pricked by the needle. She occasionally felt abdominal pains, but would endure the suffering. When she could take it no longer, she would lie down for a while, but even as she did, her hands continued to sew buttons onto garments. With Xianxian growing up as quickly as the crops, she could not afford to waste time.

One night, Shui Qin and Shunqiu were in bed reading through their deposit book. Shunqiu looked at the numbers, like snails crawling across the page, and said dully, 'It would be fine if Xianxian tested well enough to get into one of China's famous universities. She doesn't necessarily have to drink all that foreign ink.'

Shui Qin closed up the deposit book resolutely and said, 'She wants to go abroad, too. You don't need to worry about it.'

My brother knew what she meant: he was just supposed to give her any money he earned and not interfere. Inwardly, he felt awkward, and lonely too, but he did not have any way to refute her. Ever since she had married into his family, she had taken control of all household matters. Shunqiu was used to it. He admitted she was a good helmsman, a capable sailor, and an excellent navigator. She had defeated countless odds and ends in life; their large ship would soon be brought home to the ideal harbour.

Calculating according to their current income, there would be just enough money for Xianxian to go overseas for high school, if the parents continued to work like beasts of burden without letting up. Shunqiu did not quite understand it all. Sighing deeply, he turned over and went to sleep. Shui Qin turned his body over, wanting to discuss it further. She said that there was a farmhouse restaurant that had its own vegetable garden and fish pond, and they wanted to hire a few capable people to take care of them. 'Farming allows for freedom, and it's your strong suit. If you caught frogs at night, it would meet both areas of need.'

My brother mumbled, 'I doubt I would be up to it,' but did not make any further comments. He knew it was useless to do so. Shui Qin only believed in practical results, even if he worked until he was dead tired. If he were a hired hand, she would not trust him completely, but he was Xianxian's father, so she knew he would not hold anything back. At that moment, she would naturally believe that it was too much for him.

My brother turned back over to go to sleep. After a moment, he asked, 'Who opened the farmhouse restaurant?'

Shui Qin said, 'I don't know. An old customer recommended it. It doesn't matter who opened it, as long as it pays your salary.'

My brother thought this made sense. One need not know the hen personally in order to eat her eggs. He spent the night in dreamless slumber after that.

My brother went to take care of the vegetables for the farmhouse restaurant. When he came back to see his family a few days later, he was quite happy with his work. He seemed more cheerful and chatted more. Shui Qin said, 'Looks like the workers at the restaurant know how to take care of you.'

My brother said, 'They're mostly old women.'

'I can't believe there's not one decent person there,' Shui Qin replied.

'I don't care if they're decent or not. That's got nothing to do with me,' he said.

'So there are some decent sorts?'

'If you're worried, I'll quit.'

Shui Qin said, 'I was playing with you. Who would be interested in an old, sick fellow like you, and . . . '

She had inadvertently poured out what was really on her mind. She stopped suddenly, then told a few jokes to try to cover up her mistake.

My brother's face did not turn red. He slowly added, 'That's right. And a reformed prisoner.'

'Don't say that about yourself,' Shui Qin said.

My brother confirmed, 'But it's the truth.'

'I don't like to hear it.'

My brother looked at her. 'I'm a reformed prisoner. You married a reformed prisoner.'

Shui Qin reached to put her hand over his mouth, but missed, instead twisting his face until his mouth and eyes were distorted. My brother did not move, but just repeated those few words, as if he was under a spell. Growing anxious, Shui Qin slapped him. He stopped talking.

In all their years of marriage, this was the first time they had got angry with each other.

Shui Qin's monthly cycle was irregular. When it was ten days late, she went to the hospital and learned she was expecting. She sat in the corridor, thinking everything through. Before long, she had made her decision. She privately went for an abortion, then after sleeping for half a day, got up and went back to work. A month later, she had still not recovered. She experienced excessive blood loss, making her limbs weak and her lips pale. She lost a dozen pounds and could not walk upright. When she really could not carry on, she went to the hospital. The doctor said she was haemorrhaging, and he suspected it might be a tumour. Shui Qin was suddenly in a state of chaos. For several days, she was uneasy, cutting clothes to the wrong measurements or messing up the fabric while cutting. She wanted to weep, to nestle against Shunqiu and take a long holiday in his embrace, letting him carry the weight of the world for a while.

On the day of the diagnosis, Shui Qin felt she was like a frog, jumping and hopping all the way to the hospital with her heart. She jumped up the steps of the hospital, jumped past the lobby, jumped along the corridor, and finally hopped onto the stool, her abdomen heaving. Her eyes bulging, she looked at the doctor, a woman with very dark features and thick lips.

'The situation is not very good,' the doctor said, opening the thick valve. She rolled out these words like glass marbles, letting them lightly graze the surface of the table.

'Just say it. I've prepared myself mentally.' Shui Qin did not say anything, but the frog croaked.

'It really is cancerous.' Seven glass marbles were all lining up in a row now. 'It's a rare sort of condition.' Seven marbles at the back squeezed out the seven before them.

'So what is it?' Nineteen glass marbles glittered with a strange light, making Shui Qin a little dizzy.

'It's like this. It's choriocarcinoma, a very malignant tumour that usually occurs after childbirth or an abortion.'

A heap of crowded glass marbles caused Shui Qin's mind to be more confused than ever. 'How much longer do I have to live?'

It is instinct for a drowning person to grasp for something to hang onto. She wanted to calculate how much she could earn before her death, and how much she lacked for Xianxian's foreign education fees.

'Don't worry. You won't die.' The doctor removed the lid from her teacup and took a sip. Her thick lips looked even fluffier after being in contact with water. She licked her lips and said, 'We can treat it slowly, but it will take up to two to three years for you to recover.'

Shui Qin heaved a half-sigh. The belly of the frog deflated. 'What sort of treatment does it require?'

'You'll have to be admitted right away. Where is your family?' The doctor spoke haughtily, the two thick lips expanding so broadly they covered half of her face.

'I need to go home first and discuss it with them.' Shui Qin was like a defeated hen, wings drooping as she turned and walked away.

To Shui Qin, removing money from her savings was worse than death. As soon as she finished sewing the pile of clothing that was accumulated at home, their savings would hit six figures. She had intended to celebrate a little that day.

She walked beside the wall, she could still jump and hop like a frog when she had come to the hospital, but now, she had no strength, feeling like a fat, ugly toad, wriggling on the ground. She walked a few steps, stopped, then repeated the process. Finally, she stood beneath a tree, with nobody around, and started weeping.

Chapter 42:

Li Chuntian, Elder Sister

In taking care of Zhima, my sister started to neglect Sun Xiangxi. Thinking it through, she knew that, though Sun had his good points, he was, in essence, a playboy who was not to be relied upon.

Having had a taste of what other men were like, my sister now felt Zhima was even more annoying. He was 80 per cent ill, but pretended an extra 30 per cent on top of it. He was using the chance to rule over her with vigour, and she played the role properly.

When Yicao came to the hospital, she was chewing bubble gum. She blew a large, egg-shaped bubble. When it exploded, it left the gum stuck all over her mouth. She rolled out her tongue to pull the gum back between her lips, whispering, 'Ba, are you using bodily suffering to keep Ma by your side?'

Zhima was so angry he blew his beard and glared at her, then spat out a wad of phlegm.

Yicao went on, 'Don't tie my mother down. If you really are crippled, Yihua and I will take care of you.'

My sister stopped her quickly. 'You bad girl! Hurry back to school now. Don't hang around here talking that sort of nonsense.'

Yicao had no intention of hanging around. She said, 'Ma, we're all women. I'll definitely help you. What right has my father to ask for a 100 000 *yuan* divorce fee from you, when it should be you asking him for money? Even I feel it's shameful.'

My sister smiled bitterly, 'Your help is only making things worse.'

Yicao said to Zhima, 'Ba, if you keep making things difficult for our mother, Yihua and I won't have anything to do with you. We'll do as we say. Why do you think Yihua didn't come back? It's because she's already angry with you, you know.'

Zhima displayed a weak, pitiable look. Chuntian chided Yicao as she pushed her, 'Go on, you bad girl . . .'

But inwardly, she was especially pleased. Watching Yicao make her way down the stairs, she even leaned on the windowsill and smiled faintly. She wanted to watch her a little longer. Then she saw Yicao walk out of the building. A boy walked toward her, and the pair walked out of the hospital hand in hand.

When Zhima received the medical expenses from the contractor, he wanted to be discharged. Chuntian did not want to go back to the village. Disheartened by Sun, she no longer felt the urgent desire for a divorce. She muddled along and agreed to let Zhima stay and squeeze in the same bed as her.

Yicao's warning had been effective. Zhima said to my sister, 'I'll treat you well. I'll do some small business in the city, and we can save money to buy a small house. The leeches won't bite your legs anymore.'

In so many years of marriage, Zhima had never said one intimate word to my sister. Now, he just blew lightly, and she cried uncontrollably. She had a whole basketful of the past that she brought up, rebuking Zhima until her throat and tongue were dry, then the clouds dispersed and the sky cleared. Her body gradually became light. She could not help but ponder quitting her job at the teahouse, since she had broken up with Sun. As soon as she saw Sun, she would no longer be master of herself. She could not let this playboy continue to make a mess of her life.

When Chuntian went to the teahouse in her free time, she happened to bump into Sun, drinking tea. A woman sat beside him, as pretentious as a queen. Sun was trying to please her – apparently he had not yet taken this woman. My sister bit her lips, turned around, and left. The owner of the teahouse stopped her. Sun likewise called generously, 'Hey, Chuntian. Come here! Have a cup of this new blend.'

He had not even bothered to slide his own arse away from the woman's.

My sister stopped at the door and said to the owner of the teahouse, 'I need to apply for another week of leave.'

Her boss said, 'No problem. Just come back when your family matters have been arranged.'

On the spur of the moment, she decided to stay at the teahouse. At least that would prevent Sun from carrying out any monkey business on the premises. She suppressed the fire of jealousy within her and desperately forced herself not to look at Sun, feeling both nauseated and sad.

After she left the teahouse, about half a mile down the road, she grew confused. She did not know what she wanted to do. She thought as she walked.

In the distance, she saw the words *Beautiful Tailor Shop*, and envy of Shui Qin suddenly sprang up in her. She envied her happy family life and her work. She felt herself like duckweed by comparison, her body and feelings rootless and floating with the current. My sister walked into the tailor shop, half in a trance. There were no machines whirring like machine guns. It was very quiet inside. Shui Qin sat on a chair sewing buttons. She had become skin and bones.

My sister asked, 'Are you sick?'

Shui Qin said, 'May my ancestors protect me. I won't die, but it will be difficult to recover. I don't know how much this is going to cost.'

Chuntian said, 'Health is what matters. It's far more important than money. What sort of illness is it?'

'Choriocarcinoma. A one in 100 000 chance of getting it. My odds of striking the lottery would have been better,' Shui Qin said.

Chuntian did not understand. She asked where the illness was situated. Shui Qin repeated the diagnosis as if she were a doctor.

'You should have had the baby. Maybe it would have been a boy.' My sister felt it a real waste.

Shui Qin said, 'You're a woman yourself. Why do you favour boys over girls?'

Chuntian replied, 'Everyone thinks this way . . .'

Shui Qin's face reflected her feebleness, but it did not affect the look of pity ensuing from her eyes. It flashed like lightning, then disappeared. Chuntian had not taken the slightest notice.

'If Xianxian's grandfather hears of it, he will certainly curse me.'

'Be glad you aren't his daughter. If you were, you'd be like me, praying to the gods every day to curse him.'

'Chuntian, you shouldn't always remember your parents' wrongs.'

'That year, I really had no way out, so I married Liu Zhima. I spent my life working like a beast of burden, and now I'm stuck with this good-for-nothing.'

'Think of it from another point of view. You have Yihua and Yicao, two beautiful little wadded jackets. That's a respectable harvest.'

'Yeah. A grown daughter has her own mind. Just wait until Xianxian is grown and you'll know what I mean.'

'Her? She's started to manage us already.'

When they talked about their daughters, the atmosphere was gentle. Smiles appeared on both Shui Qin and Chuntian's faces.

Chapter 43:

Li Shunqiu, Eldest Brother

When my brother got home, dinner was ready. Chopped peppers with boiled mud fish, chilli rings fried with vegetable stems, fried salted fish, and another plate of peppers, deep-fried. These were all of his favourite dishes. He turned it over in his mind. It wasn't his birthday, nor was it their wedding anniversary. He was suddenly on guard, even deeply disturbed. What had he done to deserve Shui Qin going to all that trouble to make a table of almost flattering dishes for him? She was still sick. My brother was not stupid. After he came out of prison, his brain might have seemed a little rusty, but he could put two and two together, especially when some strange phenomenon occurred. There might be a bit of a rattling sound when his brain powered up, as the rust was shaken off, but there was still a bright steel machine underneath.

My brother quickly erased signs of his first misgivings and turned with a happy expression to face the food. He would not expand his emotional territory. He was used to keeping the range of his emotions within the train of Shui Qin's skirt.

'Where's Xianxian?' he asked.

'She went back to the village,' Shui Qin said. 'Your parents are always hoping she will go back over the weekend.'

'They're old. They only have this little thing to look forward to.' My brother's sarcasm had some pity in it. 'Actually, they don't really love anyone.'

He placed chopsticks and two bowls of rice on the table.

'Are you like Chuntian, always remembering your parents' wrongdoings?' Shui Qin sat down and picked up her rice bowl. 'Which children in the village did not grow up like animals?'

'Chuntian will never get rid of the shadow cast over her life. Even when she is doing well on the surface, she's definitely still struggling inside.' My brother was helpless on all fronts, and this made him feel somewhat ashamed. 'And Zhima is a bastard. Fortunately, Yihua and Yicao keep their mother in their hearts. Xianxian also takes your side. If you were to have another, it would weaken my position even further.'

Shui Qin had been wondering how she would bring up the subject of her own illness. She never imagined he would throw her a line like this. She grabbed it. 'Yes. That's why I got rid of it.'

My brother thought she was joking. He picked up a mud fish with his chopsticks, put it into his mouth, pursed his lips, sucked and dragged out its whole skeleton.

'I'm sick now . . . It was caused by my recent abortion.' Shui Qin knew she could not conceal it, so she thought it best he heard it straight from her.

'You had an abortion?' he asked.

'Yeah. I know you all wanted me to have a boy, but I didn't want to have another child.' She searched for the right words. 'Of course, I should have at least talked to you first. But I knew you would support me.'

Shunqiu paused for several seconds. He then picked up

another mud fish and started sucking on it. He slowly dragged its skeleton out, just like the other.

He remembered well that over the last two months, he had only slept with Shui Qin once. It had only lasted five minutes, and he was sure he had pulled out in time.

'I have cancer now . . .' Shui Qin went on.

The skeleton slipped from his chopsticks. He was suddenly alert. 'Cancer?'

'I won't die. It's still at an early stage.' Shui Qin put the word 'die' right out in front, wanting to use the cruel word to stop Shunqiu from discussing it with her further – for example, whether she could have gotten pregnant when he had pulled out.

My brother said, 'Admit yourself to a hospital. We can always earn back the money.'

His voice sounded sleepy. He was still digging through his memory, wondering if they had done something one night when he was half asleep. After he had fallen ill, the doctor had advised abstinence. His heart was insipid, and his body indifferent. It was hard for him to say for sure whether there had been a mishap.

'I . . . did I do something in the middle of the night . . . make some mistake?' he asked carefully, as if making a review.

'Shunqiu, what do you mean? I'm in this state now. Can you act like a man?'

Shui Qin immediately got angry, and even started to cry. She was also confused about what the tears meant, but she could not think of what else to do, so she just cried. She was acting, and she felt ashamed.

She regretted the time she had done it with the 'old customer.' At the time, she had been like a girl, head over heels, not knowing north from south. She even forgot to remind the 'old customer' she was ovulating. The 'old customer' was in his prime of life, and he must have thought that a middle-aged woman would have some experience. Perhaps he even assumed she had on a contraceptive ring, so he shot with all his might, sending millions upon millions of wild chargers into Shui Qin's territory. But the sound of the hoofs told her that it was a huge mistake.

My brother said nothing. He continued sucking the mud fish, a large pile of skeletons in front of him.

'What will happen to Xianxian while I'm hospitalised? Will you ask your mother to come look after her?' Shui Qin said.

My brother grunted in agreement. 'I'll go back tomorrow morning to get them,' he said.

'Don't let your father know I'm sick,' but what she actually meant was, *don't let your father know I had an abortion.*

'If my mother knows, there's no way to keep my father from knowing,' Shunqiu said.

Chapter 44:

Li Xiaohan

The news had wings. It filled the air, firing the nation up and generating discussion about the C&R systems. Scholars jointly wrote letters, demanding an examination of the violation of the constitution in the Custody and Repatriation system.

Yu Shuzhong's office was filled with smoke. He chugged away at his cigarettes, as if the solution to the problem lay at the end, where the smoke clears. But the mountain range shrouded by the smoke was indistinct, its expression vague.

I stood at the door, in a dilemma. Yu waved away the smoke hovering before him. He said he was looking for me.

We sat by the coffee table, and he brewed a pot of fermented tea. Several old photos were added to the wall, taken during Yu's university days. My brother appeared in them. They looked quite different from today's university students; the gap was as obvious as that between the Tang dynasty and the Qing. In the space of just ten years, it was as if we had seen several dynastic changes.

'Once, Xiazhi brought a cake of fermented tea. It was harder than a brick. We had to use a hammer to knock the leaves loose,'

Yu said as he poured tea. 'Do you like the fermented tea from your hometown?'

'I don't know much about tea. As long as it can quench thirst, it's fine with me. But I don't like men in striped T-shirts, especially those with wide stripes.'

Yu looked at the shirt he was wearing. 'Are thin stripes acceptable?'

'T-shirts with wide stripes are funny. They either make you look Western, or like a country bumpkin. What you're wearing falls in between the two.'

'Rural-urban fringe zone?'

'The rural-urban fringe zone leans slightly towards town.'

'Even though you both came from the same mother, Xiazhi was kinder than you,' Yu said, laughing. 'But when Xiazhi criticised the current political situation, it was like he drove the nail so deep, it hit the bone.'

When we were small, Xiazhi had said that a gentleman would speak, but stay his hand, reasoning things out rather than resorting to force. But he said, words were like a stream of bullets, whizzing towards the bad guys. He would never have imagined his own ending.

'Didn't you quit smoking three months ago? Why are you smoking again now?' I was more concerned about the living Yu than I was about my deceased brother.

'Smoking is certainly not going to solve anything. I've got some good news and some bad news. Which do you want first?'

'The bad,' I said.

'I just had a meeting. In the Ma Lujia case, we've become peace-breakers, and were criticised and cursed. With the first report of the SARS incident, we're in big trouble. I might be transferred to a new post, and the *Today Newspaper* might become a walking corpse.'

'In Ma Lujia's death, we brought the criminals to justice. We set things right for an ordinary man. We took the lead in breaking through the forbidden zone of reporting on SARS, and we can round that off to be a good deed.'

'Also . . . they told me to fire you.'

I was caught off guard for a moment, then overjoyed. 'I never imagined an underling like me would be included in their net. It's an honour.'

'I won't dismiss a good journalist without an appropriate reason from them.'

'They don't need a reason for anything they do.'

'As long as I'm here, you stay,' Yu said.

I immediately recalled a stage line from wartime, *As long as I am here, the battlefield is here.* I almost blurted out, 'I'm your battlefield, but you've never fought on this battlefield,' and realised then that I had not had any romantic affairs in a long while.

I tilted my head and drank my tea, suppressing my confused thoughts. 'Tell me the good news,' I said.

'The good news is, the central leadership has already looked into the Ma Liujia case, and the shelter system will soon be abolished.'

I nearly slipped off my seat. I was completely shocked.

'I didn't expect it to be done so quickly either. This is from the Xinhua News Agency.' He handed me a copy of the report as he spoke.

The new prime minister convened a meeting of the State Council to discuss the abolition of the shelter system, and it was decided that action must be taken immediately.

I read the title.

'More than seven hundred shelters will be closed nationwide,' he said.

'You succeeded,' I replied.

'We succeeded.'

We should celebrate in bed. I didn't actually say that out loud.

'Now there is a new battle to be fought. Medical personnel will also contract SARS and die from it. We need brave reporters,' he said.

'As long as I'm on the battlefield, I'll work. I'll go.'

'Promise me you will be careful, no matter what happens.'

'If I am quarantined, you send me spicy crawfish. If I'm killed, you write my obituary.'

At that moment, I received a call from Yehe Nara. The C&R system had been abolished and she congratulated our paper on accomplishing a great feat. Because she was coughing, she was currently in the Xiao Tang Shan SARS quarantine area. Tang Linlu had worn a mask thirty-two layers thick in order to see her. Whether it was a misfortune or blessing, she finally had some quiet time to read *The Golden Lotus*. She talked about some matters coherently. In the end, she asked how my sex life was going.

I glanced at Yu. I said I was rereading *Love in the Time of Cholera*.

'Tang always boasts about your chief Yu. You haven't given that a try?'

'*Love in the Time of Cholera* is really better than *One Hundred Years of Solitude*.'

'I'm especially eager to find out if an idealistic youth is lustful.'

'The people's names in *One Hundred Years of Solitude* are too long.'

'Is it inconvenient for you to talk now?'

'Right, I'll be happy to let you know my views on it when I've finished reading.'

*

After three consecutive days of interviews at the hospital, I started coughing on the fourth day, and I had a slight headache. When I was working late that night, I suddenly got a high fever. Something roared inside me, and my walls collapsed.

SARS has found me, I thought. *I'm going to die. I'm not married, I have no children, and I've never experienced a real romance. The little ghosts will taunt me if I go to the grave like this.*

I was so frightened, I wanted to cry. But I forced myself to stay calm. I had just made a name for myself at the news agency in these past few days. It would be a terrible loss of face to fall apart now. On the way to the hospital, I joked with my colleagues, saying, 'If I die, I want everyone to burn spicy crawfish often as an offering to me. They surely won't have the real thing in hell.'

I thought about how Yu looked when he was so anxious his comb turned dark, and about the obvious difference in the frequency and magnitude of the heaving of his chest. He did not really look bad in thin-striped T-shirts. Each of his dimples was valued at a million dollars – and if I'd had any money at all, I would gladly have paid that price for him.

I thought my symptoms were not those of SARS. Most illnesses had similar clinical responses, but had different causes. It was lovesickness that gave me a high fever, depression and suppression that caused the illness. If Yu would just embrace and kiss me passionately, my fever would subside. Just one night of passion would make me a new person.

The fever made my mind more active. All sorts of legends were floating through my mind, and Yu was always the protagonist. I did not want to die. I was afraid being lovesick in hell would be like being grilled over a fire. Inwardly, I was extremely anxious, but in order to keep from making a fool of myself, I fell asleep on my way to the hospital. When I woke up, I saw a huge floral arrangement with a couplet hanging from it, like at a funeral. I thought I really had died. A few people in space-suits, and carrying oxygen tanks and wearing masks, surrounded me. I thought paradise was on the moon. Only when they spoke to me did I realise I was in a hospital ward on Earth. I had felt faint, and when I was admitted, I was shivering all over and my skin was so hot you could fry an egg on it.

Then Yu arrived. As he looked at me through the glass that enclosed the intensive care ward, I watched him discuss matters with the doctor. He rejected wearing the astronaut suit, refusing even to wear a mask. The doctor called a colleague over. They continued talking. The doctor lowered his head to think, looking very solemn. One of the doctors lifted a bottle and sprayed Yu all over, as if he were a pest. I envisioned an insect becoming dizzy amid the insecticide, then falling over and dying. I wanted to laugh, but a tear fell down my face.

The giant insect was not knocked over by the insecticide. He did not say anything, but just sat and looked at me.

'What do you feel like eating?' he asked.

You, is what I didn't say, at least not aloud. I just wiped the corners of my eyes and smiled.

'You're very popular now. The doctor said you won't be accepting any interviews.'

'I'm leaving them for myself.' I looked optimistic.

'Yes, there's no reporter better than Li Xiaohan. I'll give you a whole page. You can let go and write,' he said.

'Are you abusing your power for personal gains?' Yu's words made me guess how serious my situation was, and how few days I had left. My self-interview would be my posthumous work.

'I've been thinking about what I could do for you, but you do everything yourself.'

'I can't get what I really want.' I imagined my confession on my deathbed, pushing against my tear-ducts and flooding the twelve pipes. If I were a poet, I would also recite a love poem and leave it in his ear to be held for the rest of his life. He could hold onto this secret, deep, tragic love while he lived his mundane life, and his wife need never know.

Yu did not ask any further, which was sufficient evidence that he knew the meaning behind my words. Sick people and drunk people are the same, they say what they really mean. When you're going to die, you pour out all the rubbish you held inside all your life. That way, the burden of the spirit is unloaded and one is free to become a ghost.

'Some things that you attain at all cost may not be what you really want anyway.' He was an experienced person, after all.

'There's another possibility. You can make things clear,' I said.

'OK. You're the Ministry of Truth,' he said, not arguing with me.

'The Ministry of Truth specialised in manufacturing false news,' I said, not letting him off.

'George Orwells's Ministry of Truth collapsed.'

We laughed silently, and as gloomily as the ward. Everything was all white around us.

'I've got good news and bad news. Which do you want first?' he asked.

'Bad.'

'They're trying to get the courts to clean up the *Today Newspaper*.'

'The defendant's stand has an outstanding offender. Greatness can withstand judgement,' I said.

'The knife won't fall on stone. They know where to strike a blow.'

'Do we have financial problems?' I asked.

'He who has a mind to beat his dog will easily find a stick.'

'The whole world is watching. They can't do anything underhanded,' I said. 'What's the good news?'

'The good news is that our colleagues at the News Department are waiting to meet their new director, Li Xiaohan.'

Getting the appointment at that moment was like adding on to a martyr. It increased the ominous feeling inside me. *I was going to die.*

Chapter 45:

Li Chuntian, Elder Sister

The five- or six-square-metre single room had been converted from a warehouse. There was no toilet and no kitchen, and only a small window allowed in the slightest shimmer of light. Rent was 100 *yuan* a month. My sister had pasted a layer of newspaper on the walls. Down the centre of the room, she had run a rope on which she could dry clothes. Zhima and Chuntian had acquired some pots and pans, and an induction cooker. Their little room was like a tiny sparrow equipped with all the necessary components. When she cooked, the sound of her spatula hitting the wok was loud. When she fried peppers, she could hear the neighbours coughing over and over, but anyway, everyone needed to eat.

Occasionally there was laughter, like a bird bursting from its cage and settling on a tree. The neighbours came and went, asking this or that. All of them were villagers, so they naturally felt quite close. As they mixed with their neighbours, they soon knew what cost least, what was most profitable, and where the risks lay. Zhima had shed blood. He had received his wages and, now that his body was recovering, he was actively planning for his new life. He decided to sell kebabs. He would first work as an apprentice, so he could learn the ropes.

Chuntian continued working at the teahouse for a while. Sun did not take other women there anymore and, in fact, seldom went there himself. Chuntian guarded the teahouse like it was her turf. She had won, but the victory was a little boring. The city was so big, so there was no lack of places for Sun Xiangxi to fool around. Before long, Zhima mastered the barbecuing process and got his stove and charcoal ready. My sister would quit working at the teahouse, and when he was ready to venture out, she would start working with him, selling kebabs.

On the day she meant to resign, Sun showed up at the teahouse, looking for Chuntian. He wanted to take her to the riverside to eat live fish. He did not mention where he had been all this time, nor what the hell he had been doing. She said, 'You didn't reply to my texts and didn't answer my calls. I assumed you were dead.'

Sun asked, 'When did you call?' He quickly pulled out his phone, and then spread his hands. 'Oh, my phone fell into the toilet a few days ago. I just had it repaired, so a lot of the information was lost. Also, I had to go to Beijing.'

Chuntian said, 'You can find someone else to take care of your last minute "crotch time" now. Don't come looking for me anymore. My husband beats people up blindly.'

Sun pretended to be furious, 'He hit you again?'

She laughed silently, then said, 'You are so pale and delicate. I'm afraid if he raised a fist at you, you'd be reduced to tofu residue.'

It was beginning to dawn on him what she meant. For a moment, he could not believe she would leave him. He always thought she was dead set on him and would allow him to fool around with her.

'Chuntian, if you start to regret your choice, you can always come back to me. I'll be here for you.'

She had seen such performances many times before. She was no longer impressed.

Fortunately, she had Zhima as an excuse. If not, it would have been difficult to get rid of Sun. It wasn't that he loved her, but that he felt it was a real loss of face to be ditched by a woman from the village.

On the way home, Chuntian let out a huge sigh. She almost cried several times, but she managed to force back her tears.

Zhima was preparing bamboo skewers and placing them all around basins and baskets. He was working alone, and working quite hard.

'Are you going to open your stall so soon?' she asked.

'There's a big movie being released at the cinema today. There will be a lot of people. Let's give it a try and see how it goes.'

Zhima had even given careful consideration to the location. He was worthy to be called someone with experience in the world.

Chuntian found a stool to sit on and started skewering leeks, mushrooms, chicken gizzards, tendon slabs, lamb, and bread.

'A lot of people use rat meat or the meat from dead cats sprinkled with cow urine to pass off as mutton. We have to have the real deal. We might earn less, but we'll let word-of-mouth advertising do the trick.'

Zhima had even done market research. Apparently, he was quite a genius.

Chuntian said, 'We need to have peace of mind as we earn money, then we can sleep easily at night.'

'Yeah. And once the word gets around, we can save a bit of capital. We can get a small shop front then. You'll be the boss.' He had a long-term plan.

'You really think big, don't you? Let's not start daydreaming just yet. If we do enough to get by, that will be good.'

Chuntian was afraid Zhima was getting overly eager. She thought it best she pours a bit of cold water over him.

'What do you mean? We can get a bunch of leeks for one *yuan*, enough for at least twenty skewers. If we sell each skewer for half a *yuan*, you do the math. How much will we earn?'

'I'm just afraid no one will want it.'

'How could that be? There are bamboo sticks on the ground everywhere. People have obviously been eating grilled food, or they wouldn't have discarded the sticks here.'

Chuntian thought about it. She gained confidence and her hands worked harder.

At dusk, she and Zhima pulled their wooden handcart to a spot across from the cinema and started their charcoal fire. Smoke danced above the flames. A group of primary school students came over, their first batch of customers.

Chapter 46:

Liu Yihua, Niece

Liuzi's case was settled quickly, and the main perpetrator, Qiao Feiyan, was shot. Many others were sentenced, and a bunch was given their dismissal notices. Yihua did not come to see me any more. She had good looks, but did not know how to use a computer or how to speak English, and she had no skills. Was there any more suitable place for her than a nightclub? I imagined her lending her lustre to the assembly line at some factory. Apart from sexual harassment from her boss, factory manager and the like, generally I felt it would be a waste of her youth. She would be worn down in a matter of years, and that would truly be a regret. The good fortune to attain the right path seemed to elude innocent girls like her who had nothing besides their looks. They were born to be property.

I did not interfere in Yihua's affairs. After all, every plant must grow in its own way.

When it comes to repaying a favour owed, a noble person will always keep her promises. Yihua's path was not destined to be anything ordinary. She took the initiative to contact Hu Lilai to settle her debt with him. No lion will let a deer just pass by in his line of sight – Lilai only hesitated for a few seconds before pouncing.

Early on, Yihua had figured that if she gave her first time to Lilai, that would be worth more than ten times in compensation, and Lilai would not be able to give her change, so she thought she would have to find someone else to be her first. The fellow she found was a white man, around thirty years old. He could not speak Chinese, but was very gentlemanly, not like the Chinese men who touched and pinched the girls all over as they laughed wretchedly. His name was Mike, and he kind of looked like the character Michael in *The Godfather*. It was rather a novel idea to allow a foreigner to take her chastity overseas to distant lands all over the world, like carrying off some small daughter she never had a chance to meet. Yihua chose him. In bed, he treated her gently, as if she really was his lover. They did not speak – did not make any noises – even remaining silent as they climaxed. It was like struggling with a disease, bearing it patiently, though it was unbearably painful.

When they had finished, Mike poured two glasses of red wine. Yihua could not move. She felt her body had been torn into a ragged cloth, fluttering in the wind. She lay in bed for half an hour, looking at the banknotes on the pillow beside her. She mustered her strength, got dressed, smoothed her hair, and felt like she had been reborn. There, with Mike, was her first time. She was at peace. She left the money, and even said 'thank you' as she walked out.

She did not have small change for a taxi, so she went to a small shop, bought a bottle of water, and got some change. She felt both liberated and relieved.

Lilai took Yihua straight to his house. He lived in a two-story home, and there was a plot of land full of banana trees in front of the door. She could hear his mother coughing inside. His room was upstairs. Clothes were strewn everywhere, and it smelled like someone had spent all his time jerking off in there.

As she took off her clothes, she asked, 'Do you want to do ten times separately, or finish it all today?'

Lilai said, 'Depends on the situation.'

Yihua lay down, then said, 'Let's do it all today. Your house is far away. Let's save on travel costs.'

Lilai was in a rush, crying out almost as soon as they had started. After ten minutes, he started again. This time he showed more restraint, going slowly, and even trying to get Yihua to participate. When he had finished the second time, he decided to save the remaining times for a later date. If he gobbled up everything at once, he might later find himself hungry with nothing to consume. But in the end, he could not hold back, and before he knew it, he had used up five times.

Yihua actually climaxed. She was surprised, but also disdainful. Climaxing changed the quality of the relationship. She was no longer returning a favour. She should not do that. It was blaspheming Liuzi's name.

But Yihua's body felt good. After the tenth time, she continued to see Lilai. He told his mother Yihua was his girlfriend. The old woman was so happy, she kept having asthma attacks. Yihua sometimes brought small gifts for her. Lilai's mother was quite satisfied and urged him to marry Yihua, giving his mother a chance to receive a cup of tea from her daughter-in-law's hand at the wedding ceremony before she died. Lilai told Yihua, but she said did not want to get married and have kids. She had many things she still wanted to do.

Putting aside his mother's wishes, Lilai said he would wait for her. His feelings for her ran deep, and he did not want to marry anyone but her.

This was a threat. Yihua knew she would have to be vigilant.

Chapter 47:

Liu Zhima, Brother-in-law

Zhima set up his stall. As he fanned the charcoal fire, sparks burst into the air. My sister acted as his assistant, taking out spices, propping up the foldable stool, hoping that the thin and deflated waist pouch would be inflated by the time they closed shop at midnight.

The couple chatted as they worked. Chuntian said, 'Yicao was eighth in the placement test. Maybe our house will produce a female university student. This ball-breaker, she doesn't even work hard at her studies . . . If she would just put forth a little more effort, she might even do as well as Xiaohan and study in Beijing.'

Zhima was more concerned about his kebabs. 'We better cover these or ash will fall onto them.'

My sister put gauze over the kebabs. 'What's the big deal, even if a little ash gets on them? It's like that's more important than your offspring.'

Zhima said, 'The ash will affect the taste. The spawn in Yiyang is big, so it doesn't taste good. If they don't taste nice, people won't come back to us, and they won't bring others to come with them.'

Of course, my sister agreed, but she just wanted to talk a little about Yicao. The girl was dating young, and did not emulate good habits. Once, Chuntian even saw her smoking. If she would just test well enough to get into university, my sister would leave her to her vices.

Zhima was more accepting of the situation. 'Don't bother about things you can do nothing about. Even when she gets married and has kids, they won't be in the Liu family. We may not even see them. What do they really have to do with us? Parents are like distant relatives, if even that.'

Chuntian thought about her own relationship with her own immediate family. Wasn't it just as Zhima had described?

A couple of young fellows came to the stall and ordered a bunch of kebabs and some beer. Chuntian got up and went to the canteen to buy the beer. When she came back a couple of minutes later, the stall seemed to have been crashed by wild horses, with the charcoal and sparks spread all over the ground. The small foldable stool had been thrown far away, and the young people were helping to pick up the sticks.

'What happened?' she asked.

'The city inspectors came,' Zhima said.

'For what? Why did they overturn everything?' She bent over to pick up the kebabs, as if they were their own currency.

'They said they won't be so nice next time they see us.' Zhima took the charcoal in his tongs and put it back in the stove. He turned to the young people and said, 'I cook only with non-toxic green carbon. My lamb kebabs are all genuine. If you don't find me here next time, I'll be somewhere nearby. Anyway, I'll always be in the area.'

One young man said, 'It's best if you have a lookout. When they see the city inspector's car, you can quickly pack up and go.'

The second added, 'You should hide the kebabs. That way, even if you are a little too late, you won't lose much. Sometimes they might even take away your grill with the kebabs.'

The first one replied, 'True. You'll have to learn to play cat and mouse with the city inspectors, then you can really be an outstanding kebab guerrilla troop.'

The kebabs were delicious. They said they would be back.

*

Listening to the young men's advice, the first thing my sister and Zhima did any time they reached a spot to sell was hide the kebabs among nearby bushes, only taking them out when someone placed an order. The foldable stool, stove, seasoning tins, and brushes were not worth much money, so there was no real harm losing them. Chuntian was responsible for handling the money, taking the kebabs from the bushes, and serving as a lookout. The weather was quite mild, and the curtain of night was like silk, embroidered with stars. The charcoal fire and light smoke danced happily.

Even on such a harmonious and peaceful night, Chuntian never let down her guard. She looked about her, eventually developing outstanding instincts, to the point that even if she was not at the stall, she was habitually on the lookout. They successfully avoided the city inspectors, always escaping unscathed. Every time Zhima boasted to others, he described it in quite thrilling terms, as if he and his wife were agile martial arts masters, the Barbecue Knights. As soon as the city inspectors' vehicle left the spot, the Knights landed lightly on the ground and continued cooking. The customers who had been temporarily scattered would gather around like onlookers and resume drinking, laughing, and talking, as if the false alarm had all been a performance to add excitement to the diners' evening out.

Zhima was good at coaxing people in, and he had developed a large corps of regular customers. Some would start calling when they were a long way off, 'lamb kebabs,' 'roasted bread,' 'aubergine,' or 'crisp chicken bones,' as if they were calling Liu Zhima's name. They received orders by phone too, from people who were drinking at home and were too lazy to get out. When business was good, the couple was so busy they could barely cope.

On this particular night, Zhima's hands had been going nonstop, and his legs were numb from standing too long. Chuntian's waist pouch had long ago filled to the brim.

'Did Yicao finish her exams? Ask the ball-breaker to come help tomorrow night,' Zhima said.

'Let her relax for a few days. She's exhausted from her studies,' Chuntian said, protecting Yicao.

Zhima and my sister liked to call Yicao 'ball-breaker,' just like many women called their sons 'smelly son of a bitch,' or some women called their men 'one who deserves to be chopped to a thousand pieces.' Such phrases were not to be taken for their literal meanings, but contained some special affection.

Zhima did not have time to argue. He had a cycle going, roasting mutton as he sprinkled oil, sending sparks flying. He was afraid of Yicao, this 'ball-breaker,' who also encouraged her mother to pursue a divorce. He liked his daughter, but he really could not handle her.

Chuntian was even more determined to work hard, like she wanted to make up for Yicao's share, too.

At around eleven o'clock, my brother pulled up to the stall on his motorcycle.

'Something's happened,' he said. 'Pack up your stall.'

'Business is just picking up. What's so urgent?' Zhima asked.

They could not make out if Shunqiu was trying to tell them,

or trying hard not to say what had happened. His expression was complete chaos.

'Did something happen to Shui Qin?' Chuntian asked, thinking of Shui Qin's illness.

'You . . . you two need to be prepared . . .' my brother stammered. 'It's Yicao. She . . .'

'What has she done now?' Zhima said.

'She jumped,' Shunqiu answered.

My sister and Zhima were shocked.

'She jumped from the tenth floor of the hotel. Dead on impact,' Shunqiu said.

'There must be a mistake. Our Yicao might do a lot of things, but she wouldn't commit suicide,' Zhima said, as if trying to convince himself.

'She was in a bar with four male classmates, celebrating her freedom after taking the college entrance exam. They went to a hotel and got a room together. It's quite likely she was . . . harmed by someone.' Shunqiu was careful not to use the words *gang rape*. 'The police are still investigating.'

My sister's legs gave way under her. She plopped down to the ground.

Just then, there was a screech of brakes. The city inspectors descended, and a few burly men dashed over. Without a word, they started overturning things. Spurred by the news of Yicao's death, Zhima's reaction became abnormal, and he was desperate to protect those worthless belongings. At first he just objected, but a fight soon broke out.

My brother had been at the losing end of fights, so he didn't dare help now. He squatted helplessly to one side, shivering.

My sister shouted, 'Zhima, forget it. Don't fight. Let them do what they want.'

Even if he didn't want to fight, Zhima had no choice by this point. He was knocked to the ground, and three or four people kicked him and stomped on him. One jumped on him with both feet, stomping on his head.

Chuntian howled fiercely. Pulling at them, she said, 'He just recovered, he can't take all this beating. I beg you, let him go.'

Chuntian was shoved to the ground.

Zhima did not resist further. He curled up and covered himself as best he could, letting them get on with it.

He was not moving. It was like he was dead.

They stopped beating him then. They spread out. One of them bent over to check on Zhima, to see whether he was still breathing.

Zhima suddenly raised himself up, stabbing the guy. No one could tell what sort of weapon he had in his hand.

The body of the city inspector convulsed and trembled as he lifted his head. Everyone saw something jutting out below his lower jaw.

It was a bamboo skewer, rammed into his throat.

Chapter 48:

Li Xiaohan

As I lay dying, I wrote a final letter. Its style was optimistic and its content bright. This was not at all contrived. I really did face my own death without any regret, and did not know what I would do with myself if I lived. I had no interest in my new position at work and had no real aspirations. When it came to being married and the life after that, I had no clue at all. I was used to making a living amid adversity.

My last letter was quite long. I tried to persuade my father to apologise to my sister, and I asked my mother to unashamedly dry her newly washed underclothes in the sun. I wanted my brother to know how extraordinary he was, and wanted Yicao to study history, master a foreign language, and learn to play a musical instrument. I told Yihua not to gamble with her body, and to beware of the devil. Finally, I mentioned Yu Shuzhong, represented only by the letter Y. I said love was my private matter, and I felt no need to let him know my feelings. A person's love will never be invaded by bacteria; it has nothing to do with mundane things, and there will not come a day when we see its residue at the bottom of the cup and feel disappointed.

But I did not die. I did not tear up my 'final note,', either. Instead, I wanted to copy it with a brush and mount it on the wall as a way of encouraging myself. Life after my sickness was a trial. I was not loyal to the ideals of my final note, itching to have a go when I was with Yu and trying to test him or provoke him. In my final note, I had hypocritically sublimated myself, and was insincere in the part about love. In fact, I hated one-side affections, crushes, unrequited love, or seeing little of each other even though we were in close proximity. Any love two people could not simultaneously participate in was deformed. And to call it love was a disgrace to love, just as you could not call masturbation 'making love.'

Early that morning, Yu picked me up from the hospital and drove me straight to the Pearl River. Boats were floating in the river, and we walked along the banks. The beard and eyebrows of old banyan trees dragged on the grounds. The river was wide. My heart was full of love. For the first time, I felt Guangzhou was not so bad. Yu's breath was like a crawfish, reaching out with its countless fine, soft hands to entangle me. I controlled my own urge to embrace him.

When we came upon another banyan tree, without a word, he suddenly took me in his arms. My heart immediately felt like a group of sparrows caught in a net, turning into a messy collision. The crowded sparrows were noisy, struggling with each other, but also amicably stroking one another's feathers.

It was difficult for me to extract myself from our embrace. His body seemed to be expanding its territory, and a seed burst from the ground, instantly strong.

I raised my head to kiss him. He avoided it. My kiss fell on his cheek.

'Why?' I asked.

'For me, it is enough that you are still alive. Anything more than that is a luxury,' he answered.

'I don't mind.'

'She minds.'

His answer made me feel ashamed.

I pressed my crotch against the seed that had sprouted in his groin. 'It disagrees.'

'I'll have to keep it in check.' He kissed my cheek and loosened his hold on me.

I was like a deserted island, lonelier than I had been before he embraced me.

We walked in silence for a while. There were plenty of people out doing their morning exercises. The birds chased each other beside the river.

'They're collecting evidence against me everywhere. Yesterday, one of our advertisers told me the police went to her office. They were especially interested in learning whether there were any irregular financial dealings between me and our clients. In fact, all the big advertising clients that have dealings with our newspaper office are being investigated,' Yu said, breaking the silence.

'This attack is a diversionary tactic, a distraction from the real attack.' I was back to reality, as if I had just walked out of a warm living room.

'We won't have any problem,' he said. 'Our only problems are that we are too sharp and too brave.'

'If the leading bird is shot, it's better for the rest of us to just bury our heads in the sand and think with our arses.'

Laughing, Yu said, 'They want to detain me for suspected financial offences, for privately dividing state-owned assets. You know, 100 000 *yuan* was the newspaper's bonus, and it was all legal income. They had to let me go.'

'They won't give up until they get you.'

'I don't have any issues – unless they choose to dig up old accounts, of course.'

'What old accounts?'

'The year Xiazhi died, a lot of things happened.'

I knew what he meant.

I thought of many things in that moment. Finally, I imagined Yu in jail, a fallen hero captured, and his wife abandoning him. My passion for him would not change. I would visit him every day –

'I always wanted to marry a hero,' I said.

'I hope our generation doesn't need heroes, and that everyone can just live happily as ordinary citizens.'

'You want me to be a spinster?' I asked, revealing a fear I seldom admitted even to myself.

'The sooner you sober up, the sooner you'll get married,' Yu said, a double-edged remark.

Chapter 49:

Xiao Shui Qin, Sister-in-law

Zhima had not intended to take a life, but the bamboo stick he had wielded had not had eyes, and even though he had not intended it, the blow was a fatal one. The police handcuffed him. When he asked to see his daughter's body, they rejected the request. He wept as he walked away, staggering along a crooked path as if he were drunk.

I got word of what had happened and hurried back. My mother wept the most bitterly, and my sister seemed to be inventing all sorts of ways of expressing her grief that went beyond just weeping. She was like a scientist lost deep in thought. Yihua sat with her mother, looking a little dumbfounded.

At first, there were two theories about how Yicao had died. One said she had committed suicide for the sake of love. The other was that she had jumped because she could not bear the humiliation after being gang-raped. The school was pushing for the argument that she had committed suicide for the sake of love, hoping to preserve the reputation of the school with this explanation, and to contain the influence of the act while the officials settled matters quietly. Four boys confessed to drinking until they lost control, and to forcing Yicao to have sex with them. The school said the students were usually excellent both in studies and behaviour, and that the pressure of high school had been too great. They had used the wrong approach to let off steam, and they hoped to receive leniency. The mothers of the four boys came as a group to my sister, begging for mercy and offering to pay whatever price my sister asked as compensation. My sister said honestly that the state had its laws, and that there was nothing she could do about it.

Our family lacked the ability to console anyone else. Each person managed his or her own grief well and did not lose control. My mother cried for a while, then calmed down. She remembered that it was time to cook, and she needed to go to the shop to buy meat and to pick vegetables from the back garden. My father picked up his fishing nets and spread them on the pond, catching two grass carp. Soon, the kitchen was full of noise, and my sister instinctively joined in, preparing delicious food for the reunion of those family members who were still alive.

After the thunderstorm, a cloud of fire rose over the horizon, as if a giant wound had opened in the celestial body and a blood-red glow flowed across the sky. The ground was bathed in gold, warm and bright. It was completely unlike the human world which had just undergone a tragedy.

Shui Qin had just finished her first round of short-term treatment. Her family rushed over before lunch. Xianxian was dressed in Western-style clothing, like a city girl. She occasionally showed how pampered she was.

My father kept his face straight as a board, but not because of Yicao's tragedy. She was a daughter of the Liu household and had nothing to do with the Li family's fortunes. Rather, he was angry with Shui Qin. She had acted on her own, aborting the Li family's offspring, and ended up with this lingering illness. The cancer was a punishment from the ancestors, her just reward.

My brother went about things cautiously, trying his best not to make a sound. He picked up a chicken's foot and sat alone in the corner gnawing on it, then swallowing the crushed bones. The yellow dog lurking nearby went away disappointed.

For a while, we did not speak at all, or spoke only about Guangzhou. Xianxian had many questions, and she was filled with curiosity about the outside world. She was smart and lively, and would not tolerate a perfunctory answer, so I had to give her my full attention. She asked what Yihua did in Guangzhou, and expressed her frustration that she could not immediately grow up herself. Yihua lowered her head and turned her attention to extracting the meat from a fishbone. I replied, 'Your cousin is a line leader in a factory. A line leader is a group leader in charge of one production line.'

Xianxian said she wanted to go somewhere even further away. She wanted to go to a university in the US, and she wanted to bring her grandparents travelling in the States.

Shui Qin sat quietly. This was the dream she had lit in Xianxian. She could not snuff it out now. But the dream was like a balloon that had escaped from her hand and was currently drifting further and further away. She had to catch hold of the string again.

Shui Qin had thickened her skin and gone to speak to her 'old customer.' She had hoped he might offer some financial support on account of their night of passion, since he was, after all, the cause of the incident.

The old customer laughed uncontrollably. He said, 'You sleep with your husband every day. How can you say I'm the one who knocked you up?'

Throwing away any semblance of dignity, she did not hold

back. 'He's in poor health. We haven't slept together in more than six months.'

'If your husband will say that to me himself, I'll believe you.'

The old customer had her there. There was no way she would tell her own husband she had slept with another man.

Thinking of Xianxian's future, she said, 'If you really want, Shunqiu will come and tell you in person.'

The old customer said, 'Even if Shunqiu is willing to be made a cuckold, it just means you two are conspiring to frame me.'

She said, 'You can't behave like this. That's heartless.'

He said, 'I'll just pay you for that night, then. How much do you want?'

'I'm not a whore,' Shui Qin retorted.

'Where's the difference?'

She was enraged. 'Give me 10 000 *yuan*.'

The old customer said, 'Even a virgin doesn't cost that much.'

'That's my price,' she said.

The old customer pulled 1000 *yuan* from his wallet and placed it in front of Shui Qin. 'Be realistic. Your market price is at most 200.'

To simplify her complex feelings, it was best to treat this like a transaction. Shui Qin was humiliated and felt annoyed, so she simply lowered herself and treated this old customer as a john to whom she had made a sale. At any rate, she had slept with him; there was no need to erect a memorial archway. As she accepted 1000 *yuan,* she suddenly felt enlightened. She had inadvertently found a way of making money. If her body couldn't do it, she could use her hand or mouth. That didn't count as selling herself. It was just paid labour, like tailoring or working in the fields. One always got paid for one's labour, and that had nothing to do with morality or chastity.

Disgusted with her own train of thought, Shui Qin put down her bowl and chopsticks and went into the washroom. She lathered her hands with soap and started to wash slowly. She brushed her teeth, up and down, back and forth, inside and out, vigorously. As she scrubbed, in her mind there suddenly emerged a constant stream of wild rabbits, emerging from trouser crotches. Their ears stood erect. They were wretched, ugly creatures, and their animal odour assailed one's nostrils.

She was always washing, scrubbing, and brushing in this manner. We all assumed it was part of her prescribed treatment.

Chapter 50:

Liu Yihua, Niece

The death of a young girl is like bait, attracting all sorts of fish. They surround it, take measure of it, poke at it, and discuss it, spitting bubbles all the while. They are suspicious, thoughtful, curious, and secretly excited. For those several days, our home was like an exhibition hall. The viewers brought their families, coming in and out. When they had viewed the free exhibition, they dawdled beside me and Yihua, offering a variety of praises and asking quietly about the outside world, particularly inquiring whether we could help their idle children find a way out. Regardless of whether or not we promised to help, they showered us with gifts. We barely escaped having them bring livestock into our courtyard. Some of them came to my mother, begging for her help. Because of her relationship with her neighbours, my mother asked me to see what I could do. I said, 'If they don't have the academic qualifications, I can't help.'

She replied, 'Isn't Yihua doing just fine?'

I said, 'She has some assets.'

Ever vigilant, my mother said, 'Tell me the truth. What is Yihua doing in Guangzhou?'

I told her, 'She's a decent girl. She's not doing anything bad.'

My mother's sorrow seemed to multiply before my eyes. She knew what sort of jobs required girls with 'assets.' Those from neighbouring villages who did not have academic qualifications but had assets were working at bars in Shenzhen, showing cleavages, lips painted blood red, and eyes painted jet black.

Yihua was humiliated that I had concealed her real occupation. She felt it was upright work, and there was no need to lie about it.

'I'm not a line leader. I work in a nightclub. I sell drinks and accompany customers while they drink. You can sleep with the customers if you want, but if you don't want to, no one forces you to do it. That's the situation. Wherever a person is, she can go wrong. When it comes down to it, it all depends on the person,' she said loudly.

The person who had come to ask for help was slightly embarrassed, and the faces of our family members went paler than ever. That night, my mother and sister had a talk with Yihua. Chuntian said, 'Why did you have to publicize your work in a nightclub?'

My mother said, 'First of all, you shouldn't have gone to a place like that. Who knows what sort of disease you might contract?'

The two older women's advice was humiliating, like a whip striking Yihua's face. She tolerated and tolerated, on account of their bereavement and suffering. In the end, she could not stand it anymore. She finally let loose.

'I do honest work. What have I done wrong? You two never bothered about me before. Just continue doing that, and leave me to live my own life. So what if I work in a nightclub? It's much cleaner than the work I could do elsewhere! Do you think bureaucrats are clean? Or people who work nine to five? Does carrying a briefcase make someone clean? Do you think "decency" means "clean"? You're wrong. You don't understand me. It's for the best that you never do.

'You all live in this small place, never going out. You only see the superficial good or bad of things. You jump to conclusions. You don't even know what's going on in the world. I'm a bull in the open field. Why do you want to bother about me now?

'Why didn't you take Yicao in hand before it was too late? She was smoking, drinking, and fooling around with boys. Didn't you know I had put all my hope in her? You go and look. See how many letters I wrote her and how many books I sent back. None of you cared at all about what I had become, as long as I didn't make you lose face!'

My sister and mother were speechless.

Yihua felt like crying, but she also felt crying was no use. None of her tragedies could compare with Yicao's death.

Chapter 51:

Xiao Shui Qin, Sister-in-law

The telephone pole half blocked Xiao Shui Qin. The fourth man that evening passed by.

'Hand job, fifty *yuan*. Blow job, eighty. Old customers get a 10 per cent discount,' Shui Qin popped those words out of her mouth suddenly. The fourth man looked like he had been hit by a stone. He suddenly stopped and looked at her, not understanding what she had said, though in the sultry night air, he could easily guess with 80 or 90 per cent accuracy.

Shui Qin's eyes lit up. What she saw was not a man, but money. She wanted to seize every banknote that passed before her and integrate it into her account. She had calculated that based on the number of men in Yiyang, if each one took just one hand job or blow job from her, she could earn enough to send Xianxian overseas to study. But most of these men were quite stingy, or their sex drive was not strong enough, or perhaps they had their needs met elsewhere. They held on to their noble sentiments, only making deposits in their own wives' accounts or their lovers' passbooks. They had very little interest in a 'craftsman' of Shui Qin's sort.

Tonight was an exception. The fourth man followed Shui Qin into an alley. He chose the eighty *yuan* package, but paid her 100.

He looked good – clean, and somewhat cultured. Before he got excited, he chatted with her, saying, 'I know you must have run into hard times. . . you'll do anything to survive.'

Shui Qin squatted in front of him and said to his lower body, 'You're a good man.'

'Is business good?'

She pulled the thing out, as if pulling out a carrot from the ground. 'I can't talk while I work.'

He shut up. Looking down, he uttered quiet moans. Before long, his mouth was crooked, his eyes moving sideways, and he looked up and cried out.

He pulled up his zipper and tidied his clothes. 'I think all men should do this, helping a woman in difficult times, no matter through what means.'

'This is my phone number.' Shui Qin handed him a business card. It read: *Flowers Reservation: Lady Thatcher*. She used this pseudonym at work.

The way the fourth man talked nauseated her, but she appreciated his patronage.

Late that night, Shui Qin cleaned herself up and went to bed. Her hands were tired, and her mouth felt like it was still holding something.

*

My brother came home early in the morning. He wanted Shui Qin to give him 500 *yuan* to give to the family of his friend Li Ganzi, who had just passed away.

Ganzi had died while he was fishing in the pond. He was carrying an electric prod. It was unclear whether it was suicide or an accident, but it didn't matter, really. Either way, he was dead. Since he had got out of prison, he had not found a wife, but lived alone, sleeping each long night on a bed made of bricks, poor and dirty. After my brother moved into the city, the two had rarely met.

Shui Qin said, 'Five hundred *yuan* is a lot. You two were just regular friends, so 200 should be enough.'

My brother said quietly, 'A few of us talked about it and decided we would each give 500. That will at least cover the cost of a coffin. If I only give 200, it will be unacceptable.'

Shui Qin curled her lip. 'A favour given to other people can still be returned to you. A favour used on Li Ganzi's body will come to nought. We aren't rich. Ganzi's ghost will understand.'

My brother said nothing. As usual, he could not persuade Shui Qin. Lacking this ability, he merely dawdled, waiting for her to change her mind.

Every time money was extracted, it was like carving on Shui Qin's heart. This was especially true since her illness – her heart was covered with scars from the various extractions made to cover her medical fees. She wished silk could be made without the need to feed the silkworms, and she wished she could eat once every three days instead of three times a day.

In the end, Shui Qin gave my brother 300 *yuan*. Not wanting to lose face, he secretly went and borrowed an additional 200 from others.

*

The words 'reformed prisoner' were written all over the demeanour of Li Ganzi's corpse when it was recovered from the water. Shunqiu carried the coffin, his legs shaking beneath Ganzi's weight. Many thoughts came alive in his head, *Ganzi was forever living in prison. He never really came out. What about me?*

Shunqiu bowed his head, sweat falling from his body onto the soil beneath him. He thought of Shui Qin, wondering which man she had been with. He felt sorrowful for a while, then unconsciously became proud of her. *Wang Mazi's woman is always smoking and playing cards. Zhang Niujing's woman is always lazy. Li Banjin's woman is always running back to her parent's house. . . They aren't half the woman Shui Qin is. Ah, she's a good woman. Diligent, deft, organised. If I didn't have her, this family would have collapsed long ago. . .*

The coffin came to a stop at the pit's edge. Loess showered down, and several strange birds screamed as they flew across the sky. Children stood by, watching this final scene. The brawny men took hold of the ropes and let the coffin descend slowly, then started to shovel. A new grave quickly emerged from the ground as they piled the soil on top of it.

My brother broke a pine branch and inserted it into the soil at the tip of the mound.

Chapter 52:

Liu Yihua, Niece

When Yicao's university admission notice was received, it was like seeing her remains. The family was thrown into sadness once again but, at the same time, their outlook on life did not change. Life went on as usual.

Yicao's death most impacted Yihua. Something inside Yihua had died with her sister. It was like her support had been taken away, and now the whole body slackened. She changed, and became uninhibited. Returning to Guangzhou after her sister's death, she no longer simply sang or sold drinks, and she went beyond sitting on the guests' laps, too. She now spent the night with them, taking their money before she left in the morning. Neither sad nor happy, she simply disappeared from their lives without a trace.

In the private rooms, Yihua was like everyone else, wearing long, black muslin gowns, standing in a row. They were dark or pale, their skin peeping through their gowns, all there for the guests' choosing. The girls wore badges on their breasts, displaying their work numbers instead of names. Yihua was Number Eight. The girl who used to be Number Eight had gotten married and was a mother now. Yihua had replaced her.

On this night, Lu Mingliang had brought the girls into a private room, and they arranged themselves in a line. Four or five men sat on the sofa, puffing on their cigarettes and whispering in each other's ear. They looked like hawkers with bulging waist pouches, preparing to take away a robust, sexy young cow.

Mingliang whispered in Yihua's ear, 'I'm getting ready to resign.'

'Why?'

'I am going to have a baby.'

'Whose is it? That truck driver, Han?'

'Yes. He said that after my son is born, we'll settle in Hong Kong.'

'He has a wife. Don't be cheated by him.' Yihua was straight-forward. 'I don't quite trust Han.'

While they were whispering, Yihua was selected. They had to call 'Number Eight' a second time before she snapped to alertness. She walked over and sat next to the man who was waving to her. She poured him a glass of wine and clinked her glass to his, feeling very much at home.

Mingliang was chosen as well. She did not look well. As soon as she had had a couple of beers, she ran to the washroom. Yihua followed her and saw her leaning over the toilet bowl, retching.

'If you're not feeling well, don't drink. Go home and rest.' Yihua caught her loose long hair and pulled it back.

'I'm pregnant,' Mingliang said, raising her head. 'I can't keep doing this.'

'Are you sure it's Han's?' Yihua asked.

'Of course it is,' Mingliang replied.

'Tell him to get you out of here quickly.'

'He's already arranged a place for me to live. . . At first, I wanted to finish this month, then go.' Mingliang wiped her mouth.

'If I were you, I wouldn't stay another day,' Yihua said. 'You mean you can't bear to leave?'

'If I say yes, you can't laugh at me,' said Mingliang. 'He only comes by once in a long while. I'm used to a lively scene. I'll feel stifled living alone.'

'You're not alone. You've got the baby in your belly. You've got to think of him.' Yihua tidied Mingliang's hair, then helped her out of the washroom.

*

At one o'clock in the morning, Lilai was waiting for Yihua at the door of the nightclub. He walked back and forth under a tree, occasionally glancing at the entrance of the club. The red neon light blinked on and off, alternating between lighting and darkening his face. The effect was like a film montage.

Yihua finally appeared. She was only lightly made up, and her hair was tied high on her head in a bun. Her skin was tight and glowing. A gust of wind blew at her long sky blue spaghetti-strapped dress. She had consumed a fair bit of alcohol and was a little drunk. She fell onto Lilai, giggling. She alternated between several poses, as if propositioning a stranger. Lilai carried her and put her on the motorcycle in front of him, wrapping his arms around her. He started the engine and accelerated. The motorcycle roared away at top speed in a cloud of dust, heading to the night market for a late night supper.

Business in the market in Guangzhou did not slow down even in the early morning. Weary young people sat beside the stalls, continuing to drink, eat, and enjoy themselves. This was real life, spitting bones into the darkness, their laughter soaking into the dawn. But it was also illusory, like an underwater world.

Crab congee, fried noodles, fried clams. . . Yihua was still giggling as the dishes arrived.

'Why aren't there any peppers in the dishes?' She wrinkled her brow. 'How can I eat anything without peppers?'

'Hey, can we get some chilli sauce?' Lilai called to the stall keeper.

'I don't want chilli sauce,' Yihua said, annoyed. 'Chilli sauce is chilli sauce and peppers are peppers. You have to add the chilli peppers when you cook the vegetables. It's completely different from seasoning with chilli sauce. You don't understand chili peppers, just like you don't understand me.'

'Both make the food spicy. Can you really tell the difference?' Lilai asked perfunctorily, yawning.

'It's like I'm playing music for a cow,' Yihua called to the aproned stall-keeper, 'Give me some pan-seared green chilli peppers!'

The stall-keeper ran over.

'What is it you want?'

'Pan-seared green chilli peppers,' Yihua repeated.

'I don't know how to make that. Never heard of it.' The man laughed. 'Here in Guangzhou, we think it's best to eat less chilli. Bumps on a pretty girl's face are not nice-looking.'

Yihua used the chilli sauce, but was not satisfied. Her temper flared.

'The crab's dead,' she said, tossing away the crab shell. 'I mean, it's been dead for a long time.'

'It's been cooked thoroughly. How can it not be dead?' Lilai teased, 'Would you dare eat a live crab?'

'A person who can't discern between good and bad food won't have the ability to discern other things,' Yihua said. 'I would rather die than eat such bland food every day.'

Lilai put on an expression to please, carefully protecting Yihua's fury, preventing it from igniting. He still wanted to marry her. His mother had urged him again just that day not to delay, so as to prevent trouble. If she got angry, there would not be a chance of her agreeing, and he would not even be able to propose.

'My sister jumped because she didn't have chilli peppers,' Yihua said, giggling. 'I knew she could get into the university. She was smart, and she had quick reactions. She was so damn smart.'

'I've never met a girl cleverer than you,' Lilai said sincerely. He was confused, and not sure whether Yihua was drunk or sober.

'How many girls have you met?' Yihua wanted to make things difficult for him. 'A lot?'

'The treatment centre used to take in a lot of girls. . . Those who were somewhat clever found ways to escape that place.'

'Those girls don't count. Must be those you've touched and slept with.' Yihua giggled again. 'Then you'll know what's good and what's bad, or what's dull and what's spirited about them.'

Yihua wanted Lilai to talk about other girls he had screwed. Finally, she forced it out of him. He had been with two other girls; one was his middle school classmate, and the other had escaped from the treatment station. He had long ago cut off contact with them. Now, he only had Yihua, and she was the only one he loved.

He said, 'Huahua, marry me. Move into my house. I'll cook for you, and I'll put chilli peppers in every meal.'

Yihua thought that was hilarious. 'I might as well marry a pepper,' she said.

'I'm serious. I wish you would be serious too.' He did look serious.

'I'm not joking. Getting married, having kids, and washing nappies is boring,' she said.

I love you. And you love me. Why not get married?' he reasoned.

'Do you want to hear the truth?' she asked.

'Tell me.'

'I've never loved anyone but Liuzi.'

'I don't believe you. As soon as I touch you, you're wet. That surely means something. I don't believe you don't love me.'

'Sometimes, all it takes is seeing a carrot, and I'm wet. But I don't love carrots.'

And with that, Yihua put her chopsticks down. She had had enough.

Chapter 53:

Li Chuntian, Elder Sister

My sister went to the detention centre, taking clothing and other daily articles for Zhima. Zhima could not stop crying. If he had known how things were in here earlier on, he would have never driven the bamboo stick into that fellow's throat. Shunqiu had brought them the news at the wrong time. If he had missed the time by just a little, Zhima not only could see his younger daughter one last time, but could also weep to his heart's content, and finally bury her himself. When Zhima thought back on things, he remembered that he had had a strange anxiety that morning. His hand had slipped, and he had broken a bowl. He was very super-stitious. He wanted to take the day off, but my sister called him 'lazy bones' and said he was returning to his old ways.

Chuntian was full of regret, too. She had disregarded Zhima, not listening to his sense of foreboding. Zhima was like a black crow, with the air of a sorcerer about him. The night before their son died, he had had a bloody dream. Ever since then, he had paid special attention to his intuition. When he felt a stirring, he would stop to test the wind direction, pondering carefully before he made a move. He stuck out his sensitive tentacles as he crawled around every day. The facts had proven that he did not, in fact, escape catastrophe, even though he had done all that. He had been sentenced to death for murder.

He felt this was unfair. In court, he had cried, 'They started the fight. It was four against one.'

He showed the judge his teeth. 'Look, they knocked out my front teeth.'

He even raised up his shirt and acted like he was pointing at the acupuncture points. 'Here, here, it's still painful. They hit me over and over with rubber batons. I've been wanting to massage them with saffron oil.'

The judge pounded his gavel, the long wings on both sides of his cap shaking. 'If you want to appeal the decision, the petition must be submitted within ten days from the day the court verdict has been received. If it is a written appeal, you must submit an original copy, along with two photocopies. This court is adjourned.'

'I refuse to accept the decision! They had weapons! There were four of them! Of course, I can't accept. . .'

The judge stood up and left the courtroom. Zhima continued to shout, his eyes searching all around him, looking everywhere for the gigantic drum of injustice. It was like he was part of a period drama, beating on the drum to draw out the legendary hero Justice Bao.

The gallery was mostly empty. The faces of the court workers and few spectators were expressionless.

On the wall, there hung a sign reading, *Leniency for those who confess their crimes*.

Zhima was deeply disappointed. He obediently stretched out his hands, and was handcuffed and escorted from the room.

*

When my sister went to see Zhima, she had to talk to him through a glass panel. As soon as he saw her, Zhima started to cry. He said, 'I don't want to die. I like putting out our kebab stall every day, working and chatting with our customers. The most exciting part was watching you count money behind closed doors each night. I've lived so long, but I'm just now starting to find a little meaning to my life. I don't want to die.'

Zhima dried the tears from his face and went on, 'There were four of them fighting me. I'm not satisfied. I want to appeal. Even if I die, you've got to continue to appeal.'

Chuntian thought, then said, 'Lawyers are too expensive. We can't afford one. Cheap ones are just puppets. It's like throwing money away if you hire them. From the time you were picked up, I've pooled all the money we earned together. Even so, I only managed to scrape together such a small sum.'

'Yihua didn't send money back?' Zhima asked.

'She's paying a lot to maintain herself outside. Living on her own in another place, and we never sent money to help her. . . it's best we don't add to her burden. I've only got one daughter left.'

'You're already treating me as dead?' Zhima was stunned. 'You really wish me to die?'

'You and I are both partly responsible for what happened to Yicao.' My sister was like a yoked ox, slowing pulling the weight behind her. 'I don't want you to die, but the law won't listen to me.'

Zhima bowed his head in despair. His face was covered with snot and tears. He pleaded with my sister, 'Chuntian, find a lawyer for me. No matter what, you've got to find a lawyer for me. Oh yeah – isn't Sun Xiangxi a lawyer? Get him. You're close to him. He won't charge you anything.'

Chuntian was secretly startled. It seemed Zhima had known everything all along. It was the first time she realised her husband was actually quite shrewd and deep.

'I do know Sun. . . I'll ask, but I can't say for sure that he'll help.' Now that Zhima had brought Sun out of the shadows, Chuntian felt a huge moral weight on her. She was both ashamed and angry.

'People should consider their sentiments. If he wouldn't help you with this little favour, doesn't that mean you've slept with him for nothing?' Zhima said, taking an even more direct approach.

Chuntian's face tightened, and she pursed her lips as tightly as a chicken's arse. 'Don't talk like that. It wasn't like that.'

'Then what was it like? He didn't sleep with you? Right. . .' He laughed. 'I know all about your affairs.'

My sister gritted her teeth. 'I'll go back and see what I can do.'

'If he doesn't agree to help, tell him you'll sue him for rape,' Zhima lowered his voice as he made suggestions. 'He won't risk his delicate flesh.'

Chuntian looked at her man in amazement.

'. . . Also, if he's willing to give you money instead, that's fine. Collect 500 *yuan* for each time he slept with you. That should be not less than a hundred times, right? That should be enough money to hire a lawyer even more reputable than Sun.'

She said nothing.

'After that, if you want to divorce me and be with him, I won't object at all. . .'

Chuntian threw a hard slap toward Zhima's face. The *pop* was loud, and the glass tremoured.

*

My sister did not want to bother about Zhima. She wanted to tear his despicable face to bits in that instant. Her heart softened, then hardened, sometimes sad, sometimes angry. She moved her feet woodenly, leaving the prison and starting to make her way home.

The world was dry, like an empty teacup, and she could see the residue at the bottom of it.

Her legs grew increasingly tired. She stopped and leaned against a camphor tree for a while. She heard Sun's voice echoing in her ear, *If you start to regret your decision, you can always come back to me. I'll be here.*

A little warmth oozed into her heart. If she didn't ask him for help, what could she do?

What took her by surprise was Sun's affected tone. There was no gentleness; he was cold and meant business.

A woman's whining voice came over the phone.

'Take it as me begging you. In any case, save his life.'

An image came into her mind, of a naked woman on a bed. She struggled to get those words out, her hand shaking lightly.

'I've been very busy lately. I can't help now. I've got to go to Guangzhou tomorrow for a business trip. Let me remind you, in cases like Liu Zhima's, there isn't much hope.'

Chuntian suddenly increased her volume, 'Sun, is the woman you're fucking now as stupid as me?'

'You're welcome. Give me a call again when you're free.' Sun hung up.

Her mind was a complete blank, snowy white under the glare of a thousand-watt lightbulb.

Chapter 54:

Xiao Shui Qin, Sister-in-law

Shui Qin had become a familiar face at the hospital. Every time she went for treatment, there would always be doctors who greeted her with, 'Oh you're here' and 'You're looking well,' and other similar courtesies, as if Shui Qin were their colleague.

Looking well? They were just being polite. She saw herself in the mirror every morning and saw her skin growing darker and gloomier every day, and the number of spots increasing. Her eyes had no spark, and there was a dull pain in her lower abdomen. She knew her body better than the doctors did, and she was prepared for the worst.

Recently, the pain had increased. She had endured it until her next checkup and test. Then she was told that the tumour had grown and was spreading. Even a radical hysterectomy might not be enough to take care of it now. On this day alone, there had been dozens of patients admitted for uterine or ovarian cancer, so many, in fact, that beds had to be brought in and placed in the corridor. The doctors were so overwhelmed that they did not wait to determine whether it was necessary to remove each uterus, but just removed all. The surgery cost at least 10 000 *yuan*.

A woman without a uterus was like a bedroom without a bed. The emptiness would be disturbing. If a woman did not have a uterus, she was like an abyss, both physically and emotionally.

Shui Qin left the overcrowded hospital, giving up her bed there for someone who had more hope of recovery.

Having had past experience, life and death were no longer a blow to Shui Qin. Her heart felt like a stone finally falling to the ground. At last, she did not have to give her money to the hospital. She would not have to spend time in desperate struggle anymore. Sometimes, hope was more torturous than despair.

Shui Qin heard the happy clacking sound of the sewing machine as she fell into a trance. It was like she was hopping between the twin worlds of yin and yang. Thinking about her present life, about the mysterious underworld, about her relatives and friends, in this trance she inadvertently walked towards Xianxian's school. The iron gate was closed; it was school hours. She looked through the iron rails. In the past, when she was always busy at the tailor shop, she seldom came to Xianxian's school. She had always been proud of Xianxian. Ever since the girl was small, she had been very independent, not needing anyone to take her to school or pick her up. Other children would skip school and go to an internet cafe, but would she sneak online without approval? Xianxian had taken in all the ideals her mother tried to instil. She was clever and got good results, giving her parents peace of mind.

It occurred to her that she had not spent enough time with Xianxian. She had not even taken the time to go with her daughter to fly kites by the river. Now she had so many things she wanted to do with Xianxian, including bringing her to Beijing to see the Forbidden City, Tian'anmen Square, and the Great Wall. She wanted to bring Xianxian to Tibet and climb the snowy peaks there, meet the lamas, and experience all of its snowy charm.

Shui Qin wiped her eyes. Having lived to this age, she had never been so sad. In her mind, she saw a grassland green and vast, with the sun rising over the horizon. The sky was a radiant glow, and she was running non-stop towards the sun – but suddenly she was shrouded in dark clouds, the grassland turned grey, and in the distance all she could see was a dark abyss.

A needle slowly pierced her flesh, and it hurt. The pain spread through her chest, flowing to her lower abdomen, ultimately settling in the uterus. The countless needles formed into a steel knife. Her uterus was a vast farmland. The knife grew into a plough and cut deep and endlessly into the land. She clenched the railing and bent over, as if looking for something on the ground.

Suddenly, the bell rang and the students flooded out, breaking her trance.

The iron gate swung open automatically. Shui Qin followed the gate as it swung toward the wall. She raised her head, but remained hunched. It was an awkward posture.

Xianxian came out. She looked like she had not got over some unhappiness that must have arisen at school.

Shui Qin called her, and forced herself to straighten her body. Xianxian was caught off guard.

'What are you doing here?'

'I was passing by. Let's go to a restaurant. What do you want to eat?'

'Didn't you say we should eat at home? It's more hygienic, and we can save money.'

'Just for a change of taste.'

'You can stand to spend the money?'

'Xianxian, I was too harsh towards you all before. You're right. I used to be a miser.'

'Pa is harder on himself. He picks up other people's discarded cigarette butts from the street to smoke. Sometimes it puts a lot of mental pressure on me.'

Shui Qin hid her surprise. She forgot her pain for a moment.

'I study hard, and I don't participate in extracurricular activities. I don't play with other students, and I don't go online. My classmates call me *Freak.*'

Shui Qin lowered her head, as if looking for something. She felt deep regret. For so many years, she had actually imprisoned her daughter. She had put a life plan in place, but it was like a huge prison cell, depriving her daughter of her free nature. She had imposed too much on the girl. She was not a good mother or a good wife. She was just a cold, rigid housekeeper, chief of a machine, keeping the machinery of home running steadily.

'. . . but I don't care what they call me. We'll see who will have the last laugh.' Xianxian had grown up strong amid the discrimination of city people towards village folk.

With some difficulty, Shui Qin smiled. She was comforted, but also a little worried. If one sought to prevail over others, it would only bring more suffering to oneself. This she knew from deep experience.

'Are we really going out to eat?' Xianxian asked.

'Of course.'

'Then I'll tell you what I really want. I want. . . Yang's spicy crawfish, grilled carp, fried snails, stewed chicken feet. . .'

'OK, OK. Let's go to Yang's.'

'What about Pa?'

'Call him.'

Xianxian took out her phone, hesitated for a long while, then said, 'I want to show you a photo.'

She flipped through her phone, then held it up in front of Shui Qin.

Shui Qin looked, and her heart was like a tiny boat floating on the surface of the water. The sudden added weight made it sink a little deeper.

Although the resolution was not high, and it was the side view, it was night, and the lighting was dim, but an acquaintance would recognise her at first glance. She was half squatting, giving a customer a blow job.

'Where did you come across something like this?' she asked, pretending to be calm.

'My classmates took the photo,' Xianxian said, taking her phone back. 'They didn't know it was you.'

Shui Qin remained silent.

'I don't want to use such dirty money to go abroad.'

Shui Qin was stunned.

'You'll do anything to realise your own ambitions.'

'My own ambitions?'

'You mean I'm wrong? Going overseas to study, distinguishing oneself – that's your dream. I'm just a tool for achieving it.'

Shui Qin could not say anything. Her lower abdomen was starting to ache once more.

'You're ruthless to everyone, including yourself.'

'Don't speak to me in that tone. I'm your mother.' Shui Qin put forward the dignity of a mother.

'I wish you weren't.'

Shui Qin raised a hand but did not slap her. Her hand remained in the air for two seconds, then dropped.

She did not say anything else. Sadly, she turned and walked away, alone.

Chapter 55:

Li Shunqiu, Eldest Brother

My diligent brother changed jobs again. Every day, he donned a yellow jacket with fluorescent stripes and stood on the sprinkler truck. Using a water gun, he watered and fertilized green belts around the city, or sprayed insecticide. Sometimes he carried a garbage can and cleaned advertisements stuck to poles or walls. He liked the job. When it came down to it, he liked working outdoors, especially early in the morning when it was quiet. In the gentle breeze, he woke the sleeping street, like waking a child, washing her face, and helping her dress, then watching her happily bounce off into the crowd. It was a pleasant feeling.

He had nothing much on his mind. He had work to do, and he was satisfied with that. His wages were like a mud fish, slipping through his hands straight into Shui Qin's, where it ran no further. He said there was nothing more natural than a man earning and giving his wife money.

After a storm had passed, the weather suddenly turned cold, the leaves yellow, and the world tighter. The sloppiness left by summer seemed outdated. Shunqiu was sensitive to autumn. As soon as it came, he felt the ache in his knee joints, an old soreness.

Pinching, resisting, squeezing, pressing, pricking, massaging, he applied different methods to ease the pain.

He turned and twisted as he walked on the street, sometimes bouncing a few times with each step. Stopping to shake the soreness from his leg, he accidentally knocked over an old woman's shopping basket. Tomatoes and potatoes rolled everywhere, some lodging beneath the wheels of cars, and others dropping into the drain. The buxom, large-hipped old woman grabbed hold of Shunqiu's waistband and refused to let go.

Coming into contact with the opposite sex in such a large crowd of people made him blush. He quickly took out five *yuan* and handed it to the woman.

The old woman spewed flames from her red lips, but she spoke with a stammer, 'My tom. . . tomatoes aren't ordinary tomatoes. My potatoes a. . . aren't ordinary po. . . potatoes. They're organ . . . organic.'

'They have organs?' shocked, Shunqiu looked down to observe the round things scattered across the ground.

'You are. . . laughing. . . at. . . me,' she said angrily. 'These tomatoes cost three *yuan* a piece, and the potatoes are two. . . two and a half *yuan* each. I paid fifty *yuan* in total.'

He dug through all his pockets, and each pocket stuck out its tongue at the old woman, proving the five *yuan* was all he had. He had saved it by skipping breakfast for the past two days.

'Far. . . Farmers!' The woman snatched the five *yuan* and picked up the potatoes and tomatoes which were still good, scolding and cursing all the while.

My brother raced away like pedalling on hot wheels, escaping from the scene.

*

When he told Shui Qin about the incident – and the five *yuan* – that night, he said it was good he had not had fifty on him. If he had had that much, that old woman would have dug it out of him. She was not rich, but acted like she was, even saying that the potatoes and tomatoes had organs.

Shui Qin had just finished washing her feet and was drying them on the rim of the basin. At first, she had only listened with one ear, but hearing this, she suddenly laughed so hard she over-turned the foot basin, spilling water all over the floor. My brother rushed to get a mop and rag and started mopping and wiping the mess up.

Shui Qin curled up on the sofa and watched her husband clean up the mess. She said, 'The woman said *organic*, not *organs*. It means they were grown without pesticides and fertilisers. Rich people eat that sort of thing. One tomato costing three *yuan* is not considered too much.'

Shunqiu wrung out the rag, letting the water drip into the basin with a ringing sound. He spread the rag on the floor, using his hands to push it and turn here and there all over the whole room, swiftly wiping the whole floor. The floor sparkled delight-fully. Since Shui Qin had fallen sick, he had meticulously taken care of all the housework, developing a method of his own.

Shunqiu said, 'Whether they're organic or not, they're not worth that much. When I grow vegetables at the farmhouse restaurant, I just pour urine and dung over them. It's a natural fertiliser. It makes them taste better.'

Shui Qin did not answer. Her body began to contract gradually. Eventually, she sat on the sofa, curled up like a shrimp.

When Shunqiu had finished washing the rag and mop, he went into the washroom and cleaned up the wash basin and toilet. After he busied himself for a while in the washroom, he dried his hands and came out. He noticed Shui Qin's strange position, and when he came nearer, he saw she was trembling slightly.

'What's wrong?' he thought she was crying.

Shui Qin did not respond.

My brother touched her. Her forehead was covered in sweat. He cried, 'It's not hot today. The hot spell of autumn is over. Why are you so sweaty?' he handed her a towel, 'Are you feeling sick?'

Shui Qin tried to pull herself up. Looking at him, she intended to tell him her condition, but then changed her mind, feeling there was no point causing him unnecessary anxiety. She decided to downplay it. 'I was a little chilly just now. I'm afraid it's malaria. I'll go to bed and sleep it off.'

'I'll boil some ginger water for you,' he said, and went to prepare it.

After a while, he carried a bowl of ginger water into the room. Shui Qin was reclining on the bed, studying their cash and account books. Her face was dull.

Shunqiu put the ginger water down and sat timidly on the edge of the bed, as if the money were pigeons that would fly off at his approach.

'Drink it while it's hot,' he urged.

Shui Qin took a spoonful, then put it aside. 'I'm going to put all of this in your keeping. The PIN is Xianxian's birthday.'

'Why?' It was as if he had been stung by an insect. He was a little flattered.

'Whether it's in your care or mine, it's all the same,' then she changed her tone. 'I mean, if I want to relax a bit. Isn't that OK?'

She said the last phrase in a tender tone, like she was being coquettish. Shunqiu was not used to that. He touched her forehead to check if she were in some sort of fevered confusion.

She grasped his arm and pulled him to her side. 'Shunqiu, look, we only bother about making money. We never go out together as a family. This weekend, let's bring Xianxian to the Changsha Zoo.'

He rested his arm behind her, letting her lean on it like pillow. 'That costs money.'

'I've realised that you can never save enough money. You have to work for a living, but you also have to live. In the blink of an eye, we'll be old. Once that happens, it's too late to enjoy ourselves.'

'But we haven't saved enough for Xianxian's studies. . .'

'Actually, I was wrong. Our way of doing things may not be what she really wants. We shouldn't put pressure on her. We should let her pursue her own destiny.'

'Yes. I feel the same. It's good if she stays close to home. She can't go a day without peppers fried with meat. What would she do if she went far away?'

Shui Qin smiled silently. 'True.'

My brother was relieved. He felt his life was truly a happy one.

*

On the weekend, all three of them got up early. The atmosphere was cheerful. Food and everything they needed for the outing was ready.

Shui Qin was in too much pain to walk. She did not say anything, but stood, doubled over and with huge beads of sweat rolling down and hitting the floor, where they gathered into a puddle. It reflected her soon-to-be extinguished flame, and darkness was like a group of crows, gradually gathering.

Xianxian looked at her mother, not sure what to do. From the time she was three years old, she had dressed and fed herself. At six, she washed her own clothes. When she was eight, she learned to cook for herself. She had not grown up acting like a spoiled child in her mother's embrace. She had not heard fairy tales as she was tucked in at night, and she had never cried for sweets. She had given Shui Qin's arms that freedom very early, never asking to be held or carried. She did not know how to return to her mother's embrace now.

'We'll go to the hospital,' Shunqiu said, putting down his back-pack.

His wife waved him off and lay on the sofa. 'No, there's no need. I think I got a chill last night, and my stomach hurts now.'

Xianxian gave her mother a glass of warm water. Thinking of the photo on her phone, she was unhappy.

'Xianxian, how about if Baba takes you?' Shui Qin said.

'I'm not as bad as just being concerned about enjoying myself, not caring whether you live or die.' Xianxian wanted to help her mother, but she could not draw near her. This barrier made her feel fear and anger.

Feeling her tone was inappropriate, her father criticised, 'Xianxian, is that any way to speak to your mother? If we can't make it this time, we'll just go another time. The zoo will always be there. It's not going anywhere, right?'

'It doesn't matter to me. It was the two of you who wanted to go,' Xianxian insinuated. 'I don't have too many expectations in life. It's just a bunch of animals, right? It's no big deal whether we see them or not.'

The three of them stopped talking. The room was still.

Suddenly, a wailing cannon shot out from Shui Qin's mouth, whooshing as it rushed towards the ceiling, and after a few explosions, silence quickly resumed. The writhing Shui Qin, and the father and daughter struck dumb by the cannon, stood among the smoke and fragments in the room, forming an equilateral triangle, unmoving in their separate positions.

Chapter 56:

Li Chuntian, Elder Sister

My sister found a lawyer after all. Aside from eagerly pocketing the attorney fees, everything else the lawyer did was just going through the motions, as if he came especially to chime in with others' views.

The retrial appeal upheld the original judgement. Zhima wept when he heard the verdict.

The day before his scheduled execution, Chuntian went to visit him. He was still weeping. She wanted to capture a last photo of him on her phone, but it was not allowed.

She just sat there, listening to Zhima cry through the glass. Thinking of how this person would be reduced to a heap of ash the next day, she was a little horrified. After all, they had shared a bed for more than twenty years. Many couples were like this. Neither partner belonged to the other, but after sleeping together for some time, they did.

For the past several days, she had been rushing about on account of Zhima. She did not have time to mourn for Yicao, so she held her sorrow inside like a rolling snowball. By the time Zhima's execution was set, this snowball suddenly broke through the barrier and crashed and struck her head. The snowball exploded into fragments, becoming snowflakes filling the sky.

My sister did not cry. Rather, she laughed. She giggled, then stopped, alternating between walking and resting, and always looking like she could not hold back a smile.

She thought of the time she gave birth to Yicao. It had been a difficult delivery, breech. The lives of both mother and daughter had been at risk. Yicao had entered the world with great difficulty, just for the sake of sixteen short years.

Chuntian laughed. She thought of the scene of her own birth, how her father had held her upside down, intending to drown her in the river. She laughed again.

She thought of the first time she had gone into the field and several leeches had attached themselves to her legs and sucked her blood. It scared her so badly she had screamed and cried. She laughed again.

My poor sister's laughter sounded like she had a cough with a cold. She had to cough intermittently between the laughter, causing the people on the street to look at her in surprise. Past events which cost her pain and sorrow could only make her laugh right now. She felt that she would never finish laughing as long as she lived. So she became worried, wanting to cry, to shed a few tears, or to scream her sorrows to the world around her. She wanted to tell everyone that she had collapsed, that nothing was left but a skeleton of her. She also wanted to ask why all these things had happened to her, too.

Everyone seemed to be hurrying, completely disinterested. Chuntian could do nothing but continue laughing. The corners of her mouth cracked from too much laughing, and her brain ached from it too, so she leaned on the fence and took a nap.

When she came to herself, it was dusk. She found she had taken the wrong route. Everything around her was unfamiliar, and she did not know the way home. She walked aimlessly, trying to get her bearings. She asked directions from passersby, but she could not remember her own address, nor could she recall the name of the neighbourhood, so she could only sit on the ground and wrack her brain.

Chapter 57:

Liu Yihua, Niece

Yu Shuzhong was sentenced to ten years in prison. The leader of the *Today Newspaper* was replaced, and the newspaper renamed. We were all sacked.

I did not wish to stay in Guangzhou. Yehe Nara and Tang Linlu migrated to Canada, leaving the Xingke Book Garden behind. They invited me to return to Beijing to manage it.

The temperature in Guangzhou suddenly dropped. The moist, lingering heat finally exhausted its own moisture, like a plaster cover being torn open by the wind, and a trace of coolness poured in.

I sat in the departure lounge at the airport, looking at the floating clouds. They kept broadcasting news about flight delays.

I had not seen Yihua often, and she never took the initiative to look me up. Our relationship was left undeveloped.

The day we met, I asked her to a café beside the Pearl River so I could say goodbye. She had gone through a great change. She was all grown up, looking like a woman instead of a girl. The experiences she had undergone showed, and there was a certain seriousness in the way she talked now. She did not sound at all like a girl who worked in a nightclub. I suddenly felt a little guilty. I should have shown more concern for her, especially after so many things had happened. As I listened to her talk, the idea came to me that maybe I should take her to Beijing with me.

Yihua said she had slept with Hu Lilai, and that he was very good to her. He wanted to marry her, letting her rule the roost and take charge of the passbook. She, on the other hand, did not want to continue the relationship. She did not love him, but out of boredom, she had slept with him several times.

Yihua was the most innocent girl in the world. I regretted having despised her relationship with Liuzi.

She talked about Zhima as well. When the time came, she would go back and accompany her mother to collect the ashes.

As I sat in the airport thinking of these things, the clouds turned grey and thickened, pressing the distant sky very low. The plane was still slowly taxiing on the runway. The lift brought the food containers to the door, and a man went back and forth, carrying it aboard.

Yihua had said that the problem she encountered was that Lilai did not agree to the breakup. He would not give up.

She did not ask me for help, but just spoke frankly about her troubles. If I had cared about her a little more, if I had realised how crazy Hu Lilai was, or if I had taken her away from Guangzhou early on, I would not have read about her death in the newspaper: *Unsuccessful breakup, girl chopped to pieces by boyfriend.*

Rain poured down, suddenly turning everything white. After two or three hours, the rain was still falling fiercely and there was lightning and thunder, as if the sky were enraged. The airport started to flood. The work crew cleaned up in the rain, their figures like insignificant road signs.

All airlines had stopped their flights. The exits, halls, and waiting areas were all crowded with stuck travellers. The airport was like an ant bed. The cafés, restaurants, and even the toilets were too crowded to enter. Everywhere you looked, there were thighs, behinds, arms, mouths, and faces. Many people were making phone calls, speaking in all different tones with different attitudes, and after they hung up they all seemed lost.

The wind was very strong, torturing the trees to their limits, they moved hysterically, as if they wanted to crash dead somewhere. For a while, hailstones the size of eggs fell, denting cars and making a loud racket. There was a giant, light-polluting screen advertising a new movie about a girl and three men. The actress's lips were red and her cleavage was exposed. Her eyes were bewitching. Her expression and the egg-sized hailstones in some ways enriched the boring wait. Some people cheered.

*

As I dozed in my chair, I dreamt of Yihua. I dreamt she had just bought a train ticket. Hu Lilai called, agreeing to the breakup, but said his mother wanted to see her again. Yihua agreed to see her. Lilai rode on a cloud, carrying Yihua with him, rushing all the way to his house. He suggested going upstairs first, saying he had something to give her. Since they were breaking up, she agreed to whatever he wanted to do.

Lilai's room was spotless, and there were red roses in the vase. A plastic plate held a pineapple, bananas, and apples, and a knife lay beside it.

Lilai closed the door. He led Yihua away from it and asked her to have a seat, as if afraid she might run away. He smiled at her mysteriously, then reached into the compartment behind the headboard and brought out a box. He opened it carefully and showed her a sparkling diamond ring.

'It's inlaid with diamonds,' he said, looking at the ring.

Yihua replied, 'I don't want it.'

Lilai admired how she looked when she got into a huff, like he was indulging his own naughty daughter. 'I went to Hong Kong and had it specially made. It's pretty, isn't it? Come, try it on.'

Yihua pushed it away. 'I've said all I have to say.'

Lilai was still smiling and said, 'Huahua, I'm not going to let you go.'

'I don't love you. How many times do you want me to say it?'

'But I love you. I can't live without you.'

'That's your problem.'

'Huahua, don't be so cold. Isn't it good when we're together?' he said, still smiling.

'Having sex is having sex. Marriage is marriage. They're two different things.' Yihua got up and walked toward the door.

Lilai rushed to the door in a flash, turning the built-in lock.

'Huahua, don't leave.' He suddenly knelt before her, his eyes filling with tears. 'I'm begging you, don't go. Don't leave me alone. I can't stand it.'

'I don't owe you, and you don't owe me. Let me go home. I need to rush to catch my train.'

Lilai knelt blocking the door, his face turned upwards at Yihua. 'Tell me, what do you want me to do? I'll do whatever you say.'

'Please open the door and let me go home,' she said emphatically.

'Huahua, I love you so much. Let's get married, OK?'

'Let me go back. My father just died.'

The word 'died' seemed to give inspiration to Lilai. He looked like he wanted to die. Suddenly, he banged his head against the doorframe, making a loud sound.

Yihua looked at his forehead, slowly oozing with blood and swelling.

'Do you want me to die before you'll promise me?' Lilai cried as he banged his head.

Yihua turned her back towards him. Lilai continued banging his head patiently and rhythmically.

Yihua shouted, 'Lilai! Enough!'

He stopped pounding his head. A ray of hope slowly blossomed on his blood-caked face, like a sky clearing up after the rain, brightness shooting onto the muddy ground.

Yihua took a glass and banged it against her own scalp. The glass broke into fragments on the floor, and blood in red streaks as long as earthworms crawled from the corners of her forehead to her mouth.

The room was silent.

'Can I go now?' Yihua said, looking at the floor.

Lilai was like a shark, drawn to the scent of Yihua's blood. What he sniffed from the blood was none other than love. He did not believe what Yihua said, but he believed her blood.

He moved his rusty joints, stood up and embraced her firmly, patting her and licking the blood from her face. He laughed and cried at the same time, his mouth never stopping. 'Huahua, I won't let you harm yourself. I know you love me. . . Huahua, it's all my fault. Let's not fight. We'll be OK. Let's not fight anymore . . . Eh?'

Lilai acted like a blind man touching Yihua all over, his mouth professing his love for her. His grip became tighter and tighter. He kneaded Yihua's neck like he was kneading dough. She found it hard to breathe. Her mouth opened, and a strange sound was coming from her throat. Her response excited him. He closed his hands tighter around her throat and kissed her, sucking her tongue vigorously, blood filling his mouth.

Yihua's body gradually grew limp. Her hands drooped, falling to her side. Lilai knelt on the floor and continued to kiss her.

Chapter 58:

Li Shunqiu, Eldest Brother

Shui Qin wanted to live. In the past, she had always been at odds with reality, sometimes defeating it, sometimes being defeated by it, but always knowing there would be another opportunity to test her skills against it. There were no more such opportunities now. Reality had dealt her a heavy blow and she had half collapsed into the loess. All it would take now was a single pat to her head, and she would disappear completely from the earth.

Shui Qin had never in her life been passive. Sitting and waiting for that final blow was almost too shameful to bear.

It was deep into winter and all the leaves had all fallen. When the wind blew, the trees had nothing with which to welcome their guest, but trembled with their naked trunks. Not hearing any rustling echoes, the wind was angry, and it kept shaking the trees, questioning them. From a distance, it plunged at the trees, tearing them until they fell left and right. The trees suffered silently, able to keep quiet better than ever.

My brother got off work and went to buy some boiled assorted beef giblets with a wheaten cake to take home, since the stove at home was always cold these days. He put the food on the table and opened the refrigerator. It was full. There were vegetables, fish, pork ribs, milk and fruit juice. . . clearly, Shui Qin had gone to the supermarket that day. She very rarely bought so much, usually buying milk but not juice, or juice but not milk; fish but not meat, or meat but not fish. If something was on offer, she bought it. If there were buy one get one free offers, she would buy those items, or sometimes even just pick up the free items.

My brother looked at the clock. Xianxian would finish school soon. He quickly tied on his apron and started cooking rice. He thought about whether it was better to braise fish or pork ribs, finally settling on the ribs. It was best to eat ribs fresh, and the carp would actually be tastier if it was pickled in salt for a while.

When Xianxian came in, the rice cooker had just finished cooking, and the house was full of the fragrant smell of meat.

'Go find your mother to come back to eat,' Shunqiu said, waving his spatula as he let the vegetables slither into the wok.

'Even though she's sick, she runs about. Why don't you rein her in?' Xianxian was impatient.

It got dark early, and the wind outside the window was strong. Plastic bags swirled along the ground.

Placing the vegetables on the table, my brother took off his apron and set the bowls and chopsticks on the table. In the bedroom, Shui Qin's phone rang. It was my mother, saying she had made pickles, the hen had laid eggs, the yellow dog got sick and died, and Li Ganzi's mother had drowned in the latrine pit. Her rambling was endless. My brother did not pay attention.

He saw a note from Shui Qin pressed under the phone. It read:

I'm sorry. I have to go. I can't stand it anymore. I didn't tell you about the condition of my illness because I knew there was nothing you could do to ease my pain. Even more, there's nothing you can do to save my life. It would only add to your pain and anxiety. I don't need to exhaust you, and I certainly don't want to consume our hard-earned money. Money should be used where there is hope. It need not be used on the dying.

To bury someone in the village takes at least 20 or 30 000 yuan; the villagers can't even afford to die. They are poor all their lives, and don't get to eat or wear anything good. But in death, they are extravagant, letting their relatives take out loans, perpetuating the poverty. They don't know how to live well, but they want to do well in death. I don't like the idea of extravagance or the display of splendour in death. I'm tired. I want to go far away, as if on a trip. Don't look for me. You won't find me.

Xianxian has her own mind. Don't force anything on her, but discuss any decisions with her. It is best to let her live a happy, healthy life.

Forgive me for everything. I love you both.

Shunqiu and Xianxian ran beside the river, shouting. The wind distorted their voices. They ran on the bank, stopping at the wharf to inquire among the fishing boats, asking if they had seen a woman with short hair. They ran for a long time. Their loud panting covered all other sounds, while the water rose and fell with it.

'She hides everything from us. . . I must find her and bring her back,' said Xianxian, though she did not cry.

My brother had never entered so deeply into the dark night. It was like he was walking down a very long tunnel. He could hear only his own footsteps. Shui Qin was his lighthouse, and now that the light had gone out, he would run aground on the reefs. He needed to see her again. He wanted to know where the reefs lay, how deep the river was, how quick the rapids, and what precautions a helmsman needed to take. He felt he was a tiny boat swaying in the wind, his oars were tired, and even a small whirlpool could make him turn circles on the spot. He was dizzy from the spinning. He plopped down on the long embankment. The river was dark. The lights of fishing boats glittered in the middle of the river. On the opposite bank, the city curled up like an animal entering a dreamland.

Shunqiu felt like he was in a desert. The year he had gone to prison, the iron gate had clanged shut and the lock had tumbled shut, as well. A corresponding lock had been shut at the same time and had since grown rusty, and it had no key. But now, because of the rust, the lock cracked open on its own. The sound was weak, producing slight reverberations, like a rippling current moving in all directions.

Throughout his life, it seemed there was always someone behind the scenes who wanted to make life difficult for him. Someone who wanted to do him harm or destroy him.

'Who's trying to make life so difficult for me? Who?'

Perhaps he had committed some huge sin in a past life. He had been to the temple and burned incense to all sorts of deities, but his hand was burned by the incense. It was a bad omen.

A woman's body was fished out of the river. My brother went to see. It smelled horrible. The face had been decomposed, and the teeth were exposed. After just one look, he vomited onto the ground. He retched until his stomach was empty and he could not eat.

As he made his way home, he tried to think of all the things that might happen to Shui Qin. He imagined her suddenly pushing the door open and entering the room, carrying her bags, full of discounted items. He listened to the footsteps on the stairs, tidying her clothes and putting the cooking utensils away the way she had always kept them.

Xianxian did not come back from looking for her mother, and the police could not find her, either. She had run away.

Exhausted, my brother closed the door and wept. The rusted lock on his heart broke and fell to the floor. The world was like an image of something floating in the water, shimmering.

The only thing he could do was go back to the place where he was born.

Chapter 59:

Li Chuntian, Elder Sister

The stream rinsed the tree roots and stone on both sides, passing through the arched bridge and flowing deep into the forest. There was a smell of rotten leaves. Lovebirds were whispering to each other among the bamboo clumps. My sister looked around like someone from a different village, even though she was familiar with the vegetation here, the shape of the stones, and the sound of the river. Every wildflower knew her. She could tell time by the shadow of the trees, and her voice had echoed through the valley. She had stepped on the dew to go to the fields, lugging her heavy burden up the ridge.

The dreary scenery of the past flew like dust, kicking up a residue. Touching the swaddled urn, she quickened her pace.

A column of smoke rose above the roof. Liu Zhima's mother was starting a fire in the kitchen, while his father chopped firewood on the terrace. Seeing my sister, his father stayed his axe midswing, as if considering whether it was better to let the blow fall on the wood or on her.

My sister did not dare go near. By right, she should greet her father-in-law 'Ba,' but the sound would not come out. Her relationship with her in-laws had always been a source of discomfort, like having grains of sand in her shoe. When she returned to this environment, she was, out of habit docile and stiff. She looked at the axehead and squeezed out an embarrassed smile, like a traveller asking for a drink.

'You, you, you . . . Who do you think you are?' Zhima's father held the axe in his hand, and even though he stammered when he talked, his tone was cruel. 'You . . . you still dare to show your face here?'

Chuntian continued to smile, but she kept her distance from the axe.

The neighbour's back door creaked open. The neighbour, Chai Fengying, stuck her head out, exposing her upper body. Seeing the woman she had betrayed so many years ago when she slept with Zhima, she slowly stepped out the door, displaying her full length. Her posture showed she lived a nourished life.

'Aiyoh, Chuntian. Chuntian is back! I thought it was some important guest coming to visit you all.' Chai did not like to talk at such a distance, so she moved to the wall by the fence and parted the withered vine from the fence. 'You're dressed so fashionably, Chuntian. It's like you're getting younger by the day.'

The previous year, the woman living next door had died of liver cancer. Chai had grabbed the opportunity to fill the house the neighbour had left.

'Don't forget to stop by for a visit, Chuntian.' Chai released the withered vines, and the mottled figure went back into her house, leaving the back door open.

'Hussy,' Zhima's father whispered, spitting. 'That fell . . . fellow's wife had been dead just two months and that . . . that hussy is sleeping in her bed. Wo . . . women . . . there's no . . . not a good one.'

Chuntian said nothing. She held the urn in her hands, hoping to draw her father-in-law's attention to it.

Zhima's mother stepped over the threshold and stood on the base. She scattered cold rice and called to the chickens. The cockeye stared at the tip of her own nose, ignoring Chuntian.

Compared to the axe, the cockeye seemed to pose no danger. My sister walked through the clucking, pecking flock, with the chickens parting to let her pass.

Zhima's mother had not ever looked Chuntian directly in the face, but stared in deadly fashion straight down her own nose. The whites of her eyes were cloudy.

'Zhima is home,' Chuntian said gently, holding out the urn to her mother-in-law.

The whites of the cockeye's eyes widened quickly, in a split second forcing the black pupils to an impasse. They looked like startled children, hiding in the corners of the eyes.

Chuntian could not gain any accurate information from the pair of cockeyes. She did not know whether Zhima's mother was sad, shocked, or angry. If she was sad, my sister did not mind crying with her. If shocked, she could have extracted all the details, recounting the whole tale for her. If angry, she wanted to take two steps back to avoid being hit with that porcelain bowl of chicken feed.

She stood still, trying to get a read on her mother-in-law's emotions. The porcelain bowl fell to the ground, scattering the clucking chickens, and bouncing a few feet away. The old woman slowly took the urn, and the black pupils half-hidden in the corners of the eyes suddenly rolled around. Those tiny black balls rolled about on the white screen, faster and faster, more and more randomly, until they finally came to an abrupt stop. They trembled on the spot for a while, then the owner of those tiny black balls raised the urn and struck my sister with it.

'You ill-fated bitch. . .'

Her eyesight was not good. It would have been better for Chuntianif she had not dodged. One clumsy dodge and she absorbed the blow full-on instead. There was only a blunt sound, as if Zhima were sighing inside the tight confines. A wound opened on Chuntian's head, and blood started to flow from the parting of her hair.

Zhima's mother possessed some sheer animal strength. Chuntian squatted, but was off-kilter. Her behind fell on the rice grains left uneaten by the hens.

Zhima's father tossed the axe aside and grabbed the urn. Looking toward the sky, he cried, 'The only son for three generations in my household gone, leaving our house barren!' He said this smoothly, without stammering.

Chai Fengying rushed out of her house at this moment and pulled Chuntian up. She said to Zhima's parents, 'Why treat her like this? Your son is dead, and her husband is dead. You're all grieving. Why should you treat her this way?'

'She's grieving? Ask her, is she saddened by this at all? If she didn't go to the city and mess around, my son would not have. . .' Zhima's mother closed her cockeyes, wailing.

'You're her mother-in-law. That's true. But don't forget, you're also a woman. Women should have sympathy for other women.' Chai pulled my sister up by the arm and took her home.

There was a buzzing sound in Chuntian's head. Woodenly, she curled up on the sofa without a word. Chai wiped the blood from her face with a warm towel, muttering about how inhumane Liu Zhima's parents were. She even called a 'village doctor' to come from the clinic to clean and treat the wound.

At midday, Chai cooked a few dishes. Chuntian did not once open her mouth.

'Chuntian, you weren't knocked silly, were you? That old woman is ruthless. She really wanted to kill you,' Chai said indignantly. 'They're always fucking bullying honest people!'

When Chuntian heard that, she laughed.

'The stammerer and cockeye are both unkind sorts. Zhima was

nothing much to speak of either. Chuntian, you should be happy to be rid of the whole bunch.'

Chuntian sat motionlessly. Chai shook her. 'Chuntian, are you OK? Don't scare me. Say something if you're all right. If you want to eat something, my husband just caught a fish. I don't know how to make salted fish. I'm not sure if it's too salty, or too bland. Will you taste it for me?'

Chuntian sighed at length, her breath rolling the chopsticks over and over.

'All I did was bring Zhima home,' she said, crusty blood sticking to the corners of her mouth, 'and they hit me.'

Chai said, 'The Liu family owes you a lot, especially Zhima. Chuntian, I want to tell you something, but don't be angry.'

Chuntian laughed. 'Why would I be angry?'

'I slept with Zhima.'

My sister smiled as she looked at Chai.

'It was when you threatened to divorce him,' Chai explained, embarrassed by Chuntian's expression.

Chuntian lowered her head and started to eat. She looked like she was simmering with

laughter and might cough the rice out at any moment.

*

My sister found a new job cleaning hotel rooms. She washed toilets, replaced the toiletry items, and topped up the supply of condoms. There were many rooms taken at hourly rates, so she had to wait onsite to clean up the battlefields, day and night. Men and women came in puffed full of energy, then left deflated an hour or so later, living their lives as they pleased. Chuntian was always all smiles, acting like she was very contented.

The guests were very liberal. If there were no paper towels or not enough condoms, the toilet bowl blocked, or the hot water was not hot enough – if anything was not to their liking, they wrapped a towel around themselves and stood at the door shouting for the staff. The staff members always huddled together to talk about this couple or that, who this man or that woman was, whether or not they were married, how many times they had visited, and with how many partners. The happy chatter went on endlessly.

Chuntian did not join in gossiping about who had slept with whom at the hotel. She was constantly busy, knowing only how to work. She was always sought out to take over for someone on leave. Sometimes she got a headache, but she would just rest in one corner for a moment, then carry on working. The others whispered behind her back, saying that she was an odd widow, frigid and reserved. Those who had some compassion tried to talk some sense into her. She only smiled in denial and said she just wanted to make a little extra money so she could touch up the house, then Yihua would be comfortable when she came home and would want to stay longer.

The old newspapers pasted on the wall were stained black by grease and smoke, crisp and torn, and crumbled like confetti when they were scrapped. They were quite ugly. Every day, Chuntian took old newspapers home from the hotel. When she had gathered enough, she spent her day off scraping and cleaning the wall, then boiling some glue. She then would take up a brush and go to work repairing the wall, pasting new paper on it. In consideration of Yihua's tastes, she chose photos of celebrities, sticking them to the wall. She also fixed a few nails for hanging things at the entrance of the house. She put a floral print quilt, which Yihua liked, on the bed. The room looked brand new, shiny and clean, and ready for Yihua to come home.

When Chuntian kept buying rag dolls to put at home, people started to realise something was wrong with her. It was like the rag dolls reproduced automatically, forming a lively crowd in the tight space.

The landlord, a plump elderly woman, said, 'Chuntian, what do you want these useless things for?' She was very sympathetic towards Chuntian's situation, and had even cried with her.

Chuntian smiled. 'My girl Huahua likes rag dolls. She always wanted one when she was little, but I never bought her one. She cried and cried, but I still wouldn't buy one. What use is a rag doll? But Huahua likes them.'

*

The snow came again that winter. It fell on my sister's body as if falling on broken brick walls and withered foliage.

The houses were fattened, the people bloated. The streets became mysterious, the cars moving slowly along them as if afraid of startling the snow. The snow fell without reservations.

Chuntian walked on the street, her hair a puffy mess. She looked like a wild bush making its way down the road. She took no interest in her surroundings, and did not appreciate the snow. She seemed anxious to reach some destination, and also seemed like she was just strolling. She was not dressed very neatly, revealing three layers of clothes, the innermost longer than her outerwear. Her scarf was grey, and her pair of tennis shoes were scuffed up. The muddy snow splashed onto the legs of her pants. Her face was dirty, her nails black. It appeared she had not bathed in a very long time. She did not care about such trivial matters; she had more important things to do – like walking. She walked as if walking into the past or the future, or perhaps as if walking in place. She walked down from the long decline of the peach blossom warehouse to the crossroads, then continued northward to the river. There, she turned left and continued walking along the bank to the South Bridge. She looked at the Pei Gong Pavilion. The mountain peak was white with snow. Occasionally a flock of blackbirds scattered like seeds.

The river was flowing, and snow fell on the centre of the river, where it disappeared without a trace. Boats covered in snow were at rest on the bank, but there were no people. My sister faced the middle of the river and stood staring at the snowy sky, as if she was absorbed in the sight, but also as if she saw nothing at all, but simply stood there considering a difficult problem. In fact, she no longer had difficult problems. She did not need to worry about her daughters, and Zhima was also gone. She had let go of everything, and had nothing left to do.

The north wind blew, turning my sister's dark face red. She puckered her lips as tightly as a chicken's arse, then occasionally stretched them wide, smiling knowingly at the river. She had reconciled herself to many things in life, and she did not have to listen to anyone else's orders anymore. As she walked, she looked but didn't see anything. Spring, summer, autumn, winter, the fickleness of human nature, changes of fortune – none of it had anything to do with her. She walked, looking at the sky and clouds, and watching the busy people who passed her by. She was quite satisfied with her way of life. There was always a smile on her face, as if she meant to share her contentment with others.

The sky cleared. There was a clearing in the city square, and snow lay at the roots of the trees. A passionate soprano voice floated from the speakers. Women danced along to the rhythm, waving red fans and wiggling their hips. They stomped to the left and stomped to the right, holding their hands upward, then downward, raising and lowering their fans in a great red tide. Chuntian walked into this patch of the sea, walking into a maze, and could not find her way out. She turned circles inside, like an instructor reviewing the choreography. She avoided their fans, their buttocks, their legs, stumbling about as if she had been kicked here and thrown there.

'Chuntian, dance with us,' one woman cried.

She ignored them. Ever since she had heard the news of Yihua's death, she stopped communicating with humans, even her colleagues at the hotel. She refused to accept that Yihua, too, was gone.

She was excreted from the dancing crowd like a turd, rolling to one side. The sun on the snow was dazzling. With eyes half-closed, she smiled, her expression kind.

The sun drew shadows of trees on the snowy ground. A dog dug at the snow with its front paws, digging up mud and grass roots.

Seeing her, Sun Xiangxi walked toward my sister. Her eyes swept past him as if he were a tree.

'Hey, Chuntian!' he called.

She ignored him. She had long ago stopped noticing other humans.

'What's wrong?' Sun asked, following. 'Chuntian?'

She continued to smile. She stripped the snow off the holly tree, tearing off a fat green leaf, shredding the outer layer of the leaf as she walked, leaving a stem mesh as thin as the wings of a cicada.

The juice from the leaves stained her frostbitten hand green.

Momentarily surprised, Sun had lagged behind. He caught up now. He did not speak, but continued to follow Chuntian, eventually even entering her small room.

Still, she ignored him, standing and reading the newspapers plastered to her wall. She read slowly, taking half a day to move to the next line.

It was even colder inside the house than outside, and the light was dim. There were a few pieces of rickety furniture, looking like they might fall apart any minute.

The papers plastered to the wall were always new. She pasted new leaves every time she found them. When Sun supported himself with his hand against the wall, he felt the softness of it.

Just then, the landlord came in. She looked sad. Sighing, she said, 'Chuntian, I've already let you stay here rent-free for a month. If you can't pay, I can't help you. Oh! If I were rich, I would let you stay. Poor woman. . . If it were me, I don't know how I'd go on.'

Sun was surprised again.

The landlord sighed again. 'I thought I was miserable. I didn't know there was a woman even worse off than me.'

Sun pondered for a moment, then said, 'In future, you can look for me and I'll pay Li Chuntian's rent. And if you'll look after her, I'll cover the expenses.'

Chapter 60:

Li Shunqiu, Eldest Brother

My brother looked more and more like my father as he got older. He spoke little, keeping his mouth tightly shut. He did not lift his head from his work, and started chasing chickens and kicking dogs. The villagers pitied him, and those who were soft-hearted shed some sympathetic tears. They patted his shoulder, gave him cigarettes, and said a few words of comfort, or sometimes offered unspoken comfort. Their sympathies only reminded Shunqiu of his failures in life, and his flawed fate. My poor brother tried to forget the past, but the villagers would not allow it. They would not give up if they could not completely dilute their compassion. Shunqiu had to hide from them, just as he had done when he just got out of prison, using his hat to create a sort of safety zone for himself. When he saw anyone coming, he turned and walked the other way.

> *My life has nothing to do with any of you. It's best you don't take me as a place to perform your virtuous acts. . . When I was on trial in the village, you all stood around as spectators watching with interest, not saying a word. No one*

stood up and spoke for me. . . You all remained silent. Your silence makes you accomplices.

He had never been so sick of everything in this village. Ever since he came back from prison, he had worked hard to be a normal person, marrying and having a child, and living a life approved by everyone. He had a wife and child. Being a husband and father had gradually weakened the hold the past had over him. He thanked Buddha for this just compensation. There was an image of Mao Zedong in the central room of our house. Shunqiu had prayed to it every time he came home, and had taught Xianxian to do the same. To his way of thinking, prayer did no harm and nobody would complain about someone being too polite, and the gods liked it. He was full of gratitude towards life then, and even wanted to pray to the tree stumps. But the reality was that prayer did no good either. If Shui Qin was alive, she was nowhere to be found; if she was dead, her corpse was nowhere to be seen. There was no news at all of Xianxian.

My parents' hair had turned grey, and their faces were creased. My mother's hearing had weakened, and her responses got slow. She was showing early signs of dementia. Every day at dawn she stood at the corner of the house, watching some imagined distant figure draw near the house and trying to determine if it were one of her own family members.

My grandfather looked at the dwindling number of family members in the house, thinking they did not like to come home and must be more comfortable living elsewhere. Some bored people would occasionally stop by and chat with him, and he would express this sentiment to them. Sometimes naked, he would carry a bucket of water to the terrace and take a shower there, or sit on the bricks of the wall and play with himself, frightening the village girls and women. He was like a child, arguing with my father, complaining about the food being too hard to chew, asking for new shoes, and moaning that the bed was too hard and his mouth had no sense of taste, but he wanted to eat crispy biscuits.

*

On the first day of the Spring Festival, according to our old tradition, my father placed a few big tree stumps in the central room and burnt them until the whole house was brightly lit. The stumps were sizzling with white smoke, and the water bubbles on the surface of the bark exploded softly, giving off a thick sticky fragrance of wood. We sat together around the fire. At dawn, the winter's third snow fell, coming in starts and stops. The sky was darker than usual, as if it wanted to collapse at any moment. My brother constantly stirred the tree stumps with tongs, knocking down the parts which had already burned through, adding them to our grandfather's small stove. My mother was cooking pig's trotters in the pressure cooker, and it was making sizzling sounds. In years past, when Xianxian, Yihua, and Yicao smelled the trotters cooking, they would yell in excitement as they ran about the house. They would put several glutinous rice cakes onto the fire to roast, then fight over who got to eat them.

Our family listened silently to the sound of the pressure cooker now and watched the tree stumps burn. No one spoke. My father got up and brought in more stumps and stacked them at the corner of the house, but we all knew we would not be able to burn so many.

Chuntian had bathed and put on new clothes. She smiled quietly at the flames, as if listening to them talk.

My father busied himself for a while, then sat down by the fire, spreading his fingers before it. He was not very comfortable. He stood up, made one round of the shed, pig pen, and vegetable garden, then carried a piece of dry wood, added it to the fire and went on stoking the flames.

A northerly wind came in through a crack in the door. My father did not have much hair, but the few remaining tufts were blown about his head.

My sister stood up and took a couple of steps. Like a little child, she dawdled to my father's side and carefully touched his white hair, her lips counting, 'One strand. . . Two. . . One. . . Two. . . Huahua. . . Caocao. . . Huahua. . . Caocao. . .'

The flames leapt and warm light in the house glistened. My father did not move. Tears glistened in his eyes.

Chuntian continued laughing and counting my father's white hairs.

My grandfather was standing on the terrace, leaning on a cane. Snow fell on his brown beret. In two months, he would be 100 years old.

'It's cold this year. Aren't Xianxian and the others coming back to celebrate New Year?' my grandfather mumbled to himself. He pinched a few cards in his hand. 'I don't see Yihua or Yicao either. . .' he said, craning his neck as he looked inside the house. Snow fell on the back of his neck.

There was much smoke from the tree stumps. It was trapped in the house, causing everyone to wipe their watering eyes constantly.

Chapter 61:

Li Xinhai, Grandfather

By the time the cole flowers were in bloom and the bees were buzzing, my grandfather could not get out of bed, and could not recognise anyone. He had no appetite, but he clasped all his earthly possessions in his hands, all 1020 *yuan*, as he lay silently, while his right hand kept grasping the air, pushing it back and forth. At intervals, he would shout, 'My money! Where's my money? Who took my money?'

We would dig his money out from his right hand and place it in his left. Then after a while, he would shout again, 'Zhang owes me 500 *yuan*, and I owe Li 300. Tell them to return it.'

We would then take the money from his hand once again and stuff it back.

My grandfather was filled with joy, revelling in the wealth of a constant flow of money, as he engaged in unrestrained gambling in his confused state. He would yell, 'Sixty thousand.' 'Hold!', or 'Ninety.' He jumbled up a variety of cards and called out in confusion, looking like he was squandering gold like dirt.

In times of clear-headedness, my grandfather would look for his brown beret. He did not want other hats. He would pass three or four days like this, then his voice would grow hoarse, his energy gradually sapped, and he would become quieter. His eyes remained closed, while his hands grasped at the air solemnly, as if selecting cards from a hand only he could see. He rubbed his thumb and fingers slowly, as if staking everything on a single throw, pledging everything of value in an attempt to win back the capital. At this point, his face was turning green, his cheeks were sunken, and his eyes were covered with a layer of white mist.

People who had experienced such things said, 'He'll be 100 years old in ten days. Looking at his condition, it doesn't look like he'll see his birthday.'

My father had a lot to say, but controlled himself. He spat at him non-stop, but still harboured an overflow of bad feelings.

The colours of spring were all around us. The brilliant sun was warm, and the wildflowers were blooming. The willow trees by the pond swayed lazily, while the ducks moved up and down happily.

My grandfather suddenly called, 'Shufen! Is Shufen here?'

Shunqiu was cleaning his body, changing his wet, soiled clothing. My grandfather caught his hand and said, 'Go call her!'

'Who is Shufen? Where do I go to call her?' my brother asked.

My grandfather shook his head, his mouth shrunk, and he cried like a baby bird, 'I want my mama.'

We bought the coffin and set it on the terrace. Several people helped us paint it, black on the outside, red inside, with the character for 'blessings' affixed at the top of the casket. The smell of new wood came from the coffin. The onlookers stood around laughing and chatting, talking about the ridiculous things my grandfather had done in his life. It was a festive atmosphere.

At three that afternoon, my grandfather suddenly stood by the door. He looked outside with unseeing eyes and said, 'I want to sit in the sun.'

Those standing around helped him to a chair. He sat with his head drooping. His body gradually looked like it was sun-dried, curled into a ball in the chair, and he was barely breathing.

That was a momentary recovery of consciousness just before death. Afterwards, my grandfather lay on his bed and never spoke again.

My father only focused on preparing for my grandfather's death. He had prepared everything, no matter how big or small. He was simply waiting for the final breath so he could get things underway.

It was like my grandfather was teasing my father, refusing to die, suspending that one breath.

The villagers told my father it was because father and son had been fighting their whole lives, and it was time for my father to acknowledge his wrongs and let my grandfather go in peace.

We waited a couple more days. It was my grandfather's birthday. My father brought a bowl of hot water and cleaned my grandfather's waxen face. As he washed, he said, 'Ba, I'm sorry for the things I've done wrong in the past. Please forgive me.'

My grandfather did not respond.

'I've thought through that matter clearly. I was wrong. . . No matter what, Shufen was your own daughter. . .'

My father helped my grandfather put on his brown beret, then stroked the old man's face. 'I'll call her right away and ask her to come. Don't worry, Ba.'

A tear escaped from the corner of my grandfather's eye and disappeared in the creases on his face. He stopped breathing.

When the funeral was over, my grandfather's memorial tablet hung high, his two eyes spying on everything.

More from Sheng Keyi...

Man Asian Literary Prize Nominee

Abandoning her Hunan village in the wake of a family scandal, 16-year-old Qian Xiaohong heads for the glitz and glamour of Shenzhen – a place she believes will be the perfect antidote for a young woman seeking to flee a stifling rural community. But Xiaohong swiftly discovers escape brings its own dangers, and the dual threat of vulnerability and violence, which hangs over the arrival of exuberant young migrants, is brought into stark focus.

Translated from the Chinese by Shelly Bryant

For more information visit:
www.penguin.com.au/authors/keyi-sheng

*More from
Sheng Keyi...*

PENGUIN
SPECIALS

FIELDS OF WHITE

SHENG KEYI

CHINA SPECIALS

On eBook Only

Jason is a thirty-something, white-collar salesman on the verge of
a mid-life crisis. The threat of redundancy and the demands of the
multiple women in his life   compound the symptoms of a mysterious affliction that appears to be taking over his body. When the
seemingly separate strands of Jason's life start to converge, he discovers that the reality he knows never existed in the first place ...

Translated from the Chinese by Shelly Bryant

For more information visit:
www.penguin.com.au/authors/keyi-sheng

More from Penguin. . .

A Story of Friendship and Trauma by Chi Zijian

Ji Lianna passionately tends to her flower garden and avoids looking back at her life with remorse. Xiao'e does not know the first thing about plants and cannot stop thinking about her past. Eighty-year-old Ji Lianna is a child of the Jewish diaspora, and young Xiao'e is not sure whether she is human at all. The two women could not be more different. Yet, in a numbingly cold Harbin flat in an old Russian villa, an unlikely friendship blossoms between them. Soon their dark histories come back to haunt them as they realise they have more in common than just a shared address.

Translated from the Chinese by Poppy Toland